THE HER

Paddy Kelly

THE HERMES PROJECT

FICTION4ALL

A FICTION4ALL PAPERBACK

© Paddy Kelly 2021
All Rights Reserved.

The right of Paddy Kelly to be identified as the author of this work has been asserted by him in accordance with the Copyright, Designs and Patents Act of 1988.

All rights reserved.

No part of this publication may be reproduced, stored in or introduced into a retrieval system, or transmitted, in any form, or by any means electronic, mechanical, photocopying, recording or otherwise, without the prior permission of the copyright holder.

Any person who commits any unauthorised act in relation to this publication may be liable to criminal prosecution and civil claims for damages in accordance with the Copyright Act of 1956 (as amended).

ISBN   978-1-78695-845-7

Cover Design & Graphics by Pedro Sperando

This Edition Published 2023 by
Fiction4All
https://fiction4all.com

The Hermes Project

This work is dedicated to:

The unknown policeman who, in 1964, carried me over 1 mile home with a broken leg.

Fortunately there are those who are dedicated to helping others.

Paddy Kelly

"Giving money and power to government is like giving whiskey and car keys to teenage boys."

- P. J. O'Rourke

Paddy Kelly

PROLOGUE

Late 19th and early 20th Century America saw the rise of industrial power and wealth. In turn the late 20th Century witessed the rise of space exploration and computer technology while the early 21st Century is seeing firm steps to establish mankind as an interplanetary species.

These technological advancements have, along with social progress, also given way to a new breed of criminal. Criminals who in lieu of guns use keyboards to steal the work and secrets of others. These activities are labelled "Cyber Crime".

American Telephone and Telegraph grew out of what Americans like to call 'Ma Bell'. The corporate name has gone through several incarnations as successive CEO's have manuevered it into becoming the largest telecommunications conglomerate in the world.

As always in American big business, like hungry lions chasing a wildebeast, an array of Asian, European and Third World companies are constantly nipping at their heels. The failure or compromise of its communications technology is a sure sign a nation is in trouble.

The fall of great empires usually comes from within and always as a result of weak or dodgy leadership.

America's press is and has been failing for a long time.

> "No science is immune to the infection of
> politics and the corruption of power."
> - Jacob Bronowski

CHAPTER ONE

**Trinity Prison
HMP Wandsworth
Heathfield Road, South London
Friday 21:45, 20 January, 2023**

Having proven himself with good behavior Anakin Banbury, former CEO of Hamlet Security who is serving 25 years for accomplice to murder, malfeasance, grand larceny and misleading the authorities, awaits his transfer from A Wing to the Trinity scection, a Category C wing reserved for 'low risk of violence' offenders, forgers, fraudsters etc . . .

The armored car heist back on New Year's Eve 1999 in which two security guards disappeared along with several billion in cash had been largely forgotton. By most.

Now, years later, nearly all the money has been recovered as well as the missing armored car. However, of the two guards only one body was fished from the Thames years after the fact. The other guard was never found and was presumed dead.

At approximately twelve minutes before evening lockdown in the prison, as the diminutive Banbury was preparing his personal property to vacate his cell next morning, his cellmate wandered off to the toilet. Two other prisoners slipped into his cell.

Next morning during breakfast the wing's lockdown alarm blared and amongst the shouting of the guards and the wailing of the alarm all prisoners were shuffled back into their cells again to be locked down as extra guards hurridly flooded into the wing.

Banbury's cold, rigor-ridden body had been discovered tucked neatly in his bed. He apparently had been garrotted.

The required investigation was launched.

No one would ever be charged.

But Banbury's cellmate earned an extra two cartons of cigarettes for sleeping above the corpse that night.

The British Prison authorities would never discover, or much care about, the fact that the people who paid Banbury to supply the information required for the 1999 crime for which he was inprisoned were apparently none too happy that the electronic spoofer device they paid him for never found it's way into their hands.

CHAPTER TWO

New York Times Building
620 8th Avenue
Manhattan, New York

The Domino's Pizza motorcycle maneuvered between the short silver bollards lining the sidewalk and parked right in front of the huge, circular glass door which stood sentry in front of the seventy-five story skyscraper in Lower Manhattan.

The fact that the driver parked up on the sidewalk, two feet from the main entrance was to allow the night guard to keep an eye out for his motor bike. The odds of getting a ticket at 11:58 at night were virtually nil however in a town where the entire population save the city's administration realized that crime was out of control, the odds of his bike being stolen were pretty good. Even with the night guard keeping an eye out. All the cops on the late shift, now operating at 20% less manpower curtousey of the 'Defund Police' campaign, were prowling around the poorer neighborhoods where 80-85% of all the crime occurred.

More importantly, if the execs got their pies piping, hot it translated into an extra ten buck tip.

From behind the four man reception desk inside the spacious lobby the sole black, middle-aged guard glanced over the bank of monitors in front of him and casually watched the delivery guy scurry to the rear of his bike and pull out two extra-large, pepperoni pizzas. After all, it was New York City not one of your dinky little New England villages and so the only respectable sized pizzas were extra-large pizzas.

"Yo, your guys pies is here!" The night guard declared into the phone as he simultaneously buzzed the Dominoes guy in.

Send him up Jimmy would ya? The intercom growled back.

"Not supposed ta do that Mr. J.! New rules this year!"

The year hasn't officially started yet Jimmy! But if I'm looking at pizza on my desk in the next ten minutes, you'll be looking at a twenty in front of yours!

Jimmy the guard hung up the phone and motioned the kid nearer. Coming around from behind the desk he then opened the top box and took a slice out, folded it in half and took a bite catching a dribble of hot mozzarella with his other hand as he did.

"Security check kid." He garbled as he juggled the hot cheese in his mouth. "Company policy, you know, make sure there's no bombs hidden in the dough. Take the elevator, fourteenth floor, board room, door marked 'Legal Department' end of the hall."

At the same time upstairs in the modern highrise, there was a clandestine, late night meeting of a small group of PR lawyers for a major cable news network gathered to concoct a plan to combat the network's sagging ratings and to figure out how best to make use of the new sat com technology due to come on line next month plus how to exploit its potential benefits to the broadcast industry.

With all the hallways and offices, save those in Conference Room C turned out, the four figures, mostly lawyers, huddled in the shadows at the oversized conference table were reminiscent of *Macbeth's* witches in Act IV, scene 1.

"We need to decide what we're going to recommend to the execs upstairs so they can brief the on-air talent who we're going to back after Biden has been replaced by his own party and is out of the picture." The lone female pointed out to the guy at the head of the table.

Reinforced by a weekend game of paintball he effortlessly exuded the false machismo so often mistaken in the corporate world for manhood. It was clear he was the honcho at the midnight conference.

"I say we go with Harris." The bleached blond suggested much to the objection of the bald guy a PR account/lawyer type brought in to babysit the fading numbers.

"Word Salad Harris?! You can't be serious! She's the only one worse at public speaking then he is!"

"Yes but she doesn't confuse Sweden and Switzerland, refer to Michelle Obama as vice president or misquote the Constitution!" Blondie countered.

"Okay, let's see how many dozen Dems throw their hat in the ring this time and go from there." Macho Man directed. "Let's get down to the main mission."

"Good idea, I say 18." She quickly spouted.

"18 what?" He queried.

"18 Dems announce their candidiacy sometime after the midterms."

"I'll lay $20 on that!" Bald Guy threw in.

"Put me down for fifty!" Macho Man ventured.

"I'll take both those bets!" She defiantly boasted .

They all turned to the guy sitting quietly at the other end of the table taking notes as the pizzas arrived and they all dove in.

"Now guys, business please!" He pleaded.

"Yes sir." Blondie responded. Macho Man resumed.

"As per orders from the top no more boosting, paddding or faking reports! Sources will be quoted on all stories."

"You mean like the two reporters broadcasting 'live war' news from Bagdad making believe they were broadcasting the initial bombing from a downtown hotel?" The accountant quipped.

"Personaly I think it was the plastic Arica palm and fake helmets that gave it away!" Blondie added.

"Did the producer staging that thing ever get caught?" Macho Man queried as he cradled his chin as much to emphasise his interrogative as to flex his right bicep as he did so.

"Oh yeah! It was even posted on line." Blondie affirmed.

"How come I never heard of it?" He pushed.

"They quashed it. Plus the American public has the memory of a goldfish." She added.

"Well from now on word is nothing that can be

branded Fake News!"

"Chief that might be easier said than done." She countered.

"How so?"

"Well the idea of fake news has been around forever and is pretty ingrained in the zeitgeist at this point."

"Actually it only dates back to 2015 when Alphabet, the parent company of Google, published it through First Draft. Obama while giving a speech at Carnegie-Mellon used it to apply to the mass media when he said: 'Somebody has to step in and corral this wild west Media environment.'" Bald Guy informed.

"Well we will avoid it like the plague! What did we find out today on the viewership survey?" He asked.

"Pew Research reported 83% of liberals are satisfied with their news coverage. Less than 30% of conservatives reported being satisfied with same. How are we supposed to close a more than 50% gap?!" The diminutive guy with the horn rimmed glasses and extra-large forehead was quick to respond.

"We're not. Our strategy is going to be to continue to pander to the 83% while planning a transition strategy for when the numbers change."

"And how are we supposed to know when the numbers are going to change?" He asked as he looked up from his notes.

"Hello! Tuesday November 8th?" Macho Man snapped back.

"Between the supply chain screw ups, gas and food prices and rising inflation. . ." Blondie opined.

"Not to mention the border and the laptop from hell!" Bald Guy interjected.

"Those are just side shows. No one is ever going to see the inside of a jail cell because of their economic and business ties with communists or opening the border." Macho Man confidently spewed.

"But we openly backed Biden and the Dems!" The accountant countered.

"Guys, let's keep our eye on the ball! We are here to figure out how to get our numbers up to support our required revenue stream. And we can't do that with less than half a million viewers! We've already lost half a dozen sponsors. Now is there anything else?"

"The suits." Blondie prompted.

"Shit yeah, the suits. Very briefly, before we break and finally call it a night. The suits from Santa Clara are coming in on Monday! They're going to want to know how we intend to shape the news leading up to the midterms. We need to minimise the bloodbath Biden's people are likely to face. Be ready for the suits' input on which spins to apply!" He cautioned.

"That it? What about inter-departmental coordination?" She asked.

"The Chief has an all-hands meeting planned in two weeks depending on what happens with the guy the SecDef recommended for DIRNSA. He's a 98% chance of getting nominated, it all depends if he gets the Senate's approval."

"He'll get through, he's a hardcore Dem!" Accountant Guy insisted.

"He'd better at the abysamal ratings they're going into their third year with!"

"I wouldn't put money on that boys!" Blondie interjected. "Especially given the rumors of the House Intell Committee cover-up and shifty Shiff!"

"That's fake news! It's just disinformation." The big guy sarcasticaly blurted out with a chuckle.

"Yeah, Russian disinfomation!" She mockingly quipped.

The macho guy at the end of the table closed over his notebook and spoke up.

"Get your aides on the phone first thing in the morning, I want a detailed legal search of the FCC codes, any pertinent state and federal regulations regarding communications sale and transfers and it might not be a bad idea to brush up on the D.O.J.'s latest modifications and interpretations of the *Sherman Act*."

"That all? Why don't we stage a revival of *Jesus Christ Superstar* while we're at it?!" Blondie made no attempt to hide her sarcasm.

"It's been done." He shot back. "Also reports to my secretary by Thursday close of business!"

"What's the name of this company that we're negotiating with?" Bald Guy asked.

"AstroCom Technologics."

****

Dulles International
Dulles, Virginia
Thursday, February 9th

The twin pom poms of his Peruvian winter hat bounced off his chest as the fifty-something, clean-shaven gentleman in open black rubber goloshers and grey herring bone overcoat made his way to the luggage claim area. He carried only a brown leather briefcase such as a 1950's school teacher might cart aroud.

After collecting his single bag from the luggage carousel he made his way through the terminal out into the cold but clear winter day to a taxi.

"U.S. Capitol Building, please."

"How many capitol buildings do you think we got here pal?" The driver quipped looking into his mirror.

"Then take me to the largest one, please." The man politely snapped back.

Inspector Nigel Morrissey had been flown over from Scotland Yard in London to Washington D.C. to testify before a Department of Homeland Security senate sub-committee regarding the security of the formerly classified portable spoofer devices such as the one stolen from the Hamilton armored car in London back in New Year's 1999.

In route he marveled at his first sight of the city's world-famous, pristine monuments formerly seen only in movies.

One thing you can say for the Yanks, he silently

mused as they passed the imposing Lincoln Memorial. *They don't do things half measure!*

On arrival at the Capitol Building, as he paid the driver he was taken aback by the soldiers patrolling the partially cordoned off streets and all the fencing he saw.

On arrival at the front entrance he was required to present his I.D. then again at the entrance to the actual chamber where he was asked to set his bag aside with one of the D.C. policemen at the door before being scanned with a detection wand. An easel mounted sign to the side of the door read:

'House sub-Committee on
Communications, Media & Broadband'

He was escorted into the large hall where a hearing was already underway.

Inside the two large oak doors, in the front of the room, sat twenty-eight high-backed, padded chairs which were arranged around and behind a large horseshoe-shaped desk. Seveal of the seats were unoccupied.

A panel of senators, 12 from the Minority and 12 from the Majority, were seated around the desk with a 12 foot long, mahogany table in the center. Behind this table were seated four men in business suits.

In the center of the large horseshoe desk sat Massachusetts Democrat Sen. Burman. The plaque in front of him read: 'Chairman'.

A smattering of photo journalists sat on the floor at the foot of the large horseshoe desk and there was a small gallery with seating for perhaps fifty visitors.

The men at the long table represented two tech companies, AstroCom Technologies and Nexus 6, the latter of which were seeking approval of the Communications committee before they could apply for licencing from the FCC to launch their latst product, a constellation of communication satellites designed specifically to bring internet to parts of the globe where it was now lacking.

Their competition, AstroCom, sought to block their efforts.

One of the committee was posing a question regarding the *Sherman Act* on monopolization to one of the businessmen at the table who appeared to be a lawyer representing Nexus 6.

Morrissey was quietly shown to his seat on the right side of the visitor's gallery.

"Senator, *the Statute of Limitations* ruling under 18 USC 3282 (a) clearly states it is 5 years." The lawyer at the table responded.

"On what legal grounds does AstroCom intend on filing against the Nexus 6 V.P.E. system?" A second senator asked. A second suit, this one from AstroCom took up the question.

"In its 2017 ruling The Eighth Circuit applied the Continuing Violation Doctrine thus extending the time under 15 USC 15(b)." He confidently responded. "We intend to do likewise senator."

Morrissey was always befuddled by the incomprehensibly complicated American legal system. Particularly given that it was theorhetically evolved from the British system. Convinced no one on the planet had access to all the laws of the U.S. much less knew the majority if them, it seemed that no matter what law one side presented in court the fast talking lawyers on the other side, providng money was no object, could magically pull an opposeing law out of their hat.

The Chairman spoke up.

"Dr. Parker how do you intend to deal with the fact that before your first customer pays any money for your service your company will be required to have 100% of your investment not only in place but invested in the right locations?"

"Already arranged Mr. Chairman." The forty-something year old Dr. Parker CEO of Nexus 6 shot back.

"Enough of the legal arguments I'd now like to direct questioning to the technical details and applicability if the uh, the . . ." Burman announced as he shuffled through some papers in front of him. ". . . ah The Vacuum Pulse Emitter. The Chair recognises Senator Nadlinsky." Senator Gerry Nadlinsky, (D-CA) switched on his mike.

As Morrissey took his reserved seat near the front of the gallery he caught sight of Frank Mahone seated on the other side, back to the wall eating a large submarine sandwich, bits of shredded onion escaping the back end of the roll, as fellow audience members kept their distance.

Morrissey glanced back at the entrance at the 'No Food or Drink Permitted' sign on the wall, shook his head and smirked.

"Thank you Mr. Chairman." The short, fat

Nadlinsky said. "Dr. Parker, you are a professor at the Department of Electronics and Computer Engineering at Cal Berkeley, is that correct?" Nadlinsky asked.

"No, I formaly held the chair of that department but I am no longer with the university." The well-dressed forty-something at the table answered.

"How is it you no longer hold that posistion Doctor? Were you dismissed?" Nadlinsky probed.

"No senator. I felt obligated to give someone else a shot at the university chair so they could advance their career."

"Is that the only reason? I mean do you expect this committee to believe you walked away from a well paid, highlty prestigeius position as a tenured professor just to give someone else a chance?"

"Not only. After I was awarded the *Rumford Prize for Astrophysics* I decided to use the money to expand my own private laboratory, hire some young up and coming scientists and persue several other projects I believe could benefit mankind." He politly explained. "Which is why we developed the The Vacuum Pulse Emitter."

"So you're an altruist?" The vertically challenged, generously obese senator made little attempt to hide his sarcasm.

"No sir. Just a scientist." Parker answered.

"The university chair yes." Nadlinsky repeated as he fumbled through his notes. "You are familiar with this Nexus system?" Nadlinsky asked.

"I believe you mean the Omnibus satellite system? I should be. I wrote the navigational program."

"Omnibus, yes." Nadlinsky mumbled. Parker took up the question.

"In 2019 half the world was still without internet." Parker explained. "In terms of coverage we've made little progress since then. The third world wants and needs technology!" He continued. "A large part of why 911 succeeded for them but failed so tragically for us was because the FBI and Intelligence agencies were technologically behind. While Americans were posting pictures of their breakfast on Facebook and trading tweets about their favorite shoes, our enemies were making significant strides and military advances in technology. The technology my company is working on has unlimited applications to the entire internet system. The time sensitive nature of the finance industry alone is a perfect example."

"How is that Doctor?" The chairman queried.

"Sir, if we can reduce the latency transferring of information from ground to satellite by just five seconds as opposed to the undersea cables currently being used in either the *Hibernia Express* or the *Atlantic Crossing* cable, we can save 300 million dollars in those 5 seconds!" Suddenly the room became more attentive. "The undersea cable system we now use to transmit information was revolutionary in its time but now gentleman, it's time is past. Undersea communication systems are an open invite to sabotage by our enemies. Not to mention the possibility of future attacks on supply systems such as witessed with the Nord Stream pipe lines.

Because our economic system is so time sensitive that five seconds saved by using ground-to-space technology versus trans-Atlantic cables, translates to billions per day on the international market. Millions being moved in fractions of seconds, all as a result of decreased latency!" He continued with mounting enthusiasm.

"Not to mention the benefits that will be incurred when we bring in the whole rest of the world." Parker sat forward in his chair and made deliberrate eye contact with the committee members. "Imagine it ladies and gentleman, a day when every household in all the third world countries can say, 'we have internet!' It would be a quantum leap forward for civilization! If anyone ever questioned why we came down out of the trees and walked across the Serengeti standing upright looking for something better . . . this is it! This is something better!" He pleaded.

Senator Nadlinsky, a clandestine stockholder in AstroCom, was not about to throw in the towel.

"A key feature of the GPS system lies in its ability to successfully navigate it's assigned orbit does it not?" Nadlinsky challenged.

"To an extent yes." Parker replied.

"Well then doesn't your Nexus system's navigational ability also depend on the reliability of our GPS satellite constellation?"

"Yes but that's not the critical technogical breakthrough which makes the V.P.E. viable."

"And should one of your units come on course to

collide with a piece of space junk or a satilite not belonging to the United States? Say the Soviet Union for example. What then? World War Three?"

"Probably not. With all due respect senator that will never happen".

"What makes you so sure doctor?"

"Well for one thing, the Soviet Union has been extinct for well over a decade." Sporadic laughter filtered across the room. "But more importantly Senator, each of the 3,000 satilites Nexus is seeking to launch is equippted with individual navigational abilities. In other words should a unit somehow intersect the trajectory of another satilite or piece of space debris both units, in coordination with each other, will replot new courses to avoid collision. The replot will then be sent to the control center, tagged and permanently recorded."

A second committee member, Representitive Natalie Farmiga, a republican from New Jersey, interjected with a query.

"Dr. Parker should the committee decide to pass this on to the FCC for approval how long do you anticipate before you will have had the full constellation of 3,000 units in orbit?"

"We have planned for 180 days to have completed all launchs than an additional 30 days to co-ordinate all 750 satellite quad clusters and work out all the bugs. At that point 94.5 per cent of the Earth will have access to the internet."

"Three thousand satellites!" Nadlinsky exclaimed.

"That is correct, senator." Parker answered.

"Dr. Parker we already know it's getting pretty crowded up there without adding to the nearly 4,600 satellites already jamming the earth's outer atmosphere. Don't you think the addition of three thousand more satellites will increase the chances of a mishap?"

"Not actually senator."

"Why not?"

"In addition to the avoidance system already described our satellites will be restricted to the L.E.O., the Low Earth Orbit, that is altitudes below the 2,000km pathways."

Senator Burman interupted the back and forth.

"Gentlemen, I'm due in the House for a vote in twenty minutes, so if there are no objections, I would like to hear from our two police witnesses so they can go about their business and I can duck out and vote. After that, we'll take a thirty minute recess then resume." There were no objections. "Good, then I'll start. As there were earlier some questions of overlapping functions with the spoofer mechanism stolen from the London Hamlet Security van heist over two years ago and I am now informed that these so-called 'spoofer' devices are now widely used by several militaries to transmit false VPN locations through dedicated satellites, let's move to the subject of illegality.

Doctor Parker, would this Vacuum Pulse Emitter system, if approved and deployed, not afford the criminal element the opportunity to scramble or disrupt large numbers of VPN locations?"

"Mr. Chairman my company has also had the

opportunity to closely examine current spoofer devices and we believe we have come up with a safety system whereby should one or more VPN's be suspected of disruption, a notification will alert base control and allow a blocking program to be activated.

Additionally Mr. Chairman I'd like to point out that, according to the FAA, there are currently over 24,000 aircraft in the comparatively tiny space of our stratosphere and they seem to manage quite well."

"Not if you're flying out of Newark!" Someone in the gallery called out. Sporadic laughter filtered across the room.

"Mr. Chairman, if I may?"

"The chair recognises Representative Farmiga."

"Thank you. Dr. Parker, my staff informs me and in reading through your proposal here, you're predicting far-reaching implications in economics for your VPE system?"

"Yes ma'am that's correct."

"Could you please elaborate on that for us?"

"Be happy to. Many people are under the misimpression that all of our internet interactions are carried out by satellite. This is false. The majority of our online and internet interactions are still carried by fibre optic cable. While a quantum leap from electric transfer, fibre optic cable is still five times slower than information transfer through a vacuum. The delivery time of information from point A to point B is known as 'latency'. The latency time of transfer through the vacuum of space will reduce communication time by 75%. Ergo the VPE."

"How will VPE in turn improve overall commerce?"

"Not just commerce but **all** communications madam. By improving latency time by 75% we will add an estimated 1 to 1.5 billion dollars per day to the open market. Political communications would be near instantaneous, treaties and political contracts could be decided upon and signed the same day!"

"I think you give us politicians too much credit for efficiency Dr. Parker! But if you can somehow invent a way to reduce latency time in between politicians, I believe we'd all be better off." Reresentitive Faemiga added.

Again mild laughter rippled through the gallery.

"No comment madam."

Nigel Morrissey was finally called on to testify and related his knowledge of and participation in the events of 1999-2000.

"I head up a special homicide unit in Scotland Yard who were called in to investigate the disappearance of two Hamlet Security guards. The fact that no hint of the guards was found for 19 years is testimony to the cleverness of the planning by those who perpetrated the crime." Now speaking from the center table Morrissey relayed.

"So you are convinced the robbery of this prototype electronic device was a professional job?" The Chairman asked.

"Correct sir. The fact that we lost one of our best

detectives in the course of our investigation in conjunction with the fact that the perpetrators were solely focused on the electronic spoofer device, neglecting the £600,000,000 sterling contained in the van is testimony to the potential financial value of such electronic devices."

"And we still have no hint who set this robbery up?"

"We've apprehended and successsfully proscecuted the London backers but there is some suspicion that, being as these spoofers were such a sought after piece of hardware at the time, there may have been international implications as well."

"Inspector, do you feel there is a likely possibility that we will see more of these high profile cyber-type crimes in the future and that we should rethink our secuurity in these areas?" Burman asked.

"You'd be negligent in your duties if you didn't, Senator. I have no doubt cybercrime will only increase in frequency and audacity as time progresses. I am absolutely certain as we speak another such crime is being planned."

"Is there anything else you'd like to add Inspector?"

"No Senator thank you for inviting me."

"Thank you for comng all this way to testify for us."

Morrisey returned to his gallery seat.

"Call Detective Frank Mahone please." Chairman Burman took note of the fact that Frank had about a quarter if his hoagie left.

"Detective Mahone would you like us to rearrange the order of testimony in order to allow you time to finish your lunch?" He sarcastically asked over the room's open microphone.

"No thank you Senator." Mahone called back across the room as he stood to come forward. "I'll finish it later." He answered as he wrapped the last of the sandwich in its paper and crammed it into his over coat's side pocket and proceeded to the witness table. "It's not that good any way, too much mayo." There was mild laughter as the chairman ignored his return sarcasm and Frank took a seat at the table.

"Mr. Mahone would you please state your name and occupation for the record?"

"Frank Mahone, Lieutenant Detective, NYPD Homicide Division. Currently on rotatioal duty."

"Is that for diciplinary reasons Detective?"

"No sir, that's because some bright sparks in the politcal establishment decided it would be a good idea to defund the police! Perhaps some of you have seen this story in the news?" Mahone's comments briefly blanketed the room with silence.

"What can you tell us about this new VPE device?" Chairman Burman pushed on.

"Absolutely nothing senator."

"What about the spoofer device stolen from the Hamlet Security people?"

"Except for the fact that they went through a shit load of trouble to steal it, not much."

"Then why have you been called here to testify?"

"It's your show senator. I have no idea why I'm here. I'd much rather be back up in New York cleaning up the criminal mess that scumbag DiBlasio left us."

Sporadic laughter erupted across the gallery.

"Detective Mahone if you could modulate your speech it would be much appreciated!"

"I was told I was asked to come down here and talk about computer crime not space technology."

"Very well. Based on your experiences in London what can you tell us about the computer crime situation you and Inspector Morrissey encountered?" Representitive Farmiga asked.

"Like I said, I don't know anything about the tech side of the house but I do know that whatever the tech guys can dream up to make life better and help people, some low life prick can twist around, exploit and turn into a criminal enterprise particularly if they have the backing of some politicians. I trust the committee has no objection to my use of the pejorative word 'prick?' Its pretty standard vocabulary on the force."

"Very illuminating." Nadlinsky commented.

"Look I don't want to take up any of your time repeating what Inspector Morrissey has already stated but the fellas that pulled off that heist were not what you call your local neighborhood punks stealing hubcaps for a few bucks. They were well financed, highly organised and most importantly had high up political connections."

"What led you to that conclusion detective?" Rep Farmiga asked.

"The fact that they weren't afraid to do long stretches in prison means only one thing, they had political pull. Either that or they knew, even if caught, like that asshole who shot up all those people in the subway or the deranged prick who drives at full speed through a holiday parade they'd be out on low bail or get off easy."

"Are you insinuating that politicians were involved?" Senator Nadlinsky the California Democrate challenged.

"Of course not senator! We all know politicians are above board and would never indulge in illegal activity!"

Again laughter peppered the room.

"If there are no more questions and if you are through enlightening us Detective, I think we can take a thirty minute break." Burman announced.

During the recess, out in the vestibule, Morrissey approached Mahone.

"Have you always had such disdain for your government's rules?" Morressey asked Mahone as he approached and they shook hands for their first meeting in well over a year.

"Rules no. Government yes." They greeted as they shook. "You're looking pretty good for such an old man!" Mahone chided.

"ME?! Don't you lot have some sort of rule here about mandatory retirement? And if so how did you elude it?" Morrissey shot back.

"How are things in the Big Smoke?"

"Wet! For some reason we can't get the hang of freezing rain into snow like you Yanks. How are things up in the Big Apple?" Morrissey asked.

"At the moment in flux. Finally got a new Mayor,

but it's still a democrat run city so, not much is likely to change."

"The new Mayor, still pounding the race drum?" Nigel asked.

"Remains to be seen. He talks a big game but still shows no apparent attempt to crackdown on crime. How's The Squad?"

"Doing well. All send their regards."

"How are they coping without Dunn?"

"As well as can be expected. We're due to have a replacement soon."

"Any word on who?"

"No but for certain it will be a girl."

"She'll have a big bra to fill!"

"Maureen was a good woman and a sharp cop!" Morrissey stated looking down.

"Your mother still doing well?"

"Oh yes, eighty-two and fit as a fiddle! Still gives the local green grocers hell about his veg prices."

"How long you over for?"

"Funny you should ask! I've taken two week's extra holiday. Thought I might fly up to New York and have a snoop around, see what you lot have done to our colonies since you've moved in!"

"Ah well you're in luck! I just happen to know someone who's a cop! Might be able to put you up for a couple of days."

"Invitation accepted."

"Here," Mahone passed him a business card. "Call me when you land."

CHAPTER THREE

Jacob Javits Federal Building
26 Federal Plaza
Manhattan, New York
Saturday, 0530, 11 February

It was early morning, still dark when the two FBI agents, one of which, Special Agent Jim Ames, was a fourteen year vetern of the National Security Branch of the FBI, the branch that dealt with inernational crime. A branch to which the other, a dusky blond, Ukrainian-American female accompanying him had been temporarily assigned.

The two left their offices on the 23rd floor of The Jacob Javits Building in Lower Manhattan to head Uptown to Central Park.

As reward for her outstanding performance in London, on the back of the Hamlet armored car heist, Agent Irina Kuksova was given the opportunity to choose her next duty station. She chose the NSB and was posted to the Manhattan office in Downtown New York on a ninety day prorbationary period.

As more and more terrorists commited crimes to finance their subversive activities against vulnerabilities in the system the traditional distinction between national security and criminal matters had increasingly become blurred.

To combat this evolving situation the Federal Bureau of Investigation formed the NSB, the National Security Branch.

The Hermes Project

Now less than a month on the job, Irina was pulled for a special assignment: the apprehension and arrest of a man who had been selling secrets to the People's Republiic of China.

The two agents descended to the underground garage and headed over to a dark, late model sedan.

"Do you know the city?" Ames asked.

"Not really, I've never lived here."

"Well then, no time like the present to learn!" He tossed her the keys over the roof of the car.

"Not sure how comfortable I am driving for the first time in New York City!"

"Piece of cake! Streets go east west and the avenues go north south. So easy anybody could do it. Even a-"

"What?!" She snapped shocking him. "You were going to say a 'woman'. Even a woman could do it! Weren't you?"

"I was gonna say 'rookie'." He calmly defended as they climbed into the car. "Or maybe newbie. I could have also said neophyte or F.N.G." He quietly explained. "You're not one of those left wing, nutjob, blue-haired feminist freaks are you? I mean that respectfully of course!"

"I'm sorry!" She embarrassingly recanted. "Really I'm sorry, I apologise. It's just that the bureau guys I worked with in London where kind of, you know, assholes."

"Apology accepted but. . . about your profanity?"

"What about it?"

"I find it a bit offensive. But . . . if I could ask you a question?"

37

"Yes, of course anything!" She replied. He turned in his seat to face her.

"Have you heard the word of the Lord?"

Initially taken aback she quickly realized he was joking.

"Good one Ames!" She conceded. "Good one."

"Loosen up Champ, we're on the same team." He encouraged. She smiled and nodded. "It's an easy enough straight shot north up to Central Park." He advised.

"How long we been tracking this guy?" Kuksova asked as she started the car then turned on the dashboard GPS.

"Don't use that!" He said as they pulled out onto Thomas Street. He reached over and switched off the GPS. "It will take you by way of Jersey. I'll give you directions, better to learn the streets as soon as possible. Turn right here on Church Street." Traffic was sparse at that hour. "The Bureau was alerted by the State Department about two years ago, but I've suspected him since 2015. I've been working the case in my off time since then."

"Why'd the Bureau take so long to act?"

"Veer left here on to 6th. We're heading over to West Side Drive." He instructed. Irina complied. "Misallocation of resources. First it was the Bengazi fiasco and the loss of the ambo in Libya. Then Obama and Clinton had us tied up chasing the phoney Russia Gate thing which strained the hell out of our man power resources. We had agents all over the place!"

"What's the general mood in the rank and file

these days?" She ventured.

"Here, west on Canal and that'll take us up the West Side Drive. Then just keep heading north." In lieu of an answer to her question he stared straight ahead.

"Agent Ames? You okay?" Kuksova pushed.

"They had me assigned to The Hunter Biden investigation but when this bust came up I told them I wanted in on it. They said no. I had to threaten to turn in my badge. They gave me a week off from the Biden thing."

"Where'd this guy slip up anyway?"

"About six months ago he approached a Russian diplomat in the embassy's parking garage."

"Who reported him?" She pushed.

"The Russian he approached."

"Seriously?!"

"There's an unwritten rule in embassy circles that if a diplomat is approached unsolicited in the open the individual is likely to be a freelance double agent or a nut job. So out of professional courtesy we report such incidents to each other."

"Well that's cordial!"

"Besides, they probably already had what he was trying to sell them."

"You never hear about that in the nightly news. What happened, exactly?"

"A cursory investigation ensued and the guy was cleared."

"But . . . ?"

"But when there was yet another information leak a few months later and the Bureau investigated further they falsely accused and suspended an innocent agent named James Kelly."

"Jesus, how embarresing was that!" She blurted out.

"It wasn't until last year that one of our tech guys, McNeill, was able to hack into his computer and find the tip we're following up today."

"Which is what?"

"Specific details of a dead letter drop to be executed sometime between yesterday and tomorrow."

"Wow! Real life spy shit!" Irina quipped.

"It's why you signed up isn't it?"

"Why yes it is Agent Ames, yes it is!" Kuksova smiled broadly and sat back in her seat.

Traffic was still light at that early Saturday hour so they were south of the park fifteen minutes later.

"Get off on 59th then head east across town then north on Madison to 63rd."

They turned East on Central Park South then North on Fifth Avenue to approach the zoo's back entrance.

Entering through the 63rd Street back gate on the 5th Avenue side they arrived and were greeted by a zookeeper where they parked and were escorted deeper into the zoo to their stake out positions. Ames continued his briefing as they walked.

"Twenty-four-seven observation has been established and you and I are acting as a relief team."

"Why me, a rookie?" She asked as they walked through the cold and dark.

The Hermes Project

"It was a last minute thing, my regular partner's in the hospital so you drew the short straw which is why there was no time to brief you yesterday."

"What's wrong, was he shot?" She asked.

"No 'he's' in labor. Expecting a girl."

"Oh."

"We suspect the drop is to occur in one of the multiple animal houses located around the Central Garden." He informed. "Central Park zoo is quite small and all of the four major buildings are within easy sight of each other with the sea lion pool in the exact center of the layout." He went on to detail the plan. "Two agent teams will be stationed to observe the front and rear entrances of each building with an additional four teams as floaters. You and I are Team #2 and are assigned to pose as a couple."

"Okay." She acknowledged.

"But don't get any ideas! They'll be no kissing!" He added.

"Not a problem." She replied. I'm gay. He pulled back and stared at her.

"I never would have made you for playing for the other team!" He was stupefied at the beautiful blonde's responce. She stared back as they walked.

"Gotcha!" She said with a smirk. He smiled in appreciation of her gag.

The zoo's gates would not open to the public until ten o'clock so Ames suggested they get some coffee and eggs at one of the small kiosks the zoo director had ordered set up for the agents.

By 9:45 a last-minute radio check and orientation had been given by the mission chief and all operatives where in position.

"I just hope there's no gun play!" Kuksova quietly said to Ames as they slowly strolled through the plaza.

"Why you scared?"

"No, it's a zoo! Children!"

"Of course!" He nodded. "The crowds and potential gaggles of kids scurrying around is likely one reason the zoo was chosen for the drop."

"Good point." She agreed.

It was a cold but dry day and much to the agent's satisfaction they did not have long to wait.

The gates opened on time and at 11:15 the target was spotted, a box of popcorn in hand, nonchalantly wondering towards the sea lion pool in the central garden.

"Talley ho!" Ames quietly spoke into his lapel mike to radio the others.

He and Kuksova slowly worked their way arm-in-arm over to the opposite side of the sea lion pool where Ames produced a cheap disposable camera and had Kuksova strike several poses as the other surveilence teams watched their mark move on and enter the large enclosed aviary opposite.

Exiting the far end of the building he was then observed moving across the path towards the reptile house.

"The snake house! How appropriate." Irina commented.

Inside the reptile building Team #3, unseen by the subject, observed him as he quickly and clandestinely stashed something behind one of the info plates on the snake terrarium before moving away.

"He's made the drop!" The team leader quietly reported into his lapel mike just before the voice of the mission commander sounded in their ear pieces.

Two, follow him out. Three keep eyes on the drop. Four maintain surveillance for his cut out. Five, maintain cover on the rear door. We're gonna take him on the other side of the sea lion pool in the open. All we have is that his contact is a middle-aged Chinese male. Likely in civilian casual atire.

Outside several agents shifted positions while Ames and Kuksova followed him out while Team Three as back-up entered the reptile house to observe and secure the drop site.

Outside the number of visitors began to increase. The operations coimmander had to judge when their subject was as clear as possible from any civilians in the event the subject carried a weapon. Finally as he was about five meters from the exit but still in the open . . .

MOVE IN! MOVE IN, MOVE IN! Came the order.

Eight agents including Ames and Kuksova, 9mm's drawn, apeared from nowhwere moved in and effected the arrest. He surreneded without incident.

Minutes later with two agents escorting the handcuffed prisoner across to the exit a muffled shot echoed across the plush garden plaza and the meat and bone on the right side of the suspect's head was torn away.

By the time Robert Dunlap's lifeless corpse crumpled to the ground both escorting agents had their service weapons drawn, were crouched down and scanning the area for the perpetrator.

It was amongst screams and pandemonium that the small handful of visitors scattered, the remaining agents closed ranks around the two escorts and likewise faced outward.

"BASTARD! SON-OF-A-BITCH BASTARD!"

Special Agent Jim Ames, the man who had tracked Robert Dunlap all these years, was left pacing back and forth repeatedly cursing a blue streak.

A short time later, with the help of the NYPD the plaza had been evacuated, an ambulance had arrived and the area sealed off then combed but the sniper was never found.

About twenty minutes or so after the pandemonium had subsided and Dunlap's body had been taken away Kuksova and Ames wandered over to some uniforms to get an update as they and a pair of detectives were questioning a group of about a dozen witnesses who had been in the plaza.

Suddenly Irina backhanded Ames on the arm.

"What?"

"The guy, second from the left talking to the black cop." She whispered and nodded.

Ames looked up and spotted the middle-aged Chinese gentleman in a brown leather jacket and New York Yankees baseball cap Kuiksova was referring to.

"That's our contact's handler!" She declared.

Just as she did the guy made eye contact with her and hastily started for the garden's exit. On cue Ames and Kuksova it was with a distinct sense of purpose that they worked their way through the people towards him.

Once at the gate he bolted.

"SHIT! It's too early for this shit!" Ames declared as both agents hurriedly weaved their way through the remainder of the crowd then broke into a sprint.

The chase was somewhat abbreviated when the runner made the last mistake of his life. Out on the main path he stopped and drew down on his pursuers. Kuksova instinctively grabbed a young kid and his mother and protecting them with her body tucked them down behind a large rock formation off the path while Ames got off four shots to the Chinaman's two before both men fell to the ground.

Kuksova moved towards her downed partner. He'd apparently been hit.

"Disarm him!" Ames ordered from down on the ground.

Kuksova, weapon drawn with a steady bead on the subject, made her way to the critically wounded Chinaman as the mother and little boy scurried away from behind the rock.

As she retrieved his weapon from beside him she noted he was hit twice in the chest and grazed once in the head. He was struggling to speak.

"Se supone que. . . no debes usar munición real! . . . no debes usar munición real!" The

Chinaman moaned.

"Lie still, an ambulance is on the way!" She instructed as she patted him down for other weapons. Ames wandered up alongside her holding his right shoulder. Kuksova undid her scarf and moved to dress his wound.

"You okay?" She asked Ames.

"Se supone que no . . . no debes usar . . . munición real." The Chinaman repeated as he released a long deep sigh, his chest deflated and his open eyes glazed over.

"Yeah, I'm not hit. I banged my shoulder when I hit the deck to avoid his line of fire."

"Good thing he didn't have the same reflexes! That's some pretty good shooting." She complimented Ames.

"Former Marine." He shrugged off the compliment.

"Se supone . . . que no . . . no, was that guy speaking Latin?" Ames asked.

"Spanish I think." She confirmed.

"You find anything on him?"

"He has no I.D. a handfull of subway tokens and take a look at this!" She passed him the Chinaman's Tokarev54 pistol and magazeine which held only blanks.

"Huh, fuckin' blanks! Guess he was worried about the kids too." Ames commented. "What tipped you off about this guy?"

She bent down and retrieved his new York Yankees baseball cap brandishing it to Ames. "Notice anything peculiar?"

"Yeah, the logo's all fucked up. The letters aren't overlaid on top of one another."

"Exactly! And it's the wrong font. Somebody screwed up the New York Yankees logo in New York? What are the odds of that?" She turned the ball cap inside out to expose the label. "It's a Chinese knock off!"

Later in the car on their way back downtown to file their reports Irina asked about their primary subject, Dunlap.

"Do we know much about this guy? Exacty who he was selling the secrets to?" Kuksova asked.

"Yeah we know about everything." Ames responded as he stared straight ahead and drove.

"Who was he, what'd he do?"

By way of an answer Ames passed her Dunlap's rap sheet. She was shocked.

"He was . . ."

"Yeah, one of us!"

"Special Agent Robert Dunlap." She read aloud.

Later they were able to examine the single piece of paper taken from behind the placard in the reptile house.

It was some kind of electronic schematic accompanied by some kind of a software code.

****

13th Precinct
230 E. 21st Street
Gramercy Park, Manhattan

As per Frank Mahone's invitation, after completing his testimony in D.C., Nigel Morrissey flew north to New York and was met at JFK by Mahone. Not having seen each other for over a year there was some catching up to do in the car on the way into Manhattan.

"Things good with the squad?"

"Din, Ali and FNG send their greetings. We keep an empty desk and an unopened bottle of Irish on it in memory of Dunn."

"Tough break, she was a good kid."

"Crack detective as well. She was a month or so into a pregnancy to boot. We only found out after the funeral." Morrissey informed.

"That sucks! Husband?"

"Don't know. Vanished from London after the funeral."

A full hour and twenty minutes after leaving JFK, far from the glitz and glamor of Broadway or Fifth Avenue they entered the chaos and clatter of the unassuming station house designated the 13th Precinct tucked away in Lower Manhattan between 2nd and 3rd Avenues in the middle of 21st Street.

Visitors and passers-by to the 13th are greeted to the 1960's styled glass and aluminium front entrance with a large piece of twisted wreckage from the 911 bombings of the Twin Towers mounted on a low pedestal to the left of the door. The words "Never Forget" sit below the photos of the three officers from the 13th who, along with 409 other police and emergency workers sacrificed their lives in those attacks.

The Hermes Project

Upstairs the early morning clatter of the Major Crimes Division faded behind them as Mahone, accompanied by Morrissey, knocked then entered the Division Chief's office and closed the door behind them.

Perusing the cluttered office, Frank was not pleased at the indicative sight which greeted him. Disarray usually signalled dissatisfaction with the general state of things with his boss.

"Chief this is Inspector Morrissey, the fellow I worked with in London. Inspector Morrissey, Chief Detective Wachowski." Wachowski didn't bother standing.

"Glad you decided to come to work today!" Wachowski greeted. Mahone ignored the dig.

"Pleasure to meet you sir! Heard a great deal about you." Inspector Morrissey complimented.

"100% of it charitable I'm sure!" Wachowski smirked. "Pleasure to meet you too."

"I was just giving the inspector the ten cent tour of the station house. He was curious to see how we do things over here." Mahone interjected.

"How long you in town for?" Wachowski played along with the small talk so as not to be rude but was obviously pre-occupied with getting back to work.

"A few days, possibly a week, no more."

"Good to hear." He turned to Mahone as he tore a sheet from a pre printed pad on his desk and scribbled a note. "I don't care how much of a hero you are over in England, you're back in the U. S, of A. now. This ain't no foreign country. This is New

York!"

"Yeah New York, where almost no one speaks English!" Mahone quipped.

"Here." From across his desk Wachowski thrust the sheet of paper at Mahone.

"What's this?"

"A trip ticket. That's a reminder that you're on the tax payer's dime. Take the inspector back to his hotel and get your broke ass up to that address on the Upper West Side and get a follow-on statement from this robbery victim. And mind what little manners you have left. She's a city councilman's daughter. Bad enough all I got to send up there is you! She's already been through enough trauma this week!"

"I thought-" Mahone straed to say.

"Nice meeting you Inspector." Waschowski said as he brandished a mechanical smile.

"Likewise Chief."

Once out of the office they headed back downstairs.

"Nice chap, seems you two have a loving rapport." Morrissey mocked.

"Yeah, like husband and wife." Mahone grunted as they took the stairs. "Forced to stay together by court order!"

"Well, so long as it doesn't affect the children!" Morrissey shrugged.

They made their way out onto the street.

"You want to come up town on a ride along?" Mahone proposed. Morrissey momentarily considered the offer. Mahone noticed his hesitation.

"If you're not up to it I perfectly understand."

"How do you mean?"

"I mean, what if we get diverted or get a follow-on call?"

"I don't know, seeing as we hardly have any violence in London." Morrissey quipped unsuccessfully masking his sarcasm as they reached the car.

"Your chief said to take me back to my hotel room."

"Do you want to go back to your hotel room?"

"I didn't say that."

"So you want to come on the ride along?"

"I didn't say that either."

"Well for fuck's sake man, stop speaking English and speak American!"

"Alright, I'll go. BUT strictly for observational purposes!"

Ten minutes into the trip Frank made small talk as they drove.

"So how are things in London?"

"It's a city. Like here. SNUFU'd I believe you call it."

"FUBAR'd would be more accurate!" Frank added.

Twenty minutes into the drive they had just passed the 106th Street exit and were heading north in Upper Manhattan past the Museum district on the FDR when a call came in.

Central Dispatch to any unit in the vicinity of 117th. I have a 10-52 up in East Harlem. Uniforms *requesting a 10-13. Address is 1-7-1-4 East 117th, third floor. No apartment number reported. Uniforms at the scene. Over.*

Mahone grabbed the dash mike.
"Dispatch be advised, 13 Adam One diverting from routine call and responding to your 10-52. ETA three to four minutes. Out.

Acknowledged 13 Adam, Dispatch out.

"I think we're coming upon 111th." Morrissey contributed.
"There's an off ramp on 117th but it's a one way going west." Mahone noted "That address is in the middle of the block. We'll get off on 119th and come back around." He instructed as he activated the fleshing blue and red lights lining both windscreens.
"The President is furious because someone had written 'Fuck Joe Biden' in yellow snow. 'I want to know what son-of-a-bitch did this pronto!'" Mahone blurted out of the blue as he sped along.
"This a joke?"
"Yes it's a joke! You do have jokes in England don't you?"
"Yeah, bloody Parliament's full of them!"
"A few hours later, the FBI presents the results of their investigation. 'Mr. President,, the urine is Trump's. That figures! Biden cursed. But the handwriting is Dr. Jill's."
"Not bad!" Nigel chuckled .

The Hermes Project

Despite the fact Nigel Morrissey spent more than half his life in London he remained in awe of the sheer expanse of New York City as they raced to the call.

"What did you mean when you asked if I really wanted to come along?" Nigel probed as they raced past a delivery van then overtook a :exus on the wrong side.

"I wasn't insinuating anything! You seemed hesitant, that's all!" Frank explained.

"Well, I was just thinking of you."

"Me?! How were you thinking of me?!" He challenged as they turned off the FDR.

"I had no desire to get you in trouble with your chief that's all! I'll have you know I still have three full years until I intend to retire." Morrissey affirmed. Mahone focused on his driving as he offered no response.

Save for the screaming of the siren, and screeching of tires as they weaved and bobbed through traffic, there were several minutes of silence.

It wasn't until they reached the middle of the block on 117th where two black and whites had the street cordoned off, traffic blocked and several uniforms were setting up a perimeter outside the tenement.

"Which doesn't mean I have to put in for my pension I'll have you know."

"Good to know." Frank asssured.

"By the way, what's a 10-52?" Nigel asked as they double parked the car in the middle of the street and climbed out.

"Terrorist attack. Multiple explosives involved, possible dead children."

"SERIOUSLY?!" Morrissey blurted out as he stopped dead in his tracks.

"No! Just a domestic dispute. Routine shit." Mahone snickered as he took note of the small crowd which had been corralled across the street from the tenement building as he approached one of the squad cars and spoke to the uniform standing aside the vehicle.

"Lieutenant Mahone, homicide from the 13th. What'a we got?"

The NYPD squad car was parked across from the six story, c.1930's, apartment house. In contrast to many of the tenements in the Spanish Harlem district this building was quite well maintained with red brick and white sandstone window frames.

"The 13th?! A little out'a your sector ain't you?" The uniform officer challenged.

"Yeah, we heard there's a new Starbucks just opened around the corner and we were in the neighborhood so we thought we'd drop by."

Just then a gunshot blew out a window on the third floor. Bystanders screamed and cops ducked behind their cars as glass fragments crashed to the pavement. Mahone remained standing as he smiled down at Morrissey's hunched over body.

"Of course if you'd rather wait for the next gold badge to come by, we'll just go get our coffee." Mahone proposed to the patrolman.

A series of female screams emanated through the

shattered window.

"Okay what's the play Mahone? SWAT?" The uniform asked.

"No, not yet. Anybody go up there and try to talk to the guy?"

"Yeah, he demanded to talk to the press when we first answered the call. If you wanna go up there you can still see the bullet holes in the apartment door!" He nodded over to his partner sitting on an adjacent door step whose upper right arm was being bandaged by a fellow officer. "It's just a graze wound but the fact that he has no compunction to pop rounds at cops is usually not a good sign." The patrolman expounded.

"Can't argue with you there. Do you know how many he's holding up there?"

"Best we can determine after talking with the maintenance man she's his baby mama and they may or may not have a kid up there. We haven't heard anything."

Mahone removed his overcoat and tossed it onto the back seat of the police cruiser. Then unsnapping the stay from his shoulder holster he removed his 9mm Glock, tucked it into the back waistband of his trousers and smiled at Morrissey standing next to him.

"Officer, eject the mag out of your service weapon and give it to me." The patrolman complied and Mahone tucked the empty 9mm into his holster.

"You're not going in there with an empty gun in your holster are you?!" The Morrissey challenged.

"Do you want us to block the press when they

show up?" The officer asked.

"Yeah, hold'em down on the corner. I'll send word when you can let them through. Good question though! Where are those little root weevils! They're usually on the scene before we are!" Mahone pointed out.

Morrissey became visibly concerned.

"Surely you don't intend to venture up there without at least a plan?!"

"I do have a plan. I'm goin' up there and talk to the man and ask him to surrender."

"And if he doesn't surrender?"

"Then I'm gonna shoot him."

"What's the idea of the empty gun?"

"If I have to kill him, which I may have to, the best way is too lull him into a false sense of security is by relinquishing my weapon."

"You're a bloody Neanderthal!" Morrissey declared as he stripped off his overcoat, tossed it onto the backseat and addressed the uniformed officer.

"Patrolman, does that microphone cable to your car radio disconnect?"

"Yeah, it's a standard jack cord, why?"

"May I borrow it please? Mahone, give us the loan of your mobile and ear phones as well."

"What the hell are you doing, you wing nut?!" Mahone asked as he complied.

The officer returned with the patrol car's microphone, spring cord dangling below it. He passed it off to Morrissey who did a quick recording check into Mahone's cell phone, held the cord to the bottom of the phone and plugged only one of the ear phones into his ear while tucking the extra ear plug and cord into the breast pocket of his tweed jacket.

"Your man said he wanted to talk to the press?" Morrissey said as he held the cell phone to his mouth and spoke with a received pronunciation dialect. "Detective Mahone, Hugh Edwards here, BBC News at Six! Can you tell our audience at home exactly what's happening here?" He then held the phone to Mahone's mouth as if he were recording.

"Yeah! I'm about to confront a crazed Puerto Rican gunman with Monty Python as back-up!" Mahone said. The patrolman smiled.

"I'll lure him into the hallway away from the hostages and you can arrest him." Morrissey offered.

Mahone turned to the patrolman. "Once we're in the building pass the word to your men to hold their fire!"

"Will do Lieutenant."

"We got a name on this guy?"

"Apartment's rented under the name Maria Gomez. We think the perp's name is Jesus."

"Of course it is! Okay where're we going?"

"Apartment 307, it's on the left, top of the stairs. The one with the bullet holes in the door."

"Encouraging!"

Mahone and Morrissey scurried across the street to the shelter of the main entrance doorway.

"You know this is supposed to just be a ride along. You don't have to do this!" Frank said to Nigel.

"Let's don't start that again! Besides, if something happened to you I'd have to pay for a hotel for the rest of the week."

"Fair enough."

They cautiously made their way up to the top of the third floor landing to just outside the apartment door but stayed crouched down in the stairwell.

"JESUS! JESUS, IT'S LIEUTENANT FRANK MAHONE." They braced for fire but none came. "JESUS, YOU SAID YOU WANTED TO TALK TO SOMEONE FROM THE PRESS! I GOT A REPORTER HERE TO TALK TO YOU."

There was no response and they began to fear the worst.

"HE'S HERE ALL THE WAY FROM LONDON AND HE'S-" Mahone stopped shouting as they heard the half dozen locks on the inside of the door being undone.

From a few steps down in the stairwell Mahone could peer over the floor, look up and see the door crack open as far as the safety chain would allow.

Morrissey stepped out from behind Mahone and brandished the rigged-up microphone and cell phone.

"I just want to get your side of the story Jesus."

"Jew are from London?" A faceless voice came from between the cracked open door and the hall wall.

"Yes, I'm with the BBC news."

"Why jew come all dis way from France to talk wit me?"

"Actually I was in New York doing a story on

poverty in American big cities." Again there was silence. "Jesus, I'd very much like to get your perspective on why so many Hispanics are having financial problems here in America."

"What eez that?"

"What is what?"

"Respective!"

"**Per**spective. It means you're take, your idea. Your opinion."

"If jew want to talk wit me why jew bring a cop wit jew?"

"He's merely here for my protection. He is unarmed." Morrissey nodded to Mahone who pulled the empty gun from his holster and slid it across the floor frtom the top of the stairs.

"There's my gun Jesus! I'm not here to shoot you! We just need to know if everybody is alright in there."

"I want to talk wit dee reporter guy."

"I'm here Jesus!" Morrissey moved up to the landing but was careful to stand to the side in order to keep Mahone's line of fire to the door open. "Jesus, it would look better if you come out in front of the camera so people can see. They'll listen to what you have to say with more interest if they know who's talking to them." He faced the cell phone to the door.

The door slammed shut and again there was a moment of silence. Then without warning the clinking of the safety chain being undone was heard and the head of a visibly dishevelled Hispanic, thirty-something man cautiously peered out.

Unseen by Morrissey Mahone was very impressed.

"We are doing a series on violence in America and how it unfairly affects so many Hispanic citizens." Morrissey coaxed.

Jesus was lost for words but quickly returned to his natural state - suspicion.

"That don't look like no microphone to me!" He challenged.

"It's an IPhone 176 with camera and a radio mike, it transmits directly to the station. There's a TV van down the block. The police won't let it through until they think it's safe." Morrissey could see he was losing him. "You're live on the air right now! Say something."

Dressed in loose panama bottoms, a sweat-stained white T-shirt and with his Colt 9mm loosely dangling at his right side Jesus stepped out into the hall just past the door.

"Ladies and gentlemen I'm here talking to Jesus, Jesus what's your family –"

The explosive report of Mahone's Glock deafened all three as it rebounded off the narrow hall walls while the single round shattered Jesus' weapon and continued on through into the side of his right thigh causing him to collapse on the floor, grab at his wound and howl loudly.

"And that, ladies and gentlemen wraps up today's broadcast." Morrissey drolly spoke into the cell phone.

Several uniforms, guns drawn, rushed up the stairs as Mahone, his weapon at the low ready, moved in to clear the apartment.

He found the young mother on the floor cuddling her crying child, the infant's wailing heavily muffled in the stunned ears of Mahone and Morrissey.

The police tended to Jesus as Mahone guided the mother and child out of the apartment.

As they got to the door she looked down and saw the blood puddled on the floor under the now semi-conscious Jesus and went ballistic.

"WHAT DID JEW DO TO HIM JEW BASTARDS?!" She screamed following it up with all manner of chastisement in all three languages, English, Spanish and Spanglish.

Morrissey was taken aback at how quickly she turned on them screaming and cursing them and their children as she had to be pulled back from trying to comfort her blood-soaked, near comatose man.

"I don't speak Spanish, what did she say?" Morrissey asked loudly.

"That's Puerto Rican for 'Thank you'!" Mahone casually explained to Morrissey as he retrieved the pistol and they descended the stairs leaving the uniforms to tend to the scene.

By the time they reached the street and exited the building more police, the paramedics and the press had arrived.

Mahone and Morrissey had to swim their way through a gaggle of locals and reporters to get back to their car.

"In America less than a day and you're already

famous!" He commented to Morrissey.

"Yes, land of opportunity! So much for a quiet holiday! I don't suppose there is anywhere nearby to get a pint?"

It was back in the car as they were once again on the FDR that Mahone spoke first.

"An IPhone 176 with camera and a radio mike?!" Frank laughingly challenged.

"One has to think fast in a tight situation, my good man."

"Morrissey . . . I don't want to get all sentimental, but, it means a lot that you had my back."

"Don't read too much into it old boy. I was primarily concerned about getting back to my hotel room." Mahone glanced over at him quzzicaly. "I haven't a clue how to navigate the bloody underground here."

CHAPTER FOUR

Police Plaza
Lower Manhattan

That cold and blustery Monday morning Irina Kuksova left her Bryant Park apartment in Midtown to make her way across to the 8th Avenue subway line to travel south to Chambers Street. Twenty-five minutes later she entered 26 Federal Plaza to complete her report on Saturday's shooting incident at the zoo.

In the elevator on the way up to her office details of the gun duel ran through her mind.

Once in her office Irina had no sooner removed her coat when her intercom buzzed and she was requested to report to the Director's office.

As she stepped off the elevator on the 16th floor Agent Jim Ames buzzed past her completely ignoring her greeting and heading for the stairwell where he disappeared behind the fire exit door which he slammed shut behind him.

Huh! Morning to you too Agent Ames! She mumbled to herself.

Upstairs she was shown directly into the Branch Director's office.

"Agent Kuksova." He coolly greeted as he reached across his desk and passed her a typewritten form, "I need you to read this and sign this please." He directed without emotion.

Puzzled she quickly perused the two paragraphs.

"This is a suspension order!"

"Correct. Please sign at the bottom. And also I'll need your gun, badge and I.D."

"That's it? No explanation?! I'm not signing anything until you explain what's going on!"

Branch Director Christopher temporarily retreated from his hard-ass mode, sat back and took a deep breath before he methodically informed her that the exact reason she and agent Ames were being put on paid suspension pending an investigation was for losing a valuable prisoner and killing a suspected witness.

"A SUSPECTED WITNESS?!" She made no attempt to control her outrage. "HE WAS THE GOD DAMNED COURIER AND DUNLAP'S HANDLER!"

"That is yet to be determined." Christopher calmly rebutted. Kuksova was besides herself.

"He fired on us during a foot chase!"

"The gun was loaded with blanks."

"And how exactly were we supposed to know that at the time?!"

"A complete and thorough investigation will reveal the facts." He countered.

"The FBI where no good deed goes unpunished!" She swore aloud. "Andrew McCabe commits treason and gets promoted to Acting Director, Ames and I bag a bastard **actually commiting** treason and we get sidelined?! I'm beginning to understand why the Republicans called to revamp this organization!" Tossing her holstered Glock and badge on his desk Kuksova didn't bother to wait to be dismissed but made for the door without signing the form letter where she turned and spoke.

"Why aren't Ames and I being kept on the case?"

"Two reasons. Neither of you is the lead on the case and any agent-involved shoooting automatically disqualifies said agent from further involvement in said case until a full OPR investigation into the shooting has been completed."

She realized there was no further point in arguing. "Besides, there are already people on it." He added from across the room. "Of course under the Employees' Rights Act you're free too file an Objection to Action letter which will be duely reveiwed by the board."

"How long will that take?" She challenged.

"About two weeks."

"And how long for the OPR to complete their 'investigation?" She pushed.

"About fourteen days." He calmly informed. There was nothing more to say.

Once down on street level an array of options ran through her head.

Go to breakfast up in Midtown? No, she was too upset to eat. Contact Ames? No, too obvious. Find a bar and drink? Ummm . . . no, too early.

Once down on street level as Irina was trying to decide what her next move would be and after walking for a short while, she passed a corner kiosk where the headline on the cover of a magazine caught her attention;

'Shake-up in D.C. Intel Scene'

"May I have a copy of that *Vanity Fair* please?" Minutes later she was sitting in a window seat at the *Blue Moon Café* with a cappuccino reading.

'Investigation Launched Over Leaked Secrets'
House Intelligence Committee members are being considered for investigation over suspicion of leaking classified information. Although the Chairman of the HIC, Representative Burman, a Massachusetts Democrat, has been contacted for comment as of the date of publication of this article no response has been received.

The bulk of the magazine story centered around the fact that the FBI and NSA have had an unusual number of misses in the near past along with lax production in anticipating terror attacks compounded by the latest controversy surrounding the agency's data collection methods both of which have apparently caused the former Director to resign.

Eventually she found herself in another café in The West Village where she wrestled with an idea for the next three and a half hours and finally decided to sleep on it before committing herself to it.

But as she ordered her third latté she browsed through the magazine then back to the investigation article.

Just because she stopped carrying a gun and a badge didn't mean Kuksova stopped being a federal cop.

The Hermes Project

She noted the magazine's business address and the reporter's name, Sam O'Neill. She rummaged through her purse for her phone and stored the information.

"4 Times Square." She mumbled to herself. "That's handy!"

"You say something mam'am?" The older gentlemen sitting at the table across from her asked.

"No, no. Just talking to myself."

"Well, as long as you don't answer back is all that matters!" He joked.

She then headed back up town to her Bryant Park apartment to change, have a shower, a glass of wine and a think.

Kuksova's area of expertise being computer crime and the zoo operation being her first 'real' violent criminal encounter, it was by mid-morning Tuesday that she had made her decision.

She picked up her cell and dialled.

"Frank its Irina."

Agent Kuksova! How are you gorgeous? How's the country's eighteenth best Intel agency treating you?

"Very funny! You know very well there are only seventeen intel agencies! I'm on suspension."

What happened?

"I'll tell you when I see you."

You asking for another date?

"Frank I need help."

Why are you moving house again?

"Don't be a wise guy! I'm asking for help asshole!"

67

At the use of the compliment 'asshole' Mahone realized Irina was serious.

Where do you want to meet? Mahone asked.

"There's a new place called *Gramercy Bagels* over on-"

What'd you turn into a Yuppie since we came back from England?

"I represent that remark! I'm still the same smart, intelligent, devastatingly beautiful-"

I get the point! Pete's Tavern on 18th and Irving over in Hoboken, Friday. Be there by four.

"Cordial as ever! Oh and Frank?"

Yeah?

"Good to know you're still a bastard!"

I'll bet you say that to all the boys!

Having begun her week as a talented FBI agent helping to break up an international spy case Irina Kuksova, daughter of Ukrainian immigrants, now found herself unappreciated, unemployed and under investigation.

*

Vanity Fair Magazine
4 Times Sq. NYC, NY

Being the good government agent she was it was right after a light breakfast that morning that Kuksova had hit the internet to start the little personal project still coalescing in her mind.

When she had seen a brief on a rolling chyron on NBC News a week or so ago that the current director of the NSA was stepping down and no reason was given she was prompted to poke around. When the story appeared to fade from the news next day she dug around a lttle more aggresively. Finding still nothing she made a mental note to dig more later when she had more time. After spotting the VFM article, she told herself now she had some time.

It was mid-morning when she dialled her cell phone.

Vanity Fair front desk, how may I direct your call?

"I'm looking to speak to one of your staff writers, a Sam O'Neill?"

I'm sorry Sam's in a meeting right now. Can I take a message? The young sounding receptionist chimed.

"You're on Broadway at Midtown, yes?"

Yes ma'am, we're right on Times Square. Just look for the sign that looks like a 140 foot high soda can stuck on the corner of the building!

"Thank you."

When out-of-towners think of New York City most picture Manhattan. When they picture Manhattan they are likely to visualize Times Square. Times Square is dominated by the building that over several billion have seen on any given New Year's Eve broadcast surrounded by packed streets, noise makers and cops.

That building is situated at 1472 Broadway between 42nd and 43rd Streets, a structure whose footprint occupies an entire New York City block, 1/20th of a mile, and features four 70 by 70 foot square, illuminated roof panels which blast the H&M logo seen across the city from Central Park south to The Village and as far away as New Jersey.

Twenty-five minutes after leaving home Irina emerged from the the 42nd Street and Broadway subway station leaving the squeal of steel wheels and the odour of ozone behind her and emerging out into the din and chaos of Midtown traffic.

A long way from Kiev! Irina mused as she walked one block north to the H&M building.

The fifty-two story high skyscraper featured a 40 foot high glass façade resting on a set of five double doors and as she passed underneath the 14,000 square foot NasDaq sign and entered she was compelled to weave her way through a gaggle of tourists being led across the expansive lobby.

". . . over a million and a half square feet of floor space!" The tour guide informed with just enough gusto to enthral the smal group while suppressing his frustration at not being 'On Broadway' in the sense he jhad intended when he left Muncie, Indiana seven months ago.

Still adjusting to her first stateside big city Irina shook her head at the fact that they actually give tours of office buildings and once again was overwhelmed by the 'Bigger is Better' idiom which personifies America.

Up on the 16th floor she found the magazine's offices which occupied the entire level. She made her way over to the twenty foot long reception desk and asked to see Sam O'Neill.

The receptionist buzzed and a minute later a

The Hermes Project

petite, late twenty-something sporting short, brown hair, dressed in a smart business suit with matching jacket and skirt, white blouse and glasses cocked back on her head appeared from around the corner.

"Yes?"

"**You're** Sam O'Neill? The writer?" Irina challenged.

"They call us journalists. But . . . well, you know . . . Yes, I'm Sam."

"Sorry I didn't mean to be obtuse it's just that I thought you were a guy."

"No problem, I get that a lot. Dad wanted a boy. But I can throw a baseball if that matters to you!" She joked.

Kuksova smiled as she flashed her illegal spare badge. O'Neill's smile melted away.

"What can I do for you?" She nervously asked, the color visibly draining from her face as she took a step back.

"I'd like to have a chat with you about this month's issue and the interesting article you wrote. You might be able to help me out with a case I'm on."

"A federal case?"

"Not really, well sort of. I'm doing some work for the government." To Irina's relief O'Neill didn't ask to see any further proof or I.D. "I'm only interested in your story about the intel services."

"Oh thank God!" O'Neill was visibly relieved. "I thought you were here about my ex-boyfriend! Total whack job!"

Given that scrap of information, Kuksova saw

her opportunity.

"I know exactly what you mean!! She said. "Been there, done that, got the Tee-shirt!" Irina spouted in faux confidence touching the younger woman on the arm as reinforcement.

"RIGHT?!" Sam said aloud. "You can never tell a book right?!"

"You are absolutely right! I totally get where you're coming from!" They laughed a little too long and finally Kuksova spoke.

"Just a quick word."

The constant buzzing of phones combined with sporadic foot traffic made for disruptive surroundings.

"Is there someplace else we can talk? This won't take long. I'm actually here regarding the article you wrote, about discord in the alphabet agencies?"

"Oh, I see! Well in that case why don't we take the lift down to the cafeteria on the 4th floor and get a latte?"

"Sounds good!"

Sam leaned in over the reception counter and plucked a pen and paper from the desk. The pen was dry so she grabbed another.

"$37 million sign, 18 million LED's on the entrance way and I can't get a God damned pen that writes!" She cursed. "Janice, I'm leaving you my new cell number. I'll be down in the cafeteria if anyone needs me." She informed the receptionist.

Focused on her keyboard, Janice didn't bother to look up but instead just grunted in response.

As it was only mid-morning the cafeteria wasn't crowded so they settled on an isolated table off to the side.

"What can I help you with?" Sam started.

"What prompted you to write the article?"

"I was assigned it from the Editor. She's a 'never Trumper' and hates the government! Besides, we don't work freelance here like *Cosmo* or *Rolling Stone* we're given assignments by desk."

"By desk?"

"Yes, Fashion, Current Affairs, Beauty. I'm recently promoted to Politics. Took me a year to get out from behind Entertaimment! Hated it!"

"At least you got to meet the celebs, no?"

"Yeah, as long as you like self-rightous, holier-than-thou assholes!" Sam spat.

"I noticed there were no names in your piece." Kuksova questioned.

"The three or four people I was introduced to and spoke with asked not to be named. Probably for security reasons. Plus they're supposed to be getting a new director soon. At least the NSA is anyway."

"You really didn't cite much in the way of evidence that there's discord in the three major agencies."

"Well it was only a filler article and I didn't know what to write exactly, it being my first real assignment. The piece I submitted came in at 3,000 words! J.J, my editor cut that in half straught away."

"I see."

"But in regards to the people, every time I was referred to someone for a quote or an opinion I'd get the run-around. The only solid name I walked away with was one from a House Rep."

"Who was that?"

"A congresswoman who asked not to be named in the article, which I thought also kind of strange."

"Why?"

"Well, I mean she is in the public eye being in the Congress and all. In addition to which she is on the House Intel Committee and has direct control of funding for the NSA and I am writing an article in an international publication wanting to give a little insight, maybe get the security services some good PR. I mean let's face it, after their Russia hoax scheme fell apart it's not as if the general public has any faith in them anymore, especially the FBI!" She became wide-eyed and stared up at Kuksova. "Oh, I'm sorry! No offence intended."

"None taken. Please, go on."

"Well you read it. It's only a 1,200 word piece. It was originally supposed to be a puff piece lauding the security services. But with the security scandals from the last administration and the shit this administration has gotten into it's a wonder I could write anything positive at all!"

"Is that why you focused so much on the NSA?"

"Partially, but mainly because they're getting this new director and they're rumored to be the most productive of all the agencies. Largest, biggest budget, blah, blah, blah."

"What was the congresswoman's name?"

"I won't get in trouble?" She cautiously asked.

"Sam, I'm FBI."

"That's what worrries me! You know, 'I'm from the government, I'm here to help you!' Again, no offence."

"None traken. Besides she's in public office, unless she's a criminal she can't hide her identity."

"Makes sense. Her name is Natalie something. I have it and her contact details up in my office. Come back up and I'll get them for you."

Having finished their coffees they stood to leave.

"I'll get this." Sam insisted as she fished her wallet from her shoulder bag then drew her credit card from her wallet. Irina slid a fiver over to her.

"Sorry, we're not allowed." Irina smiled. "Could be misconstrued as a gratuity."

"Oh!"

Back upstairs Sam flopped her purse on her desk, manned her keyboard and started to pull up the contact's name and number when her intercom buzzed.

"Yes?"

Sam, need you at the front desk to sign for a package!

"Shit! Be right back." Sam scurried out of the small office and Kuksova waited as O'Neill went out to reception to sign for the delivery.

Irina couldn't help but notice O'Neill's purse had partially spilled out onto the desk. Of the half dozen items which caught her eye the most prominent was Sam's UPI Press Pass.

By the time Sam re-entered clutching a bouquet of flowers the Press Pass was in Irina's left hip pocket.

"Nice bouquet!" Kuksovo complimented.
"Isn't it?!"
"Who is it from? Him?" Irina teased.
"Yeah, great isn't it?!"
"Yeah. Great. Maybe he's not that bad of a guy after all."
"Ya think?!" Sam laid the flowers aside and retook to the computer to retrieve the name. 'Congresswoman Natalie Farmiga.' Sam scribbled the name on a Post-It. "She's a Republican from northern New Jersey." She added as she passed the note over her desk to Irina. "I have to tell you agent Kuksova, it's a breath of fresh air."
"What is?" Irina read the paper then tucked it away in her pocket.
"The fact that you wouldn't let me pay for your latte because of the law. It's a breath of fresh air to know there's at least one honest agent in our government!"
Irina half smiled uncomfortably and bid O'Neill good-bye.

****

A Hot Dog Stand
Corner of Sixth Avenue & 14th St.
12:30, Wednesday, 13 Feb

Immersed in the blare of horns, the staccato of a distant jack hammer and the din of Sixth Avenue traffic Nigel Morrissey stared in amazemet as Frank Mahone devouered the tail end of the second

Sabrettes hot dog before Morrissey had lfted his first to his mouth.

Mahone caught his stare.

"What's wrong? Why ain't you eatin'?" Mahone mumbled as he chewed.

"You do realize that you're supposed to chew your food?" The Inspector quipped as Frank took a long swig of his Yoohoo then attacked his third saurekraut and brown mustard drenched hot dog.

"Thanks mom!"

"You want I make you usual four?" The short, stubby Greek at the push cart asked Mahone.

"Yeah!" As he swallowed the other half bottle of Yoo-hoo.

Morrissey took a tentetive bite of his hot dog just as the radio in their unmarked sedan crackled to life.

Attention, attention. Any unit in the vicinity of Seventh and Christopher we have a report of a car jacking in progress. Victim reports three black males, held her at gun point. Stolen vehicle is Burgendy Ford SUV. Plates to follow. Over.

With a string of saurkraut dangling from his mouth Mahone was immediately in the car and manning the mike.

"Dispatch, 13 Adam One responding. ETA three to five, Out."

Acknowledged 13 Adam. A black and white will meet you there. Will keep you advised. Out.

"Let's go Jeeves! Sounds like the indians are attackin' the fort!" Frank directed.

Morrissey spit the half chewed bolus of frankfurter into the waste basket on the corner as he made his way to the car.

"New York City hot dogs! Made fresh monthly! Bloody thing tastes like it was leftover from when we were here!"

Mahone sped away west on 14th then skidded through a left hand turn on Seventh Ave and headed south.

"This one could get messy so –"

"Mahone, don't start that malarky again! I-" Morrissey protested.

"SHIT!" Frank declared.

"What is it?"

"I forgot, you're not carrying! I don't suppose you still have the gun I -"

"No, couldn't bring it home it was in your name."

"Shit! And I left my back-up piece on the night stand!"

"But I did a year's rotation on an ARVO unit ten years ago."

"Armed Response Vehicle Officer. So you know how to handle a gun? If you had one!"

"Well, not really."

"What are you talking about?" Frank sought to clarify as he slowed slightly to clear the next intersection at 11th and Greenwich.

"Regulations. We're required to store the weapons in the boot of the vehicle and only take them out when required while on a call."

"So how many calls did you get in a year?"

"Well 'calls' per se are divided into potentially lethal fire arms and 'other then fire arms', in which case we'd need to park in a safe zone, unlock the boot, select a weapon then-"

"Christ Almighty man! How in God's name did you ever shoot anybody?" Mahone argued as he weaved around local traffic.

"Oh, I never shot anyone! And there's no need to get snippy!" He snipped. "We're not a gaggle of cowboys in England! We don't man our weapons to shoot people! We man them to deter!" Morrissey sensed Mahone's mountng frustration.

"How many times?!"

"I think about three."

"THREE CALLS?!"

"Three or four yes."

"London, a city of over ten million and you only got three or four calls?!"

"Oh I wasn't in London at the time. I was in Bromley Borough."

"And in Bromley Borough how many times were you required to spend an hour digging your weapons out of your trunk?"

"Well, let me think."

"Never mind we're here!" Looking around he slowed the car and spotted the black and white unit up the block.

"Dispatch, 13 Adam 4. Relay to the black and white east of me to cut his lights and siren and to cruise down to West Broadway and Sixth."

13 Adam 4, be advised, second black and white now west of you approaching north from SOHO.

"Dispatch, identify units please." Frank requested.

13 Adam 4, unit to your south west is 2 Adam One and unit to your east is 4 Adam Three.

"Dispatch, direct 2 Adam One to Varick Street. Tell him to monitor the tunnel entrance. Have 4 Adam Three maintain position, work his way south and meet me at Varick. If we haven't heard from the Tunnel Authority yet we'll have a chance of boxing them in between us. Maybe even flush them out. Over."

Acknowledged 13 Adam, will relay.

As each NYPD dispatcher only handled the radio traffic from two precincts, Mahone was unable to speak directly to the two black and white units assisting him to search for the carjackers and so had to relay through Central Dispatch.

"How do you know they're heading for the tunnel?" Nigel innocently asked.

"Reason these scumbags struck where they did was so they cold hit and then dash cross the river to Jersey thinking we can't chase them across state lines."

"Can you?"

"Yes. But we don't have to. Once they cross state lines it becomes a federal rap. Besides, New Jersey has cops too! That's why we always catch the dumb ones."

"But how can you be sure they're-"

13 Adam 4, be advised, victim has relayed Bluetooth tracker code on stolen SUV which now indicates suspects driving at legal speed just north of Holland Tunnel on Washington.

"Dispatch, advise 4 Adam that 13 Adam is moving to intercept." Frank transmitted.

Copy 13 Adam. 4 Adam is also moving to back-up.

"Copy Dispatch." He turned to Morrissey. "Little bastards must have a portable police scanner! You were saying?" Mahone mildly boasted.

"I was saying how impressed I am." Nigel attempted a recovery without completing his query about how Frank knew about the tunnel location.

Of the half dozen tangle of streets that lead to the entrance of the Holland Tunnel it was a toss up as to which street the car thieves would be found on. However, knowing they were armed not only upped the ante but gave a strong indication that, once discovered they would attempt to evade.

Meanwhile, inside the stolen vehicle, the three black thugs congratulating themselves believing they were home free, suddenly became subdued as the driver spotted the black and white unit from the 4th Precint further down on Varick Street. The stolen SUV rounded the corner and suddenly turned left onto King Street.

13 Adam be advised suspect has made a quick turn, now heading east on King.

"Shit!"

"You seem to say 'shit' a lot!" Nigel observed.

"No shit!" Mahone replied as he swung a 180 in the middle of the intersection cutting off a delivery van.

"They know they can't chance racing through

tunnel traffic, not at this time of day." Frank explained as he grabbed for the radio mike. "Dispatch, 13 Adam here. Get some units over to the entrances to the Williamsburg and Brooklyn Bridges."

Roger 13 Adam, will comply.

"Is there no way to evade in this part of the city?" Nigel asked.

"Leave it to to a bunch of out-of-town Mullies to pull a car jacking in the city sector only a mile wide, with the most convoluted streets!"

"How do you know they are from out of town?"

"Easy! They're too stupid to remember we're on an island that's only a mile wide!"

All units be advised, call recieved reporting erratic driver on Broadway just crosssed Spring Street. Bluetooth sig of stolen SUV indicates vehicle now approaching Grand.

Inside the speeding SUV the three inept car thieves, realizing they were no longer in a movie, argued vehemently about what to do.

"Nigger I told you not to drive south!" The one in the red track suit chastused.

"SHUT THE FUCK UP JAMELE! YOU FROM JERSEY TOO! WHAT THE FUCK YOU KNOW ABOUT MUTHER FUCKIN' MANHATTAN!" The driver in the L.A. Lakers track suit shot back.

Near the end of Broadway the streets narrowed and so a decision was made.

"Dwayne, turn here! We go back to the tunnel area and ditch this bitch!"

"Then what?" The driver challenged.

"Then we split up, hop on the subway and go the fuck back to Newark!"

Now deep in the convuluted, narrow streets of SOHO, they turned west on Howard Street with the intention of heading back north out of The Village.

At Greene and Canal they continued arguing distracting the driver just long enough for him to overshoot the turn causing the SUV to tilt up onto two wheels, careen off the side of a large delivery van, flipping the SUV onto the passenger's side and skidding it through the intersection before taking out the corner lamp post and finally coming to a halt up on the side walk against an abandoned corner storefront.

The youngest and most spry of the hole-in-the-floor-gang quickly emerged through the side window and disappeared up Canal Street.

Dwayne the driver and his second accomplice kicked out the fractured windshield and high-tailed it up the two lane residential Wooster Street just as Mahone and Morrissey pulled up in their unmarked sedan.

"You take the little one, I'll take the Lakers!" Mahone said as they too headed up Wooster as a small crowd gathered around the wrecked SUV.

Morrissey, with no hope of catching the younger man, slowed only minutes later as he fought to catch his breath.

But karma was with him as the thief reached the middle of the block where a full four story scaffolding held several construction workers looking down and who had witnessed the crash scene.

Looking over his shoulder to check on the inspector's progress the carjacker was stiff-armed by a significantly larger hard hat and now fought to catch his breath as he looked up from the ground, wide-eyed and realizing the game was up.

Morrissey caught up, cuffed the theif and confiscated his snub nosed .38.

"Much obliged old chap!" Morrissey spurted as he thanked the worker and marched the thief back down the block towards the patrol car.

A second hard hat climbed down from the scaffolding.

"That cop English?!" He asked his colleague in surprise.

"I guess the NYPD is recruitin' from where ever they can these days!" His buddy answered.

"That defund the police shit must really be hittin' hard!"

Meanwhile, Mahone had chased the driver to the next corner where he saw him duck into a corner art gallery.

Gun drawn, Mahone followed the suspect into the *Leslie-Lohman Art Dealers* on the corner.

The massive open floor premises occupied the space of three standard shop fronts and rose several floors from street level.

The space appeared unoccupied until seconds later he heard rythmic tapping of wood on wood growing louder until a purple and yellow haired female sales attendant in a stone washed denim dress suit with a hemp tie and platform shoes appeared clip clopping from between the large abstract sculptures towards Mahone.

"May I help you?"

Unsuccessfully trying not to be distracted by the dozen piercings puncturing the left side of her face, he holstered his weapon.

"Looking for a black guy, purple track suit, L.A. logo on the back."

"Ah yes! Follow me." She calmly said as she turned and walked off towards the back, the puzzled cop close behind. "Two years ago we had an incident and were held up at gun point. Several Banksy's were taken."

"What's a Banksy?"

"You don't follow the art world, do you?"

"Look lady, under different circumstances I would love to know all about the latest art fads and how many cats you have at home but right now I need to know where the black guy in the Laker's track suit-"

"The guy you're looking for is back here." She nonchalantly answered leading him to the back store room. Mahone again readied his 9mm and clicked off the safety as they entered the rear storage area.

"You'll not be needing that." She informed him as she indicated a one foot square monitor screen up on the wall in the corner opposite. "Banksy is an artist."

On the screen they watched from an overhead CCTV cam displayed a long, rectangular, sealed off room as the culprit pounded on the door he had entered through then in turn focused his frustration on each of the solid walls of the ten foot by eight foot windowless space, all with no luck.

"The owner had a panic room installed. Walls are an half an inch thick solid steel." She informed. "One way in, one way out. Once activated you need the voice code to get out."

"Biggest rat trap I've ever seen!" Mahone observed as he reholstered his weapon.

"OHHHH! That's a bad idea!" She declared as they watched the not-so-bright thief step back and fire off a round at the door he had come in through.

He immediately fell to the floor and curled into the fetal posistion, covering his head as the slug richoshayed off the walls several times before dropping to the floor.

His luck held and he remained unhit.

"Who is he?" She asked.

"Some asshole who carjacked a woman at gunpoint about a half hour ago."

"Nice guy." She commented.

"You sure he can't get out?"

"Not without the code."

"You got the code?"

"Of course!"

"Mind if we leave him in storage while I go see what happened to his bros?"

"No problem but I have to leave and lock up here by six."

Mahone smiled.

"He got enough air in there?"

"Yes there's a ventilator. Why?" She answered.

"In case I'm not back by six. Meanwhile I'll call

it in and try to have a couple of uniforms come by and collect him." He turned to leave.

Back out and up the block the other thug sat handcuffed in one of the black and white units which had arrived while Morrissey waited by their unmarked cruiser.

"You okay?" Mahone asked of Morrissey.

"A bit winded but yes, all's copestetic. You?"

"Our boy's contained."

Ten miutes later they were heading back up Canal Street to return to the 13th when again the radio crackled to life.

13 Adam say your 80 please?

"13 Adam here. In route to base."

13 Adam, we have a message relay from your precinct.

"Dispatch 13 Adam. What's the message?"

13 Adam Inspector Morrissey is requested to call his unit in London as soon as he returns to base.

"Roger Dispatch. Will see that he gets the message. Out." Frank responded.

Acknowledged 13 Adam. Dispatch out.

Frank turned to Nigel as he drove,

"Nigel, call home when we get back to the precinct house."

"Much obliged Frank. Don't know what I'd do without you."

On their return to the precinct Morrissey placed his call back to London and spoke to his chief in Scotland Yard.

CHAPTER FIVE

**Tower Hamlets
East London
Thursday, 14 February**

Having flown into Heathrow the night before Nigel Morrissey had not gotten much sleep.

It was less than fifteen hours ago while still back in New York that the Inspector got word his elderly mother had passed away in her sleep.

Years ago after his father died, he being the only child, Nigel grew closer to his mother and had taken her in for these last few years.

Although in good health until a month ago, she was never dependant on him. The news of her unexpected death came as a shock just a day ago but, having seen more than his share of death, he had now come to deal with it.

Having had little contact with the members of the Squad in the last week, it was through Sergeant Enfield, a.k.a. FNG, that he received word of his mother's death and impending funeral.

It was hardly twenty minutes later that he received a text back telling him that, after he landed back in London, he should meet the Squad at their operations room in Scotland Yard an hour before the funeral.

From Heathrow he taxied straight to The Yard and made his way up to room 601 the former AV room he and the Squad had 'commandeered' when first organized and found themselves essentially homeless in the New Scotland Yard.

When he arrived the Special Homicide Investigations Team, Ali, Din and Enfield were all there to welcome him back and extend their condolences.

As a morale booster to help cheer him up the guys had placed a black reef and a bottle of Jameson's Irish whiskey next to a framed, color photo on Maureen Dunn's desk then cordoned it off with police tape and posted a 'No Tresspassing' sign on the front. The fact that Sgt. Dunn was killed in the line of duty while in Paris had hit Morrisey particularly hard and not only left them without the required female member but minus a skilled investigator.

More importantly, knowing that he was without blood relatives and now completely alone, it was imperitive that Morriessey be reminded he still had a family in The SHIT Squad.

The funeral service at Tower Hamlets Cemetary Park was brief, drizzily and sparsely attended.

Save for the four members of the Squad, a couple of neighbors, a vicar and the family lawyer no one else was in attendance.

Following the short grave-side service Morrissey politely thanked the attendees and waited until they left before joining the three squad members off to the side under a giant willow.

"I appreciate all your support! I just want you all to know-" Morrissey attempted to profess before being cut off.

"Right lads!" Ali the token black interrupted. "If we're going to devolve into all the sticky, touchy feely sheit we'll need to have the proper surroundings!" He declared.

"Couldn't have said it better meself!" Din the token Indian seconded.

"So let it be written. So let it be said!" Boosted Enfield the token white guy.

"I guess its the pub then!" Nigel Morrissey concluded.

*

Dirty Dick's Pub
Off Great George Street
Central London

They parked the car in the Met police yard and took the five minute walk across the Thames embankment along Westminster Pier past the tube station and onto Great George Street.

Dirty Dick's Pub in close proximity of the Yard was established as their after hours haunt or 'regular' since formaton of the Special Homicide Investigation Team almost two years ago.

The two hundred and fifty year old Tudor styled pub was wedged in between two glass and chrome business buildings wth its entrance just off the laneway.

"With 40,000 offices and approximately 20,000 civilian employees the NYPD are the largest intercity police force in the United States. Last year

The Hermes Project

they affected 184,652 felony arrests with the average arrest rate of-" Sergeant John Enfield, a.k.a, FNG, lectured as they ducked into the pub out of the light rain.

"Enfield, give it a rest will you?!" Ali blurted out as they hung their coats and Morrissey slid his umbrella into the brellie holder by the door.

Being only half past two in the afternoon the after work crowd was yet to filter in so attendees were sparse allowing The Squad to take their usual booth in the back of the place.

"So Inspector, how did you find it working with the Americans?" Heath asked as they headed in towrds the back.

"Quite informative Sergeant, quite informative."

No sooner had they taken their seats when a late-twenty something woman with close cropped blond hair in jeans and a dark blue, light Kagool came in. Though dripping wet she carried no umbrella, wore only a polo shirt under the windbreaker and appeared impervious to the cold. She headed straight back to their booth.

"Sorry I'm late Sergeant Heath!" She apologised as she peeled off her wet Kagool to reveal several arm tattoos. "I went to the squad room, found your note but had to find this place first." She apologised as she nodded over to Din.

"MacIntyre." Din nodded back.

"Mac!" Ali also greeted her. "A bit wet aren't we?" He added.

"It's fuckin' London then, it'n it?" She greeted in return. "I brought me things up to 601 and was going to move into a desk in the back but it's all taped off with a black wreath on top and a . . . bottle of whiskey!"

"That'd be Maureen's old desk." Ali informed.

"Maureen?" She questioned as she slid into a chair.

"Sergeant Dunn." Enfield added.

"Oh, the officer you lost in Paris." She affirmed.

"The officer **we** lost in Paris." Ali corrected.

"Yeah, yeah that's what I meant." She corrected.

"Lads, it was a nice gesture but, I think it's time we took down the memorial." Morrissey suggested. The three lads nodded in agreement.

Ali stood to make the introductions.

"Inspector Nigel Morrissey, may I introduce Sergeant Amy MacIntyre. MacIntyre, Inspector Nigal Morrissey, the only senior officer you are likely to meet who has no compunction about telling the higher ups where to stuff it! Inspector our newest member of the SHIT Squad."

Morrissey stood and shook her hand.

"Pleasure to meet you sergeant, welcome aboard. Apologies for not having read your jacket yet. Been a bit busy."

"Perfectly understandable sir. Fuckin' pleasure to be aboard!" He instantly recognised her accent.

"What part of Glasgow you from?" Morrissey asked.

"Knightswood mainly but after Da lost his job at the ship yards with BAE we moved out to East Kilbride where I done most'a me growin' up."

"Rough area that!" Enfield pointd out."

The Hermes Project

"How is it you got the short straw?" Morrissey asked her.

"Hardly a short straw Inspector! Soon as I found out about youse bein' formed up and crackin' some of the wide open cases youse were bein' given, I put in me application! Whether youse know it or not youse're the talk of the U.K. Police Service from here to the Midlands!"

At her unexpected compliment the four traded looks of pride and praise. MacIntyre continued.

"Apparently they was four other women considered for the slot. But they was all married, two with kids. Mayor's office was a feared of the bad PR what might come should another woman snuff it whilst on duty especially if she was a mother."

"More like not wanting to pay the extra family death compensation!" Enfield opined.

"I wouldn't dispute that as well!" She argued in agreement.

"MacIntyre, as you're only just in and this is your first drink up with the Squad, we usually start with a small quiz." Morrissey enlightened her. She was unsure of what to make of the exasperated reaction of the other three sergeants, all with smirks on their faces.

"Right then lads, first question. What's wrong with this table?" The Inspector threw out.

"Allow me!" Enfield quickly volunteered then began a slow perusal of the thick oak trestle table. "Well, we can tell by the joinery that it is hand made, not factory produced. It at least dates from the pre-war era and –"

"And it's missing bloody pints that's what!" MacIntyre quietly declared as she slapped the table top and rose to go to the bar.

"No, no Mac!" Morrissey stayed her with a hand to her arm. "Those who dare don't always win!" He nodded over at Enfield who assumed a frowny face before heading off in the direction of the bar. "Wrong answers buy the first round." Morrissey informed.

"FNG, make mine a stout!" Din called after him.

"So as this is the first time we're all gathered allow me to introduce you." Morrissey said to MacIntyre. "Sgt. Rohan Rankor our token Asian is known here as Gunga Din. Our token black, Muhammad Ali is Sgt. Franklin Heath and the FNG up there doing the honours is Sgt. John Enfield."

"Inspector, is it still proper to call Enfield the FNG?" Heath proposed. "I mean now that we've a new FNG?"

"What the sheit is an FNG'?" MacIntyre inquired.

"Fucking New Guy! In your case, Fucking New Girl I suppose." Din said. "Enfield was the last to join the squad so the Inspector tagged him FNG."

"Sir if I might ask, why do you not use everyone's proper names?" MacIntyre asked.

Ali and Din smirked at her question.

"Because my dear girl when our not so subtly racist mayor decreed the ethnic composition of the squad, more level-headed individuals, we four that is, resented his directive that we adhere to his identity politics driven agenda. Ergo in an effort to maintain control of our own identity it was decided that we develop aliases. In essence relabeling ourselves." He expounded.

"Nom de plumes as it were." Din added.

"Speaking of which we're going to have to do something about getting you a name." Morrissey decreed.

"Like what?" She challenged just as Enfield returned with the pints.

"What are we on about lads?" He asked as he set the tray on the table and proceeded to pass out the pints.

"We were talking about a handle for MacIntyre."

"Why don't we all have a think on it and decide later?" Enfield suggested. "Right now I'd like to propose a toast." They all raised their glasses. "To the return of our fearless leader! Welcome home chief! Glad you're back!" Enfield complimented.

"Glad to be back!" Morrissey modestly toasted.

"Tell us about New York Chief. See any action while you were abroad?" Heath proded.

"A bit."

"Like what?" Din pushed.

"Nothing much. A hostage scenario. A car chase following a car jacking and a couple of attempted murders."

"Bloody hell! In less than a week! That's more action then we see here in a month!" Din declared.

"Are you sure you weren't on a film set sir?" MacIntyre quipped.

"There were times I wondered. Very different approach over there."

"How so?" Enfield asked.

"They call it a Police **Force** not a Police Service. Affects the whole approach, the way they do things."

"From what respect?" Heath pushed.

"Well, aside from being mentally prepared to get physical at any point during each day, guns are the main factor. They're all armed to the teeth!"

"So are the felons they face!" Enfield defended.

"Fair enough!" Morrissey agreed. "I read in *The Guardian* on the flight back over that to date there have been no homicides in London so far this year?"

"That's the rumor!" Din confirmed.

"We think its a crock though." Enfield added. "A clever PR ruse cooked up by His Highness the mayor!"

"Kahn's office jiggles those numbers around all the time!" Heath reinforced.

"And the Yanks?" Din asked.

"Can't speak for the entire country but New York has tipped the scales at over 400 homicides so far since last year."

"Fuckin' hell! I thought Clyde was a rowdy place!" MacIntyre threw in.

"Another thing is their technology." Morrissey continued. "Eons ahead of ours!"

"Such as?"

"They are actually experimenting with a vehicle mounted, anti-riot, sonic weapon that when aimed at rioters and fired . . . makes them sheit their pants!"

"You're joking!" Din commented amongst

riotous laughter.

"I'm not!"

"Long way from Glasgow eh MacIntyre?" Enfield challenged.

"Hell, just visit any pub in Townhead on a Saturday night you can see half the punters sheitin' their pants!" MacIntyre commented.

Up front in the pub several more customers began to drift in.

"After spending a week there and seeing what they face, I understand why the police are armed. Completely different world over there!" The Inspector added.

"I guess where there's big money to be made in a big way all the stakes are bound to be a bit higher." Enfield added.

"Still, I'd fancy a trip over!" Din mused aloud.

"Be interesting to see the place." Mac threw out.

"Be even more interesting to work over there!" Enfield enthusiasticlly added.

"Not I!" Firmly declared Ali as he drained the last of his pint. "No interest in going anywhere near the bloody place!"

"Why not?"

"If I wanted that level of violence on a daily basis I'd go back to Nigeria!"

"You were a kid when you snuck in under the fence here! What do you really remember about Nigeria?" Din asked.

"Enough to know I'd not fancy working as a cop in either place!" He flagged a waitress and signalled for five more pints.

"Well if there was a way I'd sign up tomorrow!" Enfield enthusiastically declared.

"I might consider a couple weeks holiday over there if I had the dosh!" Mac considered.

"I'd sign on if we went over to work as a team." Din nodded. "I mean think of the professional experience we'd bring back!"

"I'll tell youse in all honesty, a few weeks there'd be worth a year working cases here when you got back!" Morrissey affirmed.

"You think there's any way to get into that excahnge program as a group Inspector?" Enfield ventured.

"Not a chance in hell FNG! That's an inter-agency funded project and the NYPD has ten times the budget the Met does which is why they only send one or two officers at a time, and usually only PC's. The Met would hardly be up for sending the entire squad over, much less for one to two weeks."

"What if we raised the money on our own?" Din ventured.

"How exactly?! Bake sales and a car wash?!" Ali sarcastically spat. "Besides there's the liability issue. Who's going to pay your medical expenses when you get shot? We have to fight the Met for weeks as it is when an officer is stabbed here!"

"Point taken Heath." Morrissey explained. "Now to more important matters! We need a name for our newest member! Questions, comments, snide remarks?"

"Well, seeing as how she's a Scotty–" Enfield started but was cut off by MacIntyre herself.

"SCOTTY?! I look like an overweight Yank with a sheit accent pretending to be ridin' some phony star ship across the heavens yellin' 'I'm giving her all she's got captain! I'm a man not a machine! She's getting ready to blow!'" She spouted in a comical, mock accent. "Fuck off with your Scotty!" She spat garnering a good round of laughter.

"I sense some resistance sergeant!" Heath quipped.

"Are we to take it then that the name Scotty is a nix?" Din asked. By way of an answer MacIntyre flashed him a two fingered salute.

"The lady has a point lads!" Din agreed.

"Right, Tammy it is then!" Morrissey declared.

"Tammy?! Why Tammy?" Din asked.

"We can't go callin' her Tammy!" Enfield objected. "Tammies are for men!" He informed.

"And why not?! Sean Connery was called Big Tammy so he was!" MacIntyre vehemently protested.

"You've a long way to go to reach six foot two girl!" Rankor quipped.

"Will somebody please tell me what the hell a 'tammy' is?" Heath inquired.

"It's a Scottish traditional cap named for Tam o' Shanter, the hero of the Robert Burns poem." Morrissey explained.

"Cheers for the history lesson Inspector, but who exactly is Robert Burns when he's home?" The Nigerian pushed.

"Ahhh, now you're taking the piss, mate!" Amy MacIntyre scarfed at Heath's ignorace of the legendary writer.

"Right, **Little** Tammy it is then!" Morrissey reiterated.

"To Little Tammy!" Enfield offered as they all raised a glass and toasted.

"Now that leaves just one more bit of business. The christening!" Morrissey pointed out.

"THE CHRISTENING!" Din, Ali and the FNG echoed in unison raising their pints. Unknowingly MacIntyre followed suit.

Then, to raucous applause across the entire bar room, they christened her. With their pints.

Sgt. Amy MacIntyre was now officially 'Little Tammy' of the Scotland Yard Special Homicide Investigation Team.

The SHIT Squad.

*

Vanity Fair Magazine
4 Times Sq., NYC, NY

The main press room, the size of a university basketball gym, held a double row of five foot by three foot tables that dominated the space and housed just under one hundred people.

Like the *U.S.S. Lexington* at Midway when they spotted the first Mitsubishi aircraft coming in for a bomb run the entire room appeared to be in pandamonium as editors gathered up their sheep, reporters pulled copy and models scurried to the make-up room to prepare for their photoshoots.

The Hermes Project

It was the start of another work day when Sam O'Neill stepped off the elevator that morning at *Vanity Fair Magazine* twenty minutes late to work as usual.

Twenty minutes was enough time to duck into her small side office, drop her purse and coat on her desk, get oriented and most importantly have two cups of coffee and a protein bar and then sneak out on the employees' veranda to quickly enjoy a smoke. A smoke she bet her coworker Jimmy Page at the New Year's Eve party she would quit. Soon.

The large screen TV in the employees lounge was tuned to CNN while Sam sipped her coffee and watched along with three or four colleges. Up on the screen a gaggle of commentators were crammed in and were ganging up on a reporter from *Breitbart News* named Ben Shapiro.

"The current problem with the mainstream media is blowing things out of proportion to garner ratings." Shapiro argued, the black yamulke precariously perched on his black hair.

*"What happens in the future when a politician does some things that are really bad, and you know there's a strong possibility that's going to happen, and you've already started out at level 10? Where will you go from there? At that point you are in real danger of blowing your credibility and losing the confidence of listeners. I mean to see your reporters reporting minor things as **disasterous**, then when you report actual bad things that are things that are **real** disasters, you won't be taken seriously by anyone."*

"Who's that guy?" One of the middle-aged copy writers asked to no one in particular.

"It's that Jew kid again. What is he like twelve years old?" Another challenged.

"Does his mother know he's not in school?" The older one quipped.

"News flash cretins and those who aspire to such heights," O'Neill entered the fray. "That 'Jew kid' graduated Phi Beta Kappa, summe cum laude from UC and is a cum laude graduate of Harvard Law School."

"Sounds like somebody's got'a boy crush!"

"So he's got a lotta 'cums' on his name, what's he doing tellin' the *Most Trusted Name in News* people how to run their show?" The older guy challenged.

"Yeah! Who's he when he's home?" Another chimed in.

Sam shook her head while slowly losing patience.

"You mean aside from the fact that he wrote his first book at the age of seventeen, a year later became the youngest nationally syndicated columnist in the country then was one of the youngest Editors-in-Chief ever to run a news agency in the U.S. and now owns *The Daily Wire* where he has his own news show, a weekly editor's column and has written seven books all by the age of thirty-two?"

"Huh." One of the copy guys grunted.

"Snappy comeback!" Sam remarked. "And if that was too much of an earfull for you medium achievers, I'll give you the *Reader's Digest* version.

That's more than the other three of those CNN news monkeys up their on the screen sitting with him combined."

The room sat silent as she ducked back into the kitchenette, popping back out again as soon as she grabbed a cherry cheese Danish from the large box on the counter.

"Those so-called 'most trusted names in news' are in for a rude awakening boys! You can take that to the bank! I don't know where and I don't know how, but the days of corporate news in main stream media, along wiith the corporate network stations are numbered."

Sam made her way to her desk to get to work. No sooner had she switched on her keyboard when her cell phone line buzzed with a text.

You're presence is required in the throne room.

Sam quietly cursed, angrily slid her chair from under her desk and headed down the aisle to her boss' office.

The standard stereotype of an Editor-in-Chief is usually portrayed as a gruff, street-wise, battle-weary, white middle-aged male, always yelling at his secretary, into his phone or at his employees. But J.J. Johnson was different.

J.J. was a gruff, street-wise, battle-weary, middle-aged white female always yelling at her secretary, into her phone or at her employees.

There was a rumor that once you got to know her she didn't yell as much.

"Christ! Everytime I pick up a paper, magazine or surf the net I come across another 'news network' broadcasting their version of the what they call the news!" J.J. griped as soon as Sam entered her office.

"I'm good J.J. How are you?" Sam greeted as she came in and took a seat in front of the desk.

"Funny, I didn't hear you knock!" She snapped

"I forgot."

"And tell me this O'Neill, how come it always looks like these on-line channels are broadcasting from their mom's basement?"

"It's still a new game J.J. Everybody from the Editor-in-Chief on down got screwed when printing went automated in the Sixties. Now that reporting is computerized, it's everybody's turn. Every Tom, Dick and Sally with an opinion has an on-line site, and with crowd funding they can get their own show, read the headlines some where and post their version of the 'facts'!"

"Thanks for the update O'Neill! I never could'a figured that out on my own!" She barked.

"In keeping with the fact that it's always a team effort, and you're always open to new ideas, suggestions and your door is always open . . . happy to help, J.J.! It's one'a the perks of working here. That's why the whole office chipped in and got you that trophy last year."

She nodded towards a tiny, two inch high, plastic gold cup on the desk. The wooden base held a small, crooked, brass plate: 'Boss of the Year'.

"Very funny smart ass. Now since we're on the subject of asses why is yours in here? Because I

The Hermes Project

don't remember my door being open?!"

"Because you sent for me a whole two minutes ago."

"Oh yeah!"

"You do know Alzheimer's isn't supposed to hit until you're in your Sixties?" J.J. knew full well that O'Neill knew she was sixty-two.

"Well, you just made my job a lot easier. You're going to do a piece on this political battle over the new satellite system languishing in Congress."

"The Nexus 6 and AstroCom stuff? A little out'a my wheel house ain't it? Besides, Page does the Science and Tech stuff. When there is science and tech stuff. I don't know anything about satellites and computer tech!"

"It's not science and tech stuff I want. It's the politics of it all. Who's shmozing who? Who's making back door deals about what?"

"You want D.C. gossip! Castle intrique stuff?"

"Exactly!"

"Aw come on J.J.! I'm on the follow-up to the mid-terms and got my next column to finish by Friday!"

"No problem, you'll finish your column by Wednesday, Franklin will take the next two weeks on the changing political situation and the new girl, Janie's gonna take the Obits."

"Franklin doesn't know shit about the mid-terms, I need at least three more days on my column and the new girl's name is Jenny, not Janie."

"See? That's why I'm giving you the story! You've an eye for detail!" She cajoled as she came around from behind her desk, took Sam by the shoulders, stood her up and gently but firmly guided her to the door. "There's a morgue file already started on the previous hearings with all the background in your email. Graphics has been notified to work with you and I anxiously await your first draft on the potential market implications for the cable industry, future impact on consumer service and whether or not the D.O.J. is gonna gum up the works or whether the proper amounts of green are going to change hands to make sure the current projects will be rubber stamped to pass Congress as usual."

"Bye J.J. Good talk as usual." Sam nodded as she stepped through the door.

"Likewise O'Neill. Talk again next week. By the way, good job on the NSA piece."

"Thanks J.J." Sam quietly uttered as the office door closed over.

*

Currently Sam O'Neill was in the archive room scrolling through previous interviews and articles.

She was paying particular attention to articles which fell into the 'fake news' category when she came across a tape of a 'Russia Hoax' news broadcast file with feedback from celebs, stars and other left wingers. She found a full copy of a White House vid and decided to show it to her colleague Page.

"What's this?" He asked when she thrust the

USB in front of him.

"It's the raw footage of Trump at the White House. The one with Trump parading out people he says were hurt by Obamacare."

"I seen it."

"No! Just watch."

"Why is there a hidden message if you play it backwards?!"

"Just come over here and watch it, jerkweed!"

They both sat through the 30 second video which was shot in one of the reception rooms of the White House.

"Okay, so?" He pushed.

"So when they broadcasted it they chopped off the end where the reporter asked him about the NSA and whether or not he intends to stop them trying to spy on Americans!"

"So CNN got it wrong again. So what?"

"That's the whole, complete video. Why would someone edit it then put it out there?"

"To jump on the Take-Trump-Down bandwagon. You know like with Fentynol when that first entered the news cycle, before people started dying from it. Everybody was doing it. It was the thing to do. Plus it garnered clicks! Especially when you get all your news stories from Twitter!"

"You're missing the point! Not 'why would somebody do that', but WHY would somebody do that?"

He pushed back from his desk as if he came to a realization and looked up at her.

"You on Fent right now?"

"No!"

"If you got some, can I have one?!" He joked.

"You were in a frat when you were in college weren't you?" She accused.

"Why, because I like drugs?"

"Look, you just don't chop off a chunk of video before it goes national without authorization! Imagine if somebody here decided to print one side of a story and send it to the press?"

"You mean like that dumb bitch at *Rolling Stone* did a while back?"

"Exactly!"

"J.J. would have their head mounted on her office wall! So, sorry I was a frat boy, but what's your point?"

"My point is this was not accidental! Look at how fast all the lefties, and some of the others, pounced on this! Then the full 57 seconds was released."

"It was click bait for some dummies looking for 'the big story'." He mocked.

"It was a trap! The increase in term 'fake' news now being used by everyone was noticed by everyone! It was being used to devalue the network. Something's going on here!"

"There sure is! CNN is staffed by a bunch of assholes being run by a chief asshole who only cares about ratings and has no clue what 'journalism' is. So he's giving us all a bad name."

"What if it goes deeper? What if it was more about the NSA thing?!" She proposed.

"Are you jumping on the conspiracy

bandwagon!?" He challenged.

"Yeah, that's it." She mumbled unconvincingly as she walked away. "Conspiracy! The universal liberal defence!"

CHAPTER SIX

NSA Headquarters
Fort Meade, Maryland
a.k.a. 'The Fort'

Dating back to 1917 during the First World War, the NSA did not evolve into its current form until November of 1952. Since then it has mushroomed from one office with three cryptologists to an agency of approximately 32,000 employees with a budget of over 62 billion dollars.

Originating directly from an office called the Black Chamber, it was just after the First World War that intel operations were moved from Washington D.C. to New York City where it was with the cooperation of Western Union they were able to set up as a Code Compilation Company.

In a time when telegram companies charged by the letter therefore making codes extremely popular, especially to large corporations who dealt with large numbers of telegrams weekly, it was the perfect cover.

Following the Great War in 1919 when the military cryptographic section known as MI-8 was disbanded the Black Chamber was formed.

During the Thirties the U.S. administration saw the need to reduce what little funding there was and by the late 1930's with things heating up again, internationally that is, cryptologists were able to break most Japanese diplomatic codes and so were able to keep American diplomats appraised of Japanese strategies. Most important of these of course was the JN-25 which allowed the U.S. Navy to intercept and defeat the Japanese armada at Midway, a battle which marked the turning point of the war in the Pacific.

By 1952 the Cold War had settled in and Cryptology had reached its highest echelon of importance thus far.

As each of the military branches, as well as several government agencies, had all developed their own cryptographic facilities and inter-agency co-operation was not what it should have been, the AFSA or Armed Forces Security Agency was formed in 1949.

However due to being top heavy in bureaucracy which combined with continued inter-agency non-cooperation, centralisation of intelligence, particularly concerning the FBI and the fledgling CIA, the AFSA was closed down.

In 1951 president Harry Truman ordered an investigation into the AFSA and why it had failed which directly resulted in the formation of the National Security Agency.

Rampant abuse in the 1960's and 70's by several intelligence agencies including the NSA where to lead to the evolution of much oversight and the passage of several regulatory laws to include the FISA or the Foreign Intelligence Surveillance Act in 1978. This Act requires the authorities to apply for a special warrant through the secret FISA court to allow them to spy on U.S. citizens.

However, as always, there are those who believe laws are made to be broken.

Amongst their many mis-steps such as the botched raid at Waco, the disaster at Ruby Ridge, *Operation Crossfire Hurricane* and the fake *Steele Dossier* the FBI in particular demonstrated how to easily circumvent the FISA Act.

This led to the American public's already simmering mistrust of their government dropping to an all-time low during the 2016 to 2020 administration thus solidifying the low double digits in trust the NSA are still struggling to overcome to this day.

Although the NSA has had many successes, most not publicized, the 9/11 bombings of the World Trade Center in New York is now considered the worst failure of U.S. intelligence to date to include Pearl Harbor.

Unlike with the DEA, the FBI or the CIA, the NSA has no direct connection to the overall 'watchdog' of the Intel agencies, the DCI or Director of Central Intelligence. The NSA's safeguarding advisory role is completely independent. In theory the director of the NSA is responsible only to the Secretary of Defence through the Joint Chiefs of Staff who answer directly to the POTUS.

Thus having virtually no congressional oversight, the NSA routinely ignores requests from congress or other officials for information they do not want politicians to know. Acting outside Congressional review the NSA is the most secretive of all the seventeen Intel agencies in the U.S.

The current politicization of the intelligence agencies is often cited as one of the most dangerous and weakest pillars of the U.S. government.

****

In the shadowy world of intelligence there are four basic categories: SIGINT or signal intelligence which takes in information from all transmission devices phones computers etc.

HUMINT or Human Intel, which deals with all intelligence gathered by human agents.

Imagery intelligence or IMINT dealing primarily with the analysis of imagery gathered clandestinely or otherwise.

And finally MASINT, or measurement Intel which seeks to detect, identify and track intelligence sources.

Developing and testing surveillance programs the 'No Such Agency' continually encourages innovation by her employees.

One such employee could be found in the basement offices at the Fort Meade facility's Alert Center.

The Alert Center monitors relevant intelligence sources, analyzes and correlates significant facts, reports and events against existing strategies, concepts and plans.

It was in the Alert Center department of the NSA headquarters there worked a man colleagues knew as 'The Riddler'. Word was that there was no code or data he couldn't decipher given three things; enough time, enough Camel cigarettes and enough KSF Honey Blended Heirloom Organic coffee.

At five foot seven Phil Finley wasn't a big man, wasn't a rich man and wasn't what one would consider particularly good looking.

But above all Philip J. Finley Jr. was an honest man which set him as a polar opposite of 98% of the D.C. infastructure. 99.9% if you included the Congress.

Raised in the flat lands of Kansas by 'God-fearing' parents, although not particularly religious himself, Finley was drafted in 1968 during the Viet Nam War, ace'd his ASVAB exam and was recommended to be sent to Turkey where the military code center was short a man after one of their code breakers had a little too much Turkish absinth, totalled his motorcycle and earned himself a medical discharge by getting himself broke. In three places.

Finley was sent to Turkey to work on the Soviet data system which had not yet been completely solved.

It was there that Finley's hereto undiscovered mathematical talents, like Egyptian treasures in the Valley of the Kings, were unearthed.

He was there less than a week when he recognised all the Soviet traffic was mathematically based and he was able to catalouge useful patterns.

A few years earlier in May of '68 the Soviets had suddenly started some heavy training. Finley started to pick out things that were different from their

The Hermes Project

normal training. By early June he submitted a report saying they were going to invade Czechoslovakia.

No one took him seriously.

That summer they invaded Czechoslovakia.

At the time the Agency routinely looked for about 100 'indicators' before they would make a significant call and pass it on.

Finley got it down to five and those five weren't even on the approved list. Those five indicators repeated time and time again regardless of the situation.

Prior to the Tet Offensive in the late Sixties and again just before the Yom Kippur war in '73 he called both events before they happened.

In 1979 when he analysed the Soviet build up just over the border in Afghanistan he reported there would be a soviet invasion late on Christmas Eve when the majority of the West were sleeping.

It was just before midnight on December 24th that with 280 aircraft and 25,500 men the Soviets invaded Afghanistan.

Finley had missed it by one hour.

"Phil you can't be for real!" Bill Whitcome a close colleague now challenged as he stood acoss the small basement room where Finley sat at his desk.

"Why not?!" Phil Finley rebutted as he adjusted his glasses.

"There are over seven and a half billion people on the planet! More than half of them have phones and or computers. You're talking about three to three and a half billion phone numbers!"

"I estimate double that if you count that many people have more than one cell! Plus they have several computers." Finley added as he pushed his roller chair away from his desk and across the room to the console behind him.

Whitcombe followed.

"Okay, I get that. But to be able to trace EVERY phone in the world?! Be realistic will ya!"

To emphasise his argument Finley stopped what he was doing, turned from the desk and faced his collegue.

"Bill do you understand how far behind we are in technology? I'll tell you how far behind we are, at one point not so long ago management here actually debated about giving agents email! EMAIL! There are no secrets on the internet, it's all open source for crying out loud!" Finley argued.

"Sorry Phil, I still don't see it happening."

Finley resumed typing as he debated his collegue.

"Bill, humans are like any other animal, they want security and reliability. Therefore they are creatures of habit so they do everything in patterns, some simple some complicated but there's always patterns." He pushed back aross the room between consoles on his roller chair. "Analysis is just a matter of discovering those patterns." He shrugged.

"Granted but, how will your *Hermes* program deal with those kinds of numbers?"

Finley finally stopped and again made eye contact with Whitcombe.

"Look, assuming 14.5 billion phones and computers is a lot, and I'll give you that it is, you have to agree that there are a finite number of atoms in the universe, regardless of that number, yes?"

"The Law of Conservation of Matter; matter cannot be created nor destroyed. Yes, finite number." Whitcombe conceded.

"Then 14.5 billion is just a smaller subset of that! No? I mean, both are finite numbers!"

Whitcombe desperately fought for a comeback but could not find one. Finley pushed on.

"The problem here is the old mentality we operate under. We collect everything, dump it into a giant collections system and let the analysts sort it out. Under the present system the analysts are little more than highly paid garbage collectors for Pete's sake! They're being swamped with too much data and there is zreo possibility for them to get through all that information. And while they're rummagng through it more info is pouring in all the time." As Phil spoke Whitcombe stood silent. "We have to find a way to select only what's important and focus on that. That's how we catch up ond overtake the bad guys!"

"So what's your magic solution? How do you invision your *Hermes Project* helping us?"

Encouraged by his coleague's concession Finley turned and gave his full attention.

"My, our, big logjam at the moment is the God damned cryptologists dragging their asses in getting data down here to the Alert Center so I can push on with building the program!"

"Why do you need their help?"

"I need the use of their sessionizer computer to

help organize all the data to allow me to catagorize it."

"So what's the hold-up on their end?"

"Dunno! I ask for their help, they ask for a memo. I send a memo and they take it to the House Intel Committee and get more money but they don't give me a time scale on when they'll inprocess the data."

"You realise what they're doing don't you?"

"Of course I realise what they're doing! They're using me as a meat puppet to squeeze more money from Congress!"

Whitcombe took a seat besides Finley and thought for a moment.

"Can you lay your hands on a dedicated computer from somewhere?" Bill asked.

"Probably one laying around down in Surplus I guess, so yeah. Why?"

"Then why not just get one out of Surplus, set it up here and make it into your own desktop sessionizer?" Whitcombe suggested.

"Is that possible?" Finley asked.

"Yeah! All you're asking the machine to do is organize some data. All that requires is a program but it's easy enough to write one."

"You think you can do that?"

"Cost you a bottle of Johnnie Walker." Bill joked.

"Red or Black Label?!" Phil answered.

"Blue!"

By the end of the week Phil Finley had his sessionizer and was procesisng small chunks of data.

Bill was saving his bottle of scotch for a special occasion.

The Hermes Project

Like a weekend.

****

Irina Kuksova wasn't sure where to start so that morning she stopped by a local Walmart and bought two burner phones with sim cards.

Finding a quiet, West Side café she ordered a latté, took a seat in the back and pulled out her phone. There she started the info gathering portion of what she called her tentative investigation into the rumored disruption of the U.S Intel services she'd read about in *Vanity Fair Magazine*.

Her run-in with the FBI chiefs in London had not only left a bad taste in her mouth but had, at one point actually pushed her to the brink of considering resignation.

She now considered her suspension the perfect time to act on her suspicions.

Fiddling with O'Neill's stolen press pass as she dialled she was unable to reach Sam O'Neill by phone to thank her for her help and ask a few more questions, so Kuksova instead referred back to her notes to locate the name of the congresswoman that the *Vanity Fair* writer gave her at the interview.

With the first of the burner phones she dialled the number she found on line. The phone rang three times before anyone picked-up.

Central Legal, how may I direct your call? A young male voice inquired.

"Hi, my name's Sam O'Neill and I'm with *Vanity Fair*. We're doing a story on the ten biggest companies in America, we're calling it *The Next Big Step!*"

Catchy. How may I direct your call? He repeated tersly.

"I wonder if you could tell me the status of the House Intel Committee's final decision on Nexus 6's latest project?"

I'm in Legal, you want PR. If not try the FCC. He abruptly hung up.

"Decision went that good did it?" She sarcasticly commented into the silent phone.

Ten minutes later, after mistakenly being connected to The Smithsonian, the D.C. Zoo and *The Neighborhood Food Guide* she finally located Capitol Hill information.

How may I direct your call? A young female voice inquired.

"Hi, I'm trying to reach someone who can give me some info on the House decision concerning the Nexus 6-"

Who's calling please?

"My name's Sam O'Neill, I'm calling about the recent Nexus 6 decision. I'm with *Vanity Fair Magazine*, we're doing a story on the ten biggest companies in America –"

You're wanting the House Intel Committee. That would be Senator Burman's office. She politely informed.

Twenty minutes after starting her phone game of *Where's Waldo?* Kuksova was finally given the number to Representitive Natalie Farmiga of the House Intel Committee and, as an after thought, asked for the number for general information at the NSA.

Natalie Farmiga, a Republican representing northern New Jersey's 11th congressional district was a first termer with a strong reputation for being conscientious, hard working and not yet jaded by the immoral and ignoble methods demanded of conducting business inside the D.C. Beltway.

The young, intern receptionist poked her head through the office door of the rear area of the storefront headquarters.

"Natalie, call for you on line two! It's a Sam O'Neill."

"Thank you Lynn." Farmiga picked up. "Representitive Farmiga how may I help you?"

"Ms. Farmiga so glad I caught you in! My name is Sam O'Neill and I'm a staff writer for *Vanity Fair Magazine*." Irina Kuksova lied into the phone.

Representative Farmiga expressed her surprise to find that Sam was a girl when she heard Irina's voice.

"Oh, I expected a man. I mean, I was surprised to hear you're a-"

"A woman, yeah no problem. I get that a lot." Irina replied. "I'm a staff writer for *Vanity Fair Magazine*."

"Oh very nice! What can I do for you?"

"My editor has asked me to poke around and write a general info piece on women in politics in the current climate."

"Sorry, I really don't subscribe to gender or race politics Miss O'Neill. I'm one of those rare

Washington breeds who believe a person should be judged on merit and what's beween their ears not what's between their legs."

"Perfect! That would not only be the exact angle I'm looking for but express an opposing point of view that would give the Libs something to complain about!"

"Miss O´Neill, I really don't think-"

"Please, Representative Farmiga . . . Natilie! If I don't have **something** on her desk by Monday morning I'm toast and even though V.F.M. is primarily a women´s magazine J.J., that's my editor, will have no reservation about putting my slightly overweight ass out on the street! Help me out here, please? Fifteen minutes of your time that's all I'm asking, I promise! I'll meet you anywhere you need."

There was a long pause.

"You pose a persuasive agrgument Miss O'Neill. Are you down in D.C.?"

"No, Manhattan but I could fly down-"

"No need, my office is just over the river in Jersey. Do you know Morristown?"

"I'll find it!"

"We're located on Speedwell Avenue right next to the Horshoe Tavern. Just across the river then find State Route 202 and follow it straight in."

"GREAT! When are you free?" Kuksova pushed.

"Not sure. Hold on, LYNN! LYNN!" She called out to her intern.

"Yes Ms. Farmiga?" Lynn scurried back to the office.

"Lynn set this reporter up with an appointment here for next week."

"You're in D.C. all next week ma'am. The new NSA Director?" Lynn reminded her.

"Shoot, General Pravum! Okay then, anytime after my D.C. meet."

"Yes ma'am, will do."

"Thank you Lynn. Miss O'Neill, my intern is going to set something up for you."

"Thanks a million! You're a life saver Representitive Farmiga. You got my vote in the Fall!"

"But you're in New York! I'm in New Jersey!" She pointed out.

"I just thought with the current flexibility of the voting rules . . ." There was no response from the other end of the line. "Never mind, bad joke. Talk to you soon!" Kuksova smiled broadly as she hung up. "Yes! Step two complete." She mumbled to herelf.

*

Unlike Reagen's former Chairman of the Joint Chiefs of Staff General John 'Jack' Vessey, who was not only the longest serving military man in U.S. history but had worked his way up from a lower enlisted man as he fought in WWII, Korea and Viet Nam, Lt. General Michael Pravum, U.S.A.F., was what is known in the Pentagon as a 'Paper General'.

'Big Mike' was short and pudgy with a noticably receeding hairline and with the exception of acting as an administrative escort to President Obama in Iraq, had never been to a war zone in his twenty-six years of military service.

This was not by happenstance but by design.

Officially a wing of the DoD the NSA is technically directly accountable to the JCS. In reality, barring a major political scandal, the NSA are held accouountable to no one. And even then it depends on how high up the chain the scandal goes.

Of course none of Pravum's history could be properly deduced from the chest full of ribbons he brandished on his uniform as he continued the third day of his orientatation tour of The Fort.

The newly appointed Director along with his adjutant, Colonel Parva, breezed into the Alert Center unannounced to find Phil Finley, Bill Whitcombe and a junior programer busily at work.

Introductions were made and not being military, in lieu of a salute, Whitcombe stood, smiled and nodded in acknowledgment as did Finley who, head buried in his current chore, didn't bother to stand. The programmer magically vanished.

"Morning gentlemen!" The colonel greeted. "This is General Michael Pravum our new Director. General, Mr. William Whitcombe from our Codeing Section and Phillip Finley one of our top analysts, sir."

"Gentlemen, pleasure to meet you. I hope all goes well down here?" Pravum greeted.

"Yes sir, going very well, thank you." Whitcombe replied still standing. Pravum approached Finley who was deeply focused on his computer screen typing away.

"Finley, I understand you're onto something that could revolutionize the agency's analytic capabilities?" Pravum pushed as he stepped closer to Finley's work station.

Visibly annoyed Finley glanced over at Whitcombe who averted his gaze before also ducking out of the room.

"Not really General. Just running some ideas for short cuts in the collections arena. Maybe save some time for the cryptologists down the road."

Pravum was unsure if Finley's reply was due to an unwillingness to share his work or if he was motivated by a sense of modesty.

Pravum stepped forward and placed a hand on Finley's shoulder.

"Don't be shy Finley! This is the NSA, we have no secrets here!" Pravum laughed at his own joke as did the Colonel.

"I'm writing a code to interact with one of our satellite systems."

"Interesting. You have a name for this system yet?"

"Not really, it'll likely be weeks before it's finished."

"Very well then, keep me up to date." He patted Finley on the shoulder.

"Will do Director." Phil answered without looking up from his computer screen.

Pravum nodded at the colonel and turned for the door.

"Well boys, I'm told you're doing some good

work down here! Keep it up."

"Yes sir, thank you General." Whitcombe spouted.

"Yes sir." Finley echoed.

When they left Bill approached Finley.

"What the hell was that?!" Whitcombe attacked.

"What the hell was what?!"

"Didn't you tell him about the program?"

"I must'a have forgot."

"Why didn't you give him the whole spiel?!"

"What are you talking about?!"

"He's the Head Honcho, the H.N.I.C., the Top Tamalé! Why didn't you sell him harder on *Hermes*?!"

"Why do you think?!"

"I don't know, I just thought maybe you might want your department to look good for the boss man! Score some points for yourself, maybe even get a few extra bucks allocated come the quarterly budget allowance!"

Finley turned his chair and looked up at Whitcombe.

"And when he asks; 'When will it be ready?' and I say, 'Gee General I don't know' or if we run into a glitch along the way or better yet when we test it and it fails, then we, **I** look like just another Bozo." He quietly postulated.

"Yeah but, would it have hurt to be a little more civil to the guy! He is our boss after all."

"I'm suspicious of people who try too hard to be your friend when you first meet them. Reminds me of crooked cops, lawyers and judges. No thank you.

Besides . . ."

"Besides what?"

"Nothing. Pass me that calculator will ya."

Phil Finley's mental acuity was not limited to mathematics. He was also astutely aware of the office dynamic where-by some supervisors lacked compunction about stealing ideas or innovations from their subordinates and passing them off as their own to garner credit for themselves. How did he know this?

From bitter experience.

****

An ancillary responsibility as a member of the House Intel Committee is initial oversight of the Intel agencies particularly when it comes to funding which is subject to congressional approval.

In line with this job task description Congresswoman Natalie Farmiga, the New Jersey Rep, was tasked that morning with driving over to Fort Meade to meet with the newly apppointed NSA Director General Mike Pravum.

As the new DIRNSA Pravum had had the last two weeks to get oriented visa vie his new job and would by now be ready for his first face-to-face with the Congressperson who would be his primary conduit to the agency's financial support. That was, at least in theory, how it was supposed to work.

Farmiga was there specifically to gather updates on project accounaility and finances.

"Representitive Ferma, glad to make your

aquaintence." Pravum didn't bother to offer his hand as she was shown into his office.

"Likewise General, and it's pronounced Farmiga."

"Of course. Sorry. Please have a seat." The uniformed man to Pravum's right took a seat opposite Pravum forming a loose triangle between the three as he sat. "This is my adjutant Colonel Parva also U.S.A.F." Farmiga gave a cursory smile to the man in civvies and nodded across to him.

"General I only have about a half an hour to give you –" He held up his hand and cut her off.

"I anticipated you would be short on time, coincidentally so am I. To that end I've arranged for the colonel here to give you a tour of the facility."

Farmiga was well familiar with the tactic known as 'being fobbed off'. She didn't fall for it.

"With all due respect General I've been here once or twice before and unless you have something new to show me I woul d like to get down to the primary reason I'm here on behalf of the committee."

"Which is?"

"Which is finances and the string of recent failures of your agency." She clarified.

"Failure is quite a strong word don't you think congresswoman? I assure the committee that we are well aware of the negative press we've been getting and are taking measures to re-evaluate and tighten up our evaluation proceedures!" Pravum defended.

"Publiclly stating that the Biden lap top was Russian propaganda. Failure in the Afghanistan evacuation and failure to forecast the Russian invasion of Ukraine –"

"With all due respect congresswoman Farmiga," The colonel spoke up for the first time. "The POTUS was made fully aware of activities on the Ruso-Ukraine border six full weeks prior to February the 24th!"

"Very well, please fill me in on your intended approach to your lagging behind problem along with how you intend to mend fences and improve strained relations with the other agencies? This has come up more than once in at the last two committee meetings and remains a bipartisan concern." She firmly informed.

"This organization is the lynchpin that holds the other sixteen agencies together! There's a reason the NSA is always headed by a senior military man Ms. Farmiga. Without us half the intel data they all use wouldn't exist!" Pravum objected.

This guy actually believes the NSA is King of the Intel Hill! Farmiga's internal dialogue shouted out to her. At this point she realized two things; there was nothing to be gained by butting heads with Pravum and maintaining self-control was paramount.

Just then the colonel's cell phone rang. He stepped away to take the call but came straight back over and offered the phone to Pravum.

"For you sir. CEO of AstroCom."

"Ask him to hold, I'll take it next door." He moved to the door as he addressed Farmiga. "The colonel here will escort you down to the Alert Center where Mr. Finley will finish off the briefing congresswoman. Any further questions I'm sure he and his department can help you with. If there's anything else have the chairman of your committee send me a memo." Pravum left.

"This way Congresswoman please." Pravum's adjutant stood and escorted Farmiga down to the Alert Center and to Phil Finley's space. Introductions were made before the colonel excused himself and headed back to the elevator leaving Natalie Farmiga alone with Bill Whitcombe and Phil Finley in the basement room.

Finley waited until he was sure the colonel was out of earshot before leaning in to Farmiga and speaking.

"You met the Genereal I gather?"

"Unfortunatly yes."

"He comes off as a bit prickly at first but once you get to know him you find out he's really just a gigantic prick. Pardon my language." Whitcombe informed. Farmiga smiled.

"How many in your department Mr. Finley? Here in the Alert Center I mean." She asked.

"Counting Bill and I . . . two."

"That many eh?"

"So I take it you've come to find out what the hell is going on around here?" Finley jumped right in.

"No. Initially I'm here to check progress on last quarter's programs, but since you bring it up . . ."

Finely and Whitcombe exchanged glances before Finley spoke first.

"Well, in the words of the Great Bard, there **is** something rotten and it ain't in the state of Denmark!"

"You have my ear Marcellus!" She replied.

"Can I speak freely?" Finley asked.

"Of course! I'm not here to get anybody in trouble."

"Well, it's just that . . . morale in this place has really taken a nosedive ever since the Afghanistan thing."

"Yes those deaths hit everybody pretty hard." She concurred.

"Not just the deaths but the fact that we sent brief after brief to the DoD, the HIC even the POTUS directly and it seems like everything we did was completely ignored!"

"All of which put us even further behind the Reds and the Russians." Bill Whitcombe added.

"Not to mention the Afghanis who took us into their confidence and worked with us thinking they wouldn't be left behind when we eventually evacuated!" Phil angrily spat.

"The reason we missed so many of the relevant events in the last year, aside from the twelve to fourteen hour a day workloads, missing half the holidays because you have to work and are always on call should be obvious." Whitcombe interjected.

"Well it is essentially a twenty-four/seven job." Farmiga defended. There was no reply. "About all the slip-ups?!" She pushed.

"Simple, an overblown sense of confidence and superiority. Primarily in the upper echelons!" Finley said.

"Is that what happened with Snowden and Manning?" Farmiga asked.

"Well, that's apples and oranges." Finley replied. "I can't really speak to the Manning case. Chelsea Manning was an Army analyst and that was handled by the Army CIC. But he did leak-"

"**She** did leak!" Whitcombe jokingly interrupted.

"SHE! HE, IT! Did leak hundreds of thousands of documents and was pardoned strictly for political gain by Obama. Snowden on the other hand came from Dell and was then recruited by the CIA as a subcontractor. As I understand it he quit after hearing Clapper's lies under oath in that congressional hearing about surveilling civilians without authorization."

"They even offered Snowden a team slot on the TAO, Tailored Access Operations, probably as a bribe but he said no thanks." Finley added.

"Wow! Did not know that." Farmiga confessed.

"Most people don't."

"The thing that lit the fuse though was right after 9/11 when the Contract Manager held a meeting and said, 'We'll get all the money we want now! Do your part and you'll get your share, there's plenty for everybody. We can milk this cow for 15 years!'" Phil growled.

"Milk this cow?!" Finley said with extreme irritation. "Thousands dead in the worst intel failure in U.S. history and she's throwing around obscene metaphors!" He blurted out.

"Then she repeated; '9/11 is a gift to the NSA! We're gonna get all the money we want!'" Bill added.

Shocked, Farmiga sat back in abject silence. Both men breifly followed suit.

"Well if things are so bad there's got to be some way we can score a win for the home team!" She coaxed.

"We've been trying for the last five months but with little progress." Finley informed.

"Based on Phil's methods we issued warnings months before the WTC bombing."

"Get this!" Finley suddenly recalled. "**THE** J2 HIMSELF, **THE** senior military officer who reports to the Joint Chiefs of Staff, comes down from the Pentagon to the National Military Joint Intelligence Center and into our Alert Center right here and tells us we're giving him garbage, that we're wasting valuable tax payers' money!"

"After we I.D.'ed Bin Laden before the attacks as a likely candidate, he actually yelled, 'Who cares about some raghead sitting under a fig tree spouting fatwas?! That's not important. Who cares?!" Finley repeated.

"Thank God that A-hole's gone!" Whitcombe added.

"How did things get so screwed up?" Farmiga pushed.

Both men hesitated to answer.

"Please don't take this the wrong way but why

do you think you're here? You have no special expertise in Intel. You're being used as a Band-Aid. Strictly cosmetic!" Finley emphatically stated.

"How do you know I don't have any special expertise in Intel?!" She objected not bothering to mask her irritation.

Finley glanced over at Whitcombe who nodded in affirmation as if to say, 'go ahead, tell her!'

"Your primary school was St. Mary's in Camden New Jersey, a private, conservative, Catholic girl's school. A good school with a good College Prep program but nothing in the way of technology. You had trouble with another girl in the fourth grade. You were only able to finish when your mother threatened to pull you out of school if your class wasn't changed.

You did high school at Ferris in Jersey City where you graduated with a three point nine GPA. You were awarded a partial academic scholarship to Fairleigh Dickinson where you majored in Poly Sci with a sociology minor and graduated with a three point seven GPA. You hated your calculus teacher and gave up the clarinet in your second year because it interfered with your dating and social life. Your first time with a boy was-"

"OKAY, OKAY! That's enough! How did you get all those details about me?! They're not in my bio!"

"We are the NSA. If you have any secrets we'll give them to you." Whitcombe relayed.

"We're not supposed to tell you but, as soon as you were assigned to the Intel committee we were ordered to run a background check on you." Finley revealed.

"Besides, it's required by federal statute." Whitcombe added.

"What statute?" She demanded.

"It's classified." Whitcombe relayed.

"Look, we realize that since WWII the NSA was the most productive agency. But that was three or four generations ago!" Finley declared. "After the Dems took power the Agency asked for millions in a budget increase and after Pankowski retired your committee needed a new NSA babysitter, someone who didn't know the score. How the game was palyed. It would have been too obvious to appoint another Dem so you, a GOP 'er got the job."

"And with Dems in the Senate majority now its not like your vote is gonna count for anything, plus it makes them look like they're being bipartisan."

"We think, well Phil here thinks, he has something that might catapult us back into the head of the game." Bill offered.

"Talk to me." She pushed.

"Metadata!" Phil quietly declared.

"Metadata?" She questioned.

"The metadata approach! It's not important what you're looking at, ads, military schedules, porn whatever, it's what does the history of your digital fingerprints all along tell us about what you've been up to? Who you really are."

"Sounds interesting. Continue please." They had genuinely peaked her interest.

Whitcombe rose, made his way to the door, closed it over and locked it before returning to his seat.

"Phil here has developed-"

"Still developing actually!" Finley corrected.

"He calls it *Hermes*!"

"It's an application-"

"Fellas please! Metadata?!" She demanded.

"Congresswoman, say you have two suspicious parties talking to each other . . ." Phil started then reconsidered. "Look Ms. Farmiga, in all honesty this is going to take a while to explain. With your permission let us set up a well-planned demonstration with a proper Power Point presentation, perhaps-"

"Hey, nice alteration!" Whitcombe interjected.

"Thank you!" Finley returned. "Can we say one week from today?"

"I think that's a good idea! One week, ten days I'll have my office call over with a day and time, okay?"

"That'll work for us!" They agreed. She rose to leave. "Oh and Ms. Farmiga for now, let's just keep this between us. Especially if you talk with the General!"

"He doesn't know about it? Don't you trust him?"

"We prefer not to show it to him until it's tested and finished. So for now let's just refer to it as The Project."

Her suspicions were aroused but she chose not to reveal them.

Outside waiting for the elevator, though suspicious of his apparent altruism, Farmiga decided that she liked this guy Finley.

Unbeknownst to anyone in the Alert Center, up in his office earlier Pravum issued an impromptu order to his adjutant.

"I want that bitch kept on a short leash! A very short leash! Do I make myself clear?"

"Yes sir, crystal clear!" Parva parroted in response.

CHAPTER SEVEN

13th Precinct
21st Street
Lower Manhattan

Chief Wachowski only briefly looked up from his cluttered desk as Frank Mahone pushed through his office door.

"Nealon says you looking for me?" Mahone anounced as he entered.

"Yeah, get over to 21st and the River and handle this." Wachowski grunted while thrusting a pink phone message slip towards Mahone. "Came in about five minutes ago."

"Why me? I thought I was in Robbery this week?" Mahone protested as he glanced over the note.

"Only until I need you somewhere else." Chief Wachowski fired back. "That's the definition of a 'floater' Frank, you work where I need you! That's the sort of thing that happens when you take a year off to go to England on vacation."

"A year off?! Fuckin' vacation?! Was you who sent me over there!"

"Yeah, to keep you out'a reach of that bitch in Internal Affairs! You're welcome."

"But . . ."

"Take it up with the clowns over at City Hall Park."

"I'd like -"

"Consider it a promotion." He cut Frank off.

"How in the hell is being transferred from Robbery to Homicide a promotion?"

"Because you're dealin' with a rougher crowd so you got a 90% better chance of being killed and thus being put out'a my misery. Now go!"

Mahone turned to leave then paused and turned at the door but, before he could speak the Chief again cut him off.

"Because the reported body washed up in Peter Cooper Village which you know is at the end of 20th Street off the Styvasant Cove pier. The 13th Precinct, which is our Precinct, is on 21st Street. 21st Street is next to 20th Street. Thus enters into the equation what's known as 'jurisdiction'." He sarcastically spewed.

"I was just going to say-"

"You requested to go back to homicide, so I guess it's your lucky day! Besides, no one said its a homicide. In all likelyhood it's an accidental."

"I should be so lucky!"

"Also Detective Mahone seeing as how your new English best friend has gone home, and as a personal favor because you and I are so close, I will allow you to choose a partner. And because there seems to be a reward system out there in Bad Guy Land for whoever can put a bullet in you and make you finally stay down, if the partner of your choice ops to not want to work with you I will be happy to assign you one." Wachowski blandly explained.

"I was just going to ask if I have time for a-"

"No."

"Where exactly's the stiff?"

"Central just got the call five minutes ago. It's still on scene. They were told to leave her in situ until a competent policeman arrives. But you are all I have at the moment so go arrive already!"

Frank glanced down at the the slip of paper.

"The body's a female?"

"Yes Frank, women die too. So go and arrive please."

Ten minutes later Mahone was parked on the East River Greenway and making his way to a small crowd gathered around the ambulance next to the entrance to the small ferry pier. The older of the two paramedics approaching met him halfway.

"Jimmy Jones, City Hospital."

"Frank Mahone, 13th Precinct." Jones led him down the short embankment to the river's edge.

"Coroner been notified?" Frank asked.

"Yes sir, due here in about twenty minutes."

"Who found the body?"

"A couple of joggers." Jones nodded off to the side and back up the embankment where two young men in sports gear stood looking down at the scene.

"They say or see anything?"

"No. Just said they were out for their daily run when they got down there by those stumps, they smelled something and when they got around here they spotted the body and called the police. We've been here about fifteen minutes. One of them found a purse a few yards away as well."

"Where is it?"

"I have it up in the ambulance. Didn't open it yet."

Frank got the medic to help him remove the heavy blanket covering the corpse to reveal a thirty-something woman with short brown hair, in a white blouse and dark skirt. There was no obvious trauma and except for missing shoes she was fully dressed.

"This exactly where she was found?"

"Yeah. We got the word to leave her as she was just as we pulled up."

Frank thanked the paramedic and after a cursory search of the immediate area, the body and noting the area between the Queens and Brooklyn shores across the river he mentally prepared what he would note in his report.

He again addressed Jones.

"Hang around until the coroner shows up. Meanwhile go tell those guys I'll come up and talk to them in a minute."

"Will do."

"Where you taking her?" Frank asked.

"Dispatch said to transport her over to Mount Sinai."

"Sinai? That's ridiculous! Bellvue's just over on 26th! Take her there. You get any flak tell them to call Mahone at the 13th."

"Will do detective."

Facing out across the river Frank drew an imaginary azimuth from the tips of Brooklyn and Queens to where he stood.

Knowing that the East River current flows south to the harbor but has strong fluctuations both ways depending on the tides, he made a couple of rough guesses as to where the body may have been dumped should it actually prove to be a murder victim.

Additionally he noted that his triangulation crossed both the East River ferry and Astoria ferry routes.

By the time Mahone interviewed the two joggers and determined they had nothing to contribute a rep from the Coroner's office had arrived and was doing a cursory field exam in the ambulance as Frank walked over to him.

"What'a ya think Doc?"

"Early thirties, possible accidental drowning, fell overboard maybe during a party tour or something. Judging by her dress and approximate weight she doesn't appear to be a drug user."

"If she was she's pretty clean." Frank added.

"Exactly. Looks to be dead about ten to twelve hours, no obvios signs of trauma, no defensive wounds, at least none on the surface. You find any I. D. on her?"

"They found her purse but I haven't gone through it yet. I'll do that over at the station house when I do my report." Frank hesitated for a moment as he stared down at the hapless victim. "Doc, you ever known a young woman to get well dressed to go out but not wear any jewellry?"

"Huh, can't say as I have, no." He commented after a quick glance over the body. "You thinking robbery?"

"Not necessarily. Just thinking out loud. How long before I can get a post mortem?"

"Well you're lucky there, it's Wednesday so I can

probably get an open table before the weekend. As long as everything is cleared out from last weekend. Seems like it's a free-for-all in this city lately come weekends!"

"At least it ain't Chicago!" Frank quipped.

"Thank God for that!"

****

"Then I had the idea to create the system with the aim of converting it to be fully automated." Phil Finley explained to Whitcombe. The two sat off to the side of the sparsely filled NSA cafeteria.

"I wouldn't be in a big hurry to let that get out!" Whitcombe, sitting across from him cup of coffee I hand.

"Why not?"

"You serious? You'll put a dozen people out of work! You'll wind up getting run over in the parking lot accidentally on purpose!"

"Hadn't thought of that." Finley conceded. "Well even so, that's only half the battle. There's still the gremlins!" Finley stated.

Finished with lunch they stood to leave.

"Still the what?"

"Haven't you ever watched a Wold War II movie about flyers?" Finley queried.

"Speak English!"

"We still need to iron out any kinks that might pop up."

"You're talking about doing a test?!" Whitcombe suddenly realized.

"Of course! But it has to be 45% to 55% reliable, the test must be kept classified and it must operate in as near as real time as possible."

"Oh well, as long as there's no pressure!" Whitcombe quipped.

They reached the door and swiped their key cards to exit the cafeteria.

****

Vanity Fair Magazine
Main Office

Mahone showed up at the front desk of *Vanity Fair Magazine* twenty minutes before his appointment time with the Chief Editor. It was only by coincidence that J.J. Johnson stepped out of her office to stretch her legs and hand carry some memos to the front desk that she noticed Mahone slouching in the waiting area arms folded in front of him apparently dozing.

"Who the hell is that?" She demanded of the receptionist.

"A homicide cop."

"Is he here to see someone?" J.J. quietly asked Janice the receptionost.

"Yes ma'am."

"Who, exactly?"

"You." J.J. drew back and did a double take.

"Well wake him the hell up, get him some coffee and bring him in! This isn't a fucking flop house!" She stromed away.

Minutes later Mahone was sitting in front of the middle-aged editor in a spacious corner offfice with a panoramic view overlookng all of Midtown and asking questions.

Oddly enough there was a slightly older suit sitting quietly off to her left. He was well dressed in an Armani, was not introduced and sporadically jotted notes on a steno pad.

"Ms O'Neill came to us out of Columbia School of Journalism and was employed here from January 3rd 2019." Johnson explained reading from her computer screen.

"She play well with others?" Mahone probed.

"Sam attends all office functions, gets along wiith the half dozen people she regularly comes in contact with and as far as I know avoids all the usual office intrigue and has no enemies. At least not here."

"I'll need to see her office."

"As soon as we're done here I'll take you to it."

"Work habits?" Mahone asked.

"Good to excellant. Always has her assignments in on time. Save for the one that was due Monday."

"I wouldn't hold my breath on her getting you that article any time soon."

"Why not? What are you saying?"

"I'm saying that if I were you I'd get somebody else on that article assignment."

"Don't tell me she's run off with that biker bastard!"

"Mrs. Johnson –"

"It's **Ms** Johnson Mr. Mahone!"

"How did I not know that." He shrugged. "Point is Miss O'Neill won't be returning to work any time soon."

"And why the hell not?!" J.J. demanded.

"Because most folks don't report to work after they're dead."

"DEAD?!" Wide-eyed she sat bolt upright while the Armani stopped jotting notes and stared blankly over at the two.

"Yeah you know, the big sleep. Bought the farm. Taking a dirt nap."

"How'd it happ . . . when'd it happen?" Johnson was visibly shaken.

"Her body washed up on the shore of the East River and was found by a couple of joggers."

"Did she drown?"

"We are looking into that possibility."

"You think she was murdered?!"

"There's no evidence it was murder. The Coroner's office is still investigating."

"But it's a possibility?!" J.J. pushed.

"The Coroner's office is still working on it."

Frank glanced over and noticed the man had stopped taking down notes.

"Can you give me anything on her personal life?" Frank pushed on with the questions.

"She had an on-again off-again relationship with her boyfriend. According to her collegues he only showed up at her office twice, both times in the same week."

"Any idea what he wanted?"

"Not really. Take her to lunch, get some money

from her maybe."

"There appear to be any friction between them?"

"I don't pry into my employee's personal affairs."

"Would there be any CCTV tapes? I'd ilke to know what this guy looks like."

The older man continued to sit quietly, off to the side still not taking any more notes of the conversation.

After a few more routine questions Johnson led Mahone down the hall and over to Sam's office. The older man disappeared upstairs.

"Who's the Boris Karloff?" Asked Mahone once they were out of earshot.

"Head of Corportate Legal." She said as they walked while noticing Mahone's expression. "You're a cop asking questions about a posssible murdered employee. We're a multi-million dollar international corporation. Can't be too careful."

"You didn't know why I was here until I told you. He was here before me."

"Like I said, you're a cop. An experienced cop. Sleep deprived but experienced. Experienced cops don't usually waste their time unless they think they've got somebody to pin something on." She repeated as she opened the door to Sam's former office.

Frank rummaged through Sam's desk and around the small room. Johnson followed behind also going through all the desk drawers apparently looking for something.

"Did Sam have a purse on her when you found

her?" Johnson asked.

"Yes."

"Was it closed up?"

"Why?!"

"What was in it?" She asked.

"Why are you asking?" Frank pushed.

"Did you find a press pass in it?"

"No. Driver's licence, some money, hair brush, why?!"

"Because it's not in her desk and if it wasn't in her purse it's missing!"

"Meaning?"

"Sam bought drinks the night after work the day she was awarded her press pass, she was that proud of it. She never let it out of her sight."

"So?"

"So? So a press pass is like a cop's badge. It gets you access! Access to places others can't go! Crime scenes, clubs, sports events if you're into that crap."

"You think maybe her boyfriend took it?"

"Not likely but why in hell would anybody steal a press pass?" Johnson asked.

"If it's so valuable why not?!" He countered.

"Point taken!" She conceded.

"When's the last time she might have used it?"

"Not sure. As far as I know the day that FBI agent was here to meet her." Frank's gaze shot up from the desk. Johnson continued talking. "Why go through the trouble when you can just download a bootleg one on line anyway? Hell, for fifty bucks you can even send in a passport photo and get one sent back with any major publication and all your details on it!" She explained.

"Better living through technology!" Frank cracked.

"Yeah!" She agreed.

"You didn't happen to get the name of this FBI guy did you?"

"It was a girl not a guy and sorry, no."

"She must have flashed her badge, I.D., something? Did no one get her name?" Frank pushed.

"To my knowledge only Sam."

"How do you know she was FBI?"

"Please! You guys all look the same. You've practically got 'COP' stamped across your foreheads!" She growled. "Besides, Sam told me later when I talked with her."

Later that morning CCTV footage revealed the FBI agent in question,

CHAPTER EIGHT

Nexus 6 Research Center
Austin, Texas

Following the D.C. House Intel Committee hearings in February Daniel Parker immediately returned to his home, one of three, a ranch in Elroy south of Austin which had been most recently converted into his automotive research facility.

Just as Howard Hughes' father left him a small tool and die factory upon which the eccentric billionaire built his empire so too did Daniel Parker found his current space technology fortune on the hard work and genius of his father's financial foundations.

The car radio, although developed by the 1920's was sketchy at best, had limited range and was nearly 25 to 30% the cost of a new car. The obstacle to be overcome was the voltage differential.

Radio receiver devices of the time ran on 50 to 250 volts. A standard car battery could produce no more than 6 volts. Transformers had already been developed however could only provide a steady current and more often than not would short out the radio circuits.

Through his understanding of electronics Parker's father developed and successfully marketed the first pulsating transformer allowing perfect control of the electrical flow and thereby permitting car radios to be standard features in all passenger vehicles.

Parker senior patented his invention in 1938 and by 1946 there were over 9 million AM car radios in use. In 1952 FM radio was introduced and by the sixties, twenty years before Daniel was born, his family was worth well over $545 million.

Not cntent to live off his father's efforts Daniel worked constantly to build on the previous Parkers' contributions, primarily through the R&D of satellite technology.

Currently he could be found on his twelfth lap of the Circuit of the Americas' 3.4 mile, convoluted race track just north of Elroy testing a new battery configuration on his personally designed, yet to be marketed EV Zephyr 3, two door luxury car.

It was by special arrangement with the University of Texas, Austin campus that Daniel Parker was permitted to schedule time on the university owned track for experimental and testing purposes the results of which he would share with the UTA engineering department.

Of course the $50,000 annual grant he sponsored helped to persuade an initially reluctant university board as well.

At present a gruff, well built Managing Engineer named Malachi, fifteen years Parker's senior, was waving wildy as Parker zoomed past him going into his thirteenth lap leaving the senior assisitant's long, grey handlebar mustashc flapping in the breeze.

The rear of the car was emitting a whitish haze of smoke.

"Malachi, Malachi come in. You trying to signal

me?" Daniel transmitted into his helmet mike as he focused on the next turn. There was no response. "Malachi!"

Just then the big man remembered he had his mike and head set down around his neck and pulled it up.

"BOSS, BOSS! You're trailing smoke! I think the battery array's had it! Pull her into the pit!"

Slowing down coming into the last turn of the next lap Parker geared down and turned to enter the pit when the underside housing holding the lithium battery array occupying the entire undercarriage and chasse burst into flames.

From the other end of the pit Malachi sprinted towards the car grabbing a fire extinguisher enroute.

Parker, now trapped inside the rapidly burning vehicle was frantically fumbling to undue his harness and force open the door to escape.

Without warning the passenger's side window exploded inwards as Malachi smashed the window with the extinguisher, ripped open the door and with two giant hands reached in and like a life-sized rag doll dragged a choking Parker out through the window and shoulder carried him a distance away from the now fully engulfed vehicle.

From a safe distance away they both watched as the vehicle was consumed by flames.

"I don't think that's how you're supposed to use a . . . fire extinguisher Chief!" Daniel breathlessly coughed out as he peeled off his helmut and sat back on the ground.

Malachi standing over him had all he could do to

contain his anger.

"God dman it Boss! I'm tellin' you again, you need to hire professional drivers to do this shit!"

"What for?"

"WHAT FOR?! For to save you from becoming a crispy critter!"

"That's what you're here for. And you're doin' a pretty damn good job too!"

The big man offered Parker a hand up.

"I swear Boss, if I hadn't promised your old man . . ."

"Malachi?"

"Yeah what?!" He snapped as he stomped away and rehung the fire extinguisher.

"Thanks."

"You can thank me by not being stupid!" He barked.

Just then a cell phone ring tone sounded with the main theme from *Star Wars*. Malachi pullled the phone from his side pocket and read the caller I.D. before offering the phone to Parker. "It's Boca Chica!" Malachi then called back over his shoulder as he walked away.

"Don't get the wrong idea Boss! I only saved your ass because if you die I gotta go lookin' for another job and I'm too God damned old fer to go through all that interview shit again!" He growled.

Daniel smiled as the phone continued to ring several more times before he answered.

"Parker here, talk to me."

The call was the message that the last of the VPE satellite constellation had just been successfully lauched from the rented Space X launch pad at Elon Musk's Boca Chica beach space port down on the coast.

Parker turned to watch the diminishing flames of the charred hulk of his Zephyr 3.

"Thanks. Do you have telemetry?"

We expect to receive the confirmation signal in the next twenty to thirty minutes.

"As soon as it's established activate the satellites, confirm transmission and have Sally in P.R. type up a press release. I'll be down there sometime tomorrow. Out."

Will do Boss!

Parker's smile melted away as he glanced over at the smoldering ruins of his Zephyr 3.

"To bad we've no marshmallows!" He mumbled to himself as he pushed up from the ground. "Back to the drawing board!"

CHAPTER NINE

Before transferring to England for his temporary assignment with the London Metropoiltan Police Service Frank Mahone had had to give up his one bedroom on the Upper East Side. Since his return to The States and given the latest wrinkle in the never-ending New York housing crisis, Mahone was compelled to take an efficiency across the Hudson River in Hoboken, New Jersey.

Rent was a third of what he paid in Manhattan but came with a trade off of thirty minutes travel time, tolls and or public transport fees of about $100 a week to get to work.

But that afternoon as he sat on his half couch facing out towards the towering Manhattan skyline sipping a bottle of Heinekin with his feet up on the coffee table he ultimately decided it was worth it.

As he reached for the TV remote his cell phone rang causing him to quietly swear. As the ring tone blared to the sound of a mullah's call to prayer followed by the sound of an M60 firing off he lifted the phone to his ear.

"Mahone here, talk to me."

"Mr. Frank Mahone?" The male voice in a slightly tainted accent asked.

"Yeah, what'a-ya-want?!"

"Mr. Detective Frank Mahone of the NYPD?"

"Yeah! Who is this?" His annoyance began to surface.

"Sir, can I ask you if you've heard the news?"

"What fuckin' news?"

"The news of our lord and savior Jesus Chri-" Was all the caller got out before being cut off as Frank aggressively pressed the off button and returned to his beer and the football game.

A minute later the phone again sounded.

"Yeah?"

"Is this the big strong Yank what finds lost armored cars, bus loads of schoolgirls and loves politicians?"

This time the man on the other end spoke in a high falsetto with an exaggerated London, East End accent.

Mahone's face gradually nurtured a broad smile.

"Morrissey! You Limey asshole!" Frank snapped back.

"You like Enfield's impression of a holy roller?" Morrissey taunted.

"To what do I owe this annoying disturbance . . . ah pleasure?"

"Just ringing my 13th closest friend to inform him that I have officially handed in my retirement papers at the Met but I have three weeks holiday time coming. They gave me the option of cash or time off. And with my mother now gone . . ."

"My condolences Nigel, I was sorry to hear the news when it came in. I never met her but I know your mother was a good woman."

"Thank you mate. That means a lot."

"When I say 'good woman' I don't mean by how she raised you! Just by how she must have had to fight the urge to give you up for adoption all those

The Hermes Project

years!"

"Always were the empathetic one you were! So how's the second most efficient police service in the western world treating you these days?"

"You mean aside from rock bottom morale, exaggerated administrative overreach and departmental scrutiny along with personnel and pay cuts? Fine. Then there's always the question of residency."

"How do you mean?"

"The new asshole mayor wants to pass a law telling us where we can and can't live."

"Well, good thing you chaps fought a war to get away from all the tyranny of the British Empire eh?"

"Nigel?"

"Yes Frank?"

"Go fuck yourself!"

"Tried it. Didn't care for it!" Nigel shot back. *"However, did save a bundle on dinner and a movie!"*

Frank reached over with the remote to turn down the TV.

"So what's the next chapter in the life of one of the top fifty cops I've had a mild pleasure to work with?" Frank asked.

"Funny you should bring that up old chum!"

"That doesn't sound good! Should I be sitting down?"

"Not at all! I'm simply thinking of coming back to your quaint, little collection of colonies!"

"You mean like for a visit? You just left last

month!"

"Yes, I suppose you could say for a visit. But a visit with a purpose."

"Wait!" Mahone paused a beat. "Okay I'm sitting down. Give me the bad news."

"No bad news mate! Only good news! In her will my mother's sister, bless her curmudgeonly, crusty old soul, left a small plot of land and a cottage over in Parkchester to her sister."

"Okay, how is that good news?"

"The cantankerous, old sod died a week before my mother and I'm named as the alternate beneficiary!"

"Great! So now you have a healthy pension, a house and a plot of land."

"Yes and I almost feel bad for the old bird! But not quite!"

"Still doesn't answer my question. What's next?"

"I fly out day after tomorrow to go and see the property"

"Morrissey, I don't know what you're plotting to plot with you're newly aquired plot but. . ."

"I'll fill you in when you buy me a pint next week at that Pete's place tavern you were always talking up when you were over here!"

"So what you're taking the long way around the barn to tell me is you're coming back over here?"

"You are a cracker jack detective now aren't you!"

"But what about going up to Parkchester to see your property?"

*"Not **up** old boy! **Over**! Parkchester in the Bronx!*

The Hermes Project

Bronx, New York City! I'm thinking of taking my pensioner's years over there! No more cold, wet and damp for old Morrissey boy-o!" There was only silence on the other end of the line. *"Well, I can tell by your silence that you are genuinely overcome with excitement, emotion and anticipation!"* Nigel excitedly spewed. *"See you next week!"*

The line went dead.

"Shit!"

****

Uncharacteristically British Air flight 1066 landed at JFK on time and The Squad proceeded through customs to the luggage claim area. Once outside the terminal they found a taxi.

Din, Heath, Enfield and Little Tammy stowed their luggage in the back and climbed into the eight pack van.

"Where to folks?"

"Sheraton Midtown." Heath directed.

Twenty-five minutes later as they were crossing the Brooklyn Bridge, the sounds of sirens blaring and honking horns ushered them onto Manhattan Island.

"This is one exciting city! So many things going on all at the same time!" Enfield declared with the excitement of a child just arrived at the circus.

"Yeah, most of them unsolved!" Heath grumbled.

"Hey Din." Enfield called over his shoulder.

"Yeah?"

"You've been here before yes?"

"A couple of times, why?"

"I see why you like it here."

"Yeah? Why's that?"

"There's a deli on every corner!" He guffawed.

Din didn't laugh. Enfield and Tammy laughed. The Pakistani taxi driver quietly chuckled to himself.

As they drove through Times Square Enfield sat back and pretended to contemplate his words before he spoke.

"Interesting fact; the New York City Council paid Hillary Clinton four million dollars to officiate at their New Year's Eve celebration last year." He relayed.

"Really?!" Din asked.

"Yeah, they wanted somebody who's used to dropping the ball at the last minute!"

Din, Heath and the driver laughed.

"Ya bloody bowbag! In East Kilbride they kill for better jokes!" Tammy mumbled as she chuckled.

"Bowbag, is that good or bad?" Din whispered over to Heath.

"Not a flippin' clue mate!" He answered.

Enfield, face glued to the window, was now maintaining an enamored silence while taking in the surroundings of the Midtown traffic, skyscrapers and general atmosphere of organized chaos.

Heath on the other hand made no effort to hide his discomfort. He intended this to be less of a vacation and more of a trying police assignment. It wasn't as though he had any real animosity towards New York in particular, he just hated cities.

"I just can't get over how these Yanks can drive

on the wrong side of the road and not bash into each other!" Heath mumbled out loud.

"Same way as the punters in Glasgow can get pissed out of their heads each night and still turn up for work next mornin'."

"How's that Tammy?"

"Practise Sergeant Heath, practise!" She answered.

Heath quickly pulled back from the window when a bus zoomed past on his side of the van.

"Lads just remember, if we have to hire a motor car, these Yanks drive on the wrong side of the road!"

It was at the front desk of the hotel, during check-in, that they were again reminded they were no longer in England.

Tammy stepped up to the young female desk clerk to get registered and dutifully slid her passport across the desk. The clerk typed in her information.

"Do you have a cell number ma'am?" She politely asked.

"Cell number?! We's the ones what puts them in their cells!" Tammy snapped back with a smirk. The young desk clerk stared in confusion.

"I mean a number ma'am, I need a cell number."

"Well you'll have to go out and do a crime won't you then?" Tammy snidely remarked as she began to slowly simmer.

"Ma'am the hotel will need to know where to reach you in case of an emergency."

"You can reach me in my bloody room providing I ever get one!" Tammy angrily growled.

The young one behind the desk began to get flustered.

At that point the older desk clerk next to them stepped over and intervened by taking the young clerk aside and conferring with her in a low tone.

"What seems to be the trouble?" She asked.

"I'm having some trouble trying to get this guest's telephone number."

The senior clerk assumed the reins and stepped over to Tammy.

"Ma'am you do have a cell, don't you?"

"Cell? What the fuck is this, biology class? Is everyone here completely daft?!"

Heath, Din and Enfield stood quietly off to the side enjoying the show. However, the people in line behind Tammy were losing patience.

"You do have a phone number don't you?"

"A fuckin' phone number! Is that all you're after? Me mobile phone number?" She brandished her smartphone to clarify. "You're one daft mumpty you are!" She again swore.

"Yes ma'am, a mobile phone number." The clerk confirmed. Tammy relayed her number to the clerk. "Thank you, ma'am."

"Bloody Yanks!" She swore as she grabbed her card key and bag before the bell boy could and headed for the elevators. The people in line breathed a sigh of relief and Heath stepped up to the desk.

A minute later a scream blasted from around the corner by the elevators. The three lads dashed around to see what was the matter. The view that greeted them took them all off guard.

A young bell boy was sprawled out on the floor rubbing his jaw, Tammy stood over him, both fists clenched. Several other guests stood off to the side maintaining a safe distance.

"Did you whack him?!" Heath demanded.

"Bloody right I hit the lavvy-headed wank stain!"

"Why for Gods sake?!"

"Bastard suggested I keep me key card in me twat!"

The humiliated bell boy, keeping his distance, climbed up from the floor and made eye contact with Heath.

"All I said was you better keep that in your fanny pack!" He innocently pleaded scurried away into the sanctuary of the crowd.

Enfield moved to help the young lad while Heath was speechless and increasingly terrified of police involvement. Din was completely lost. Heath stepped over to the young man.

"Heartfelt apologies mate! 'Fanny' means something different where we come from lad." He explained to the hotel worker brushing off his red uniform.

"Apparently!" The boy grumbled.

"I thought these bloody people spoke English!" A dumbfounded and slightly embarrassed Tammy complained.

"They do. You don't!" Heath angrily countered as he guided her into the lift. Enfield slipped the boy a tenner and apologised for his police mate.

"First time off the farm Sergeant?" Heath

chastised Tammy.

"Bolt off, ya mangled fud!" She snapped at Din who smiled at her as she retrieved her bag and stepped onto the elevator. Tammy's embarrassment turned to humiliation as the small crowd dissipated. No one else dared enter the spacious lift.

"Off to a rippin' start here so we are!" Heath swore under his breath as he followed her on and the elevator doors slid shut.

*

Office of the Chief Medical Examiner
Bellevue Hospital
26th Street, Manhattan

It was cool and breezy but not cold as inspector Morrissey walked up 1st Avenue with Frank and looked down to read a text from his phone as they crossed 25th Street.

Frank and Nigel, now in New York, were crossing the street into the City Medical Examiner's building to confer with the Assistant Coroner Dr. Jackson.

"Just got a message from Heath. The children have landed and are all tucked in at the hotel." Morrissey relayed to Mahone as they scurried across the street between cars.

What Morrissey had neglected to mention to Mahone on the phone last week was that in line with Endfield's suggestion, Heath, Enfield, Din and MacIntyre had all requested their annual holiday leave together.

Naturally the Chief Inspector refused their request outright but once it was leaked to *The Guardian* and *The Mirror* that the crack Special Homicide Investigation Team, a.k.a the SHIT Squad, which had solved the Metropolitan's *record* number of cases in the short year and a half they had been together effectively reducing knife crime, assault and gang violence by nearly half, Mayor Sadiq Kahn had little choice but to over rule the Commissioner.

Add in the facts that elections were not far off and that formation of the Squad had been credited to Kahn by the London press, and Enfield's brainstorm about traveling together worked like a charm.

"Nigel can I ask you a question?" Frank probed stepping off the elevator out into the underground labs.

"Work away old boy."

"In God's name what was going through your head when you decided to invite your entire homicide squad over here?" He asked as they followed their escort through the narrow marble halls and made their way into the morgue where Dr. Jackson was waiting. He picked up on the tail end of the conversation to do with friends coming over for vacation.

"Nothing was going through anyone's mind when no one invited anyone anywhere! The lads, of their own volition I might add, decided to take a holiday. It was either here or somewhere such as Sihanoukville, Cambodia. But When I told them about my uncle in the Royal Navy who had his hand chopped off so they could steal his wristwatch when he was on leave there they chose-"

"They chose the city with a higher crime rate! In fact one of the highest crime rates in the U.S.!" Jackson interrupted.

"Well . . . yes. That and Enfield always wanted to see a Broadway play!" Nigel jokingly added.

"This just keeps getting better and better!" Mahone let out a long deep breath. "Please don't take this the wrong way Nigel, but I have no time to babysit a bunch of tourists even if they are a bunch of cop friends." Frank made clear.

"You'll not even know they're in town!" He assured. "Look, Enfield tells me they all have rooms booked at the Midtown Sheraton and-" Nigel began.

"The Midtown Sheraton!" Jackson repeated.

"The Midtown Sheraton?!" Frank echoed. "There's your first fuck up! The place is three, four hundred dollars a night just because they put little chocolate mints on your God damn pillow and fold the the ends of the toilet paper into little points! Only a bunch of saps would stay in Manhattan when they come to see New York!"

"Absolute saps!" Jackson again chimed in hanging and shaking his head.

"Where in bloody hell would you stay then? Miami Beach?!" Nigel defended.

"No bonehead! Across the river in Jersey. It's half the price and only a fifteen minute train ride into The City. Plus you can jump on a train, ride over and walk anywhere in the city."

"And get knifed, shot, beaten." Dr. Jackson added as they walked towards the lab. "Or take the subway and just get mugged!"

"Jackson!" Frank snapped. "No help from the peanut gallery please!" Mahone chastised. "When are they coming in?"

"They landed at Kennedy a couple of hours ago."

"Nothing like a little notice!" Mahone grumbled. "Okay, I have to get back to the precinct after we're done here, so you're going out to meet them at JFK and-"

"ME?! I don't know my way around this place!"

"You're from Scotland Yard, you'll figure it out. Start by taking the bus that's marked 'JFK Airport'. When you get them back to the Sheraton cancel their rooms from tomorrow on, then call me on my cell."

"What for?"

"I'll get them reservations at the Holiday Inn Express near the Holland Tunnel over in Jersey, about 10 minutes from my place. I stayed there a couple of nights when I was moving house. There's an in-house Cambio and rooms are $238 per night or about £195 Sterling."

"That's a $128 difference per night, nice one Frank!" Morrissey thanked.

"No problem."

"This is us." Jackson announced as they arrived at the autopsy suits in the very back of the basement.

The Jane Doe corpse, aka Samatha O'Neill, Frank Mahone and his men had fished out of the East River a couple of days ago had been autopsied and a call from the Coroner's office was put in to the 13th Precinct then routed up stairs to Homicide where the message landed on Mahone's desk.

Partially for some exercise and partially to clear his mind, rather than taxi over, Mahone had insisted they walk the short five blocks north up to 26th Street to consult with Jackson, the M.D. assigned the case and who had performed the autopsy.

Morrissey was visibly impressed by the size of the below street level lab.

The sprawling room accommodated a half dozen dissection tables each with two, overhead, multi-lamp, high intensity lights, adjoining fully stocked surgical trays and cabinets as well as ceiling to floor privacy curtains.

Only one of the tables was occupied with an autopsy in progress. The attending physician, his hands buried to the elbows in the the deceased's abdomen, nodded to Jackson while Morrissey fought back a slight gagging reflex as they passed by.

Down at table #5 Jackson peeled back the white bed sheet to reveal the cyanotic but still attractive face of the twenty-something woman.

"Cause of death?" Mahone asked.

"Drowning secondary to intoxication."

"She was drunk? You got a handle on her B.A.L.?"

"Blood Alcohol Level was zero, no liquor detected."

"What was she intoxicated on then?"

"It would appear she was poisoned." Jackson

informed.

"Poisoned?! Then dumped in the river?"

"With all due respect Lieutenant I get paid to read the present, you get paid to guess at the past." Frank wasn't amused at the dig but bit his tongue.

"Toxicology came back with slight traces of amphibian toxin."

"Never knew frogs could bite!" Morrissey opined.

"They're poisonous not venomous. They don't bite. You die by handling them. Either of you guys ever watch National Geographic?"

Mahone suddenly looked up from the clip board he was browsing through.

"Only Shark Week!" He snapped back. "Cut me some fuckin' slack here Doc will ya? I look like a fuckin' zoologist to you? What the hell would a writer from a fashion magazine be doin' handling a deadly fuckin' frog? A bet or a dare or something?!" He pushed as Morrissey stepped closer to hear.

"According to our friends up at the Bronx Zoo there are over 170 known species of South American Dart Frog. You know the kind natives use to tip their poison darts in?"

"Or ultra-rich thrill seekers bring to parties for kicks?" Mahone suddenly realized aloud.

"What do you mean 'kicks'?" Morrissey asked.

"They lick them to get high." Frank explained.

"Christ are you serious?" Nigel challenged.

"Serious as Kamala Harris' inability to form coherent sentences!"

"They ever die?" Nigel asked.

"Sometimes. We've seen a couple pass through here." Jackson informed.

"Some people!" Nigel sighed.

"Some people are idiots!" Mahone declared shaking his head.

"True but without whom we'd all be out of a job!"

"Excellent point Doctor!" Nigel opined.

"Frogs Doc, frogs!" Mahone reminded.

"Of course! Just handling any one of them can kill you." Jackson added.

"You think this chick was at an Uptown party licking South American frogs?" Mahone pushed.

"Not impossible, but because of their lethality combined with a pin prick-like puncture in the back below the neck, her poisoning was definitely not voluntary."

Mahone flipped back to the cover page of the report which featured two outlines of a human in the standard anatomical position, one anterior and one posterior. The posterior outline featured a red dot indicating the suspected point of injection to the left of the upper thoracic spine.

"How can you rule out suicide?" Frank pushed.

"There are only a couple of places you can't inject yourself especially with the amount required. That's in the lower cervical or upper thoracic regions where I found what appeared to be a needle mark."

"Why only there?"

"The toxin would hit you too fast plus . . . here, try and pretend to be injecting yourself." He grabbed an empty 20cc syringe with no needle on it and passed it to Mahone who tried to reach around behind himself to where the doctor indicated but couldn't manage.

"So who was she?" Nigel ventured.

"We've tentatively I.D.'d her as Samantha Elizabeth O'Neill staff writer for *Vanity Fair Magazine*." Jackson answered.

"Why tentatively?" Nigel asked.

"Law requires her to be I.D.'d by a relative. Her parents have been notified and are flying in tonight so I can't finish off the paperwork until they get in and confirm her."

"Where they flying in from?" Frank pushed.

"Ohio, why? Is that a problem?"

Frank was suddenly mindful of possible complications to include permissions, court orders and jurisdictional ramifications.

"They'll likely want to take her back with them." Frank tossed the white sheet flap back over O'Neill's face and passed the clipboard back to the doc. "Need a favor Doc. It's important."

"If I can, sure."

"I need you to hold her here and keep her under a Jane Doe."

"Detective, her parents? I can't legally hold her after they sign for –"

"Look, I have a very strong suspicion that her death ties into a much bigger case and I might need you to run some more tests."

"But-"

"Just tell her folks that we need a judge's order

or something before you can release her. It's important Doc, plus I'll owe you one!"

"End of next week Lieutenant! Best I can do!"

"I owe you a beer!"

"I drink scotch. Imported!"

"Nigel, I'll meet up with you later tonight and take the Squad back over to Hoboken."

"Awfully decent of you!"

"Yeah, I'm a fucking saint! Jackson e-mail me over a copy of the death cert as soon as you get it finished. And just on the off chance they might agree, ask the parents if they'll consent to letting us keep the body for a few more days. Tell them The State will pay to have it shipped back home." Mahone said as he and Nigel left.

"Gotta love a guy who takes charge!" Jackson mumbled to himself as he returned to work.

****

Just over ten days from her last visit to the Alert Center of the NSA Natalie Farmiga made her way back to Phil Finley's workspace to receive a demonstration briefing of his proposed *Hermes Project*.

It was just after ten in the morning when she was settled in, notebook in hand, ready to hear of this 'miricle' program Finley was ready to present to her.

"Won't the General be joining us?" She asked as she sat alone in the small work room surrounded by computers, printers, a slide projector and Phil Finley with Bill Whitcombe seated behind the projector.

"We actually thought we would run it by you first, just to iron out any kinks we might have missed." His answer reinforced Farmiga's suspicion of the existence of trust issues between the Alert Center and Pravum's office. Not a good sign.

Finley began.

"Last time we spoke I pointed out that, counting phones, computers and other communication devices, we guees-ta-mated there are approximately fifteen billion electronic units capable of being used for person-to-person communication."

"I would say at least that many," Farmiga agreed.

"Prior to conception of *Hermes* and still today, our agency works on the premise of collecting all information possible, passing it to the analysts and waiting for them to discover something while they wade through it all."

"Which backlogs the system for months?" Farmiga correctly deduced.

"Exactly! In essence the analysts are never able to catch up especially when new leads are constantly filtering in."

"I see."

"Instead by switching to the *Hermes System* which is based on metadata, we can-"

"And metadata is?" She interrupted.

"Metadata is the data surrounding the data!" Whitcombe added before Finley explained further.

"By way of example two parties, party A and party B, are having a conversation. We intercept their conversation and analyse it and find no informartion of any value. Which is what we find in the majority of cases. We've just wasted valuable time, resources and something you will not be happy to hear, money! Where as using metadata in lieu of the actual conversation we back out and scan all the communications of both parties within a given set of time parameters say over the last six months."

"Their connections only! Not the actual conversations about aunt Betty's birthday celebration or uncle Frankie's cookout next Saturday." Whitcombe supplemented.

"And now we're looking for a pattern. None found? The analysts can move on."

"What if you do find something. Say with party B?" She queried.

"Then it follows to suit that we'll find somethiing else such as that same contact in the given six month period contacting a known red flagged individual and we can spend more productive time following that contact! By eliminating the internal content with the relationships with people and focusing on those relationships we can make it quick, efficient and relevant."

"Sounds good in theory but, over fifteen billion devices?" Farmiga challenged.

Finley nodded at Whitcombe as he walked over and switched off the lights. The slide projector came to life and splashed a computer genertaed graphic on the screen.

The graphic was a configuration of hudreds of

white beads interconnected by single strands of white lines, not unlike a standard 3D model of a long chain molecule, all on a black background.

"Each dot or node represents a communications device. Fifteen billion nodes all with connections to others." Finley continued.

The slide changed and was replaced with one showing a large globe of the same nodes all inter connected.

"When you pull one node from the globe all the nodes it has connections with come up with it."

A third slide showed one node at the twelve o'clock position in the globe rise slightly tugging at all the ones it was attached to.

"The idea is we would start the analysts on one or more of the most likely targets and follow on from there."

Farmiga sat back and contemplated for a long while making the guys a bit uncomfortable. Finally after scratching out some notes she spoke.

"Alright let's say your *Hermès* system works, and you are able to double your analytic ability-" She postulated.

"More like triple!" Whitcombe piped up.

"Quadruple at least!" Finley added.

"Okay, so now you can theoretically tap into any communications device in the world. What's to prevent some unscrupulous player abusing the ability?"

"Glad you asked Congresswoman! It wasn't long after the first mock tests were completed, that we realized we had created the most powerful analytic tool ever developed. We, in effect had the ability to invade everyone's privacy on earth who had an electronic communications device. In near real time! Not good! We immediately agreed we'd have to do something to protect the innocents."

"What did you do about it?"

"First we had a rig a more definitive mock test."

"Mock test?"

"Yes, I invited the cryptologists down to the center and gave them a demonstration. I wrote my own program and Bill plugged it into our desktop computer. I took a random problem that the analysts had been working on for the last two weeks, put it into our modified computer and minutes later up popped the answer!" Finley explained.

"In less than five minutes!" Bill Whitcombe added.

"First thing they said was, 'Don't you think they should be in the mainframe?'. I said, 'Hell yeah it should be in the mainframe!' They said, 'Well send it up to us! I said, 'Send me a memo!' That was three weeks ago. I still haven't received a memo."

"Then what?" Farmiga asked.

"I had to improvise a sessionizer to scan the internet for red flags."

"And a sessionizer is?" Asked Representative Farmiga.

"In networking a session is a time delimited two-way link, a practical layer in the top IP protocol enabling interactive expression and exchange between two or more communication devices or terminals. In our case about fifteen and half billion phone lines."

Looking up from his child-like and joyful spirt Finley glanced over at her and saw her eyes glazing over.

"Sessionizers organise stuff ma'am!" Whitecome blurted out. "It's like setting up a direct phone line only to billions of phones." He added.

"Is that possible?!"

"We call it the *Hermes Program*!" He proudly boasted.

"Greek messenger of the gods!" The representative pointed out.

"Not only!" Finley gleefully added to Farmiga's puzzlement. "He was also the trickster!" He smilingly added.

Farmiga assumed some hidden meaning but had no desire to sidetrack the conversation.

"The failsafe in the system prevents the computer from taking in information on American citizens unless they are under suspicion of compromise in which case the contact is red flagged. As a backup the system additionally requires a FISA warrant code number to further invade the citizen's privacy."

"Well I'm glad to hear that, but we both realize the court system can easily be circumvented by unscrupulous individuals lying to the FISA Court like Comey, Struck, Page and others did during the last administration." She added.

"Exactly!"

"Glad you brought that up!" Finley declared as he continued to type and a code appeared on the screen in front of them.

"What's this?" She asked.

"You might call it a last line of defence!" Farmiga leaned further forward and focused more intently. "I haven't shown any of this to the General yet." Finley informed. Farmiga immediately pulled back.

"Why? Don't you trust him?" She asked.

"No, no it's not a matter of trust, just that I haven't finished the codeing yet!" He lied.

He finished typing in a phone number and pushed back from the console.

"Assume we want to scan number 03-501-776-6677."

"That's my number!" She exclaimed.

"Yes it is. Now I want to access your private data." Farmiga instantly shifted in her chair as he punched in a code and the screen began to flash. "You see, the program denied me entry because you have no red flags out on you."

"But what happens if somebody flags my number and by-passes your firewall?"

"You mean 'Sentinel'. I named the firewall Sentinel. Let's do that and see what happens!"

"Just make sure you take it off when we're done!" She demanded.

"Not to worry, this isn't the actual program. Its just the prototype." Again the screen flashed but only for about three seconds then shut down completely.

"Impressive!" She complimented. "What happened?"

"I call it Sentinel Vanguard! It's a back-up to the back-up, sort of."

"What happens then, after it shuts down I mean?"

"The attempted user's access code is recorded and reported to a classified access file. At least it will be when I get the whole system finished,"

"I see."

"Plus, I've developed a failsafe program as a mechanism to keep it out of bad hands. You have to show you have FISA approval."

"And the DIRNSA agreed?!" She asked. Both Phil and Bill quickly exchanged glances then looked down.

"Well . . . not exactly." Phil confessed.

"As soon as we told him about it he wanted it removed."

This last statement solidified Farmiga's hidden suspicions about Pravum.

Again an awkward silence permeated the room as Finley and Whitcombe sat silently. Finley switched the lights back on.

"The General never was coming, was he?" She deduced. Again the two men exchanged glances. "Which is why you purposely scheduled this little demo when you knew he wouldn't be around?" She added.

"You should have been an analyst Ms. Farmiga." Finley nervously commented. "I call the firewall 'Sentinel' because it requires a special card number to be issued by the Director himself or better yet a FISA court judge once he's reviewed the petition."

Farmiga stood and gathered her things.

"Mr. Finley, Mr. Whitcombe, you've done excellent work here. Based on what you've presented to me today I'm inclined to grant you the increasing funds you have requested. However there is one caveat! Hermes must include the Sentinel firewall! This is non-negotiable. Are we clear on that point?"

"Crystal clear congresswoman."

"As you know National Security Division's Office of Intelligence is responsible for preparing and filing all FISA applications as well as appearing before the FISA court."

"Yes."

"But I'm still not completely clear on how your program prevents anyone in the National Security Division from tampering with the warrants once they're in the Office of Intelligence?"

"With all due respect Congresswoman Farmiga, our task is to facilitate the flow of information analysis. Any wrongdoing on the political side is out of our perview."

"Meaning that's my responsibility not yours?"

"Your words ma'am, not mine." He quipped.

"So the primary motivation for developing the Hermes program was ergonomics?" Natalie Farmiga sought to clarify.

"Exactly! As it is, the analysts make their daily database polls and then get back hundreds of returns but are never able to catch up analysing and reporting them. Essentially, without Hermes, they would remain permanently swamped." He explained.

"You did all this on your own, unauthorised without permission?" Representative Farmiga asked. It was with some trepidation that Phil Finley answered.

"Well . . . yes ma'am."

"Why?"

"Representative Farmiga, in all my years of government service I have learned one thing above everything else; it's always easier to beg forgiveness then to ask permission!"

The congresswoman assumed a nondescript expression. Finley decided to go for broke and push it.

"As long as it's about the money and not about duty, the deterioration of the country caused by intelligence failures will continue. Look what's happened to the FBI!" He opined.

"And the DOJ!" Whitcombe added.

"Politics is the cancer. Until the cancer is treated there can be no cure." Finley added.

After a short period she looked up at Finley.

"There's only one thing I can say to you Mr. Finley. You'll get your money. On this one condition!"

"Which is?"

"You can guarantee me a fail safe firewall system."

"Consider it done! What about Pravum?"

"Don't wory about him."

After she left the two sat in a relieved silence for

a brief period before Bill spoke first.

"Do you think we should have told her about the testing?"

"Better not. Not necessary, not until we have the results. Besides, I've already contacted a friend up in Seattle, an electronics engineering professor. He's agreed to let us use his facilities to launch a large-scale test over the holiday weekend. He's already involved with military research and has a clearance." Finley revealed. "Now I just need to figure out what to use it on."

"What do you mean?" Bill asked.

"I mean we need a system to test it on." Phil explained. "Fortunately I already have one picked out!"

"Which government agency is going to let you use their satellites to test your system?"

"Not government, civilian owned. Eagle Eye!"

"Eagle Eye?! Eagle Eye as in the bazillionaire Daniel Parker's satellite system?! Did your mother drop you? He could crush us like flies on a windshield!"

"Not if he doesn't know about it!"

"How is he not going to know about it? He's got the most sophisticated hacker detection systems known to man! Hell, he invented half of them! And if he does find out about it we're yesterday's news! I'm talking not even a footnote in the archives!"

"I love it when you get all melodramatic! It's so Jack Reacher!"

"Phil, I'm serious as a heart attack!"

"Relax! He's **not** going to find out about it! I'm

going to upload it through my friend's system at the university in Seattle this Friday at 1800. We'll let HERMES collect data until 0600 Monday morning and we'll see what we come up with! I'm confident we'll collect something. The question is can we at least mine 50% of the data?"

"And then what? Hire a battalion of secretaries to check the numbers? You're talking billions of contacts!" Whitcombe objected.

"No, we don't need the exact contacts. We only need to record the percentage and latency periods. Then we'll know for sure it works!"

"But what if it doesn't work?!"

"Then we'll find out why and fix it!"

Whitcombe shook his head. "You should work for the NSA!"

"Nah, couldn't do it, couldn't work for the NSA!"

"Why not?!"

"Too many assholes!" Finley said as he returned to his work.

CHAPTER TEN

245 39th Street
Kuksova's Apartment
Friday

Irina poured her second cup of coffee as she again glanced down at the *Vanity Fair Magazine* on the kitchen table.

It was out of force of habit that she rose and had breakfast at half past seven that morning in her Bryant Park apartment despite the fact that she had no job to go to and wasn't due to meet Mahone for several hours yet.

Not quite clear what it was, an idea had been forming in her head since last evening.

She piled a generous portion of cat food onto a small plate and along with a saucer of milk set it out on the back fire escape for the feral cat she never saw, putzed around the apartment cleaning then eventually decided to dress and leave.

It was cold but clear a few hours later when Irina took the subway downtown, switched to the PATH line and rode under the Hudson over to Hoboken.

Less then half an hour after leaving her apartment she stepped off onto the subway platform on the New Jersey side of the river.

Exactly how to approach Mahone and present her case dominated her thoughts as she walked up the much gentrified residential sector to enter Pete's Tavern on the corner of 18th and Irving.

Fully expecting a lower class, working man's

dive Kuksova was pleasantly surprised by the elegant interior of the place.

The establishment was modelled in every detail after a late 19th Century New York Tavern with the central theme dedicated to the author O'Henry.

With pendant lighting down the center of the pressed stamped ceiling, the long dark wood bar, complete with brass rail, running the length of the left side of the big room and the round four-top tables surrounded by bentwood chairs filling the floor area, she felt as though she had actually stepped back into the turn of the last century.

Given their previous casual relationship, which since returning from their work in England seemed to have cooled off, meeting Frank to ask for help suddenly appeared a bit more daunting.

On the way down the middle of the sparsely attended bar room she took a second to check her hair in the huge back bar mirror when she spotted the booths along the back wall.

In the corner booth she saw that Frank had already arrived and had ordered drinks. In front of him was a half consumed pint of Guinness and a Manhattan cocktail.

"You're not looking any worse for wear since I last saw you." He complimented as she removed her overcoat.

"Frank it's not been that long!"

"Just tryin' to start things off on the right foot. Have a drink." He pushed the Manhattan over to her.

"Don't mind if I do!" She set her coat and purse aside and took a seat opposite. "Nice place you picked here. Uncharacteristically classy."

"I always like to keep the competition off balance." He said in reply. She smiled back as she sipped her cocktail. "It is Gramercy Park after all. The place was founded in 1829. O'Henry lived-" He started to relate.

"O'Henry lived right up the street on Irving, came here often when he wasn't in jail and *Gift of the Magi* was written in that booth right over there. Although that may or may it be true it brings in the tourists." She quickly spirted out.

"You ought'a join the FBI. Be a good stepping stone to becoming a homicide detective with the NYPD."

"Sorry, I couldn't work for minimum wage. How's the new mayor working out?"

"Same circus different clowns!" He grunted. "What's with this suspension nonsense?"

She took a deep breath, finished off her cocktail and slid her glass aside before speaking.

"When we came back from England I was assigned to The National Security Branch."

"You wanted that anyway, no?"

"Yes, but I wasn't prepared for all the political bullshit!"

"Talk to me." He coaxed with sincerity.

"Last week I was pulled for surveillance duty. We're supposed to stake out this guy in Central Park who's suspected of selling secrets. The agent on the case has information indicating they'll be a dead letter drop. We do the stake-out, the drop happens, we nail the guy and are taking him in."

"Well done. Case closed."

"Not quite! The schmuck goes and gets himself sniped!"

"Sniped in Central Park?!"

"Right there between the aviary and the primates!" She added.

"Welcome to the monkey house!" Mahone fell back in his seat. "Was he . . ."

"Delta Oscar Alpha! Dead on Arrival. As dead as David Koresh at Waco. Definitely a professional hit."

"Don't suppose you caught the sniper?"

"No. But it gets better!"

"Hold on!" Mahone stood, signalled for two more drinks then, like a kid about to hear a bed time story, retook his seat and refocused. "Okay, chapter two. Proceed."

"While we're waiting for Forensics to show up I spot a dodgy looking guy, Chinese type, moving towards the front gate. I move towards him and he starts running. Jim and I give chase and-"

"Wait, back the truck up. Who's Jim?" He asked with measured suspicion.

"My partner."

"You have a partner already?"

"It was only temporary, for the arrest."

"Good looking guy?"

"Why, you want me to set you two up?" She snarked.

"Just curious that's all." He fell back and raised both hands. "Forget I asked. Please continue."

"We give chase and he starts firing on us. So we

return fire. Jim, an ex-Marine-"

"UHHH!" Frank held up one finger. "We prefer the adjective 'former' Marine." He interjected. She pulled an annoyed face but continued.

"My partner nails him but when we get to him turns out not only is he not dead yet but his weapon is full of blanks!"

"Not very strategic of him, is it?" The waiter arrived with their drinks, set them out and Frank dropped a twenty on his tray. "Your runner buy the farm?" He asked her.

"Yeah, but before he checks out, while we're telling him to relax the ambulance is on the way, he starts mumbling. In Spanish!"

"Thought you said he was Chinese?"

"Exactly!"

"Any idea what he was saying?"

"Not really I don't speak Spanish. I've only got Russian, German, Ukrainian and Finish." She said.

"Is that all?! Slacker!"

"Focus Frank, focus! Blanks?!" She chided.

"Curiouser and curiouser." He took a swig of his pint. "Were you able to I.D. this traitor guy?"

"The runner no. The spy yes."

"Did he make the drop clean?"

"Yeah."

"You guys recover the dropped articles?"

"Article. There was only one. Something that looked like some kind of schematic."

"Okay, one step at a time. First off, who was the guy?"

"A Robert Dunlap. Sixteen years on the job!"

"He was a cop?!"

"FBI!"

"Wow!" He nodded. "Another senior FBI guy selling out the country! Who could'a seen that comin'?"

"Okay wise ass, your hard-on for the FBI aside, why is a Chinese agent speaking Spanish, carrying a Russian gun loaded with blanks while meeting an FBI double agent for a dead letter drop at the Central Park Zoo?"

"Nothing on TV that morning so he went out for a stroll?" Frank quipped.

"Can you be serious for one moment?! I came to you for help dammit!"

"Okay, okay sorry. Was this Dunlap guy armed?"

"Service weapon and federal I.D."

"Did you get a make on the Chinaman's gun?"

"I'd never seen one before but the weapons guys identified it as a Tokarev-54. Why?"

"Tokarevs have been around since the Thirties but the 54 is a Chinese knock-off version. Electronics technology and Ivy League professors aren't the only things the Chinese steal! If it's a Tokarev that's a pretty safe bet this guy was working for the ChiComs."

"What the hell is a ChiCom?!" She challenged.

"Chinese communist. Talk to me about this paper you guys retrieved."

"Like I said, looks like some kind of electronic schematic. There was no writing though. But I've seen a similar one before."

"Where?"

"Last year on another case. It didn't make sense when I first saw it but now that I've seen this one, I recognized it."

"Explain please."

"It was a pretty old case. On New Year's Eve '99 the CIA intercepted and 'removed' a South American operative working for the Chinese. He was supposed to have a copy of a schematic for an electronic device. It was supposed to be on the operative when they retired him but it wasn't there. It was a similar electronic layout as the one I saw when we arrested Dunlap." She continued. "He was supposed to be carrying some information about the spoofer device you guys later discovered in London along with the schematic. We had a rough idea about this schematic and our electronics people were able to piece together what they thought it would look like. But the agent they retired-"

"You mean dusted?" Mahone clarified.

"Retired! He didn't have it on him. After you and Morrissey uncovered the portable spoofer we were able to reverse engineer the schematic and it looked like the one we took off Dunlap last week."

"Huh! Can you describe it to me?"

"I can do better than that!" She reached over for her purse, rummaged through it and produced a folded over, eight and a half by eleven inch Xerox copy and passed it across to Mahone.

"It looked exactly like this!" She boasted passing the tech drawing across the table."

"You stole evidence in a major espionage case?!"

"No! What do you think I am some sort of

criminal?" She defended. "I photocopied it before I turned in the original." She defended.

"Isn't that still tampering with evidence?" He challenged.

"Well it's not like I'm going to hand it over to the ChiComs!"

"You know if you ever make it to the upper echelons of the Bureau, you'll fit right in!" He opined as he perused the drawing.

"Thanks for the vote of confidence!"

"Never mind Miss Comey! Let's stay on this." He said. "So our boy was either killed for this or for something we don't know about?" He pushed.

"I think so, yes. And it was done by professionals, therefore it was likely only one of four criminal agencies-"

"The CIA, the FBI, the NSA or the Mafia." He finished.

"Very funny! I was going to say the PRC, the FSB, Mossad or one of the South American agencies."

"Orrrrr . . .? The CIA!" He added.

"Or the CIA! Okay there's a possibility it was the Agency, however so slight!" She qualified.

"Tell me about this Chinese guy speaking Spanish. What'd he say?"

"Like I said, I don't speak Spanish-"

"I do." He said. She looked surprised. He shrugged "Almost two decades with the NYPD it's an unofficial requirement! So what'd you think he said? Can you remember any of it?"

"Something like 'Supone que . . . no . . . no usar

munición!' I think."

"Se supone que no **debes usar** munición? That sound like it?"

"Yeah, but he tagged it with the word 'ree-al', I remember that."

"Se supone que no debes usar munición **real**? That sound more like it?"

"Yeah, yeah it does. What does it mean?" She pushed.

"'They said you wouldn't have real bullets!' or 'You're not supposed to be using live ammo.' is a rough translation. What the hell does that mean?"

"You got me! That's why I called New York's nineteenth finest!" She quipped.

"Very funny! I don't have to take this abuse! I got people lining up to abuse me!" He attempted to lighten the mood. "That all you got to go on?"

"We did a walk around after they took the body away and given the layout we're pretty sure the shot trajectory came from the south side of the garden."

"In that case he probably fired from the Delecort Clock area about 100 meters away then escaped out onto 5th Avenue where he melted into the Manhattan crowd." Mahone suggested.

"We had a back-up stake-out manned by another team around the corner from the Chinese embassy over on 12th Avenue just off 42nd Street near the waterfront. Apparently he was supposed to meet another guy just outside the zoo but that guy was picked up by the NYPD on suspicion, but they had to release him on a diplomatic immunity ticket a couple of hours later."

The Hermes Project

"If this third operative was able to claim diplomatic immunity then he was definitely part of their cell!" Frank opined.

"Yes. The back-up unit was tapped into the local CCTV traffic cameras. He was later tracked going straight back to the Chinese embassy after seen disembarking a cab and entering the embassy two and a half hours after the zoo incident."

"Unbelievable!" Frank quietly declared.

"What is?"

"The Reds hack into the Office of Personnel Management to steal hundreds of SF-86 clearance forms. They had a high profile senator sleeping with a Chinese spy-"

"Swalwell & Christine Fang." Kuksova clarified.

"Senator Diane Feinstein's driver and office manager of twenty years uncovered as a high up Chinese spy who reported directly to the consulate. . ." He continued.

"While Feinstein was head of the Intelligence Committee no less!" Irina added.

"And now yet another FBI agent is busted selling secrets to the Reds! I'm getting the distinct impression we're not playin' our A game!"

"And there's one more little wrinkle in the fabric!" Kuksova added.

"What's that?"

"You remember your friend Anakin Banbury?"

"The English banker guy who helped mastermind the heist to sell the spoofer technology to the Chinese? The guy we put in prison? What about him?"

"He's not in prison anymore!" She informed.
"They let him out?!"
"Yeah, feet first!" She exclaimed.
"He got Epsteined?"
"We call it being 'Clintoned', if you're a republican! But yes, right there in his own little jail cell!"
"You think there's a connection between your guy Dunlap and Banbury getting wasted?"
"Not sure. But if there is, SOMEBODY ought'a find out." She locked eyes with him and stared at Mahone without blinking. Mahone sat back and returned the gesture.
"Is that why you called to meet me, to rope me into getting tangled up in one of your cases?"
"It's not **my** case Frank! I'm just throwing out some facts. If those facts happen to point to one of the largest criminal conspiracies since the Biden laptop and graft cover-up. I'm just sayin' ya know..."
Frank Mahone and Irina Kuksova had no established relationship per se. They had worked together for a brief time in London and though they had slept together on only a few occasions while in England it was by mutual agreement that when they returned to the States they would return with no strings attached.
But in the short time they were together Kuksova, through training and instinct, was able to formulate an eerily accurate assessment of Mahone's inner workings.
She knew for instance that, despite the train

wreck of his personal life, amidst the bureaucracy, violence and bullshit, he was a committed cop dedicated to fighting crime in a city he loved.

Above all he hated bullies of any kind, description or on any level. He especially hated political bullies, politicians who used their positions to leverage and intimidate others. Or politicians who manipulated the laws to get ahead. Or who . . . okay he hated politicians.

Having now, after working with the London Met and having been exposed to the world of international crime, Kuksova was willing to bet that he was even more determined to make a difference, 'before he bought the farm' as he so eloquently phrased it.

Irina continued to pursue her subtle persuasion.

"I just don't see how an organization with billions in revenue, secret powers and answerable to practically no one can make so many mistakes of such magnitude! Statistically speaking it should be impossible." She theorized. Mahone silently stared across at her. "Now I have to decide what to do." She continued. "I can't just let this thing go!" Irina sighed with just enough pout to matter.

"Like I said on the phone, concerning your suspension, I wouldn't worry about it, these things happen all the time. Being suspended following any shooting is routine. Once they've completed their investigation they'll call you in, dismiss it and you'll be back on the job in no time." He assured. "Meanwhile you get a paid vacation, you don't have to go to work and you can take some 'me' time."

Frustrated at her failed effort, unsure if he was ignoring her or if he really didn't get it, Irina downed the remainder of her second Manhattan and fell back in her chair. She couldn't comprehend how he didn't get her not so subtle hints.

Reading her body language he couldn't understand what she was annoyed at.

"You and I view police work very differently Frank! Besides, I'm not just talking about Dunlap and Banbury! I'm talking about something else I found."

"Like what? That Feinstein's office manager was a communist spy? That congressman Swalwell was sleeping with another spy or that Trump ordered the Russian embassy in Francisco closed when he found out it was lousy with Russian spies? Because all that's already out."

Realizing that he was using sarcasm as a way to refuse getting involved, she sat quiet for a long moment and simmered before speaking again.

"I was gonna tell you . . ." She leaned across the table and sublimely indicated he do the same. He complied and she leaned into his left ear and seductively whispered, "I think I found Amelia Earhart's plane!" She then abruptly pulled back and raised her voice. "You know you can be one sarcastic prick sometimes, you know that?!"

Grabbing her purse and coat she stormed out back past the pendant chandeliers, the mahogany bar and the bent wood chairs.

Mahone came out from behind the table and watched as she headed away until she disappeared behind the glass paneled front door.

The obviously drunk, sporadically toothed old man seated at the end of the bar looked over at Mahone now standing beside him.

"Women! Can't live with 'em, can't shoot 'em!" The old man slurred with a giggle. "Don't let it bother you son! Happens to me all the time!" Mahone glanced over at him.

"Thanks!"

****

It had just gone half past nine that morning when Mahone with Nigel Morrissey in tow strolled into the main office of The City Coroner's to again meet Dr. Jackson.

"Brought back-up with you again I see!" Jackson greeted as they entered the basement office.

"Doc, Inspector Nigel Morrissey of Scotland Yard. Morrissey you remember Dr. Jackson." They shook hands.

"Scotland Yard hey? I say, 'av we got owe selfs an international case now gov'ner?!" The young doctor affected with a terrible British accent.

"Knock if off Jackson!" Mahone snapped. "What'd you find out on the O'Neill girl?"

"Now shee here you mug! Don't be no wise guy, shee?!" Morrissey shot back with an even worse Cagney impression.

"If you two Bozos are done with Amateur Hour!" They both smiled. "Well?" Frank urged.

"It's your call Mahone but I think you gots

yourself a CSI situ here!" Jackson informed.

"A what?!"

"CSI! You know Grissom, Willows Brown! Don't you own a T.V. man?"

"No!" Mahone quietly snapped.

"You're joking! He is joking isn't he?" Jackson posed to Morrissey.

"Afraid not lad! It was stolen. Besides, his religion forbids it."

"Now if we're done playing T.V. trivia . . ." Mahone pushed.

"Yeah, sorry Lieutenant. I haven't filled out the DC-107 yet but the court order to hold the body expires tomorrow. The parents are back and I have to ask them if they want to take a copy of the death cert back with the body and they are definitely gonna check the 'yes' box on that one."

Mahone's next question shocked Morrissey.

"Jackson, what if you forgot to ask them?"

"Sorry Lieutenant, no can do! Daddy needs to be able to bring home the bacon or mommy gets mad and when mommy gets mad daddy sleeps on the-"

"Yeah, yeah I get the picture."

"Why would you want to delay sending the poor girl back home wth her parents?" Nigel ventured.

"Because when they see the Line 20 entry on the 107 they're gonna want a separate investigation and that's gonna get in the way of **my** investigation which is gonna muck things up!"

"What's on the Line 20 box?" Morrissey ventured.

"Legal Cause of Death." Mahone and Jackson

answered together.

"Which is?" Nigel asked.

"Asphyxiation by drowning." Jackson answered.

"Why should they-"

"Secondary to poisoning." Jackson finished.

"So this one is definitely a murder case?" Morrissey affirmed.

"Like I said, this one's gonna take some time and effort." Mahone relayed to Morrissey.

"Well then, I guess we'll just have to put a foot under it and wrap this thing up ASAP then won't we!" Morrissey threw out.

"What's this 'we' shit?! You got worms?" Frank asked.

Jackson fought back a smirk.

"'We' as in you, I and -" Nigel started but was cut off by Frank. Morrissey's covert intentions quickly dawned on Mahone.

"And who?!" Frank forcefully challenged. "Don't even think about it! Your guys are over here on vacation, that's all!"

"But Frank, think of the-" Nigel unsuccessfully pleaded.

"No! They might be crack investigators in London but over here the American politicians will chew them up and shit them out for political purposes, consequences to the case be damned!" Frank overtly declared.

"But-"

"No! Not no but hell no!" Mahone left down the hall repeating, "No, no, no!" Morrissey trailing behind.

Jackson shook his head, laughed and walked away returning to his work

"Two cops separated by a common language!" He mumbled.

****

NSA Headquarters
Fort Meade, Maryland

Finley remained calm but still took in a breath before knocking on the Director's door

"Come in!" Pravum yelled back.

"You wanted to speak with me General?"

"Yes Phil have a seat." Finley complied. "I want to have a few words with you about this *Hermes* program."

"Yes sir?"

"It appears to be a very strong program."

"Thank you sir."

"Of course it needs to be tested."

"Yes sir."

"Have you run a test on it?"

Finley shifted slightly in his seat.

"No sir I haven't had time to design one yet." He wasn't sure why he lied but it was on pure instinct that his internal dialogue told him to.

"Well I've just given it to the cryptologists to play around with. I'll have them run a test."

"As you see fit General."

"There's just one thing I need you to do."

"What's that sir?"

"Need you to scrub this Sentinel firewall. As the program will only be for internal use I don't see that we need it."

Finley's first impulse was to argue against removing the firewall. However, quickly realizing it might alert Pravum to his true intentions he held his tongue.

"Please tell the crypto guys that if they need anything just call down." Finley relayed.

"I'll do that."

"And please let me know what the results of the tests are."

"I'll pass the word to crypto."

"Is there anything else General?"

"No Finley you may go."

"Thank you sir."

Finley headed straight down to the Alert Center and to his computer to copy and scrub all the results and data from the test run he was currently setting up. Now more than ever his suspicions about Pravum were confirmed.

He reached for the phone and dialled.

"Bill, it's Finley. I need you down the Alert Center."

"What's up?"

"We have a priority job. I'll explain the particulars when you get down here."

"On my way."

A short time later, down in the Alkert Ceter, Phil Finley was explaining to Bill Whitcombe what the job was.

"I need you to rewrite a code."

"Okay, which one?"
"The Firewall code for *Hermes*."
"Why does it need changing?"
"I just had a meeting with Pravum. He wants the program to have no firewalls."
"That's bizarre!"
"Not if you factor in the possibility of Pravum wanting others to have access."
"What are you talking about?"
"I'm talking about others having access besides the few we talked about."
"But its an internal program. Why would he want . . . ?" As his mind caught up with Finley's thought process Whitcombe stared in disbelief. "You think he's-"
"I reviewed his record. He retires in two years."
"So?"
"So more than half of all companies like AstroCom are staffed by former FBI, CIA or NSA." Finley informed as he furiously typed away.
"And going to work for them is perfectly legal!" Whitcombe argued.
"Yes but bringing TS material with you is not!"
"I'm still not following."
"This agency took enough flak from the Snowdon and Manning fiascos not to mention all that Russia collusion bullshit! Now we had the DOJ using the FBI to take down a potential presidential candidate. Can you even fathom what kind of a shit storm we would get if the Director himself was caught selling classified material to private contractors?!"

"I'm still not sold on your theory!" Bill reluctantly confessed.

"Look. . ." Phil shifted in his seat. "He doesn't have the time in service to get a third star before retiring so he'll hang it up at the two star rate making half his base pay, $8,000 per month. His monthly mortgage payment is $2,650. He's got a kid in college with two years to go at $65,000 per year in tuition alone and they are a three car household with payments on two of the cars at $950 total per month not counting insurance."

"What about the other car?"

"Their 2021 Prius is paid off."

"You did your homework!" Whitcombe was increasingly impressed.

"Food and gas at least another $2,000 to $2,500." Finley continued. "His wife does charity work so there's no income there plus she has expensive tastes."

"So that brings him to right about $7,000 to $8,000 a month!" Whitcombe concluded.

"Not quite! He's still got to pay into their two IRA funds and cough up $130,000 in tuition! All providing there are no family emergencies."

"You forgot something!" Whitcomb corrected,

"What?"

"What size underwear he wears!"

"34 regular boxers, 32 in briefs." Finley relayed without looking up from his typing. "Now I need that code as soon as you can!"

CHAPTER ELEVEN

Office of Rep. Farmiga
Morristown, New Jersey

"I expected a man. I mean, I was surprised when we first spoke on the phone to find you're a woman." Farmiga commented as she greeted Kuksova.

"No problem. I get that a lot." Irina replied.

The northern New Jersey 11th congressional district representative may have never sought to play the gender or race card as so many of her weaker congressional colleagues routinely did however, she did count herself fortunate to be one of only two women on the twenty-one member House Intel Committee and the only female member of the minority party's team in that all important group.

With the Dems fielding twice as many members to the committee as the GOP member Farmiga, no fool to the reality of modern life versus the fantasyland some Americans lived in propagated by their D.C. reps, realized that her vote counted for nothing on the issues at hand as anything the GOP passed would not get through the senate.

At least now that the congress was again about to change hands, things might change.

Irina had finally been able to nail down a date to interview representative Farmiga. They met that afternoon in Morristown, New Jersey at the Congresswoman's town center office.

The Hermes Project

Kuksova, posing as Sam O'Neill from *Vanity Fair Magazine*, wisely opened the interview with preliminary questions of Farmiga's background and personal history.

They were briefly interrupted when Farmiga's intern came in with some messages and to offer coffee. Irina politely declined and they continued.

"The difficult history of the other agencies' rivalries aside, the fact that the NSA is not really held accountable by anyone along with the CIA still fighting to play down the bad reputation they earned in the 50's and 60's is a major bone of contention." Farmiga continued in answer to Irina's latest question.

"I see."

"The fact that the NSA has dropped the ball in what appears to be a developing pattern has also compromised the public's trust in all the government agencies in general."

"I understand there's a new director at the NSA? Is that related to the latest scandals in the agency?" Kuksova pushed being fully aware of the answer.

"Yes, but I'm not really at liberty to discuss any of those details. However General Pravum-"

"An army general?" She feigned not knowing.

"No Air Force."

"Can I use his name?"

"Yes, it's already been made public."

"Can you spell that for me?" Kuksova requested as she wrote.

"Sure, P-R-A-V-U-M, General Michael Pravum." Farmiga repeated.

"Have you met him? Do you think he'll be able to turn it around?"

"He seems very capable." Was her short reply.

"Something else my readers are very interested in, what's being done to avoid another Chelsea Manning or Edward Snowden situation?"

"Quite a bit actually. Significantly increased background checks, further I.D. verification and an increased probation time. As well as other measures I can't go into."

"What positive developments can you talk about?"

Allowing the mark to believe they are contriolling the conversation is a critical step in extractng information from what might be an unwilling dupe was a lesson Kuksova learned well from her five months at Quanico.

"As a matter of fact I just had a meeting down at The Fort and there's a promising individual with an impressive history, a guy who's come up with a development I-" Farmiga continued.

"You can't talk about!" Kuksova finished.

"Actually no I can't. But I can tell you that it will contribute a quantum leap to our analytic ability. They told me that if we couldn't read a message they'd give it to this Finley guy." She let slip. "Shoot! Please do not print his name."

"I won't. I understand, strictly off the record!"

"Anway, he would be able to extract the metadata. You see it's not about the actual conversation. It's the data about the data. Metadata is data about the data."

Of course Farmiga wasn't informing Kuksova, a trained FBI agent, of anything she didn't already know.

"By the way, all this isn't classified is it?!" Kuksova asked adding just the right amount of faux trepidation.

"No, no! It's all open source." Farmiga assured her. "Just no names!"

"Agreed. So what prompeted the General's meeting with you?"

"As hinted at I your first article, the Congressional Intel Staff is disillusioned with production at the NSA. The old director was only a few months from retirement and was finally persuaded to hand in his papers and so, along with a healthy golden parachute, did so a few months back. That's when General Pravum came on board, appointed by O'Biden as the new director."

"O'Biden? Do you mean Obama?" Irina pointed out.

"Sorry, sorry! I meant Biden." Farmiga laughingly corrected her own political joke.

"So how did your meeting go? Do you have faith that he can turn things around?"

"No way to know for sure but after the briefing I received on some new things happening I have faith that we'll get it where it needs to be!"

"For real? With no snags?"

"There's always going to be snags, but after he explained the agency would need a complete overhaul following my briefing with two of his private contractors-"

"He wants to revamp the whole system one piece at a time, like a 'just to be sure' kind'a thing?" Kuksova projected.

"Exactly. And naturally he explained it would cost several billion more than the current budget allows-"

"Billion with a 'B'?!"

"Yes billion with a 'B'! But that's also off the record!"

"Of course!" She drew a line through her last notes. "We could invade a small country for that price! Sounds a bit steep even for the government!"

"I told him outright that billions was a non-starter." Farmiga shot back.

At that point the interview shifted to a brief conversation about some new satellite research and contractors when, having obtained the information she came for, Kuksova thought it best to wrap things up. She closed over her note book and stood to leave.

"So really not that much turbulence in the intel agencies after all. And what little there is is being seen to. Have I got that pretty much right?"

"Pretty much." The congresswoman echoed. "One more thing Ms. O'Neill, I apologise but I didn't ask for your I.D. earlier. May I see it now please?" Farmiga held out her hand.

Irina smiled, set her purse on the desk and slowly dug through it.

Except for having long blonde hair as opposed to short brown hair, Kuksova bore a passing resemblence to Sam O'Neill however no where near exact. Irina was a few inches taller and had much lighter hair. She prepared herself to break cover if need be as she calmly handed over Sam's press pass.

Farmiga merely glanced at it.

"I don't dye my hair anymore!" Irina innocently added as a diversion. "Bad for the roots!"

Farmiga looked up from her desk and made eye contact.

"I know what you mean. I colored my hair once. Never got used to it so I let it grow out." Farmiga related.

"Besides, blondes have more fun!" Kuksova was careful to spert out as she took back the I.D. and held it photo side in before dropping it back in her purse.

"Of course you'll want to see the article before it goes to press, won't you?" She confidently asked as a further diversion.

"Yes please, I will need to see a draft before hand. Mail me a copy and I'll get the edited version right back to you. Just use your better judgement."

"Just like my boss at the office!" Irina joked in relief.

"It was a pleasure meeting you Ms. O'Neill."

"Thank you for your time Congresswoman. Best of luck in the upcoming elections." She added as they shook hands.

There was much to think about on the train ride back over to Manhattan not least of which was, rather than reassurance, Irina felt more certain that something wasn't right. The FBI being one of the top three of the seventeen intel agencies, she was now more convinced that something was not as it should be in the upper eschelons of the U.S. Intel services.

There was a disturbance in The Force and Luke Skywalker was nowhere to be found.

**

FBI Main Office
Police Plaza
Lower Manhattan

Kuksova sat speechless as she stared blankly across the desk at her boss.

"I'm required to inform you that you have the option to have a lawyer present if you want one." He spoke in a detached, monotone voice.

"I don't understand. You summon me here when I'm already on suspension, then start asking me questions about things I don't even know what you're talking about! Now you're throwing lawyers at me?!"

"You're being formaly investigated for breech of trust and possibly violating the Secrecy Act."

Slowly but clearly the picture began to gel as Irina recognized this tactic from past experience in other cases with other agents.

After you've I.D.'d your target, allow them to speak in their defence in the hope they'll incriminate themselves before they even know what the charge is. Then give them only the bare minimum facts of the case you're trying to build against them. After all American law does dictate that the accuser is required to share everything they claim they have against the defendant. Innocent until proven guilty.

Of course, that's only in the movies.

However, Special Agent Kuksova also recognised a hole in their plan. If they, whoever they were, had to use this approach it was fairly clear they had no hard evidence of whatever her imagined or fabricated crime was.

More importantly she took it as an indication that she was definitely on to something.

"I'm gonna need a lot more context before I answer any questions particularly questions on a topic I know nothing about!" There was a short stare-off. "So what's this little inquisition all about?" She pushed.

He leaned back in his oversized chair.

"Have you or have you not been talking to the press?"

"Absolutely not!"

"You sure?"

"I interviewed a magazine writer."

"What about?"

"About an article she wrote."

"Which writer? From what magazine?"

"It was . . . I think I need to know exactly what I'm being accused of before I start divulging information about secondary parties."

"It would be in your best interest to cooperate at this point Agent Kuksova."

She sat silent letting it all sink in.

"You mean it would be in **your** best interest for me to cooperate." She confidently countered.

"Look Kuksova . . . Irina, you've done some fine work over the time you've been with us. What ever this is I'm sure we can clear it up in no time and we can get you back on active duty!"

Her body language not only reinforced her continued silence but sent a clear message to her supervisor that this phase of the operation was over.

"As you wish." He leaned forward on his desk and took back the paper. "You will cease and desist all investigative activities and any other cases you may have been assigned until further notice. If you're found to be interfering in any case The Bureau will consider it investigative interference of an ongoing case."

"Anything else to report to the Kommisar?" She flipppantly asked before she stood and made for the door.

"No. You may leave." As she was halfway through the door he called over. "And Kuksova, I suggest you lawyer up."

Once again, mintues later Irina found herself out on the street alone. Or so she thought.

In fact she was not alone.

Emotionally consumed by what had just happened she didn't notice the two casually dressed men 100 meters up the plaza sharing a cigarette and having a relaxed conversation.

Leaving the Police Plaza Building she headed north west toward City Hall and passed through the arch. By the time she reached Broadway on the other side the two men had followed her and then split up seemingly trying to guess where she was headed.

Her inner voice reminded her she didn't know where she was headed but she knew she had to find a place to take a break and collect her thoughts.

Drifting north up Broadway for a half dozen blocks as she pondered her next move, she crossed over to Church Street and settled on a café across from the Trinity church.

Her two tails, one on either side of the street, dutifully ducted out of sight and waited.

Once settled in the nearly deserted café Irina had to focus hard and clear her head.

After a second cup of strong black tea her mental meanderings wandered into Frank Mahone territory. Not about their occassional trysts back in London but a brief review of the source of their seemingly unrelenting professional rivalry and it angered her.

She then realized that her anger stemmed from the fact that nothing appeared to bother him. He displayed his anger when appropriate but always pushed on with finding a remedy to the problem never letting his emotional state stand in the way of calculating a path to a solution.

He never took anything very seriously and was always joking at what others viewed as inappropriate times.

All this in contrast to the fact that she believed the FBI's mission was much more critical then the local city mission of the NYPD.

Mahone on the other hand, made no effort to

hide his lack of respect for her agency.

She was convinced he probably thought of her as just a glorified desk jockey. Just another D.C. bureacrat.

On the one plus side he hated corruption as much as, if not more than herself.

On top of all else he drank too much.

Fianlly she dialled her cell phone. It was answered on the first ring.

"Speak to me!" Mahone greeted.

"Frank, it's Irina."

"Irina! Glad you called. We have to meet."

Kuksova was taken off guard.

"Uh . . .okay. When and where?"

"Tonight or tomorrow, you're call."

"Uh, I . . . I've something on tomorrow." She lied. "Can we make it today? Is it urgent?"

"Well it can wait until next week I suppose, that is if you're all tied up."

"No, no! I can get away."

"Okay then, make it tonight, around eight. Nigel Morrissey is back over."

"Really?! To visit?"

"He's got business here. Pick a place, up near you. I'll call you around seven.

"Sounds good. We'll talk then."

"Okay.

"And Frank?"

"Yeah?"

"Why don't you bring Morrissey? Be good to see him again!"

"Sure!"

Satisfied with herself that she thought to invite the inspector as a conversation buffer she smiled.

Still unaware of Sam O'Neill's situation, Kuksova was in for yet another shock to both her psyche and the case she was trying to build.

****

Enzo's is a nice medium priced eatery located on the West Side a few blocks from Irina's apartment. The place avoids haute cuisine but neither do they serve spaghetti and meatballs and being able to smell the food from a block away was one of their big draws.

From where she sat near the back of the tastefully decorated bistro Irina could see Frank enter and briefly speak with the maître d' but was puzzled that he was alone.

He was pointed towards her table and made his way over.

"Hey, good to see ya again." He greeted as he took a seat.

"Where's Nigel?"

"He's running late, got lost on the subway. Took the BMT instead of the IRT and wound up over in Brooklyn."

"The poor man!"

"I texted him with instructions and the restaurant address. He'll figure it out, he is with Scotland Yard after all!"

"Good point."

"Irina, I have to ask you a question."

"Okay." Sensing a seriousness she made direct eye contact with him.

"Have you spoken to anyone since your suspension? In an official capacity I mean." He casually asked. She gave him an odd look.

"Why? Why do you ask? What does it matter?"

"Okay, so you have. Trust me, it matters." He maintained eye contact.

"Yes, I spoke with a reporter, a journalist actually."

"A female journalist? From a magazine?" He asked.

Irina's face suddenly assumed a more serious demeanor.

"Yes . . . how did you know?"

A waiter dropped three menus on the table as he whizzed by.

Frank leaned in before answering.

"I have a strong suspicion that your initial hunch might be right. Something is going on in one or more of the agencies." He confided. She was shocked

"What changed your mind?"

"Not 'what' but 'who'. Sam O'Neill."

"Sam O'Neill? You've been in touch with her?" Suddenly her nerves were acting up.

"In a manner of speaking, yes."

"How is she?" Irina broke eye contact.

"She's been better." He answered.

"What did she say to you?" Irina asked.

"She told me that either she had a dodgy background or she wrote the right story about the wrong people."

"What are you talking about?"

"You know how Shakespeare said; 'All the world's a stage and all the men and women merely players?'" He asked.

"Yeah?"

"Well today there's one less player."

"She's misssing?!"

"In the game of life, Miss O'Neill has been removed from the board."

"Holy shit!" She took a minute to digest the news. "How? She was only in her late twenties!"

"Murdered."

"Double holy shit!" She fell back in her chair and her eyes widened as he cocked his head to the side, sat back and stared at her.

"What? What are you staring at?" She challenged.

"Just giving you time to gloat."

Now it was her turn to sit up and stare as she folded her arms.

"Frank Patrick Mahone I am seriously insulted. Do you honestly think I'm so petty, so shallow as to want to sit here with such an important case and brag that, 'I told you there was something wrong!' as if we were school children?" She defended.

By way of response Mahone pursed his lips, raised both hands and smiled in surrender.

At that point a waiter approached.

"Hi my name is Chad and I'll be your-"

"Nobody cares Chad. I'll have a Manhattan, two cherries." Irina tersely ordered.

"Whiskey neat." Frank relayed.

"Make mine a double!" Irina amended her drink order.

"Be right back!" Chad the waiter cheerfully chimed.

"Let's focus on the task at hand." She suggested in a professional manner.

"Okay, okay! I was just trying to be magnanimous." He relayed.

"Well you're magnanimity does not go unappreciated."

"That's very big of you. Let's talk about a plan." Mahone proposed.

"There's just one thing I need to say." Irina said as she reached for a menu.

"Yeah, what's that?"

"I told you so! I told you so!" She chided him child-like in sing song.

"You need help Kuksova!" He just shook his head as he opened his menu. "Serious help!"

Morrissey suddenly appeared at the table.

Never having fully adapted the European custom of fake kissing while shaking hands as a greeting, Mahone just reached over and shook hands as he watched Morrissey and Kuksova engage in the ritual.

"You're looking beautiful as ever!" Nigel complemented Irina.

"Thank you Inspector. You're looking very well yourself. Welcome back to the land of the poltically confused!" She repricated.

"Things are not much different across the pond! So what's the current topic of discussion?" Nigel asked.

"Murder." Frank informed.

"Ahhh! Right up my alley!"

"We've actually just begun touching on it." She added. "You want to fill him in or should I?" Irina posited.

"Our little secret agent here seems to have gotten herself in Dutch with the the higher ups in the Big Brother agency." Mahone filled in.

"In Dutch?" Morrissey questioned.

"Screwed the pooch." Explained Mahone.

"Dropped the ball." Answered Irina.

"In trouble." Frank clarified.

"I see. Exactly how much Dutch trouble?" Morrissey probed.

"Enough to get my ass suspended!" She blurted out.

"For how long?" He pushed.

"Initially two weeks. As of now, indefinitely."

"It would appear that the last person, a magazine journalist, who our girl here interviewed, has turned up dead. The body you and I saw at the morgue." Frank prompted.

"The one doctor Jackson autopsied?"

"Yes."

"Are you a suspect?" Morrissey rushed to ask.

"Not yet." She replied. "I was about to ask, have they determined a mode of death?" She asked Frank.

"M.O.D. appears to be drowning secondary to lethal injection." Mahone answered.

"Have they traced the drug?" She inquired.

"No drug, poison."

"Have they traced the toxin?" Nigel pushed.

"I'll get you a copy of the report later."

"So what's your connection?" Morrissey asked Kuksova.

"Sam O'Neill did an article on discord in the NSA. I went up to her office to talk to her about her sources."

"Seems fairly straightforward. Where's the problem?" Nigel asked.

"I was on suspension at the time and wasn't supposed to be investigating anything. Now I am on double secret probation pending an investigation."

"Do we suspect this journalist was hiding something?" Nigel pushed.

"No but when I followed up O'Neill's story with a congresswoman Farmiga O'Neill had mentioned to me, I realized I had some even stronger suspicions that there were some dodgy dealings going on in the Alert Center of the NSA."

"And what exactly is an Alert Center?" Morrissey asked.

"Not sure. From that point on everything was classified and she couldn't talk about it."

Morrissey sat back and smiled.

"Well then, it appears to me that we have a number of tasks to complete in order to achieve the mission!" He offered.

"There you go again with that 'we' shit! What tasks?" Frank challenged.

"What mission?" Kuksova followed on with.

"The mission to get you back on the job, find out who offt'd Miss O'Neill and then, time permitting, help Agent Kuksova here launch an investigation into the NSA."

Mahone dropped his menu.

"Launch an investigation into the NSA?!" Frank snapped. "Were you a difficult birth?! Did your mother drop you?!" He challenged. "I thought we already discussed this?!"

"Discussed what?" A confused Irina asked.

"He wants to get The Squad involved!"

"The Squad involved in taking on the NSA?!" She gasped.

"Well, it's what we're trained to do, isn't it?" Nigel defended.

"**Trained** to do yes. **Paid** to do no!" Irina emphatically declared.

"Take on the fuckin' NSA?!" Frank quietly repeated.

"Well I didn't mean five guns on the high street at lunchtime!"

"WHAT?!" Irena questioned.

"It's **six guns** on main street **at noon**!" Frank corrected.

"I simply meant do it legally. What's wrong with that?" Nigel argued further.

"What's wrong with that?! Do you understand who they are?" Irina pushed.

"Yes! A powerful intelligence agency."

"**Powerful** intelligence agency?" Frank echoed. "They are fuckin' evil incarnate! Do you know who the most powerful man in the world is?"

"Yes, the president of the United States." Nigel blithely shrugged.

"EEEGGHHHH! Wrong answer Hans, thank you for playing! It's the God damn head of the God damned NSA that's who! They are the Stasi, the SS and the KGB on steroids! They've made more people disappear than David Copperfield!" Frank softly growled.

"I'm sensing some reluctance." Morrissey dryly uttered as he sat back and sighed.

"Well at least you have **some** sense!" Mahone chastised.

"You know, come to think of it. . ." Irina suddenly muttered to herself.

"Don't even think about it! Puerto Rican drug dealers, black gang members and Russian mafia are where I draw the line! If you two maniacs want to sign your own death warrants, go for it. Count me out!" He looked around for a waiter.

"There might just be a way. . ." Irina wondered out loud.

Suddenly Chad floated back over to the table.

"You folks about ready to order?" He blissfully smiled.

"Yeah! Whiskey." Mahone snarled.

"Manhattan, two cherries."

"A pint of lager please."

"I'll be right back with your drinks and to take your dinner order!" Chad cheerfully chirped and flitted away.

Irina, suddenly pleased with the NSA idea patted Morrissey on the arm and spoke softly.

"He just needs to warm up to the idea." She assured.

"Make that a whiskey neat with a whiskey back!" Mahone grumbled after Chad

****

It was just after ten in the morning when Frank Mahone, from the seat of his grey sedan, watched as the caboose of the seemingly endless freight train finally rumbled past. The red flashing lights and bells ceased and the barriers slowly raised.

Crossing the tracks he pulled off into the side street and dialled his cell phone.

"Congresswoman Farmiga?"

"Speaking."

"My name is Frank Mahone, Lieutenant Detective Frank Mahone, NYPD."

"What can I do for you Detective?"

"Congresswoman I'm working on a case that I think you might be able to help me with. Is there a possibility of meeting up to have a chat?"

Given the political friction between parties currently infecting the D.C. circuit, Farmiga felt she must be extra cautious about talking with police and so was hesitant.

"May I ask what this is in regards to Mr. Mahone?"

In the interest of truth, given her reluctance and the fact that she was a politician, Mahone decided to lie.

"It's in direct relation to a missing persons case."

"Is it someone I know?"

"I think so, yes."

"Okay. I believe I have an opening on Friday at two."

"Sorry Miss Farmiga, it's a bit more urgent than that. It won't take you any more than ten, fifteen minutes at most."

She saw no way out of it.

"May I ask how you came by my name?"

"Your name came up in the course of the investigation, during an interview with another interviewee. A publisher and editor actually." He purposely let drop.

Farmiga immediately put two and two together. Editor - magazine - interview - reporter equals a woman named Sam.

"Very well detective. I'll be in my office until three o'clock this afternoon. If you can make it in before then-"

Erroneously believing Mahone was ringing from Manhattan Farmiga banked on the possibility that he would not make it over into New Jersey by three o'clock.

"That's your office in Morristown, New Jersey? On Speedwell Avenue right next to the Horse Shoe Tavern?"

"You are a detective, arent you? Yes."

"I'll be there in 5-minutes." He said before hanging up.

"Son-of-a-bitch!" Farmiga swore as she hung up.

Ten minutes later Mahone was sitting in front of her desk.

"With all due respect detective, let's forgo all the cloak and dagger stuff and get right to the point.

The Hermes Project

Who is missing and how does it involve me?"

"You seem rather defensive Miss Farmiga."

"Humblest apologies detective. Who is missing and how does it involve me?" She persisted with increased intensity.

Mahone appreciated her straightforwardness and decided he would play along.

"Congresswoman, you did an interview for *Vanity Fair Magazine*."

"What about it?"

"The reporter's name was Samatha O'Neill."

"Yes, I remember her. Tall, blonde, good looking. Is that where you got my name?"

"No, from someone else."

"Is O'Neill your missing person?"

"She was."

"So you found her?"

"Yes."

"Where was she?"

"In the city morgue by way of being face down in the East River."

Farmiga's eyes opened wide as she fell back in her chair.

"My God! Found dead?"

"As found as Hunter Biden's laptop. You don't get anymore found in that."

"You think it wasn't accidental?"

"Jury's out, but we are looking into the distinct possibility of homicide."

"How can I help?"

"How long was your interview with her and what did you talk about?"

"Twenty, twenty-five minutes. Apparently she was writing a story about the discord in the D.C. intel agencies. At least that's what she told me."

"Did she touch on any subjects that might be considered classified?"

"Not really. Closest we came was my passing mention of Daniel Parker's VPE program."

"Parker? He testified at the D.C. hearings back in February, no?" Frank recalled.

"Yes he did, before you and the English policeman spoke."

Frank sat back in his chair and nodded.

"You were there!"

"Yes I was. I am on the committee." Farmiga confirmed.

"I remember. Who is this Parker and what is his relevance to my case?"

"None as far as I know. He's in astroelectronics. Currently working on a satellite project to bring internet to remote regions of the world, poor coutries et cetera."

"And after that he's going to cure world hunger?"

"Sarcasm is out of place detective." She chastized.

"What is this discord between intelligence agencies?"

"Same old throne room intrigue and backstabbing! The ATF doesn't trust the the FBI, the FBI doesn't trust the CIA and nobody trusts the NSA as they all compete for the same big bucks."

"Meanwhile Chinese spies are all over congress

like fleas on a dog and the country's security status continues to deteriorate and go to hell?" Mahone sarcastically interjected.

"Your words not mine!" She disavowed raising both hands in the air.

"So this VPE program, is it classified?"

"Parts of it yes. But to reiterate, we didn't talk about it. It was barely mentioned. She was more interested in the politics of the situation."

"So you don't think O'Neill's investigation could have tripped over something she wasn't supposed to know about?"

"Well I can't say for sure but I can't imagine what it could have been. She was primarily writing about inter-agency politics."

"The politics which are built on power which is based on money?"

"Point taken!" She concurred.

"Did O'Neill ever interview Daniel Parker?"

"No idea. You can ask him if you like, I have his contact number."

"That would be helpful."

Farmiga took to her intercom.

"Lynn, can you come in here please and bring me Daniel Parker's day number."

"Be right there congresswoman."

A minute later Farmga's intern appeared with a Post-it note and passed it to Mahone.

"Will there be anything else Lieutenant Mahone?" Farmiga asked.

"No but if you think of anything you can reach me over at the 13th Precinct." He said as he stood to leave placing a business card on her desk.

He paused in the doorway.

"Do you know if O'Neill finished the article?"

"You'll have to ask the magazine, I never saw it. But I do have a rough copy. She sent it to me for approval."

Mahone was impressed with Irina's thoroughness.

"Can you get me a copy?"

"I'll get Lynn to send it over to the 13th Precinct." She said perusing his card as he made his way to the door.

"You sure there's nothing going on down south inside the Beltway that I need to know about?" He took one last shot.

"Nothing that concerns the NYPD Lieutenant Mahone."

"Just on the off chance that something comes up give us a ring. Have a good afternoon congresswoman."

CHAPTER TWELVE

Museum of Natural History
Central Park West

Ali, Din, Enfield and Little Tammy all sat at the small, corner table facing Morrissey who had sprung for tea and cakes. Due to the late afternoon hour the sprawling museum cafeteria was nearly deserted.

It was getting later when Morrissey arranged to meet the Squad at the ground floor restaurant in the Museum of Natural History to, unbeknownst to them, ask a favor.

"So Chief what's so important that we need a team meeting on our holiday?" Heath asked.

"I know you lads are on your holiday and I have no right to ask you to work. But a couple of friends are in trouble and they need backup."

"Would these two friends by chance be police friends?" Enfield deduced.

"Yes. And they got themselves in Dutch pretty good."

"What does that mean, in Dutch?" Asked Din. It was Enfield to the rescue.

"In Dutch simply means to be in trouble. It comes from having a Dutch uncle which dates back to the mid-19th century."

"And what, pray tell, is a Dutch uncle?" Din further requested.

"A disciplinarian, someone who gives you hell when you need it." He casually explained.

"Why pick on the Dutch?" Heath challenged.

"It relates to their Presbyterian work ethic background. It just means-" He was suddenly cut off.

"If Cliff Clavin here is finished giving us an entomology lesson in vocabulary-" Heath began but was interrupted by Enfield.

"Actually I think you mean **etymology** sergeant!"

The whole table braced for action as Heath looked down and after a short pause responded slowly and deliberately through pursed lips.

"If this Berkeley Hunt don't stop it wif his petty sheit he'll wind up wif my bloody foot right up his bottle and glass!"

Heath slid his chair over to the side an inch or so as a moment of silence was wisley observed at the table.

"As I was sayin'. I have a question." Heath calmed down and dropped his bad boy yardie, gangsta' persona.

"Yes Ali?" Morrissey sighed.

"Exactly what are we supposed to do some 5,000 kilometers from London with no valid police I.D., no access to resources, no official badges and, oh yeah, absolutely no authority?"

"Good point Sergeant Heath. But before I answer, you all need to understand, besides having absolutely no authority here anyone of us gets in the shit, the lads at the embassy will be of no use to us! Not to mention the guaranteed repercussions back at The Yard!"

He casually glanced around the table as the four members nodded in affirmation.

"I've a question."

"Yes Tammy?"

"What are we doing sitting around here runnin' our gobs?" Tammy chastised.

"Does that mean you're in?" Morrissey pushed.

"Aye! Not sure what kind of wee spot your mates are in but be a cold day before we let some bampots get a leg up on us so it will!" She swore.

"Yeah, what she said." Din echoed.

"Tell your Yank friends we're in!" Enfield agreed.

"Marvelous! Mahone and I have a couple of things to look into." He explained as he scribbled an address and phone number on a scrap of paper. "Here are the contact details for Special Agent Irina Kuksova-"

"**Special** Agent now?" Enquired Heath. "Very nice!"

"Yes, but she's currently on suspension. I'll let her explain when you meet her." Morrissey filled in as he slid the paper across the table to Heath. "The four of you will work with her until Frank and I finish up what we have to do. Then we'll join up and see where we're at."

"Well now that we have the teams chosen, player's positions sorted and a kick off decided, I say we get to work! But first a bit of scran!" Tammy declared.

"What the hell is scran?" Asked Din.

"I think that means it wants fed." Heath answered.

Paddy Kelly

****

Hotel Lounge
Holiday Inn Express
Hoboken, New Jersey
19:30 Sunday March 13th

Now with Morrissey and the Squad on board it was a simple matter to approach Kuksova and offer a formal informal partnership.

Following a two hour long discussion, several pints and half a dozen Manhattans, an agreement was arrived at.

Irina would continue to focus on her case with Enfield and Din helping while Tammy and Heath lent a hand in tracking down O'Neill's killer.

There was only one small obstacle: Frank Mahone.

A brief phone call to Frank's apartment had him over at the lounge twenty minutes later.

"Fuck off!" Mahone blurted out once there. "Not no but **hell no**! I'm not about to condone a handful of tourists getting mixed up in a murder case even if they are friends. And if I were you people I'd be doubly reluctant about getting involved in this D.C. business as well. This ain't the junior leagues you're in here! This is the no-rules, win or die league you're flirtin' with! These assholes have seven ways from Sunday to fuck you over! That is if they don't pop a pill in you first! Which they can do with complete impunity!"

A blanket of dejected silence settled over The Squad sitting around the table. "Remember, these Federal assholes aren't accountable to anyone!" Frank reminded.

Following a long silence Tammy was the first to speak.

"So how do you really feel Lieutenant Mahone?" She asked. No one laughed.

"Sorry guys, I appreciate the offer. Not interested." He rose to leave. "I gotta go meet Morrissey, talk to you tomorrow."

A mere handful of blocks away Mahone's investigation was about to be inadvertently taken to the next level.

****

Sinatra Park
Hoboken Waterfront

With its garish display of neon and half a dozen big screen televisions *The Ferryman* on the corner of 1st and Bloomfield Streets in Hoboken was the perfect hybrid of Irish pub and American sports bar.

Only a few blocks from Mahone's new apartment close to Morrissey's hotel it was a convenient place to meet, share a pint and discuss the case that evening.

With the Squad members now tucked away in their hotel rooms at the Holiday Inn Express, it was just after a late dinner when Frank and Nigel decided they would take a walk.

As they wandered down towards the riverfront park the topic of discussion quite naturally turned towards what to do next in the O'Neill case.

Amongst other things in the course of their conversation, Morrissey had offered the assistance of the Squad again. Again Mahone declined on the premise that they were on holiday and it would be wrong to ask them to work. Plus there were too many legal considerations.

"Nigel, you sure you want your guys getting involvrd with Kuksova and her crazy scheme?"

"No but I completly understand your reticence, her having a new life here and all. Not in any hurry to muck things up as it were."

"Exactly! Glad you understand."

The two cops leisurely made their way past the closed up *Blue Eyes* café pavilion on the riverfront down onto the open plaza and took a seat among the crescent of park benches looking out over the western shoreline of Manhattan.

The prominent, night New York skyline, nearly a mile away, shown from Midtown Manhattan to the Battery illuminating the entirety of the Hudson Bay.

"I've seen some pretty gruesome things back home." Nigel, observed. "But what I am constantly surprised at is why? Why would anyone want to off a beautiful, young girl in such a devious way?" Nigel proposed.

"I've been focusing on the same question. Obviously it was somebody she knew."

"Or at least knew well enough to let him get close."

"Close enough to stab her in the back." Mahone concluded.

"You said at one point her editor mentioned a boyfriend, a biker type. Nothing there?"

"Afraid not. Ran a check on him, airtight alibi. He was up in Canada for the entire month."

"I think one of our most promising leads is to trace the origin of the toxin. There can't be that many people in the greater New York area who have access to frog toxins." Nigel suggested.

"I started a potential list, zoos, pet shops known collectors. I intend to continue tracking them down in the morning."

Hesitant to broach the subject again, Nigel took a breath and just spouted it out.

"You know Frank, this is a somewhat complicated case with a fair amount of footwork to be done."

"What's your point?"

"My point is a little help could go a long way."

Frank turned and faced Nigel.

"Help from some others? Others from an outside police agency? Such as Scotland Yard?"

"Don't take offence Frank, but of nearly three dozen major cases my squad have a greater than a 95% arrest and conviction rate."

"This has nothing to do with their ability! It has to do with understanding the American legal system and how it works. In other country's it's good versus bad. Those who obey the law and those who break it. In America all crime is political. Every case that goes into an American court is viewed through a political lens.

If it's a sex case MeToo, women's rights and feminism comes into it. Cops and robbers? Was the cop white was the perp black? If its a white collar case which political party does the cheater belong to and exactly who did he beat money out of and exactly how much?

Race, gender, ideology or political affiliation, this is how the prosecution, the defence, the court and the newspapers approach every criminal case. Lawyers all want to be judges, all judges are in training to be politicians."

"So what's your point?"

"My point is this is going to get ugly, possibly very ugly. And if it goes south and it gets too political everyone from the top dog down will be considered expendable. The last thing either one of us needs is the Mainstream Media being handed two prime targets at the same time; The NYPD whom they already hate and Scotland Yard which they will dine out on for at least a month. All that not to mention the tabloid rags back in London crucifying your squad in every issue of the *Guardian* for weeks to come!"

"Your point is well taken however, I believe there's one thing you're overlooking. There is a way to avoid all that mess."

"Oh yeah, how's that?" Frank challenged,

"By doing the job we signed up for and solving this bloody thing!"

Suddenly a large stranger stepped into view. The large man was dressed in dark civilian attire, heavy overcoat, hoodie and a wool cap.

"You Mahone?" He growled.

Both Morrissey and Mahone craned their necks to look behind and spotted a similarly dressed individual standing in back of the bench. Over their shoulders and beyond, parked out on the side street, was a dark blue sedan with a third individual behind the wheel.

"You Mahone?" He repeated.

"Yes, I am Mr. Mahone."

The one behind the bench mumbled something to Morrissey.

Mahone slowly rose from the bench but as he did he was careful to face away from the man as he reached into his side pocket and produced a blackjack.

Almost instantly Morrissey, who had also stood feigned going for the man behind the bench. As the second mugger reached up to repel Morrissey the Englishman was able to grab him by the sleeves, yanking him violently forward, bending him over the back of the bench and slamming his head onto the seat several times in quick succession. stunning him. The dazed man uttered something else before passing out. Morrissey followed this deft manoeuvre by sitting on him and pinning him down.

Meanwhile, Mahone had followed through on his black jack backhand by pressing forward with three more rapid strokes cracking facial bone and rendering mugger number one splayed out and unconscious on the pavement.

"You pack quite a punch!" Morrissey

complemented. "Looks like you broke his jaw in one swipe!"

"Yeah, ever since Hoboken has become gentrified this neighborhood has gone to shit!" Frank said to Nigel as he smiled and unfurled his fist. He also wore a set of brass knuckles.

It was then that they heard a car door from the Sedan open and watched the driver step out.

Mahone casually drew his weapon and carefully placed two rounds in the rear quarter panel of the car 100 yards away.

They watched as the third would-be-mugger recovered from behind a tree and dashed back across the road, dove into the sedan and vanished down 1st Street.

Reholstering his weapon Mahone tossed his cuffs to Morrissey who cuffed his dazed man to the bench. Producing a second pair of cuffs Mahone followed suit with his attacker.

Rifling through the unconscious men's pockets Mahone discovered something surprising.

"SHIT!" Frank declared out loud.

"What's wrong?" Morrissey asked.

By way of an answer Mahone held up the guy's I.D. The one with the badge attached.

"FBI?! What in the hell. . .?" Morrissey questioned as Mahone fell back on the bench.

Aside from their 9mm pistols and shoulder holsters the hapless tough guys both carried FBI bi-fold I.D.'s and badges.

"Are those real?" Morrissey asked referring to the badges.

"They look real enough to me." Frank said.

"What do you suppose they wanted?" Nigel asked.

"Not sure. What'd he say to you?"

"Wanted to know who I was and why I was snooping around their case."

"Their case?!"

"Then he told me to go back to Ireland." Nigel smirked.

"Ireland?!"

"Guess he slept during geography class."

"They must be FBI."

Mahone cleared then passed a Glock and two full clips to Morrissey.

"Happy Birthday! This asshole just saved you $550!"

He then handed over a badge.

"What shall I do with that?"

"A souvenir. Take it back to London, put it in your trophy case." He nodded to indicate they should leave. "Memories of Hoboken." Frank added as they headed up from the riverfront.

"What's next?" Morrissey asked.

"Now I've no fuckin choice!" Frank mumbled. Morrissey smiled.

"Does this mean you're in?"

"Yeah, yeah I'm fucking in!" He cursed. "Just one more thing."

"What's that?"

"We have to keep this away from my chief! If Wachowski finds out your people are anywhere near involved in this case he'll pull me from it faster than

Al Sharpton chasing an ambulance with Jesse Jackson driving!"

"Shouldn't be a problem! I'll make sure my people know to keep everything low profile."

****

Bill Whitcombe was still wiping the sleep from his eyes as he stumbled from the duty room into the Alert Center.

"Phil what the hell is so important you got me in here at 11:30 at night?!"

"Bill I did it!"

"Did what?!"

"I found a way around Pravum's Portal!" Finley excitedly exclaimed.

"What the hell is Pravum's Portal? Another one of your stupid video games?"

"You remember how I told you Pravum wanted the *Sentinel* firewall removed from HERMES?"

"What about it? Did you remove it?"

"Oh yeah!"

"I thought you said it would be dangerous to deploy HERMES without a firewall because it would allow them to falsify and issue FISA warrants and bypass the court!"

"I've installed a foolproof failsafe. I've christened it *Sentinel Vanguard*. Ya wanna know how it works?"

Suspecting he was about to be dragged along on the approaching verbal safari, Whitcombe poured a cup of coffee, fell into a chair and lit a cigarette before rolling his chair over to Finley's console.

"Okay, lay it on me oh god of the codes."

"The user must enter a private code based on the current FISA Court warrant registration number to access HERMES. Additionally I've set up a system for the FISA Court where they have to enter the registration number of the warrant which has been requested before it's issued."

"Ensuring that both parties know about the warrant?"

"Exactly."

"Good idea."

"Of course it is! Any, attempt to bypass the system and go straight into HERMES will trigger the release of a short term virus which will erase the accessor's access code & password."

"Interesting. Brutal, but interesting."

"Plus it will alert the main file and record the access code and username of the individual who attempted to breach the file!"

"But if a breach is attempted and your system works, how will we cross reference the access code to discover the breachee?"

"Simple! We issue no more than five access codes! Yours, mine, the Director and Assistant Director of Cryptology. More directly you and I will be the only ones able to decipher and access which access code was used."

"What about Pravum?"

"Oh yeah, of course. Pravum too." He unconvincingly reassured.

"Of course." Whitcombe echoed.

"Needless to say-" Finley added.
"But you're going to say it anyway!"
"Yes I am. Keep this between us."

****

It was only a day or so later that Finley contacted his old classmate, now a tenured professor of astrophysics at U.C. Berkeley and arranged to use the university's industrial sessionizer at Moffett Field in Santa Clara, as well as their satellite scanner and data collection bank to test the functionality of the HERMES collection program.

Finley working from the Alert Center in Maryland. would clandestinely locate Daniel Parker's deployed satellite constellation and tap into it for a predetermined period of time, in this case 72 hours, store the unknown amount of data, disengage the satellites then transfer the pirated data to an NSA storage facility.

Given that adjustments to the program would be required and that this was only the first test, Finley projected that 40 to 50% successful collection of the data scanned over the holiday weekend would be considered a good test.

Naturally following recording of all the test results the information collected would be wiped.

In view of the criticality of this test Finleydecided to spend the weekend on premises sleeping in the team room of the Alert Center. There were after all a plethora of glitches which could occur potentially negating the entire test.

The Hermes Project

Although the NSA may have led the world in electronic surveillance they were by no means the only organisation in the world able to surveil via electronics.

HERMES' intrusion into Parker's satellites was not as clandestine as Phil Finley had hoped.

*** * ***

It was a few minutes before 0600 Monday mornig when Bill Whitcombe, Starbucks latte in hand, wandered into the Alert Center to find Phil Finley typing away at his keyboard.

"Hey, how're we looking? Is it soup yet?" Bill asked.

"I just programmed it to start the download from the Santa Clara computer bank."

"How long will it take?"

"Depending on how much we captured anywhere from fifteen minutes to half an hour."

Bill pulled up a chair and made himself comfortable.

Over an hour and a half later the download indicator was approaching completion. Whitcombe and Finley exchanged glances and moved closer to the computer screen.

"So the closer we are to 50% capture the more successful we can consider the program?" Whitcombe sought to confirm.

"Yes but, in truth I'll be happy with 40, 45%. Even with that we'll be ahead of the game as opposed to the current word recognition system the cryptologists are currently using."

"Then what?" Bill asked.

"We put it through our sessionizer to be organised and sorted into usable bits of data."

The words, 'Download Complete' came across the screen.

"It's soup!" Finley mumbled as he scrolled down the screen. "Holy shit!" He declared.

"What?"

By way of an answer Finley pushed his chair aside and pointed at the computer screen. Whitcombe leaned in and quickly scanned down the thousands of lines of data.

"98.6% captured?!" He fell back in his chair. "Is that possible?! HERMES captured nearly the entire contents of the entire satellite constellation?" Finley sat speechless. "That is one hell-of-a program you wrote there Buckaroo Banzai!" Whitcombe congratulated.

"Who is Buckaroo Banzai?" Phil questioned.

"Not important, take it as an accolade."

****

At the same time, just outside of Austin, Texas at the company's electronics lab a night shift worker at Nexus 6 was casually shuffling through some paperwork when a red light began to flash on the wall-sized electronics panel behind him. Rolling his chair the short distance across the floor he flicked a toggle switch, the light went out and he rolled back to his desk where the computer monitor was flashing a warning which read; 'Intruder Detected'.

The Hermes Project

Now approaching 0630 local, the lab tech moved with a definite sense of purpose as he dialed a phone number.

"Security here, Jenkins speaking." The guy on the other end answered.

"Jenkins, Milford in communications. I'm getting readouts over here indicating that someone has hacked into the Vacuum Pulse Emitter satellites."

Over in the security office Jenkins sat up straight in his chair.

"Are you sure?" He asked.

"Positive, I double checked! The firewall alert logged in 92 minutes ago and just logged off a minute before I called you."

"The security systems for those satellites has a triple redundancy! They're supposed to be hack-proof!"

"If a frog had wings he wouldn't bump his ass so much! What'a ya want me to tell ya?!"

There was a short silence on the other end before Jenkins responded.

"So what are we supposed to do?" Jenkins asked.

"How the hell do I know you're security?!"

"But you're the lab guy!"

"Yeah but we've never had a hacker breach, all that stuff is theoretical."

"Do you have a log?"

"Yes."

"Then make a theoretical entry, try and trace the theoretical source and notify your supervisor about your theoretical finds! Let them deal with it, that's

why they get the big bucks!

"Sounds good to me!"

"Meanwhile I'll report it at the morning shift change meeting as well."

"Right!" Milford hung up and began to attempt a VPN trace.

CHAPTER THIRTEEN

State Route 32
Northern D.C. Distrct
Maryland

General Pravum quickly breezed through the Alert Center on his way out of the building that morning. Poking his head in through the doorway he called over to Finley.

"When am I going see this miracle program you've been promising?"

"Congresswoman Farmiga has consented to allocate the funds. Apparently she was impressed with what she saw. I want to run the final tests to fill in the latency times. Should be ready next week for sure General." Finley reported.

"Tell me as soon as it is!"

"Will do!"

Six days a week, just a few miles north out the back gate of Fort Meade, along State Route 32 you can find *Roscoe's* food truck. The white Step Van with the pop-open side is always parked and opened from ten until three Monday to Saturday.

The surrounding rural area is desolate and offers adequate open space for about half a dozen cars to pull over, park and grab a burger, burrito or even a beer.

Roscoe's was owned and operated by retired Sergeant Major Roscoe R. Kendal and so was well known to all the servicemen stationed at Fort Meade, to include General Mike Pravum.

It was just after ten that morning when Pravum pulled his 2022, Black Lexus off to the side of the two lane macadam road and onto the dirt shoulder just behind the food truck but didn't shut down the engine. Instead he made his way over to the side of the truck where he politely waited for the enlisted WAC in line to receive her food order then returned her salute as she passed him when he stepped up to the counter.

"General, what's shaking?" The stout, middle-aged Roscoe greeted.

"Same circus, different clowns Seargent Major!"

"What can I get you today?"

"My usual."

"Burrito supreme, a yellow jelly bear claw and a black coffee coming up!" Roscoe called to no one in particular.

Bagging the burrito and some napkins he took the twenty from Pravum who waved off the change and headed back to his heated car.

With all the technological advancements of the modern era transcending speed and distance, sometimes old ways were still the best ways. Ways such as a dead letter drop which leaves no electronic fingerprints.

Back in his car Pravum scooped the burrito out of the bag, unwrapped it and before digging in to his late morning snack read the handwriting scrawled across the paper napkin it was wrapped in;

'Howard Hills Restaurant - 1300'

The Hermes Project

****

Later that afternoon before he arrived at the Howard Hills, a four star restaurant about thirty minutes outside the Fort, Pravum had changed into a civilian three piece suit and was toting a brown leather briefcase.

"Mr. Pravum here to meet Mr. Bibou." He informed the smartly dressed maître d' behind the reception podium.

"Monsieur Wesley has already arrived sir. I will take you to his table."

Pravum was led through the spacious but sparsely populated eatery to a two top in the rear of the house where a well dressed man several years his senior sat working on his second martini.

"Michael!" Not bothering to stand the man extended his hand and greeted him warmly.

"Wesley, been a long time. Good to finally catch up to you." Pravum took the seat opposite and requested a beer.

"How are things in your neigborhood?"

"Funny you should ask Wesley."

Pravum lifted his briefcase onto his lap, opened it and produced a sheaf of papers. Maintaining eye contact with Bibou he slid them across the table. Nonchalantly at first but then with increasing alarm Wesley rifled through what appeared to be a report. The word 'SECRET' was stamped in red on all four corners of each of the half dozen pages.

The cover sheet read: '*Backdoor*'

"How'd you get this?! We, we haven't even

completed research much less started full testing!" The older man whispered in alarm.

"Wesley, Wesley, Wesley! Anyone involved in surveillance research is supposed to come to us for approval. That includes AstroCom." Pravum smugly reminded.

"Getting like the KGB in this country!" Bibou cursed under his breath.

"Yes Wes. But remember, we're the good guys!"

"Mike! You can't expect us to go running to you every time we have an idea! If it blossomed and started to show potential you know we would have scheduled a presentation!"

"Cards on the table Wesley, how far along have you gotten?"

"We have the core of the software, most of the circuitry designed but we can't seem to work out the distribution formulae."

"You understand that if you get this *Backdoor* program off the ground, there is literally no chance it will be allowed to have any civilian application?"

Wesley Bibou was the CEO of AstroCom the primary competitor in space technology not only of Daniel Parker's Nexus 6 corporation but, in the area of space communications but of NASA as well.

As outlined in the report *Backdoor* was a multibillion dollar contract originally intended to be outsourced to a private contractor.

Most critically it had no FISA filtering system.

"Of course I know that! What civilian agency has the budget much less the production facilities for launching the necessary satellite constellation?"

The Hermes Project

Bibou challenged.

The two held conversation to a minimum as a waiter approached the table and took their order. Waiting until he departed they resumed.

"So where do we go from here?" He asked Pravum.

Bibou had no way of knowing that the HERMES project, with the same capabilities, was nearing completion and that Pravum had every intention of playing one against the other.

"Keep your people working on it and when you think you have it let me know and I'll set you up a presentation in front of the usual people."

"Fair enough." Bibou conceded before there was an awkward silence. "So what are your plans?" Wesley sought to change the subject. "You're scheduled for retirement in a couple of years, aren't you?"

"I am eligible this year but I still haven't made a decision yet."

"Are you still planning on coming to work for us?"

"You can tell your boss yes. If the numbers are right." Pravum nodded while he placed the report back in his briefcase. "And Wesley." Pravum reminded as he finished his beer, stood and prepared to leave.

"Yes Mike?"

"Try and remember the rules. They are there for a reason."

"Yes Daddy!" Bibou mumbled out of Pravum's earshot as the General turned to leave.

In exchange for the promise of a high paying staff job after retirement General Pravum had made a deal with AstroCom's CEO for the NSA to use their *Backdoor* system along with all AstroCom's private contractors.

What he neglected to reveal was that he intended to scam Finley's work on HERMES selling it to AstroCom and passing it off as his own after collecting millions from congress for 'testing' *Backdoor* which would inevitably 'fail to meet standards'. He would then skim his share of the taxpayer's millions, receive a bonus from AstroCom for making the deal while still collecting his military retirement.

All done as 'Classified' procedures.

On the remote chance he was discovered he could simply refuse to comment about an 'ongoing investigation' or simply plead ignorance and point the finger at his predecessor.

Mike Pravum was essentially hedging his financial future against his own government.

*

Capitol Building
Washington, D.C.

The fact that congresswoman Natalie Farmiga was put off by General Michael Pravum when she visited his office to interview him played no part in the report she had just typed out in her D.C. office. She came by her apprehension of him with good reason.

It was common knowledge that Chairman of the House Intel Committee Burman had always worked hand-in-glove with the NSA. He considered it 'his baby'. It was by no random chance that he had been selected to chair the Intel Committee.

What Farmiga had found out about the state of readiness of the NSA and duly reported was not going to make Chairman Burman a happy camper.

However, being a member of the smallest community in the country, that is an honest politician, the freshman congresswoman saw no reason to lie about what she had found. Especially given the fact that the NSA was considered the 'premier' intelligence agency in the nation.

One week after her intensive briefing with Phil Finley at the NSA Alert Center Rep. Farmiga had completed and was rereading her final status report on the current readiness of the NSA.

In it she empathetically noted that:

"Although the National Security Agency has been the most productive intel agency since World War II, beginning in the nineteen eighties a cultural attitude of virtual invincibility, omnipotence and superiority to the other agencies has set in.

As a result tragedies such as the Marine barracks, the U.S. embassy and U.S. annex bombings, not to mention the 911 attacks, have slipped by our best surveillance.

To compound matters these deficiencies not only transcend cultural attitudes in the agency. Unfortunately they extend deep into the technological capabilities of the NSA as well.

In short we are nowhere near adapted to or adequately equipped as we should be for the digital age either technologically or culturally.

While the terrorists are communicating from secure cell phones, land lines, computers and other devices we are still not able to reliably track them down.

By 1993 the digital cold war had set in and we missed the starting gun. There are fundamental problems in what was formerly our most efficient intel agency, both technically and culturally.

Pursuant to the above facts I believe the additional funds requested buy the DIRNSA, General Pravum, specifically as applies to the *Hermes Project* should be allocated on the proviso that the firewall, code named 'Sentinel' remains a part of the program.

Additionally, any further funds requested and approved should be by transfer on an allotment basis as opposed to being issued in a lump sum."

Fully cognisant that her finished report would garner some kind of reaction, and not a positive one, congresswoman Farmiga now sat staring blankly at her computer screen for an inordinately long time.

Despite the fact that Farmiga was a Freshman congresswoman she fully understood the implications of her report. The required quarterly inspection, briefing and assessment, along with her report, would be directly responsible for dictating the NSA's portion of the upcoming budget for the Intel services.

The Hermes Project

Although never openly acknowledged by congressional committees there was a quite healthy and robust one-hand-washes-the-other, unwritten understanding between budget committees and the government agencies they supported.

The House Intel Committee was not immune to this barely concealed, under-the-table arrangement.

Having had completed her assignment to write and submit an evaluation of the status of the intelligence agencies beginning with the NSA, she was genuinely worried about the House Intel Committee Chairman's reaction once he laid eyes on it.

Now having checked all the boxes; administration, task completion and results she had come to the realization that should the U.S. be compelled to shift to a war footing under the present conditions, they would most likely lose and the defeat would largely be on the failure of the intel services to maintain the ability to furnish the defence organizations with timely, accurate enemy intel.

The current state of what the Congress, the Executive and the general public believed to be the most efficient and up-to-date intel services in the world was neither.

Under 'Conclusion' Farmiga annotated a brief note;

"Politics and political ideology appears to have usurped unbiased professionalism sorely clouding judgement and skewing protocols which now appear to be dictated by political policy."

A full hour after sitting down she hit the 'send' button on her keyboard.

*

It was becoming gradually more clear to Congresswoman Natalie Farmiga that being given the assignment to comprise a status report on the NSA had been something of a setup. A way to shed one of the two republican members of the committee while still being able to make the feeble claim that the House Intel Committee was bipartisan.

Senator Burman, now in his third term, his second as chairman of the Intel Committee, must have been fully aware of the dilapidated state of the National Security Agency if for no other reason than the fact that he had been around The Swamp for more than a decade. By having Farmiga's name on the report Burman and his cohorts could hide behind plausible deniability.

In short, Farmiga had been set up by Senator Burman.

A brief two days later, after handing in her report, the inevitable happened.

Senator Burman called her in after reading through her classified report. He read selective excerpts back to her and questioned them.

Having taken detailed notes on what she had seen and heard during her several visits to the agency, she was easily able to answer his increasingly aggressive questions and defend against his unexpected and unfounded accusations.

A few days later, amid supposedly widespread news coverage, she was again called into Burman's office and asked to resign from the Committee.

"Just until things quiet down in the press." Burman explained.

She found his claim about 'press' strange given that she had seen no press, negative or otherwise, mentioning her name and none had been brought to her attention.

This of course was compounded by the fact that less than a handful of people even knew the report existed much less about its contents.

Farmiga was then advised to step down from the committee ostensibly for talking to a reporter.

This tipped her off that she was somehow being watched, quite possibly even being surveilled.

CHAPTER FOURTEEN

Goshen, New York. There are over two dozen towns and locations around the world called Goshen to include a Hebrew area along the Nile in ancient Egypt.

However, just sixty miles north of Manhattan along State Route 6 is the American town of Goshen inside of which is the village of Goshen. With a population of about 6,000 this tiny village is the county seat of Orange County, New York. As such the town's citizens are permitted to elect a sheriff.

It is to the county building and the office of Sheriff Jimmy Abernathy that Inspector Morrissey now found himself being taken.

"Sorry mate, we're looking for the village of Goshen." Frank Mahone asked the local as he pulled his rental car up alongside the elderly pedestrian.

"Other side of that rise. Just keep heading up the main road, you can't miss it." The old farmer instructed.

"Much appreciated." Morrissey thanked.

"'You can't miss it', famous last words." Mahone grumbled as they pulled away. "Wanna bet?!"

"This is a quite pleasant Village!" Morrissey commented gazing out his window as they passed a small farm off to the left.

"Probably alot like the place you got from your aunt." Frank speculated.

"I hope so!"

With the O'Neill case seemingly to have escalated to the point that someone thought it necessary to ambush and possibly try to kill Mahone and Morrissey, Frank thought it prudent Nigel be legally armed.

"I understand why I couldn't keep that FBI thug's weapon, but I don't see why you couldn't just give me the loan of your spare weapon." Nigel casually suggested for the second time.

"Strictly illegal under New York's convoluted gun laws and could be construed by some overzealous, ambitious D.A. as gunrunning."

"Christ, seriously?!"

"Seriously! However, due to the inability of the New York authorities in Albany to keep track of all their gun laws and in their apparent misguided zeal to outlaw all guns, some sheriffs in rural areas have the authority to issue gun permits in certain cases."

"And you deem someone trying to kill me is one of those cases?"

"One of the advantages of our legal system Nigel! So many laws nobody can keep track of 'em all! For every law there's a counter law!"

Just on the edge of town they spotted a kid on a skateboard and Mahone again pulled over.

"Hey kid where's the town hall?" He called over.

"Same place it was yesterday!" The tough talking, diminutive twelve year old shot back. The two cops exchanged glances.

"You're a regular Bill Burr ain't you?!" Mahone accused.

"Never heard of him!"

"Never mind. We're looking for the Sheriff's office, you know where it is?"

"Yeah. Cost you five bucks!"

"Five bucks?! Five bucks for what?!"

"Fer the information! Guy's got'a make a livin'."

Mahone produced his badge and flashed the kid.

"You paid your skateboard fee yet?"

"There ain't no skateboard fee!" He immediately objected.

"As of the first of the year kid! By order of the governor! 20 bucks or I havta'confiscate your skateboard!"

The junior gangster wanna-be-extortionist had a short but intense think about his tactic before responding.

"Sheriff's office is about a mile up, at the intersection of Webster and Eire." He spouted.

They drove away leaving the bewildered child staring, open-mouthed, skateboard in hand.

"How old do you reckon that little street urchin is?" Morrissey asked.

"No idea but he's probably not going to live to be very old!"

"How so?"

"There's an old Sicilian proverb: When you're old you know many things. But if you know too many things, you may not live to be old."

"At least he'll make a good gangster." Morrissey deduced.

"Make a better FBI agent! Supervisor at least!"

A minute later they came on a three-storey, modern looking building with a disproportionately large parking lot. The sign read: 'Orange County Governmet Center'.

"Jesus! Looks like some drunk tried to stack a bunch of boxes on top of each other!" He commented scanning the building which resembled an off kilter stack of pizza boxes.

"Frank, it's an architectural style called 'Brutalist'." Morrissey informed.

"At least they got that right! The name fits!"

They made their way to the reception desk where they were greeted by a pudgy, little old lady.

"We're looking to talk to Sheriff Abernethy."

"Oh, but this is Tuesday afternoon!" She said with empathetically raised eyerows before returning to rubber stamping some documents.

"Yeah, and tomorrow's Wednesday so what?" Mahone challenged in return.

"Tuesday afternoon is Sheriff Abernathy's day to judge the Junior 4H Club."

Again the two cops exchanged glances.

Morrissey, sensing Mahone was losing patience, stepped up to the counter.

"Could you please tell us where we might find this 4H Club meeting?"

"Yes, that would be across the road at the FUB."

"And what exactly is a 'FUB?"

"Why the Farmer's Union Building of course."

"Of course." Morrissey shrugged and smiled.

Minutes later, across the road they were trudging through a hay strewn floor in a tall brick building at least one hundred yards deep nearly half as wide and two stories high.

In contrast to the relative quiet outside, inside the place was peopled with folks of all ages, mostly teens and pre-teens, scurrying about through a low cacophony of farm animals all blanketed with the low hum of the crowd and interrupted by occasional announcements over the inordinately loud P.A. system.

"Interesting aroma!" Morrissey commented.

"Sort of makes you homesick, don't it?" Mahone added.

The first nine or ten yards were open space but the remainder was divvied up into six foot wide, eight foot deep, temporary stalls improvised from wooden pallets.

Morrissey couldn't help but stare in awe at the wide open space and around at the largest barn he had ever seen.

"America, where bigger is better!" Morrissey quietly reminded himself.

Frank stopped a gentleman wearing a green 4H arm band.

"Excuse me, we're looking for the Sheriff."

"You'll find him at the baby pig stalls. Six down on the left."

"Thanks."

They made their way down the narrow aisle to the end stall where they came upon a uniformed sheriff, two young kids and half a dozen various colored piglets.

Sneaking up on the stocky man in uniform from behind Frank leaned into earshot.

"Fucking pigs! That's appropriate!" Mahone said

softly out of ear shot of the two young kids petting the piglets. The man spun around ready to fight but altered his demeanor when he recognised Mahone.

"Frank, you worthless piece of shit!"

"Hey Jimbo! Doris come to her senses yet and leave your increasingly overweight ass?"

"I take it you know each other?" Morrissey assumed.

"Went to high school together back in Astoria." Frank explained. Nigel and Jimbo exchanged nods.

"Jimbo, Nigel Morrissey of Scotland Yard. Nigel, Jimbo Abernathy."

"OHHH! A fer-real cop! Impressive!" The Sheriff complimented. "Pleasure to meet you Nigel. Welcome."

"Nigel and I worked on a case in London a while back where I was sent over on an exchange program." Frank explained.

"Really, London?! Who'd you piss off at the 13th?!"

"Nearly everyone!" Morrissey chimed in.

As Mahone sought to steer the conversation to a more serious matter the ambient noise seemed to increase.

"Is there somewhere we can talk?" He proposed.

"Yeah, follow me." Abernathy indicated the far, rear corner where an improvised café was set up in an alcove. "Mary Sue, stop biting that pig's ear!" He called over as they walked away.

They bought two coffees and a tea and set at an isolated table.

"What's up Frank?"

"I'm on a case right now, a hairy one and I suspect we're getting close to the bad guys."

"Actually we are **very** certain we're getting close to them." Nigel added.

"How so?" Jimbo pushed.

"They attacked us. Ambushed last week. Three of them, only one escaped." Morrissey explained.

"Need your help, buddy." Frank added.

"How can I help?"

"Nigel here is not licenced to carry. I have a strong suspicion when we catch up to these guys they're not going to come quietly. And-"

"And under the Dem's bullshit gun laws where they're trying to disarm the entire country, Nigel here needs a permit to carry!" Abernathy quickly deduced.

"Exactly!" Nigel added.

"Done!" The sheriff tagged.

"Excellent!" Frank added.

"He'll still have to take the written and do the practical. You got any training?"

"I'm qualified in Britain. Did the one week course etc. Qualified with a 9mm Glock." He volunteered.

"Well, should be pretty easy then. Come on over to my office I'll give you the test. Only twenty questions, then we'll drive over to the range and you can pop off a few rounds!"

Late that afternoon, on the drive back to Manhattan, Nigel Morrissey was a licenced permit holder to carry a pistol.

CHAPTER FIFTEEN

13th Precinct
21st Street
Manhattan, NYC

Chief Wachowski nonchalantly pushed away from his desk and strode across the room to the couch where Mahone was sitting.

The Chief raised his right-hand and put it against Mahone's forehead where it was instantly slapped away.

"What the hell are you doing?!" Frank demanded.

"Checking to see if you have a fever." Wachowski informed as he made his way back to his desk. "Because if you think I'm going to pay for you for a two day vacation in Amarillo you must have bumped your head or something."

"It's not Amarillo, it's Austin and I got to talk face-to-face to this guy Parker."

"Why?"

"I talked to O'Neill's editor, I talked to the last person she interviewed and this case crosses paths with something the Feds are working on all of which point to this guy Parker and possibly his company Nexus 6."

"This thing that 'crosses paths', the thing the Feds are working on, this wouldn't by chance be connected to the shootout in Central Park a while back, would it now?"

"Could be."

"The shootout involving this Russian female

federal agent? The same one-"

"She's Ukrainian and a naturalized U.S. citizen."

"The same one you spent a year playing footsie with over in London?"

"She's got nothing to do with it and it was your idea to send me over there!"

"Don't remind me! And by the way you're welcome."

"Come on Chief! What are we talking here, a hundred, two hundred bucks round trip? A hundred and fifty hotel room with another hundred for meals and and rental car? Hell, I'll even eat at McDonald's for two days! Four, five hundred tops! Hell, we drop that on phoney drug deals at least once a week!"

"Not anymore we don't!" Wachowski stopped writing and looked up from his paperwork. "Mahone, you remember them anti-rape ad campaigns?"

"Which ones?! There's only a new one every week!"

"The one where the girl says; 'no means no!' That one?"

Frank knew he lost that round and so rose to leave.

"Okay Chief, I get the message. But I'm sorry." Frank apologised as he opened the door.

"Sorry for what?" Wachowski's head snapped up as he made eye contact with Mahone.

"Sorry for how silly you're gonna look when I crack this case."

"Mahone, you crack this case and I'll guarantee you a week's paid furlough!"

"Deal!" He barked as he left.

"And stay the hell away from the Feds!" Wachowski called after Mahone who pretended not to hear.

****

Ten minutes later Mahone was seated in front of Inspector Morrissey around the corner in *Lunetta's Pizzeria* on 3rd and 20th.

"So, did we get the green light? Are we going to get to see The Lone Star state?" Nigel enthusically asked.

"Yes and no." Mahone answered. A puzzled Morrissey glanced up from his Earl Grey. "Wachowski shot it down."

"So how are we going anyway?"

"**We're** not. I am."

"Is it something I said? Did I forget our anniversary again?" Morrissey joked.

"Cheap bastard didn't want to cough up the money. But I really can't blame him with all this politically backed defund bullshit going on."

"Dear boy, I'm thoroughly familiar with the fact that you Yanks have completly reworked, rehashed and readjusted this beautiful language we so generously bequeathed you, however I'm going to need a clarification."

"Clarification is that I'm going around to the travel agent, buy a round trip ticket on my own dime, fly down there, question this Mr. Parker and fly back here by Monday."

Morrissey assumed an indignant pose.

"I see. So it's piss off to your old chum Nigel is it?" Nigel indignantly sulked.

"No, I just wasn't about to ask you to spend your money on one of my cases. Also, shouldn't you be spending time with your squad? They came all this way just to see you!"

"See me? Those four wankers could care less about seeing me! They're here to party in the Big Apple!"

With that Morrissey reached into his breast pocket and produced his wallet then two $50 bills and slid them across the table.

"Make sure I get a window seat!" He insisted.

*

The flight from Newark International was slightly over three and a half hours and after touching down at the Austin-Bergstrom airport in Austin, Texas they rented a car.

"The girl at the information desk said it's right in the middle of town, on main street." Mahone informed. "They call it The Independent Building. Apparently it's the tallest building in the city and looks like a stack of giant Jenga blocks. It's on West Avenue." He added as they drove.

Although The Independent was designated as a residential building consisting of only high-end condos, Daniel Parker had purchased an entire floor, knocked through several partition walls and converted half the floor space into office area with the other half serving as a centrally located residence so that the entire arrangement lie roughly equidistant from both U.S. coasts.

It was on the 27th floor that they found their destination.

"Mr. Parker I'm Lieutenant Detective Frank Mahone of the NYPD. This is my sidekick Inspector Nigel Morrissey of Scotland Yard." Morrissey mildly scoffed at the label 'sidekick' but said nothing. "We can't thank you enough for seeing us on such short notice."

"Happy to oblige detective. This is my General Manager and Cheif Engineer Malachi Melos." They exchanged nods as they all took seats in the Minimalist but spacious office area.

"What can I do for the NYPD and Scotland Yard?"

"Mr. Parker," Morrissey interceded. "What exactly is that tall radio tower we drove past and what's it doing in the middle of the road?" Morrissey inquired.

"That's not a radio tower that's a moonlight tower." Parker informed.

"What the hell is a moonlight tower?" Mahone asked.

"Back in the late 1800s there were a series of axe murders in the town. Mostly women." The big man Malachi explained. "Sixteen victims in all killed or wounded."

"Sort of your own Jack the Ripper, eh?" Morrissey joked.

"This was about three years before Jack the

Ripper. Speculation remains however that, given he was never caught, that he fled to England. Possibly took up his trade over there." Malachi casually informed.

Nigel sat back and stared at Parker.

"You're not trying to suggest that Jack the Ripper came from Austin, Texas are you?!" Morrissey challenged.

"When you get back to London look into it. The thousand dollar reward posted back in the day still stands." Malachi suggested.

"As I was saying, what can I do for the NYPD?"

"Dr. Parker, we're investigating the case of a crime that was committed up in New York sometime in the last few weeks. Your name came up in an interview I conducted in New Jersey."

"Am I a suspect? Have I been accused?" Parker shot back.

"No, no not at all."

"May I ask how my name came into it?"

"I spoke with a congresswoman Natalie Farmiga, one of the politicians from-"

"One of the politicians from the House Intel Committee. Conducted the hearing up in Washington back in February? I remember her, yes, nice woman."

"Dr. Parker, does the name Samantha O'Neill mean anything to you?"

"No never heard the name. Should I have?"

"She was a reporter for *Vanity Fair Magazine*. She was assigned a story on politics in the Intel services."

"*Vanity Fair*? I thought that was a woman's magazine?"

"Apparently due to the divorce rate wedding dresses aren't so popular anymore, now they're butting their noses into politics." Mahone opined.

"Well I can't speak to that but regarding problems in the Intel services I've got quite a bit to say!" Parker volunteered.

"How's that, exactly?" Morrissey probed.

Mahone, slightly annoyed at Morrissey apparently commandeering his interview, nevertheless held his tongue.

"We've developed what we've branded a Vacuum Emitter System. As you may or may not know Nexus 6 is in competition with another company for a government communications contract extending over ten years and potentially worth billions. As a consequence-"

A low buzzing sound suddenly emanated from where Malachi was sitting. He reached into his breast pocket and produced his cell phone and all paused as he checked his message.

He nodded knowingly then passed his phone over to Parker who quickly read the text.

"Probably those bastards at AstroCom!" He said half aloud to Malachi as he handed back the phone.

"No doubt." Malachi concurred.

"Problem?" Frank asked.

"A report from my lab. Apparently someone tried to hack into our satellite system and we're trying to track the origin of the electronic signal."

"Any luck?" Mahone asked.

"They think they may have narrowed it down to somewhere on the East Coast." Malachi volunteered.

Careful to suppress any overt reaction Mahone's interest was suddenly piqued.

"Tell us about this emitter vacuum system." Mahone pushed beginning to realise where Morrissey was headed.

"Vacuum Emitter System." Parker corrected. "I assume both of you are familiar with algorithms versus programmes?"

"Yes, a bit." An honest Morrissey answered.

"Basically." A clueless Mahone mumbled, nodded and shrugged.

Parker pressd on.

"An encryption algorithm is used to transform data into ciphertext. Ciphertext can then be transferred back into plain text via a decryption key. Naturally to decipher the data back into plain text you need the decryption key."

"Naturally." Mahone reflexively concurred.

"I suspect the stolen decipher key to my Omnibus satellite system was the document recovered by your FBI friends." He pointed out. The two cops looked puzzled. "What your FBI friends were after in the Central Park shootout?" He clarified.

"That encounter is supposed to be classified. How did you find out about it?"

"You Tube!" Parker shrugged.

"Ain't technology grand?" Morrissey joked.

"Guess I walked into that one." Frank confessed.
"Tell us about this satellite project." Parker nodded over to Malachi who assumed the narrative.

Retrieving the globe from the bookshelf behind Parker's desk along with a small scale model of one of the communication satellites, he set the globe on the desk and began an improvised demonstration.

"In the entire constellation there are 24 orbital planes in the system with 66 satellites per plane. We determined that, at the altitude given, a 53 degree incline on either side of the coverage is available. 24 times 53 equals 1,272. Divide that by 360 and you get 3.5, the X, Y and the Z axis with 0.5 of a degree allowed for deviation. Quite simple really."

"Of course! Crystal clear!" Mahone uconvincingly agreed.

Parker picked it back up.

"By bypassing the undersea fiber optic cable now used and beaming up through the vacuum of space we there-by afford a much reduced latency period cutting relay speed by 75% which translates to billions of dollars per day saved by accelerating international transactions."

"'Constellation'? That's the first time I ever heard that applied to a group of satellites." Frank questioned.

"It's standard in the industry."

"So the satellites were hacked into?"

"That's what my people have told me."

"Any idea by who or why?"

"Not for certain. But I have a pretty good hunch."

Mahone motioned over to Morrissey and stood.

"Do you mind if we have a word in private?" Mahone asked Parker.

"Please. Feel free to step into the executive washroom. It's just there on the left." He indicated.

"You want us to confer in the toilet?" Mahone challenged.

"I think you'll find it adequate." Parker assured. Malachi smiled and shook his head.

Upon entering 'the toilet' both men were shocked.

"Christ! This bathroom is bigger than my master bedroom!" Mahone declared as they stepped through the door.

The extensive room, also done out in Minimalist design, was heavily accented with polished brass fittings, a toilet with matching bidet and a two meter by three meter glass enclosed, step-in shower complete with picture window overlooking the city.

There was even an 18-inch monitor set into the wall between the double mirrors over the sinks.

Morrissey, distracted by the shower, stepped over to observe the small control panel on the wall beside the 2 meter wide shower door.

Pressing one of the half dozen buttons the picture window slowly clouded over to become opaque. The button next to it activated an overhead speaker and soothing music began to play.

Outside in the office Parker and Malachi, hearing the muffled tunes, exchanged looks of surprise, shook their heads and grinned.

Mahone stepped over to Morrissey's side and

slapped him on the shoulder.

"What the hell is wrong with you?! First time in a developed country with indoor plumbing?"

In an attempt to turn it off Morrissey hurriedly pressed another button and the shower came on. Mahone nudged him aside and found the off button,

"Come here! We're in here to decide if we should tell him or not!" Mahone scolded.

"Tell him what?"

"That it has to be some government guys who hacked into his sats!" Mahone deduced.

"We can't talk about some secret program we don't really know anything about! Irina swore you to absolute secrecy! It's bad enough you told me!"

"It's not like she gave me any details! Just said she thought it was some kind of satellite program!"

"We're not even supposed to know about it. If it gets out we'll all wind up being nicked!"

"I know but we can tell him who likely did the hacking."

"Why?" Morrissey challenged.

"Because whatever it is I'm telling there's a connection between Parker's satellite problem and someone in one of the government Intel agencies!"

"Ahh! Point taken! Unlikely but point taken." Morrissey conceded. "Well then, let's go deliver the bad news!"

Back outside Frank and Nigel resumed their seats to continue the discussion.

"Dr. Parker, I have some information I think you deserve to know." Frank started. "However, I'm going to caution you that the information is highly classified and simply by knowing it you'd be breaking the law."

"That's interesting! A cop offering to help me break the law!" He mused. "I'm intrigued, Please continue,"

"By giving you this information I am violating about 18 statutes of the *Espionage Act*. If word leaks out that any of us has this information, even if they just think you have it, they will visit your house in the dead of night, ransack the place with or without a warrant, put you in jail and possibly hold you indefinitely."

Both Parker and Malachi exchanged glances and assumed a more serious demeanor.

"Okay, make me a crimial!" Parker nervously joked.

"It was likely the CIA, NSA or the FBI that hacked into your satellite computer." Frank informed.

Parker and Malachi again exchanged glances.

"How do you know it wasn't AstroCom?"

"Because the men who did it more or less told us. Through a third party."

"And why would they do that?" Malachi challenged.

"Probably because they don't trust their boss. And because we were investigating this case which they may or may not know something about."

"Why are you telling me this?"

"Two reasons; one I trust you and two in case something happens to me." Frank emphasised.

Morrissey gave a loud 'harrumph' and elbowed

The Hermes Project

Mahone. "Happens to **us**. If anything happens to us! You can act as a surviving witness." Frank amended.

Parker was taken aback by this comment.

"You're quite serious about this!"

"As serious as Biden's Alzheimer's."

Mahone stood and turned to Parker as he and Morrissey prepared to leave.

"This is not a game. If they feel you're a threat they'll come down on you with everything they have and all your money won't matter! If they can do it to a former president and other political enemies they can easily do it to you or I! With impunity!"

Parker remained quiet as he walked them to the door. As they shook hands he finally spoke.

"What's my satellite program got to do with the death of a journalist?"

"No idea Dr. Parker. No idea."

"Then how do you intend to solve it?"

Mahone stopped at the door before answering.

"Did you or Malachi kill Miss O'Neill?"

"Of course not!"

"Well neither did I or the Inspector,"

"I don't get it?"

"Process of elimination. Now there's at least four people we know are in the clear."

"Neither did her boyfriend." Morrissey chimed in.

"See? That's five. Making progress already!" Frank added.

****

Moments after Morrissey and Mahone left Parker's office a thought occurred to Parker.

"Malachi didn't we have someone sometime last year quit here and go to work for AstroCom? Somebody in HR or accounting or something?" Parker questioned.

"Yeah, a guy in accounting, named Percy. A real blabbermouth. Paid more attention to other people's business then his own."

"Uh huh."

"But he didn't quit, I fired him. His books came up short two or three times in a row."

"Did we write him a recommendation when he went over to AstroCom?"

"Not sure I can check."

"Do that please. And if you locate him, get a hold of him, tell him his firing was a mistake. We caught the actual guy who actually finagled the books. By way of compensation we'd like to offer him his position back at an increased salary." He directed as they made their way back over to their desks.

"What?! Why?"

By way of answer Parker brandished an evil smile at his Chief Engineer.

"Ahh, you want me to play him?" Malachi deduced.

"Exactly!"

"For what purpose?"

"Something is going on over there with our good friends at AstroCom and given that this contract with NASA is in the balance, a journalist working on a story about the Intel services is dead and the NYPD accompanied by Scotland Yard is poking around in Austin, Texas tells me something is rotten and its not in the state Denmark!"

"Fair enough."

"Make it a priority will you."

"You got it Boss."

CHAPTER SIXTEEN

Won Hung Lo's
**Chinese Restaurant
Mott Street, Lower Manhattan**

Phil Finley checked out of the Alert Center early that Friday to catch the D.C. to New York flight's early hop. From JFK he taxied straight into Lower Manhattan for his. 19:30 dinner meeting.

Even a block away at the entrance to the narrow alleyway the taste tempting aromas of the Chinese cuisine beckoned.

Located in the basement underneath *Qing's* barber shop off the corner of Mott and Grand, he made his way down the stairs and into the dimly lit, cramped and seedy eatery.

Finley rarely ventured outside the D.C. area however, he didn't fly 200 miles for the Kung Pao chicken and dumplings. He was there to meet up with a contact.

Given the latest turn of events Mahone and Morrissey had had a long discussion on the return flight from Texas. They used the time to regroup their thoughts and approach to the case. One of the things they agreed upon was that Sam O'Neill's murder was not random nor committed by an amateur.

By the time they were back in Hoboken they had come to the conclusion that there was some kind of relationship between O'Neill's death, her article and

The Hermes Project

some satellites. Now in agreement that there was little else to learn from Parker they decided to return to Irina's leads, Phil Finley and the NSA.

Finley enthusiastically agreed to meet and Mahone made the arrangements. For obvious reasons he considered it best not to meet Finley at The Fort.

Finley's own motivation for wanting to meet was yet to be revealed. Mahone assumed it was to be a good citizen and contribute to solving the case.

Mahone was wrong.

The two sat at a back booth in the all but empty eatery as, with the aid of his laptop, Finley continued his explanation as he pressed a key.

"With the old program if you pulled up my number, that is my 'node', you would also pull up all the numbers I've been in contact with for the last week. Now with the upgraded program. . ." He explained to Mahone who paid close attention as he demonstrated by typing in a code on his laptop. The screen then displayed what appeared to be an infinite line of contacts.

"If I pull up your node, that is your nodes over the last day or week, it allows me to trace back any number you have contacted for the life of the device you're using."

"Jesus!" Mahone exclaimed. "You've developed the ultimate spy tool!" Mahone quietly declared. "I'm gonna havt'a start callin' you 'Q'!"

"Couldn't have said it better myself." Finley beamed at the compliment as he sat back in his seat and smiled. "Of course all of this is just a dummy demonstration set-up. My laptop doesn't have the computer power to store the whole program."

"Makes sense."

"It wasn't long after the last tests were completed, that we realized we had created the most powerful analytic tool ever developed. We, in effect had the ability, to invade everyone on earth's privacy who had an electronic communications device. In near real time!"

"Jeez, what could possibly go wrong with that?!" Mahone mocked.

"We immediately agreed we'd have to do something to protect the innocents." Finley added.

"What did you do about it?"

Finley closed over his laptop and they paused their conversation as the waitress served their meal, resuming after she left.

"There's a failsafe program as a mechanism to keep it out of bad hands." He explained moving their drinks away from his computer. "You have to show you have FISA approval. As soon as we told him about it Pravum wanted it removed."

"Wow! That's not too suspicious!" Frank commented.

"Since WWII the NSA had been the most productive agency. But that was three or four generations ago. After the last elections the Agency asked for millions in a budget increase and as when the Dems took power, they assigned for oversight a freshman female congresswoman from the House Intelligence Committee, so naturally she got the NSA Account. Her name is Natalie Farmiga."

"A Republican from over in Jersey. I know, I interviewed her." Frank confirmed.

"They picked her as one of the the token republicans because they thought she would make a good rube."

"And?"

"Well we gave her a demo, she was impressed and promised to approve the funding." He continued.

"Which means hundreds of thousands more are going to the NSA?"

"No!"

"No?"

"No. Hundreds of millions!" He corrected. "Now, even though it's tested and finished, we're not supposed to be using Hermes." He explained.

"Why not?" Frank asked.

"We were ordered not to."

"By whom?" Mahone pushed.

"By Pravum, the Director."

"I don't understand. If it's so efficient why-"

Finley hesitated to answer.

"We . . .we suspect he's planning on selling it to somebody else."

"Somebody else?! You mean like the Russians, the Chinese?" Frank blurted out.

The waitress brought their food and served their drinks.

"No, no!" He corrected. "He's eligible to retire this year." Finley explained. "All the guys that come out of the NSA the CIA et cetera go to work for private contractors. If they can bring something with them that the contractor can use they stand to reap a massive bonus." He explained through a mouthful of Mugu Gai Pan. "We think he intends to rebrand Hermes and bring it with him to wherever he's going."

"To what end? The contractor won't be able to use it. What will they do with it? Sell it on to a third world nation?"

"Not exactly." Finley continued further confusing Mahone. "They'll sell it on but not to a third world nation."

"Then who?"

"With a few minor chages they'll sell it back to the U.S. government under a new name!"

"But how. . .? Why wouldn't somebody. . ."

"Because with the limited number of people who can access it and the high level of secrecy it's easy to keep it all under wraps!" Mahone was jolted into a mild state of shock. "Besides which-"

"Besides which if they do get caught no one will want the scandal so it will be swept under the rug!" Frank finished.

"Welcome to my world Lieutenant!"

"And I thought the City officials in New York taking kickbacks from drug lords was big time corruption!" Frank declared aloud. "Gotta give it to the boys in D.C., they never do anything half measure!"

"Detective, you must understand that by divulging this situation Bill and I have put our careers at risk." Finley explained.

"Careers?! HELL YOUR LIVES!" Frank added

a little too loudly. A few heads turned but in standard unwritten New York tradition no one paid attention and just returned to their meals. "Which means we're all in the same boat?" Frank quickly deduced.

"Kind'a yeah." There was a brief moment of silence at the table. "Sorry about that!" Finley sheepishly apologised.

"No problem, that's why we get the extra $1.50 per hour." Frank cracked wise. "You or Whitcombe have any hard proof of what this guy Pravum intends to do?" He asked.

"No, but in our business we work largely on metadata."

"What the hell is that?!"

"Information about the data. Information such as the fact that Pravum has met with several contractors in the last month. But only AstroCom four times."

"So? That could have been on official business." Frank challenged.

"Could have been but, all of those times in restaurants well away from The Fort combined with the fact that he turned in no receipts for reimbursement."

"No paper trail!" Mahone pointed out.

"Which means the contractor paid." Finley informed.

"And for U.S. Government employees that's a big no-no!" Finley reminded.

"Plus three times he logged out a vehicle from motor pool to the same destination."

"Which destination was that?" Mahone enquired.

"Headquarters at AstroCom."

"The same people who he met for lunch?" Frank asked.

"Four times." Finley confirmed.

Frank reached for his fortune cookie and cracked it open.

"What's it say?" Finley asked.

"You will soon take an exciting journey!"

*

Just short of a week after being assigned Malachi had completed his mission.

"How'd you make out?" Parker asked into his cell phone as he drove.

"Nothing new on the hacking angle. Looks like our detective friends had the solid skinny. It was nobody in AstroCom. Our man on the inside checked the company records and he's certain there was no attempt at a hack."

"Do you believe him?"

"The way he fell for my spiel? Absolutely. It was the D.C. clowns who hacked into to our satellites. But there's a bonus bulletin."

"Talk to me."

"Samantha O'Neill, our dead journalist?"

"Yeah?"

"Apparently she was getting hot and heavy with a high up executive at AstroCom. They were keeping it on the down low."

"Interesting!"

"It gets better."

"I'm all ears."

"Apparently he's the last one to see her alive the night before she died."

"Huh! I wonder why we never saw her finished article on politics and the NSA?" He sarcastically quipped.

"Color me surprised." Malachi added.

"Did you get a name?"

"Name, company position and home address.

"Bring it with you when you come in."

"Will do Boss."

"Perhaps we should pass this information on to our Lieutenant Mahone of the NYPD?"

"I wouldn't get to tangled up in that investigation if I were you Boss. If there's even the slightest chance of NSA or CIA involvement in that case it would kill any chance of a government contract. Besides, the New York political scene is a bit of a sewer at present."

"Maybe you're right." He concured. "Where'd you leave it with Perkins?"

"His name is Percy. I told him you'd be in touch."

"Make a note, remind me to call him."

"Really?"

"Yeah, around the second Tuesday of next week." He joked.

*** * ***

Call Your Mom

Paddy Kelly

Internet Call Center
Washington St., Hoboken, N.J.

Having gotten wind of the fact that Natalie Farmiga had been asked to step down from the House Intel Committee, Irina Kuksova's suspicions were now all but confirmed.

As Irina was in the reading room of the New York Public Library in Midtown researching congressional law, members of The Squad were getting stuck into their individual assignments.

By agreement and to cover more ground the Squad were split into teams.

Din and Enfield would do telephone interviews with O'Neill's known friends and family members and then question a list of neighbors. She had been seen once or twice getting into a Porsche with an older man. Once in a tennis outfit.

At present Din and Enfield were seated side-by-side in the nearly empty *Call Your Mom* call center and internet café on Washington Street around the corner from their hotel which had become their base of operations.

It was mid-morning and they were two hours into their internet search and phone calls when Enfield caused Din to jump in his seat.

"WOW!" Enfield suddenly exclaimed.

"Did you find something?!" Din anxiously asked.

"Yeah!"

"What?"

"It was right here in Hoboken over 150 years ago that the very first recorded game of baseball was played! Interesting no?"

Din turned in his chair and stared.

"You must have been a joy to your parents!" He grumbled as he stood.

"Where are you going?"

"To the jacks to have a slash! Want to come along and watch?"

"No, but thanks for the offer. I've already seen that short film. Disappointing ending." He fired back without looking up from his keyboard.

As Din left and Enfield tended to his work a pair of college-aged students took up seats at the work table behind him. They sat close enough that it was impossible not to overhear their conversation.

"Okay so in 2007 she's worth 58 million and last year she's worth 120 million! Explain that please!" One of them challenged.

"I know what you're getting at but there's exactly two chances the Pelosi's will ever get nailed for insider trading! Slim and none, and Slim just left town! You can take that to the bank!" The other one declared.

Enfield's ears suddenly perked up. He turned back to his keyboard and began furiously typing. Din returned and noticed his colleague's increased energy.

"What are you on to?" He asked. Enfield continued to type as he spoke.

"Din, do you remember about four or five years ago The Yard's Counter-Terrorist Unit were looking into a case that involved weapons being supplied to a certain terrorist group?"

"Not really no."

"Sure you do, it was in all of the London papers because several MP's were implicated."

"Why would I say 'I don't remember' if I do remember?! I don't remember! I wasn't yet with The Yard then. I was working out of Essex."

"Well I was at The Yard, before the SHIT Squad were formed."

"So?"

"So, there were one or two MP's implicated as well as an American senator."

"You almost have my attention." Din quippped.

"As predicted none of the politicians was indicted but the case centered around the fact that it appeared they had bought stock in weapons companies which were illegally supplying Colombian terrorists."

"And you think if this American senator is still around he's possibly connected to the O'Neill case?"

"O'Neill was doing a story on problems, corruption whatever in the Intel community. If that politician's still around . . ."

Din suddenly assumed an alarmed look, rolled his chair in closer to Enfield and spoke in a soft whisper.

"You don't think it's that Farmiga woman do you? The one O'Neill was interviewing?"

"No, we were pretty sure it was a guy. But tracing him should be easy enough, all we have to do is remember his name." Enfield advised. "It was Herman, Lerman something like that. Listen get

The Hermes Project

online, find a full list of all the U.S. Congressional members. Then start getting a list of all of their stock filings for the last five years. They're required to publicly disclose all investments while in office.

You'll find all that in the Congressional S.T.O.C.K. Report listed by year. The company we're looking for will have some foreign name, likely Spanish or Asian."

"The entire Senate? There must be hundreds!" Din protested.

"Five hundred and thirty-five counting the women, so minus about 120! So you've only got about four hundred and fifteen to cross-reference!"

"You're joking! That's half the stock market!"

"Not 'stock' as in market, 'stock' as in the federal S.T.O.C.K. Act!"

"What the hell is the federal S.T.O.C.K. Act?"

"Google it detective!"

****

It was just after 8:00 a.m. that same morning that Heath and Little Tammy could be found standing outside an apartment house on 217th Street off Bell Boulevard in Queens.

It was Sam O'Neill's second floor apartment, a one bedroom in a three story, brick walk-up.

Their first obstacle, or so Heath thought, was getting through the vestibule as both the street entrance and hall entrance doorways required keys.

With what was clearly personal experience, Little Tammy went to work.

"Sergeant Heath, go across the street to that coffee shop, get in the queue but keep an eye out through the front window. When you see me go inside, come on back over." She instructed.

Only half trusting her over-confident instructions the six foot two Heath stared down at her. "Go on go!" She insisted shooing him away with both hands as if he were a misguided puppy. Somewhat indignantly Heath turned to cross the street and she called after him. "Bring us back a black coffee as well! Six sugars!"

Once across in the queue he was amazed as he watched Tammy standing on the steps of the building next to the door pretending to be on her mobile phone for a full five minutes until a resident exited and she deftly slid into the vestibule before the door closed over.

A minute later Heath was back across the street and inside with Tammy's coffee.

"How did you know someone would come out?" He asked.

"Sure it's a weekday isn't it? 8:30 in the morning, everyone's off to work."

"Now what?" He challenged as he nodded to the second door leading into the hallway.

Without answering Tammy perused the bell panel on their right, observed the name 'Anderson' on one of the bells and rang it.

Almost immediately the second inner door made a buzzing sound and could be heard to unlock.

They slipped through the door into the hallway and quickly urging Heath up the stairs to the first

The Hermes Project

floor landing Tammy led the way to the top where they stood quietly as a door on the ground floor opened and someone called out.

"Who's there?" An old woman yelled.

Receiving no answer the door closed over and the two cops made their way up to apartment number 27.

Setting her coffee off to Heath Tammy reached into the inner pocket of her jean jacket and produced a pocket-sized lock picking kit. A minute later they were inside the apartment.

"Why do I get the feeling you've done this before?" Heath asked.

"Seen it in a movie so I did!" She replied as they stepped through the doorway.

They split up and commenced their search.

About ten minutes into their probe Tammy came across a shelf in Sam's bedroom festooned with various sized statues, cards and photographs of elephants.

Looking further she noticed one item set aside on the dresser. It was all white porcelain, very detailed and stood nearly six inches tall.

Heath entered the room. "I see nothing of any importance." He announced.

"Looks like she liked elephants. Apparently collected them." Tammy stated as she examined the statue.

"Looks expensive." Heath commented.

There was a small gift card with it. "'Here's to never forgetting our first night together.'" She read aloud. "It's signed by 'R'" She passed him the card.

"What do you make of that?" She questioned.

"Not a clue."

"Should we nick it?" Tammy asked.

"Better not. Get a photo with your phone instead." Heath suggested. "Be sure to get the handwriting on the card."

Over the next 15 or 20 minutes, as it required no password, Little Tammy and Heath went through O'Neill's desktop but found nothing. Her home laptop had not been confiscated by the police.

"Must'a kept her work files at the office." Tammy speculated.

However clean their caper Heath and Little Tammy neglected to account for the local increase in crime brought about by the New York politicians' Defund the Police program which in turn brought about New Yorker's increased Neighborhood Watch programs,

Minutes after seeing the two strangers enter the apartment building a barista from the coffee shop across the street rang the police.

Unfortunately for the two sleuths the 111th Precinct was only two blocks away on 215th Street and so were there to greet them as they attempted to sneak back out of the building.

They were immediately arrested.

Needless to say Lieutenant Frank Mahone was not a happy camper when later that afternoon he had to drive all the way out to Bayside to sign the two culprits out of custody.

"What the hell were you two knuckleheads thinking?" He challenged on the drive back to

Manhattan.

"Sorry Lieutenant. we just thought-" Heath started.

"You weren't thinking! Otherwise you would have asked me!" Mahone snapped.

"Asked you what? If it's okay if we break in to a dead girl's flat?" Heath defended.

"No! Asked me if I had the key, since I'm the the lead on the case!" He chastised as he dangled a set of door keys in front of them.

****

Irina Kuksova phoned Frank and arranged to meet him in Hoboken that evening.

She wrapped up her second day of research in the reading room of the New York Public Library and headed across the street to Grand Central Terminal to catch the train over to New Jersey.

That evening she met with members of the Squad at their hotel and collected what information they had gathered before going to meet Frank.

No concrete arrangements had been discussed however, out of force of habit she always liked to be prepared so she packed her toothbrush and a clean pair of underwear.

They were to meet at *il Vento's* a local Italian place a few blocks from his apartment where Mahone, in the couple of months he had been a resident, had established a rapport with the wait staff allowing him to stake out a regular table.

"You seem bursting with excitement." He

commented as he watched Irina jauntily approach the table.

"Aren't you going to ask me where I've been?" She teased.

"Where have you been?"

"I've been to the Public Library!" She took the seat across from him. "Aren't you going to ask me what I was doing at the Public Library?"

"What were you doing in the Public Library?"

"Glad you asked!" She blurted out. "Ya know how when certain politicians live in a bubble they often forget the truth is out there just waiting to be found?" Irina started.

"Okay Scully, what'd you find?"

"Well Mouldy-"

"It's Mulder!"

Just then a waiter apeared with menus.

"Good evening Lieutenant, ma'am. Can I start you off with some drinks?"

"Jameson neat and a Manhattan for the lady. Two cherries!"

"Yes sir. Be right back."

Irina continued.

"Under the Stop Trading on Congressional Knowledge or S.T.O.C.K. Act governing the activities of members of Congress, officeholders and candidates are required to publicly disclose, on an annual basis, their financial holdings, including stock ownership, business interests, outside income or any other position held along with their liabilities."

"Snore."

"Stop it! Pay attention, you might learn something!" She snapped. "Although I doubt it." She mumbled. "Passed in 2012 getting around STOCK was one of the primary reasons for pushing for COVID restrictions, that is to open the market and allow insider trading to more easily slip under the wire."

"Getting more interesting." He conceded.

"Fauchi likely made millions off of COVID." She added.

"That's no secret!" He agreed.

"Altogether Congress men and women raked in over $150,000,000 during the pandemic they largely helped propagate and maintain, according to a report by Danielle Caputo of the CLC."

"Who the hell is Danielle Caputo and what is a CLC?" Frank challenged.

"Danielle Caputo is a respected journalist, which means she is out of your league and the CLC is the Campaign Legal Center." She explained.

"I knew that." He boasted.

"Sure you did. According to her, 'Congressional members strategically bought stocks in companies that could increase in value during the pandemic, such as remote work technologies, telemedicine companies and car manufacturers that were shifting their production to ventilators.'" Kuksova read from her notes.

"Huh, right out of the *Pelosi Handbook of Financial Management*!" Mahone observed. "So once COVID hit, all the rules went right out the window?" He postulated.

"Pretty much!"

The waiter appeared with their drinks and took their dinner order.

"This guy Burman and his wife alone pulled in over 6.7 million!" She expounded.

"Burman? Like the House Intel Chair Burman?!"

"One and the same!" Irina confirmed.

"Okay, so? That's a lot of cash but nobody is going to go after this guy for that, especially when he's the head of the Intel Committee."

"Maybe not. But I'm pretty certain John Q. Public would be interested in exactly what insider trading he was dealing in. It at least deserves an investigation." She pushed.

"Talk to me more about these reports." He insisted.

"They must file disclosure forms known as Periodic Transaction Reports, or PTR's, within 30 days of any stock transaction."

"Wait don't tell me, our favorite senator didn't file his PTR's?"

"No worse! For the last three years he's filed false PTR's."

"In for a penny in for a pound eh?" Mahone smirked sipping his whiskey.

Irina couldn't shake the concept of an investigation being called for. One thing Mahone had over the slightly younger Kuksova was a more realistic grasp on the workings of D.C. politics.

"How could that not warrant an investigation?" She insisted.

"Because an investigation would be long and

expensive. And the point of expensive and prolonged internal investigations. . ." He explained as he finished off his drink, ". . . is to find no evidence of wrongdoing. No one is ever supposed to go to jail or worse yet, lose their government position." Mahone espoused.

"But what if there's proof of something suspicious?"

"Irrelevant. Everything in government is suspicious!"

"Then what's the purpose of political investigations?"

"The purpose of political investigations is to kill press stories. Besides, you can't investigate everything."

"Why not?!" She argued.

"Because you never know what you might find." Mahone explained. He signalled for aother whiskey.

The dinner was finished being served and they continued to speak as they ate.

"Well Enfield and Din certainly found something."

"Like what?" Frank asked.

By way of an answer Irina fished through her handbag then slid a piece of paper across the table. It was a photostat of a stock report.

"Like a certain Senator Burman who owns large amounts of stock in a Chinese company called Ming Tao who are no doubt selling their technology. Possibly to outfits like the FARC!"

"Who the hell are . . . the . . . FARC?" He hesitantly asked. The expression on his face indicated the answer was slowly dawning on him. "The assholes you told me about back in London!"

"Give that man a cigar! See? Even an NYPD detective can sometimes figure things out." She mocked.

"I'd rather another whiskey." He quipped.

Irina signalled the waiter for another round of drinks.

"Fuerza Alternativa Revolucionaria del Común." Mahone said softly.

"Exactly!" She affirmed. "The Revolutionary Armed Forces of Colombia, a designated terrorist group, converted to The Comunes a 'supposed' legitimate political party in 2017 via treaty with the UN. In reality they're hardcore communists believed to still be deeply associated with terrorism."

"Doesn't sound lithey're very defunct to me."

"Apparently not." She conceded.

"That's why the Chinese handler you guys nailed in Central Park during Dunlap's arrest was speaking Spanish." Mahone deduced.

"Not bad! You should've been an FBI agent!" Irina quipped.

"Not eligible. My parents were married."

"Ha, ha very funny! So where do we go from here?"

"Not sure. Let's meet again tomorrow and talk about it."

"Sounds good."

Following dinner and one last drink they decided to call it a night.

After paying the bill and stepping outside into the chilled night air they kissed good night.

"I'd keep this quiet for now!" He suggested.

"I will." She nodded.

But when Irina stepped off heading towards the train station which was in the opposite direction of Frank's apartment she was puzzled as he tagged along.

Irina had no way of knowing about the attempted FBI mugging of Frank and Nigel earlier in the week as he had not yet told her.

"Where are you going?" She asked.

"I thought I'd ride back over to Manhattan with you, if you don't mind."

"I don't mind."

"I have to be in at six in the morning plus I've got some reports to file. I'll drop you off and head back down town to the precinct. I can crash in the squad room."

"Okay." She happily agreed.

As they walked a thought occurred to her.

"Now we just have to decide what the next step is." She postulated.

"I'll have a long think about it tonight." He suggested.

Neither of them could know that the next step would be decided for them.

They kissed good-bye and separated at the 33rd Street PATH station on the Manhattan side where she would take the F train North to Grand Central.

Mahone however did not head straight to the southbound platform to go back down town. Instead he took the stairs up to street level to ensure a good signal on his cell phone.

The text he sent was received Uptown by two plain clothes NYPD parked in an unmarked sedan just down the block from Irina's Midtown apartment in the Bryant Park area. He sent:

'TARGET ENROUTE, ETA 15.'

In turn Mahone received the following text:

'RECEPTION PARTY READY.'

Twenty minutes later, observing Irina emerge from the subway kitchen Uptown, the two plainclothes police made their move.

As she crossed 39th Street two other men dressed in hoodies stepped out of a nearby black Dodge Charger van but were immediately intercepted by the NYPD plainclothesmen at gunpoint and forced back against their SUV face in.

"Who the hell are you guys?!" The pudgy hooded one demanded as he was being patted down.

"NYPD. Welcome to the Big Apple!" The blond detective greeted.

"What the hell ya think you're doin?!" Pudgy again demanded.

"You're under arrest for suspected stalking and vagrancy." The other detective informed them as they confiscated the FBI agents' guns and I.D.

"You have any idea who we are?!" The other hoodie challenged.

"Yeah, you're the guys were arresting!" The cops cuffed the agents.

"Arresting for what?!"

"What's the matter? No speaky English? For suspected stalking and vagrancy."

"We're on a case here assholes!" Hoodie number two challenged.

"So are we!"

"WE'RE FUCKIN' FBI!"

"Didn't you guys get the memo?" The blond cop asked as he handcuffed the angry agent. "New York is a sanctuary city. Federal law doesn't apply here!"

After being cuffed the two FBI agents were hustled into a waiting squad car and taken away.

Oblivious to events, Irina crossed the street, rounded the corner and entered her apartment.

Downtown as he entered the 13th Precinct, Mahone smiled as he read a new text message.

Federal Fuck-ups Foiled.
Bird safely home.

*

NSA HQ, 'The Fort'
Office of the Director

It was only a day later that word reached General Pravum's office about the NYPD tactics in Bryant Park which prompted Pravum to decide it was the last straw.

A secure email was sent to the seventh floor of

the Hoover Building, Office of the FBI Director.

Under U.S. law any arrest warrant requires a judge's approval. Although this process is essentially rubber stamped on virtually every level it requires the requesting authority to submit a sworn affidavit to the appropriate judge citing the suspected crime or crimes.

This is where 'judge shopping' comes into play.

Few people believe the myth that judges are impartial despite the fact that a famous politician once declared there is no such thing as a 'Democrat' or 'Republican' judge in the U.S.

Even a cursory glance at court records clearly proves otherwise.

Once a judge receives an affidavit and request for an arrest warrant, they are permitted although not required to ask questions particularly regarding verification of the facts in the affidavit.

This is rarely if ever done.

Theoretically FISA or the Foreign Intelligence Surveillance Act, warrants are no exception.

In the case of a FISA warrant The National Security Division's Office of Intelligence is responsible for preparing and filing all FISA applications as well as appearing before the FISA court.

That afternoon, in the office of Major General Pravum, the DIRNSA, Colonel Parva diligently took notes as Pravum dictated.

"When you write up the affidavit be sure to include the fact that the subject is currently on suspension and under investigation for misconduct."

The General emphasised.

"Will do sir." The Colonel replied. "What should I put down for execution date?" Parva queried.

"Time-sensitive. Immediate arrest warranted!" Pravum dictated.

"But the court rules require requests be submitted seven days in advance."

"Stamp it 'Emergency'!" Pravum demanded.

"Will that be enough time for them to hold a hearing?"

"I'll call ahead. After I talk to them they won't have to hold a hearing."

"Primary element of the affidavit sir?"

"The compromise of highly classified information to a foreign power with intent to do harm to the United States and it's allies."

"Name on the warrant request?"

"FBI Special Agent Irina Kuksova." He answered.

"Have we been surveilling her communications long enough?"

"Several weeks now."

"I don't remember seeing a warrant for a wiretap." Parva insisted.

"Under section 702 we don't need a warrant."

"But that's intended for non-citizens. She's an American!"

"She's born in the Ukraine, that makes her Russian and that makes her the enemy!"

"Yes sir. I'll get this over to the District Court this afternoon." He shruggd.

"No! Send it up through the Second District."

"But that's up in New York!"

"I know where it is God damn it! I also know that Kuksova has an address in New York! Besides, the judge owes me a favor."

"Second District it is!" The Colonel rose to leave. "Will there be anything else General?"

"No, buzz me when it's typed up."

"Will do sir!"

****

That afternoon, one day later in Mahone's apartment his phone rang.

"Hello?"

Lieutenant Mahone?

"Speaking. Who's this?" He heard only white noise. "Who is this?!"

A little birdie told me it might aid your case immensely if you were to speak to a Mr. Reagan at AstroCom.

"Who is this asshole?!" The line suddenly went dead. "Hello?!"

There was nothing but dial tone.

CHAPTER SEVENTEEN

It being late Friday afternoon and he being a man of habit Phil Finley could be found driving North up Interstate 270 to his home in Rockville just over an hour north of D.C.

Less then a year from mandatory retirement the most important thing Finley looked forward to was the peace and serenity of the wooden, three room cabin his father and uncle had hand built years ago after coming home from the war.

Save for one small room in a shed out back, Phil was careful to ensure there were no electronic devices, computers, radios or televisions in the home to remind him of what century he was currently in. Isolation and serenity would be the order of the day for the next 48 hours.

Or so he thought.

At around 6 p.m. as dark was approaching his fully restored '67 Chevy Camaro eased into the gravel driveway under the towering pines which dominated most of the property.

Preoccupied with the bottle of Cabernet Sauvignon chilling in the fridge he casually entered the dark house, passed through the dark parlor and into the kitchen.

"AGGHHH!" Finley yelled as the light came on, his peace of mind suddenly shattered when he spotted the strange man sitting at the kitchen table facing the entrance.

"Late night at the office, Phil?" The stranger casually queried.

"Who the hell are you?!" He demanded once he caught his breath.

There was no immediate answer from the well dressed 40 year old being sure to maintain direct eye contact as he cradled his chin in one hand, elbow on the table.

"Why didn't I see your car outside?!" Finley followed up.

"I design, build, launch and sell the most sophisticated communication satellites in the world. You think I'm stupid enough to give you a heads up that we were here?"

"We?! Who's 'we'?"

That's when the outer door closed over behind him seemingly of its own volition.

Finley, startled by the noise, turned to see the large, pugnacious, bald man sporting the handlebar moustache who stepped into the light, crossed his arms and blocked the entire doorway.

"Malachi here may look a bit older but still harbors enough anger at what the Chechnyins did to his family in the Ukraine back in the 1960's to get really angry when required."

"Who are you and what do you want?!" Finley again demanded.

"I am Dr. Daniel Parker the man whose satellites you hacked into. And what I want is to know is how and why."

"PARKER?! You're Daniel Parker?!" Finley stared. "WOW! It's a pleasure to meet you Dr. Parker!" Finley declared as he extended his hand and moved forward to shake. Parker made no

The Hermes Project

attempt to move or adjust his position. Finley diverted to the fridge.

"Can I offer you a glass of wine?"

"No wine! Explanation now!"

"Okay no problem!" Finley responded as he continued to retrieve the bottle of wine from the fridge followed by two glasses from the upper cupboard. "Funny story really." He quickly uncorked the bottle and slid one empty glass across the table to Parker. "Just in case you change your mind." He smiled nervously then poured himself a glass, one eye on Malachi in the doorway the entire time.

"You're gonna love this, you really are! About two months ago we where tasked with reviewing our code systems. I was fooling around with some algorithms when it occurred to me that data input was being accumulated at far to fast a pace for the analysts to ever catch up. We needed a faster, more efficient system."

"Why didn't you approach it from the angle of metadata?" Parker asked.

Finley lowered hus glass **and** stared blankly in amazement.

"That's exactly what we did! No wonder you are who you are!" He complimented.

"Very flattering. Keep talking!" Parker grunted ignoring the plaudit.

"It took a few weeks playing around but once we solved the problem of rigging up a sessionizer to handle the projected volume we were off and running. So we set the arbitrary goal of about 45%

download to be able to declare success."

"Your next problem was to be able to test your system?" Parker extrapolated.

"Exactly! We christened it Hermes by the way! Hermes because-"

"The Herald of the gods yeah, I read Edith Hamilton in school." Parker blurted out.

"Okay. But we needed a data accumulation package large enough to give it a proper test."

"So you decided to hack into my Omnibus system?"

"And we hit over 98%!" Finley gleefully declared rewardeding himself with a celebratory gulp of wine.

Following a brief silence Parker finally adjusted his position to sit erect.

"Do you have any idea how much time and money you cost me and my company?"

"Dr. Parker, I sincerely apologise for any inconvenience or problems. If it's of any consolation, all of the data we downloaded has been destroyed. No copies or files of anything were kept. It was truly a one goal experiment."

"You know, at first we put it down to to malicious hackers. But when my guys traced the algorithms it was obvious they were too sophisticated to have originated with a Comic Con frequenting, millennial living in his mother's basement."

"Thank you that's quite a compliment."

"I was only seconds away from picking up the phone and ringing the FBI at which point they would have shown up in the dead of night, raped your house, confiscated all your electronics and hauled you off to prison."

"Please don't misinterpret this Dr. Parker but, the FBI wouldn't have done you any good."

"Oh, why not?"

"Sorry, that's classified."

"I constantly handle government projects. I have a TS clearance Mr. Finley."

Finley glanced over his shoulder at Malachi before finally deciding he was probably no threat. After pouring himself a top off he leaned forward and spoke in a low tone.

"Because we're the NSA. We monitor the FBI too!"

Parker was more taken aback then he let himself show. He stared for a bit before he reached for the empty wine glass and pushed it towards Finley who gladly poured him a healthy glass.

Finley returned the glass but offered the half empty bottle up to Malachi who gave no response.

"So where does your little project stand now?" Parker queried.

Surprised but pleased by the change in tone Finley finally began to relax.

"Well, as long as we are laying our guns on the table, there's a major hang up with finishing it up."

"If it's successful and it works what could stop it?"

"The access code."

"You mean you can't write one?"

"I can but that's not the problem. My boss-"

"General Pravum?"

"Yeah. He wants it open code, available to anyone he sees fit."

"A bit unusual but, he's the Director, what's the problem?"

"Trust! The problem is I seriously suspect he's going to sell my program to a private company when he retires next year."

"That's treason!"

"Only if he gets caught. And the rate at which criminals inside the Beltway go to jail practically guarantees he will never see the inside of a court room much less a jail cell!" Finley stated before polishing off his glass.

Parker decided he liked this guy Finley. Particularly his honesty.

"What do you intend to do about it?" Parker challenged.

"No fucking idea Doctor Parker! But you can bet your ass Hermes is not going into the system without a firewall!" He poured the last of the wine. "I can tell you this, now that we've met we both will be compelled to be more cautious of covert surveillance. Especially electronically speaking."

Parker clearly sensed Finley's encroaching anguish.

"You're not suggesting-"

"No, no I'm stating it outright. Watch your ass! A lot of these upper echelon Bozos still think there's a cold war on and so believe any means justifies the end." Finley explained.

"So I've been warned!"

Parker and Malachi briefly exchanged glances.

"I have a remote property, out in Tahoe." Parker offered. "You're welcome to fly out there for a while, keep a low profile until you can decide what to do."

"That's a great offer Dr. Parker. But if I disappear for awhile it will only look like I'm running which would make me look more guilty."

"But you haven't done anything!" Parker insisted.

"Ha! Since when do you have to commit a crime in today's atmosphere to be arrested?" Parker offered no answer. "Your proposal is most appreciated Doctor. However, there are a couple of people I believe might benefit more from your offer later on down the road."

"I'll keep the offer open."

****

Are you positive Inspector?! The voice on the other end sought to confirm.

"Sergeant, I'm in your country on a temporary visa. What would I have to gain by lying to the police? I know for a fact they left the Hoboken PATH train station not 20 minutes ago headed to JFK to catch a 08:15 Delta flight."

Okay thanks for your help. They both hung up.

But it was only Morrissey who smirked as he did so.

****

"Come on!" Mahone demanded as he slapped Irina on the ass to wake her.

Inspector Morrissey's late night phone call served two purposes; one to establish plausible deniability and two to give Kuksova and Mahone a head start.

"OW! What?! Where're we going?" She rolled over and looked at the clock. It was ten minutes after five in the morning.

"Lake Tahoe."

"Lake Tahoe?!" She sat up in the bed rubbing the sleep from her eyes.

"Tahoe with a stopover in Vegas." He said as he continued stuffing her things into a bag.

"VAGAS! What are we elopeing?!"

"You should be so lucky! Come on, I'll explain on the way."

"But what if I-"

Frank reached into his pocket, produced his cell phone and showed her the text message he just received.

FBI due to visit soon. Hit the bricks!

"Who sent it? How do you know it's not a trick?"

"The sender' number was blocked, it was probably Morrissey on his burner phone. C'mon, hustle!" He tossed a carry-on bag across the bed to her.

"I can't leave the state. I'm on suspension!" She protested.

"Not anymore you're not." He said as he

brandished a pair of airline tickets.

Mahone & Kuksova had had just enough time to pack a light bag each before taxiing to the train station.

The thirty minute train ride from Hoboken to the Newark Liberty Airport was largely in silence particularly after Frank explained to her that there was now a highly likelihood that there was a warrant out for her arrest. A Federal FISA warrant which he found out from the precinct.

When they disembarked at Terminal B it was only minutes until they made it to the vestibule where they found themselves surrounded by cops, guns drawn and shouting orders to the point of causing a confusing cacophony of deafening babble.

If Irina was overwhelmed with surprise on the train by what Frank told her, she was now slowly descending into pure shock. This is exactly why her father and her family escaped the Ukraine.

Frank counted six uniforms in all before he noticed the two squad cars parked out front and an unmarked vehicle behind.

A pair of plain clothesmen made their way over to where the two were handcuffed and being held facing against the wall.

"Who's senior man here?" The older detective asked to no one in particular.

"I am sir." A senior sergeant stepped forward.

"Assistant Commissioner Baxter." The detective announced as he flashed his I.D. "We'll assume custody of these two. Get them in the car." He ordered.

"But sir-"

"That's not a request sergeant. Your men did a good job, you'll get credit for the collar. You're dismissed."

Two uniforms led by the second detective escorted the handcuffed Frank and Irina to the unmarked sedan parked at the curb and set them in back. He then directed two other uniforms to collect their luggage and stow the bags in the trunk.

The two detectives made their way back into the car and drove off leaving the uniforms to disperse the small crowd which had gathered.

Frank, in the back seat next to Irina, gradually began to notice something was wrong when he observed the door next to him featured fully functioning latches and locks. As a general rule police cars disabled latches on the rear doors to prevent prisoners attempting to escape.

The next thing he noticed was they didn't appear to be driving towards the exit but instead headed West and turned South around Terminal C where they drove to an isolated tarmac with a handful of private aircraft, some under repair.

But it wasn't until they drove into an abandoned hangar that Frank and Irina both became seriously concerned.

Pulling up next to a white jet the cops shut the car down and opened the doors.

"You realize kidnapping is a federal offence, ten years mandatory!" Irina blurted with what little courage she could muster.

"Relax Sweetheart, we're with the good guys."

The Hermes Project

The senior detective snapped back as he turned Frank around and undid his cuffs. His partner followed suit with Irina.

A young, uniformed steward and stewardess descended the jet's roller stairs, went to the car's trunk, collected the bags and carried them on board the plane.

The senior cop fished through his pocket and passed a slip of paper to Frank.

"Call this number when you get to Vegas. You'll get instructions from there."

"Who are you?" Frank asked.

"I'm Batman!" The older cop softly whispered in a deep voice. The younger cop laughed out loud.

"He cracks me up! Isn't he a crack up? I love this guy!" The younger cop nudgged Irina.

"Yeah, a regular fucking barrel of laughs!" She spat as she rubbed her wrists.

"Don't mind her." Frank said. "She has no sense of humor when she's screwed by strangers without permission!"

Irina flipped them all off before storming off up into the plane.

"Name's Baxter. I used to work personal security for Daniel Parker before I became a cop."

"Parker set this up?" Frank asked.

"Yeah. Apparently he got a call from some jamoke in the NSA. Guy named Finley. Heard you were in the shit. Parker says to tell you he's just returning the favor. Says you'll know what he means."

Frank smiled broadly and nodded.

"Yeah, yeah I do! Thanks Baxter."

"Best of luck Mahone." Baxter climbed back into his car and rolled the window down before pulling away. "By the way, nice job on that armored car case over in London."

Mahone waved him off as the stewardess appeared and tapped him on the shoulder.

"Lieutenant Mahone, we need to button up and taxi out. Take off time is in fifteen minutes."

"Okay, on the way."

Frank involuntarily took in a deep breath as he entered the 4.5 million-dollar Golfstream G650.

"This is ridiculous!" He sighed as he perused the plush carpeted interior, wood panelling and rich Corinthian leather recliners surrounding the small, Carrera marble table. "You could live on this damn plane! I mean is there anything they don't have? It's nicer than my apartment!" He asked a reclining Kuksova who kicked off her shoes.

"The rooms at the Y are nicer then your apartment! And here they have a bar!" Irina declared as she raised her empty glass of what used to be a Manhattan. The steward quickly appeared and snatched up the glass and made for the bar to refill it.

"Jameson neat please." Frank requested of the stewardess near him.

"I don't understand. What's going on, where are we headed?" She asked as he took a seat across from her.

"Apparently I was right. To Vegas." He shrugged, raised his glass and downed his drink.

The Hermes Project

****

245 39th Street
Kuksova's Apartment
05:35 Sunday

The short convoy of three black SUV's dowsed their headlights followed by their engines as they turned the corner of Fifth Avenue and 39th Street then silently coasted to the front of #245, at Irina Kuksova's apartment house.

In under a minute black PPE clad, masked men in two teams of four were lined up one behind the other as another approached lugging a 50 pound batterung ram.

From inside the well appointed space the shards of door frame exploded violently into the room on the second hammering as the combat ready gang spilled and tripped through the opening all screaming "FBI! GET ON THE FLOOR!"

The men filtered through the four rooms, still shouting, all weapons off safe, fingers on triggers.

They found no one home.

After reporting all rooms secure the leader manned his hand held radio.

"Sir, we got a dry hole here." As his men tore through the apartment confiscating anything electronic, and awaited insturctions he glanced down at the Tabby cat cowering under the living room couch. The cat hissed back.

Unfortunately for the misguided commandoes

Kuksova had spent the night across the river in Hoboken at Frank's place.

As the wanna-be Special Forces filed out of the house and piled back into their black SUV's two men sat on the steps of a similar apartment across the street and down the block enjoying their egg McMuffins and coffee.

Watching the convoy roll away Enfield and Din texted Morrissey to report their update.

A half an hour later, up in the Bronx, a similar Raiding party burst through the front door of what was, over a year ago Frank Mahone's apartment. An apartment now occupied by a retired elderly couple who were lying in bed watching morning television.

Apparently the intel people at the FBI hadn't gotten Frank Mahone's change of address form yet.

****

"What do you mean 'got away'?! 40,000 agents, billions of dollars and the most modern tech tools on the planet and two low level cops give you the slip?!" Pravum angrily challenged the Special Agent in Charge.

"They had help!" The FBI man shot back.

"What do you mean 'they had help'? Like The Fairy Godmother swooped down and flew them away? David Copperfield threw a blanket over them and they disappeared?"

"Whoever it was it was someone off the grid, or at least someone we don't have in the files."

"How many troops did you send?"

"Two squads of eight men."

"16 troops and you couldn't catch them?!"

"The only other explanation is they were tipped off."

"You mean the information was leaked?!"

"Sure why not? The DOJ does it all the time. So does the CIA. Hell Comey did it when he was running the show over in the Hoover Building!"

"Who's this NYPD clown who apparently took off with her?"

"Name's Mahone, Frank Mahone. High profile detective back in the day, now a washed-up gum shoe. Just putting in his time until retirement."

"What's his connection to her?"

"Unknown at present. But I have men working on it."

"What are you doing to track them down?"

"I've notified all the branch offices in the tri-state area, had them notify all their local sheriffs and police chiefs to put out APB's and I've requested the formation of a dedicated tracking team."

"Uh huh. Cells?" Pravum pushed.

"We tried tracking their cell phones but couldn't find a signal. My guess is they dumped them and bought a couple of burner phones." He explained.

"God damn burner phones! I told the committee to make those fucking things illegal!" He cursed before he thought for a moment considering options.

"I've got just the man for you to head up the tech side of that tracking team!" Pravum boasted. He picked up his phone and buzzed his secretary.

"Yes General?"

"Rose, locate Colonel Parva, tell him to get up to my office, I have a job for him."

"Yes sir."

"Then ring down to the Alert Center. Tell them I'm sending a Special Agent from the FBI down to them and I want them to drop what they are doing and pitch in and help this guy. He's on a very important case and the Bureau needs our help. Thank you Rose." He turned to the FBI man as he hung up the phone.

"You'll like working with this guy, he's pretty sharp, one of our best. Been with us for years."

"Who is he?"

"Name's Finley, Phil Finlay." Pravum called after him as he left. "Once you get set up I want hourly updates!"

*

Meanwhile, 35,000 feet in the air . . .

Now just over two hours into the flight neither Frank nor Irina had the emotional reserves to logically plan their next step.

Mahone had actually dozed off in the aisle seat while Irina stared at the clouds through the window.

Suddenly she was moved to elbow him in the side.

"Hey!"

"WHAT?!" He growled startled awake.

"I need you to know something."

"Right now?!"

"Just let me talk!"

"What? You really did steal secrets?"

"No!"

"You were once a man?"

"I'm trying to be serious here asshole!" She pouted in mock annoyance.

"I'm sorry, I'm listening." He apologised as he sat up straight. "Talk to me, I'll be serious." He repented. "Promise."

She took a moment to gather her thoughts and choose her words.

"I need you to know how much it means to me that you're sticking by me and really going out on a limb. I realize it could mean your career, your pension. Maybe prison. Thank you."

"Look, last time I was laid up in the hospital-"

"Last time? How many times you been shot?"

"I don't know, three or four. Like I was saying, last time I was laid up I had a lot of time to think. I knew it was only a matter of time before my wife bailed. She wasn't a bad woman, she just wasn't cut-out to be a cop's wife."

"Frank you don't need to-"

"Quit interrupting! I'm trying to be serious here. Asshole!"

"Sorry!" She tightly pursed her lips closed in an exaggerated manner.

"I swore off women, told myself they were too much trouble. Too high maintenance, not worth it." He took a long pause. "Then I got roped into the London assignment and just when I thought it was safe to go back in the water you had to happen. I guess what I'm trying to say is-"

She held up her finger for him to pause and flagged for the stewardess.

"Yes ma'am, what can I get you?"

"Stewardess, how long before we land?"

"About another two hours ma'am."

"Thank you."

At that Irina stood, took Frank by the hand and headed towards the back of the plane's executive bedroom.

They had to pass by the steward and stewardess sitting in the last of the rear seats.

"She's a federal agent, she wants to show me some FBI stuff." Frank quipped as the two passed by the crew members. "Hold all our calls would ya?"

They disappeared into the executive rear cabin.

*

Being on the lam and as the NSA had immediate access to everyone's travel information across the country, Mahone and Kuksova couldn't use their real names. This presented no issue using Parker's personal jet however, having now landed in Reno-Tahoe International they were still 45 minutes north of their destination Lake Tahoe, so a car rental was necessary.

Fortunately Irina still carried Sam O'Neill's Press pass.

Mahone had to wait outside the Hertz office and

the young clerk did several double takes at the photo I.D. but, being a millennial, was afraid to appear politically incorrect by questioning Kuksova so he said nothing.

A short story about her mother's credit card and 20 minutes later Irina exited the rental kiosk dangling the keys to a silver Ford Galaxy MPV.

Mahone followed her around back and was shocked to see the size of the multi-purpose vehicle.

"What'd you tell her, we brought the whole Girl Scout troop?!"

"A family vehicle attracts less attention, less suspicious." She casually informed. as she thrust him a sheaf of papers. He pulled the single pink sheet from the folder.

"What's this with the contract?" He asked.

"An LDW. Limited Damage Waiver." She explained. "Just because we're dangerous felons doesn't mean we can't be insured."

"Makes sense." He shrugged.

"By the way you're not insured for injury." She informed.

"Why not?"

"The clerk would have wanted to see your I.D."

"That's okay, when this is over I don't expect to be injured. I expect to be dead!" He commented as they climbed into the van.

The leisurely, scenic cruise down State Route 580 heading to South Lake was the first time in nearly eight hours either one of them had a chance to clear their heads and really relax.

As Irina drove they took in the stunning

mountain landscape generously painted with dense clusters of towering western pines. The crisp, clean alpine air was a welcome relief from the big city smog they'd left behind and a renewed sense of hope temporarily seeped into their future.

"I did some digging around on this guy Parker before we interviewed him." Frank let out.

"Uh huh?" She grunted as she negotiated the gently winding black top.

"Apparently his father is the reason we have functional radios in our cars. Some kind of electronic genius."

"Never really thought about that, how radios came to be in automobiles."

"Apparently he had some side enterprises as well."

"Like what?"

"The most famous hotel here is *Harrah's* converted from *George's Gateway Club* in the early 40's. Parker's father fronted half the $150,000 to build the place. Then back in '44 he was a major investor when they converted."

"I thought all the casinos were started by the Mob?!" She questioned.

"Not all of them. But Mob guys need backing investors too, not to mention front men."

"Questions best unasked, eh Watson?" She joked.

"Exactly Holmes!"

Just south of Lake Valley less than a mile inland where they rounded the south shore past the resorts, they found the spur road they were looking for and followed it to a custom, hand built cabin on a high point on the side of the mountain.

"Honey, we're home!" Frank mocked as they pulled in next to the rustic, two story structure.

While Frank and Irina were settling down in Parker's Tahoe cabin deciding their next move, the Squad were anything but idle...

*** * ***

Holiday Inn
Guest Lounge

After a clandestine phone call Frank received word from Parker, based on Malachi's investigation, to seek out and question a guy named 'Reagan', Mahone put the squad to work on the loose ends of Sam O'Neill's murder.

Gathered at the back table in the hotel lounge Inspector Morrissey brought The Squad up to speed and laid out his plan.

"This lad, Dr. Parker Frank and I interviewed had a problem. Coincidentally we had information to help him. We gave it to him and he appears to have reciprocated by having one of his people poke around and come up with a name. He is after sending it to us via a phone call to Frank."

"What name Chief?" Din asked.

"Nialls Reagan is the chap were looking into."

Morrissey scribbled out the name on a piece of paper and passed it around the table.

"Apparently he works for a susidiery of a rival corporation of Dr. Parker's called AstroCom. A chmical research laboratory called K&E."

"How did we track this geezer down" Heath pushed.

"Kuksova and Mahone found a list of AstroCom subsidiaries. There are three possibilities but this one being a chemical lab is our best bet. Additionally, we think he might be the last person to see Sam O'Neill alive."

"That all we have on him?" Heath asked.

"For now yes. Din, posing as a professor is going to make first contact with Reagan."

"Why do I have to be a professor?"

"Because you're Indian and, even though you're a Brit who sounds like he comes from the West End, you can do an Indian accent."

"I find that a bit racist." He protested.

"No, if I were being racist you would have asked something like, 'How was copper wire invented?' And I would have said, 'By two Indians fighting over a penny.'"

"Now that's racist!" Heath laughingly commented.

"Yeah, because Indians are so free with the money and never argue about the price, eh Din?" Tammy ribbed.

"Piss off!" He snapped.

"Pay attention!" Morrissey reminded. "You're going to ring up AstroCom and find this guy Reagan. You'll explain who you are and that you are setting up interviews with successful people in the pharmaceutical business for a lecture series for your students."

The Hermes Project

"What am I supposed to be a professor of?"

"Pharmaceutical economics."

"Oh brilliant! Why not astrophysics or better yet theoretical quantum mechanics?! I don't know anything about pharmaceutical economics!" Din protested.

"You don't have to. You're only setting up an appointment." Morrissey maintained his quiet demeanor.

"Yeah, you know like a glorified Indian secretary." Tammy again jibbed. Din was not amused.

"You know, I was just getting to like you!" Din shot back.

"Don't get too smug young lady! You're playing the student." Morrissey assigned.

"That's grand by me." Tammy shrugged.

"You've the most important job. You'll need to persuade Reagan into giving you a tour of the lab facility he works in. Being especially careful to get him to show you the lab area itself."

"What am I looking for?"

"Anything to do with or that might indicate there's work with amphibian or reptile toxin being pursued either on-premises or elsewhere."

"Can do!" She said.

Morrissey continued.

"Now, you'll need to sound like you know what you're talking about. To that end I'm having Enfield here do up a brief report on highlights in the pharmaceutical business over the last few years as well as an AstroCom business profile." Morrissey nodded towards Enfield sitting at the next table pecking away on his lap top. "That'll be your homework for the next day or so." Morrissey added.

"I should have it for you by dinner time this evening." Enfield assured her.

"Professor Din, you'll need to set up the phone interview tomorrow by ten. Here are the contact details for Reagan over at K&E Labs the AstroCom subsidiary."

"Right." Din replied.

"I won't let you down Inspector." Tammy assured her boss.

"See that you don't Sergeant! Because whether you all realize it or not, however this case turns out, it will make international headlines and that will have a profound effect on the future existence of this Squad!"

"Not to mention what the U.K. Press will write about us!" Enfield added.

The crew sat silent for a moment as the magnitude of what they were about to attempt sank in.

A group of British detectives attempting to solve a high profile murder case with no proper authorisation, legal powers, weapons or diplomatic protection in a foreign country with laws so convuluted that nobody seemed to actually know what they were. Including the American cops and lawyers.

To boot, it was a case involving the U.S. government.

"Din, you're going to hang around here and

assist Enfield." Din nodded his acknowledgement. "Tammy you are coming with me. Heath you can tag along if you like."

"Where are we going?" Tammy asked.

"Shopping."

"Shopping for what?"

"Wardrobe." Nigel replied. They all looked puzzled. "Wardrobe for our star player here." He clarified.

"What's wrong with me clothes I'm wearin'?" Tammy protested indicating her red flannel shirt, exposed tattooed forearms, faded Levis and work boots. Morrissey took in a breath before replying.

"When you eventually meet Mr. Reagan you will have to look more like a serious economics student and less like a lesbian biker."

Din, Heath and Enfield all had a good laugh.

"Fuck off the lot of ya!" Tammy snapped.

****

K&E Biopharmaceuticals Inc.
116 46th Avenue & 11th Street
Long Island City
New York, New York

The 40 minute train ride from Hoboken, New Jersey over to Long Island City required only a single changeover at 23rd Street in Manhattan.

Tammy, dressed in saddle shoes, white knee socks and a flowered dress with her short hair in twin, short stubby ponytails was seated between

Heath and Morrissey across from Enfield and Din.

She caught Din and Enfield fighting back smirks as they looked away.

"One word out of any of you wankers and that'll be me foot up yer arse!" She threatened.

The B train from Manhattan dropped them a mere four blocks away from their destination on the corner of 46th Avenue and 11th Street.

Once up on the street level they found the New York street numbering system extremely convenient in contrast to the often confusing double or repeat names of the London streets particularly when prefixed by the adjectives 'Upper' or 'Lower'.

Accompanied by Enfield, Heath and Morrissey, predictably it was Enfield despite having never set foot anywhere in New York City before, who took it upon himself to act as tour guide as they walked.

"Interesting fact: LIC was an independent city from 1870 until 1898 when it was incorporated into the city of New York. I wouldn't be surprised if the place we're looking for is an old, 19th Century factory building due to the fact that this was largely a factory area until 2001 when it was rezoned from an industrial area into residential properties which is when the current gentrification -"

"Enfield I have a question."

"Sure Heath what is it?" He answered as they walked.

"Do you ever come up for fuckin' air?"

Finally standing across the street from the six storey, 19th Century industrial building, #116 on the corner of 4 6th and 11th, Enfield leaned over to

Heath.

"Sergeant Heath, I have a question."

"Yeah, what?"

"What kind of building would you say that is? Architecturally speaking that is?"

By way of an answer sergeant Heath brandished his middle finger.

"Right MacIntyre! The lads and myself will be across the street in that coffee shop, meet us in there when you think you have what we need."

"Got it!"

"Remember, Roberta Burns, Columbia School of Economics, Junior level, Professor Din. Questions? Comments? Snide remarks? No? Good, go get 'em Girlie!"

Before she stepped into the street to cross over to the warehouse Enfield took Tammy squarely by the shoulders, made eye contact and spoke.

"GPO?" He spat.

"Group Purchasing Organisation!" She shot back.

"A.P.A.?"

"American Pharmaceutical Association."

"What is OECD data?"

"Gives the pharmaceutical economic index." She recited.

"She's ready!" He declared patting her on the shoulder.

"You sure about me accent?" She nervously asked Morrissey.

"You're an exchange student! Just think Pharmaceuticals! They have drugs in Glasgow, don't they?" He encouraged.

"Only in every pub, shop or street corner!" She shot back.

"Then I suspect they should have pharmacies as well!"

Minutes later MacIntyre was across the street and upstairs in the K&E labs where a receptionist showed her into Mr. Reagan's office.

"Mr. Reagan? Roberta Burns, third year Economics." Tammy advanced with hand extended.

"Ahh! You must be my student! Nialls Reagan, glad to meet you. Come in and have a seat." He invited.

"So you're doing economics at Columbia?"

"Yes, yes I am."

"I had a girlfriend who went there." He volunteered.

"Are you married?"

"Girlfriend, but we broke up."

"That's too bad! Was she in pharmaceuticals?" Tammy pushed.

"No, no she wasn't. Tell me, is Dr. Hendrix still head of the Economics Department?"

"Well, I only transferred in this semester, but I think I understand he's been bumped up to Assistant Dean." She lied keeping it vague enough to leave breathing room.

"So, Professor Din tells me you've been assigned a paper. How can I help? What exactly is your topic?"

For the second time in nearly as many minutes MacIntyre was compelled into some mental gymnastics.

The Hermes Project

"Well when I started the program I was interested in overall effects of pharmaceutical sales on regional economies. But since this COVID thing hit everything's sort of become a tossed salad hasn't it? Perhaps you might suggest something? A student'd be a fool not to take your advice!"

Her not so clandestine appeal to his ego worked.

"Well then maybe something with COVID?" He suggested. She feigned reluctance.

"Most of my classmates are doing something with COVID. I prefer something more original."

"Such as?"

"Well, latest breakthroughs and how they might affect the market." She casually mentioned.

"Ahh, projections! That might be interesting for you."

"Without revealing anything too secret, what are K&E playing around with these days?"

"We have a couple of projects in the works but nothing I can talk about at present." He confessed. "Why don't we take a stroll around, discuss some options then maybe something will come to mind."

"I'd like that very much, if it's not too much trouble!"

"Not at all!" He ushered her out of the small office and into the the wide open spacious room of the adjoining lab.

There were a dozen white-coated techs moving about in between the five rows of black-topped lab tables all bedecked with racks and numerous collections of glassware.

"Wow! This is impressive!" She enthusiastically

declared.

"Each bench is dedicated to a category of project, all industrial based." Reagan informed.

Carefully perusing the vast work space, MacIntyre did her best to spot anything that might be associated with frogs, reptiles or the like.

Coming on the third bench her observations were rewarded. On the shelf above the bench was a neat row of about twenty small vials all labelled with an uppercase initial followed by a Latin name.

MacIntyre may not have finished school but she recognised the labels as scientific names of animal species.

"Mr. Reagan?"

"Call me Nialls."

"Nialls, would it be asking too much if I could use my phone to take a few pictures?"

"Sure, down here's no problem, but if we go upstairs I can't allow photos. Too many classified projects."

"I understand completely. I'd just like a few mementoes and maybe one for the school newspaper. I know some of the people I work with will be very interested in some of the things youse're doin' here."

Utilising the bright light from the large industrial windows Tammy was sure to obtain close shots of the rack of vials from several angles in between a half dozen other irrelevant photos to camouflage her actions.

As a final cover she requested one of the techs take a few snaps of her and Reagan posing as if on holiday or transacting business together.

Another twenty to twenty-five minutes was spent on idle chit chat, MacIntyre manipulating Reagan into suggesting a project for her and ending in her finally thanking him for his time.

"I'll be sure to credit K&E and yourself in my paper!" She offered as they shook hands.

Forty-five minutes after departing their company Sergeant Tammy MacIntyre was back with her squad colleagues in the coffee shop.

Later that afternoon, back at the hotel, Morrissey set Enfield and Din to work on listing the Latin names from the lab vials Tammy had photographed so they could start researchig them.

Meanwhile Morrissey focused on contacting Dr. Jackson at the Coroner's office to verify the exact species of toxin used to murder Sam O'Neill.

"Dr. Jackson, Inspector Morrissey here,"

"Inspector glad you called. I sent a copy of the list and photo you emailed me of all the vials on the shelf to the National Reptile Research Centre. I was able to consult with Dr. Lillian Allen, daughter of the leading herpetologist Dr. Ross Allen of the the Herpetology Institute in Silver Springs, Florida. I got back a quite interesting report."

"You have my ear Doctor."

"All twenty are toxin extracts from reptiles or amphibians."

"Why would a small subsidiary of a space company have such a wide collection of animal toxins available?"

"Hard to say but it's not unfathomable.

AstroCom is a multifaceted conglomerate and medical research is quiet lucrative these days. Snake toxin is needed to produce anti-venom while amphibian toxins have a wide variety of applications. The treatment of infectious bites, heart disease, hemorrhage, as anti-inflammatories, certain forms of cancer. They've even had some success with the treatment of AIDS."

"Interesting. Were you able to speciate any of them?"

"Ten of the names belonged to species of reptiles, primarily snakes. The others were species of amphibians. Only two of which were frogs, both toxic, both dart frogs."

"Dart frogs?"

"Yes. *P. terribilis* and *R. ventrimaculata* both examples of the reticulated dart frog. I'll email you over the details."

"Much appreciated."

At that Morrissey signaled the others scattered around the room to gather at his table as he lay his mobile down and switched it to intercom. Jackson continued.

"Basically there are two types of biological toxins which occur in nature. Neurotoxins and hemotoxins. Most toxins are a combination of both. As the names imply neuro toxins affect the nerves shutting down vital functions such as respiratory and cardiac ability while hemotoxins attack the blood and prevent platelets from attaching to fibrinogen and closing the wound."

"So the bite victim bleeds to death?" Heath

inquired.

"Exactly."

"Did the autopsy find massive internal hemorrhage?" Enfield pushed,

"No, not according to the report. Your victim died of either cardiac or respiratory arrest, probably a combination of both."

"Anything else Doctor?"

"I sent the folks in Florida a spectrographic read out of the blood sample we took and they sent a return message stating that while it's not possible to be 100% certain which species the toxin originated from it was most likely *P. terribilis*."

"Sounds quite nasty!" Morrissey commented.

"Most aposematic features are."

"What's that, a-post-traumatic?" Heath asked.

"Apo-se-matic. Naturally evolved defence mechanisms. Spines, a slimy jell coating, bright pigmentation, repulsive odors."

"Repulsive odors! Kind'a like some'a you lot!" Tammy mumbled just loud enough.

Heath gave her a swat on the shoulder.

"It's toxin is produced by mites it ingests." Jackson added.

"How toxic, exactly doctor?" Enfield queried.

"Extracted from the parotid glands and manufactured from the mites they eat the average amount of poison can vary but it is estimated that 1 mg is enough to kill ten to twenty persons or two bull elephants,"

"Christ! And I thought my wife's cooking was bad!" Enfield declared.

"If it matters, both are generally thought to be exclusive to Colombia." Jackson concluded.

"Thank Christ for that!" Heath echoed.

"Dr Jackson, appreciate all your help."

"Glad I could be of service."

"Well boys and girls," Morrissey announced. "It would appear whe are one step closer to scoring a goal!"

CHAPTER EIGHTEEN

It was less than a week from the time Frank and Irina first arived at the cabin that, through sheer coincidence, the inevitable happened.

Irina was spotted.

The fact that Irina Kuksova stood nearly five feet nine inches tall, sported a very fit body and had long blonde hair had up until that point in her life always been an advantage. People, especially men, noticed her everywhere she went.

Unfortunately today the wrong man noticed her.

The middle-aged white guy in the dark, charcoal grey, three piece suit leaned over and nudged the middle-aged black guy in the light, charcoal grey, three piece suit as they sat in the window seat of the local mom and pop restaurant eating lunch on Lake Tahoe Boulevard which skirted the South Lake.

"What?" The black guy grunted through a mouthful of cheeseburger.

"Across the street trying not to look so blonde." He directed. "The one in the ski jacket, dark slacks and shades."

His partner briefly squinted and watched as the female turned into the *Ross Dress For Less* discount clothing store.

"You think that's one of them?" The black guy postulated.

"Only one way to find out!"

There were two things neither Frank or Irina took into account. One, although they believed their burner phones could not be monitored, Daniel

Parker's and his partner Malachi's could be.

Secondly, Mahone forgot that it ain't what you don't know that will hurt you, it's what you know absolutely for sure that ain't true that will jump up and bite you in the ass every time!

Narrowed down to a specific area and a few thousand VPNs, it is possible for the NSA to track burner phones.

A short 48 hours after Mahone and Kuksova landed in Nevada the NSA electronic surveillance unit intercepted and reported a conversation with Malachi assuring Parker the two had arrived safely in Reno. A simple series of phone calls from D.C. to the Vegas office relaying that a BOLO request for the Reno-Tahoe area be put out and the hunt was on.

Minutes after spotting her it was in traditional Hollywood style that the two agents burst through the front door of the clothing shop, weapons drawn intending to affect an arrest.

However, the expanse of the open floor plan slammed the brakes on their immediate efforts. The fact that there was a downstairs served to complicate matters.

The agents split up and searched both floors at once including the dressing rooms, toilets and underneath the clothing racks.

All their efforts yielded them was nearly being shot and arrested when, thanks to a panic stricken mother of two who manned her cell phone and reported crazy men brandishing weapons in the store, the Tahoe PD arrived.

There were two things neither of the FBI field

agents took into account.

First, they were told they were dealing with two rogue cops they were assured were not as smart as the FBI.

And secondly, they forgot that it ain't what you don't know that will hurt you. It's what you know absolutely for sure that ain't true that will get you!

Once clear of the Tahoe village center Irina texted Frank:

Stormtroopers on the prowl in Tahoe.

He texted back:

Meet me at the hospital.

This was a prearranged code should they have to abandon the cabin on short notice or become separated.

St. Vincent's Hospital was a prominent New York landmark as well as the name used in a popular film they both enjoyed. But in this context it referred to *Vinny's Pizzeria* the nearest thing to a New York pizzeria for miles.

Being early afternoon *Vinny's*, a corner eatery, was less than half full, however a corner table up front afforded them a 270 degree field of vision and the ability to detect the approach of any 'Stormtroopers'. Plus there was a back door.

"There were two of them, one black one white." She explained. "One late middle age the other middle-aged. Both closer to retirement then from the start of their careers."

"Did they call for back-up?" Frank probed.

"I didn't stick around to find out but I didn't hear any sirens or see dark vehicles closing in."

"Do they even have an office in Tahoe?" Frank speculated.

"Not that I know of but I think there's one in Reno." Irina confirmed.

"How big?"

"Not positive. But if there is I'm pretty sure it wouldn't be larger than a couple of agents, maybe a secretary." She ventured. "But there's a fair sized one in Vegas."

"They could call in back up from Vegas?" He queried.

"Only about 100 agents." She sarcasticlly quipped. "And they could be here in a matter of hours."

"That's not good!"

"More if reinforced from L.A." She added.

"This just keeps getting better and better!"

Although well out of ear shot of any other customers Irina leaned in and spoke softly to Frank.

"At some point we are going to have to go back in, you know that don't you?"

"I realize that. But we're not getting in the pool until we know the temperature of the water!"

She sat back and stared at him.

"You have a way with metaphors that makes a girl feel all warm and fuzzy inside. You know that?"

"Really?"

"NO! What the hell kind of plan is that?!" She

loudly chastized. "'No swimming until we know the water!' What are you, Elton John all of a sudden?!"

"I was thinking more like Jim Morrison actually."

As she slumped down in her chair and crossed her arms he realised she was clearly shaken by their current situation and the fact that everything she had worked for over the last decade could soon be snatched from her. All on a fabricated premise.

"Wait here. Get another coffee." He suggested as he rose to leave.

"Where're you going?!"

"To check in with Morrissey, see how they're getting on."

"You think that's a good idea now that they know where we are?"

"If their closest office is in Vegas it will be at least tomorrow morning until they can have people here."

"What about agents in Reno?" She challend.

"They always like to attack en mass, early in the morning with lots of guns and their friends at CNN tagging along. It doesn't sound like the two Jamokes on the street positively made you so they'll be hesitant to call it in without verification. So I think we're okay until the morning. I'll be right back."

Irina looked no less concerned. She ordered another cup of coffee while Frank stepped outside and took to his cell phone.

"Nigel? It's Frank."

"Frank! I was wondering when I might hear

from you! How are you two holding up?"

"We've been better. What's the latest?"

"Your plan worked like a dream. We sent Sergeant MacIntyre in posing as an econ student. She got photos in the lab of multiple vials of frog toxins."

"Fantastic! Blood-species matches?"

"Jackson at the Coroner's office cross matched blood samples with one of the species of toxins. They matched."

"So we have method. Now we need opportunity." Mahone added.

"More good news! Our friend Parker did some digging and discovered that Miss O'Neill was apparently keeping regular company with this Reagan fellow, the last one to see her alive that night."

"Interesting."

"According to Parker's man Malachi, they had a bit of a blow out that night." Nigel informed.

"Too thin. Thousands of couples fight every night."

"True, but they don't stab each other in the back with a syringe full of biological toxin."

"Also true but we still need to show clear motive." Frank insisted.

"So I've been told. Got any theories?"

"Well the obvious possibility is that she was onto something, something she wasn't meant to be onto."

"Sounds logical. But we still have to prove it!" Morrissey agreed.

"Listen I don't want to talk too long on this line.

The Hermes Project

I think the feds are on to us."

"You mean you think they know where you are?"

"Yeah. Have a couple of your guys write up a preliminary report on everything we've got so far. I'll be in touch." Frank hung up and returned to an anxious Irina.

"Well?" She pushed.

"Morrissey thinks they located the poison used to kill O'Neill."

"Really?!"

"Additionally, Daniel Parker connected O'Neill to this Reagan guy."

"Who?" Irina questioned.

"Head of the lab they found the poison in."

"At least there's some good news!" She quietly sighed.

"Yeah, but now I need to find a motive."

"She was a reporter. Maybe she was digging too deep? Came across something she wasn't supposed to see?"

"That was my first guess but . . ." Mahone lurted out.

"But what?"

"The Columbian thing. The dart frog, the frog that makes the poison is only found in Colombia." He suddenly realised.

"So?" She asked.

Without warning Mahone jumped up and ran back outside. A dumbfounded Irina just stared and shrugged.

"I'll just wait here then, shall I?" She quipped to his empty chair as he ducked back out the door and redialed his phone.

"Nigel?"

"Frank?"

"Irina told me last year about some rebel insurgent group down in Colombia the FBI were looking into."

"The FARC. Yes, MI6 were on to them as well. So?" Nigel added.

"Nigel hold one!" Mahone said before ducking back into the pizzeria. He leaned over the table close in to Irina.

"Can you still get access to INTERPOL?"

"Probably not now no. Why, don't you?"

"Not without going through my chief. Be right back!" He ducked back outside. "Nigel, do you have access to INTERPOL?"

"Yes why?"

"They always say follow the money!" Mahone declared.

"You been drinking?"

"Not yet. INTERPOL has access to the International Bank. The IB has access to international transactions. If all AstroCom is getting from Colombia is some poisonous frogs for medical research no big deal. But my genetically embedded Irish suspicions thinks there might be something else."

"Like what?" Morrissey pushed.

By way of an answer Mahone sang his response to the tune of the song *Cocaine*.

"If you wanna hang out, you've gotta take her out-"

The Hermes Project

"Take who out? You sure you're not on the John Barleycorn?"

"Drugs, illegal arms deals, human trafficking I don't know Nigel! I'm making this up as I go along! Work with me here will ya? You're supposed to be one of the best so help me out!"

"Okay, okay! I think I see what you're at. Bank records from INTERPOL."

"Give that man a cigar! With **you** contacting INTERPOL anyone who might be snooping around asking questions will not likely connect what you're doing with the NYPD."

"I've worked with several of the senior officers down in Lyon. From which angle do you suggest I approach them?"

"Request a check on any reports or investigations into illegal activity between the U.S. and Colombia including drug transactions or busts in the last six months."

"Easy enough."

"One small favor when you get time. Pop over to the precinct and explain to Chief Wachowski what's been going on. That is if I still have a job."

"If you two are coming back any time soon how are you going to travel? You obviously can't take commercial air and they are no doubt canvassing the rental agencies for your car."

"Haven't figured that one yet brother. But keep a light on in the window, we'll contact you as soon as we can. And Nigel?"

"Yes Frank?"

"We're on the clock on this one partner!"

"Then we should stop wasting time flapping our gobs!" Nigel hung up.

"Asshole!" Frank smiled and shook his head as he hung up and headed back inside.

Just as he took his seat his phone buzzed to indicate he had an incoming text message.

Given that the only person who had the number to his burner phone besides Morrissey was sitting at the table across from him, Frank and Irina exchanged startled glances.

Seconds later Irina's burner phone received a message as well. They compared phones.

The messages were identical.

*

Working down in the NSA Alert Center Phil Finley had located and been monitoring Mahone's phone on and off.

When Finley tracked the detective's phone to that of an FBI agent, namely Kuksova and then the number of a man tentatively identified as being from Scotland Yard, Phil's inner amateur sleuth got the better of him.

When Mahone's phone stopped transmitting a few days later Finley became suspicious so he fired up HERMES and, claiming to be working out bugs in the system, scanned traffic until he found a burner phone number that suspiciously activated within a minute of Mahone's regular phone shutting down. Utilising his knowledge of metadata Finley came to a conclusion.

The Hermes Project

What began as an innocent game of Cat and Mouse to test his HERMES program had now deepened into a more serious unauthorised adjunct to a well publicized murder investigation. Mr. Finley now found himself between the proverbial rock and a hard place.

That evening on duty in the Alert Center, he had just picked up Morrissey and Mahone's second telephone conversation.

Being fully aware that the FBI had received a BOLO report as well as an APB and given that he worked for the NSA, if he didn't report what he knew he would be SOL.

However, given what he thought he knew about his boss General Pravum, he was conflicted about what he was about to do. But he did it anyway.

Quickly retrieving Mahone's burner phone number Phil typed out a short message. Then locating Kuksova's burner number he repeated the same message.

Feds have ur 20.
A friend. For S.O.

Finley had been ordered by Pravum to work with the FBI on locating Kuksova and Mahone.

Now he not only had their phone numbers but a set of six digit geo-coordinates as to their location in the Lake Tahoe area.

After sending the warning to Mahone and Kuksova he dutifully forwarded the following location coordinates up to Pravum:

39.0968° N, 120.0324° W

****

Two hours and fifty-five minutes after Finley's message to Pravum a fully loaded Black Hawk helicopter, launched from Travis AFB, was racing in at tree top level gradually climbing the mountain side deep in the Sierra Nevadas.

Careful to keep pace with the two black SUVs below him speeding up the single lane dirt road towards the sole mountainside structure, the pilot maintained radio communications with the ground-based strike force.

"Cabin compound cited! 500 meters ahead. You'll see it on your right hand side in a minute." He transmitted.

The chopper gently maintained his hover over the parking lot as the two SUVs skidded to a halt in front of the single storey wooden structure. The 16 agents, all dressed in combat gear surrounded the building while a breaching team burst through the front door.

The lone Hispanic worker in the white apron looked up from mopping the floor, dropped the earphones from his ears, leaned on his mop and stared.

"We no open till six!" He called over. "Meeting start then!"

Following a 20 minute, in-depth search of what appeared to be some kind of improvised holy-rollers church, the assault commander declared the place a dry hole and ordered a full withdrawal.

The last thing he saw in the SUV's rear view mirror as they headed back down the mountain was the the club's sign.

The Truth Cartel
Experimental Reggae Club
5th Re-Born Productions

Unbeknownst to Pravum and his cohorts Finley had correctly located the fugitives at Lake Tahoe as ordered. However, in sending the coordinates upstairs to the General's office he accidentally-on-purpose switched the latitude and longitude with each other.

By that time Mahone and Kuksova where safely back in their mountain cabin miles away tucked in for the night.

During his unauthorised scans, Finley also picked up some of Pravum's calls with AstroCom as well as two traced back to a known FARC leader.

What Phil Finley had no way of knowing was that he really didn't know half of what he thought he knew about his boss Pravum.

He would soon find out.

****

It was just before 2 a.m. when the black SUV Suburban cut its headlights as it took the last turn on the dirt road before slowing then stopping just short of the cabin's driveway.

A passenger disembarked and gingerly made his way the last 100 meters up to the driveway and crept quietly up to the rear of the parked car at the top.

Being careful to maintain a low profile he produced a pen light from his pocket and examined the rear licence plate. He then returned back down to the SUV.

"That's it alright!" He queitly reported to the driver. "Silver Ford Galaxy MPV. Plates match."

FBI policy strictly prohibited any agent or two man team of agents from attempting to apprehend armed suspects without clearance or backup.

However, the tenacity and quest for glory of the two agents who had spotted Irina earlier that day and chased her through the clothing store far exceeded their loyalty to bureau policy.

Besides, the mounting frenzy back at The Bureau would magnify their heroism if they were the ones to bag this double collar!

At the same time as visions of grandeur danced in the two agents' heads egging them on, Mahone lying next to Irina was startled awake by what he thought was a noise outside.

Clapping a hand over her mouth she awakened to see him signaling for her to keep quiet.

"Where's your weapon?" He quietly whispered. She pointed to her Glock lying on the night stand next to her. "Ammo?" He whispered as they both climbed from the bed already fully dressed. He donned his shoulder holster.

"One mag." She whispered back. He passed her a box of shells from his coat draped over a chair next to the bed then gingerly proceeded to climb out the window. She moved to follow. They heard muffled but obvious footsteps on the front porch then moving around to the rear of the house.

He pointed to the wooden chair. She passed it out the window then climbed through herself.

Signalling for her to wait on the side of the house it was with his weapon drawn that he crept around front when he heard the front door creak closed followed by the rear door.

Now confident whoever they were were inside the house he returned for the chair and Irina and they quickly but quietly made their way to the front pausing only enough time for him to place the chair lying down in the dark at the top of the front porch stairs.

Stealthfully making their way over to their MPV he spotted the agents' SUV through the trees down the hill and indicated for Irina to head down to the intruders' suburban.

Meanwhile he quickly crept into the rental car, inserted the key into the ignition then broke it off before heading down the driveway to climb into the black suburban with Irina just as they heard the two hapless agents noisily rummage around in the cabin.

Frank carefully released the emergency brake and shifting to neutral drifted the SUV back down the hill as far as possible before reaching under the dash and yanking the wiring array down and hot wiring the ignition.

They drove off in the direction of the lake.

"Where did a cop learn to hot wire a car?" Irina asked.

"I wasn't always a cop. Besides, I had a Puerto Rican partner once."

Meanwhile, finding no one home the two agents dashed out of the house tripping over the chair on the porch in the dark.

At the bottom of the drive the two men discovered their SUV gone and quickly scurried, one scurried one limped, back up the drive and into the rental silver rental van.

Quickly producing a Leatherman tool from his pocket the pudgy one attempted to insert the flat head screwdriver into the ignition slot. It wouldn't go.

Undaunted he reached under the dash and yanked down the wiring then hot wired the vehical.

"Where'd you learn to hot wire a car?"

"I'm half Puerto Rican!" He joked.

Almost two miles away, backed up into the forest away from the road,sitting in the SUV, Irina finally began to calm as, 10 minutes later they watched from up the hill, between the trees as the silver Ford rental van whizzed past 100 meters away down on the road.

Frank and Irina exchanged glances.

"That was too God damned close!" She sighed.

They sat quietly in the dark for a few minutes to collect themselves until Mahone finally spoke.

"Comments, suggestions snide remarks?"

"Whatever we decide we should make a decision

before sun up." Irina suggested.

"Agreed. What's the time?"

"Nearly three."

"Which gives us about three and a half, four hours to find a way out."

"Well, Parker's plane is gone and we can't fly commercial. A bus would take a week." She pointed out.

"And we can't drive a stolen FBI van around the country." He pointed out.

"Who said this was an FBI van?!" She asked as she quickly opened and dug through the glove box papers. "Shit!" She cursed.

"What'd you find?"

"It's an FBI van!" She brandished the registration papers. "Out of the Vegas Office."

"Vegas?!" Mahone parroted.

"Must have been a couple of cowboys gone rogue trying to get themselves a medal!" She speculated.

"Now they know how it feels to have their private shit raided and stolen." Mahone quipped.

"Yeah, yeah, blah, blah, blah! Tick tock Mahone, tick tock!" She made no attempt to mask her mounting irritation. "How do you see us getting out of here?" She pushed.

He thought for a moment.

"Now that Morrissey and The Squad have uncovered this guy Reagan maybe it is time to go back in and fight it out."

"Thank you! How exactly?"

"Well . . ." He pondered. "Sometimes old

technology is the best!" He opined.

"What the hell's that supposed to mean?"

"I'll explain on the way." He put the van in gear and headed back down the narrow dirt road.

"Where're we going?"

"To hideout until it's time for the train to leave. "

****

After driving the SUV into the deserted town they pulled into a Cadillac dealership lot with a van section, parked among them and shut down the van.

Not far from the train station they walked leaving the van in the lot but, just before departing Mahone snatched the small sign from one of the used cars and stuck it under the wiper blade of the windshield of the SUV.

"Brand New. Low Mileage. $9,998! Over priced if you ask me!" Irina said aloud.

They walked in the chill of the night opposite the lake front past closed shops for about ten minutes until they came to the train station.

Essentially unchanged, architecturally speaking, since the 1940's the single storey Amtrak station in Tahoe was occupied by one drunk asleep on a bench, several vending machines and a ticket window with a sign which read, 'Closed'.

From a schedule pamphlet on the wall Mahone read the timetable. Out at 06:10 and due in to Moynihan Station in Midtown, Manhattan at 0700 Thursday morning, they both now stood just inside the door of the single platform of the mini-station house.

Reno Nevada to New York City travel time by train, two and half days, was not the most expedient mode of transport but required no I.D. to purchase tickets. Additionally, they felt the time could be utilised to mentally organise events to date, catch their breaths and construct a defence for the legal hell they knew they were both destined to face.

"I'm still not clear on this text we got? Who could have sent it?" Irina puzzled staring at her phone.

"'20' is PD speak for location." Frank answered keeping an eye on the rest of the small station. He spotted no CCTV. "So it was either Morrissey or our new best buddy at the NSA."

"Finley?! Why would he-" Frank waited for the answer to crystallize in her mind. "Then 'S.O.' must be Sam O'Neill! Which means Finley's actually ready to turn whistle-blower!" She mumbled half to herself half aloud.

"So easy even an FBI agent can do it." Mahone quipped. "It may take you some time but you get there in the end."

"I'll tell you what else is going to take some time wise guy! The next time you and I get to fool around under the sheets!"

"Only joking! Don't go getting all sensitive on me now."

"Not sensitive, just being wifely. I assmed we're supposed to be posing as a married couple!" She challenged.

At twenty minutes before the train's arrival time an attendant slid open the shutter on the single ticket window and they made their way over.

"Two tickets for the 6:10 to New York."

"You do know the 6:10 goes by way of Chicago sir?"

"No problem. Two for coach please."

"Ask if the train has internet!" She quietly egged on.

"Yes ma'am." The ticket clerk informed. "Car D has a dedicated office work space in the rear half of the car. However, there is an additional $40 per ticket surcharge."

"No problem, my husband will be glad to pay, won't you Honey?" She said as she hung on his arm and smiled broadly up at him. 'Honey' was not amused.

"Sorry sir, if I may suggest, for the price of two coach tickets you can purchase one sleeper compartment and access to the office car is included as is breakfast."

"Sounds good." Frank agreed as he slid his Master card across the counter.

The Hermes Project

CHAPTER NINETEEN

Somewhere between Reno, Nevada & Salt Lake City...

As Frank and Irina hadn't slept since two a.m. that morning they retired to their sleeper compartment in Car B, showered and slept until dinner time.

Next morning after eating breakfast they sat out in the lounge car to discuss their plan and refine the details. Following that they retired to the office car which was essentially a converted Pullman partially insulated to minimize external noise. The space featured five work stations each with a keyboard, a monitor, small table and chair.

Alone in the car they pulled up two chairs to one of the available computers and set to work.

"So where do you want to start?" She asked as she entered the access code on her ticket stub.

"Well you're the computer genius so I think you should start by tracking down the list of all the subsidiaries of AstroCom we aalready have and see where that takes us."

"Glad I thought of that!" She chirpped out.

Irina dove into the keyboard and started her search. Fifteen minutes later she located a list of the licence certifications for AstroCom Corporation Inc. There were three: AstroCom, K&E Pharmaceuticals and Excel Electronics, Ltd.

"Ltd? That's interesting. You don't see too many Ltd's in the U.S." Frank pointed out.

"Maybe they're British?" She speculated.

"Or Canadian." He added.

"Could be. I'll call it up, let's see what they do."

"Probably something to do with electronics." He quipped.

"Can't get nothin' by you detective." She then read from the homepage. "'Excel Electronics is one of the nation's top suppliers of LED drivers, industrial ballasts, transformers, blah, blah, blah and industrial GPS control systems'."

"GPS control systems?" He questioned.

"With the commercial market in GPS unit components dominated by the car manufacturers and aeroplane companies they've come to be primarily used in satellites now." Irina explained.

"AstroCom specializes in satellites so no surprise there." Mahone noted. "I thought you were a code systems analyst? Where'd you learn about satellite components?" He asked.

"A few years back, before I was posted to London, there was an investigation into the illegal sales of electronic components to a known FARC associate."

"Details please?" He pushed.

"In the port of Cartagena, Colombian customs seized an unregistered container with various contraband items inside."

"Such as?" He pushed.

"Various guns, mainly second-hand Kalashnikovs, some drugs and a bunch of electronic devices Interpol tech people listed as LRA's." She explained.

The Hermes Project

"What the hell's an LRA?"

"A Laser Range Amplifier. They're primarily manufactured to be fitted onto satellites."

"What the would a terrorist organization do with satellite parts? The FARC cases you were working on certainly didn't reveal any satellites! Hell, I don't even think the Colombian government have satellites, do they?"

"They have a pilot program but no rockets or rocket capability. So no, not really." She informed.

"So, what happened?"

"So we were never able to put it together. We concluded either the Colombians had a secret program we didn't know about, they were planning one or they were selling the components off to somebody else."

As they worked a 30-something entered the car, took a seat at the end of the row and started up playing *Grand Theft Auto*, Frank and Irina moved in closer to their monitor.

"So the investigation just fizzled out?" He guessed.

"Not exactly. The FBI team working on it were reassigned."

"Reassigned to what?" He pushed. "What's more critical then stopping the commies or terrorists from getting satellite lasers?"

She looked down with embarrassment as she answered.

"They were . . . reassigned to Shiff's Trump Russia hoax investigation."

"OH PERFECT!" He slapped the desk causing

the gamer to jump. "80 to 100 agents off on a political snipe hunt! Good thing that fucking base was covered huh? How'd that work out for you guys?!" He demanded.

At Mahone's outburst the over aged video game player briefly lifted his headphones and looked up from his game but immediately turned away when met with a confrontational stare from Frank.

"Don't blame me!" Irina vigorously defended. "I wasn't in on that hoax shit! I wasn't even in London until I got tangled up in your armored car bullshit!" She snapped back. "I was just out of training at The Academy in 2016!" She defended.

Mahone breathed in deeply and sat back in his chair.

"I'm sorry." He sighed. "I know you had nothing to do with it. It was all the upper echelon assholes who propagated that shit."

Irina nodded in affirmation of his apology.

"Why do you hate the FBI so much?" She probed careful to make direct eye contact. He met her gaze.

Having never openly delved into this territory before, Frank hesitated before he spoke.

"Rollo Tomasi." He answered.

"Rollo Tomasi? From the movie? *L.A. Confidential*?"

"When Ed Exley explains to Jack Vincennes that his father was murdered and how the killer got away with it and was never caught, he goes on to explain that he assigned the guy a fictitious name so he could -"

"Yeah, Rollo Tomasi, but I'm not following." She shrugged. He resumed.

"The FBI are supposed to be the world's premier law enforcement agency. Growing up and reading about them was one of the things made me want to be a cop. Now that I'm grown up and wearing a badge, I find out the upper echelons of the Bureau are not only riddled with crooks but refuse to investigate the Rollo Tomasis in government."

"Like who?" She pushed.

"Shiff, Harris, Pelosi. . . Fauchi!"

"Because they always get away with it?" She ventured to ask.

"Exactly! The only thing that seems to change are the names!" He spat out as he glanced across the space to see that the video gamer geek was still draped in his over-sized headphones chasing unarmed pedestrians down a city side walk. "I fuckin' hate bullies, of any kind. I get even more pissed off when I think of the political manipulation of things that hurt innocent people!"

"Like what?" She sought to keep him venting as a means of catharsis.

"Like this defund bullshit. The self-imposed border 'crises' Mayorkas has propagated!"

"Propagated and gotten away with!" She unexpectedly reinforced. Mahon pulled back in surprise and stared.

"Is someone coming over to the dark side?" He joked to her.

"I meant 'getting away with it'." She defended. "Just like these assholes are going to get away with it if we don't do our job, agreed?" She coaxed.

He smiled and nodded.

"I guess there really are times when a man should never argue with a woman." He jokingly confessed.

"This is definitely one of those times!" She admitted. "Back to work!" She whispered.

"Of the three company names on that list of subsidiaries is there a way to back check companies AstroCom has dealt with directly?" He asked.

"It would take some time but, yes I can do that."

"Good. First off, where were these LRA's heading?" He asked. Again she typed away for awhile before sitting back and smiling.

"Found one!"

"Who?"

"I'll give you three guesses but you're only gonna need one!" Kuksova said.

"The Red Chinese!"

"Bingo! Our good old friends at the PRC!" She confirmed.

"FARC wasn't using the technology! They were selling it on to the PRC!" Frank deduced.

"It gets better!" She announced after about another minute or so of searching. "It appears the Interpol investigators in Lyon reported the receiving address on the shipping docket was redacted but, the port of origin address was in New York."

"Is there a street address?"

"One one six 11th Street and 46th Avenue." She read from the screen.

"Son-of-a-bitch!" He quietly sighed.

"You know it?"

"Not for certain but I'll bet dollars to doughnuts that's the same building where Morrissey's folks traced the frog toxin to."

"And that guy Reagan!" She realized aloud.

"And that guy Reagan." Frank affirmed.

"We should be cops!" Irina declared offering a high five. "Okay, what's next?"

"See what else we can find as far as companies dealing with AstroCom."

She again typed away and searched.

"WOW!"

"What?"

"This list is five pages long!"

"Well it is a big company." He reminded.

Just then the train's public address system broke into their discussion.

Ladies and gentlemen at this time we would like to remind passengers we will be pulling into Chicago's Union Station in approximately fifteen minutes.

Our layover time will be forty-five minutes and if you are travelling with us on to Boston or New York and plan on deboarding the train, please be aware that we will be leaving in exactly forty-five minutes. Please be on time as the next train to New York is in 24 hours.

Thank you for travelling Amtrak.

It was just after nine in the morning when they realized they had worked through the last eight hours.

Irina glanced out the window to the station and saw the shops in the main concourse opening up.

"Hey, we've got until nearly 10. I'm going to duck into one of the shops and get a few articles of clothing. Besides, I could do to stretch my legs a little." She stood to leave. "You wanna come along?"

"You go ahead. I'll catch up with you. I'm gonna do a quick perusal of this list, see if anything jumps out at me."

"See you in a bit." As she left Mahone took her seat and began to cruise the long list. Not minutes into his search Mahone struck gold.

"Hello!" Halfway down on the second page was the Chinese company called Ming Tao! The only Chinese sounding company name on the entire list.

"What a coincidence! Thank you Senator Burman!" He mumbled.

*

That morning gathered together in back of the hotel lounge, Morrissey et al batted around details of the case as they anxiously awaited word from Mahone.

"Whatever the motive it must have been compelling enough to commit murder." Heath pointed out.

"Especially such a high profile murder." Tammy observed.

"That just means a bigger motivation!" Enfeild

declared.

"We still have to show motive." Din reminded.

"Personally I'm still a fan of the digging too deep theory." Enfeild threw in.

"Okay but what was she digging too deep into?" Tammy challenged.

"Well, who knew about the murder?" Din asked.

"In the course of our interview with Daniel Parker the topic of AstroCom's rivalry as well as their chasing multi-billion dollar government contracts came up." Morrissey added. "So we've determined that it was related to money, AstroCom and this guy Reagan, do we agree?" All nodded in concent.

"Given what we found in Reagan's lab I don't see any alternative." Tammy observed.

"Whatever Reagan and AstroCom were doing it must have been as big as hell!" Heath added.

"And as illegal as hell!"

"The question now is where is Mahone and what's he doing?" Din pushed.

"Oh don't you worry about Frankie boy! I'm sure he's got things well under control!" Morrissey assured.

****

As Mahone cruised the list he was distracted by something he spotted through the window out across the station's plaza.

A group of four men were huddled together just inside the main entrance and were apparently discussing the train.

What initially caught his attention was the fact that they were identicaly dressed; dark suits, white shirts and dark ties. But the dead giveaway was what Tom Wolfe the writer termed 'Black Shiny FBI Shoes'.

"God-damn it!" Mahone cursed.

He hurriedly slipped off the train to go and shepherd up Irina. Across the platform and out and around the plaza he headed as the four men spread out and made for the train.

Peering off to his left he failed to notice one of them heading directly towards him.

With a split second decision he mounted one foot up on a nearby bench and pretended to tie his shoe. Although the agent passed within inches he appeared to be too preoccupied with the train to notice Mahone.

Frank quickly scanned the shops and decided *la Ladies Boutique* was his best bet.

He spotted Irina in a shop at the counter paying for a top and some underwear where he stepped up to her, took her by the arm and spoke into her ear.

"Come on Sweetheart, we're going to be late!" Frank coaxed.

"What do you mean late? We have at least 25 minutes until-"

Leaning in he whispered into her ear.

"The Men in Black are here. We have to leave." He insisted as he led her by the arm and nodded out towards the station's mall.

Peering through the shop's front window Irina

spotted two of the men. She quickly followed along snatching the decorative bag from the counter as she left.

"Keep the change!" She called back to the cashier as they headed out the street side entrance and on to West Adams Street on the north side of the station.

"Now what?" She pushed as the cold wind swirled through the city street.

"I'm thinking, I'm thinking!"

"We have nineteen minutes, think faster!"

"You get all your shit out of the compartment?"

"Yes. How close is the next station?"

"Hammond, about twenty miles!" He informed.

"Off course!" She grunted in despair.

He suddenly had a thought. "A Bittium Tough 2C! I should have thought of it before! All the drug dealers use them! They have a tracker blocking mechanism."

"What the hell are you mumbling about?" She snapped.

"I can buy a new phone later. What's in the bag?"

"A bra, panties and and a top."

"Is your phone on?"

"No you told me to keep it off."

He turned his phone on and had her do the same.

"Stuff the clothes in your coat pockets, loose the bag. Put your hair in a bun and pull your hat down low to cover your hair."

"Then what?" She asked as she complied.

"Go into the lady's room, change your top and once you see all four men back out on the platform, meet me back in the office car."

"Where're you going?"

"To catch a different train! Give me your phone." He said as he walked from her around the block to the South entrance.

Irina cautiously re-entered the station and ducked into the ladies toilets to change.

Mahone meanwhile carefully entered the station back through the south portico and snuck down onto an adjoining train scheduled to leave just before his own while the agents went car by car searching his train.

Once aboard the adjoining train he located an empty cabin and stuffed the two activated phones down behind two separate seat cushions.

Realising his train would not depart until the agents were off he waited out of sight at the far end of the track until he again saw all four huddled together up near the locomotives.

The one who appeared to be the head agent was on his cell phone just as the train with the phones on it was pulling out.

Frank watched as the four agents suddenly ran for the other train then, realising they couldn't catch it, reversed direction and scrambled for their parked car outside as the NSA tracking center apparently informed them that their two fugitives were escaping on another train.

In aother five minutes Frank and Irina would be on their way to New York while their burner phones were on their way south to Springfield, Illinois, four FBI agents in hot pursuit, driving like a *French*

The Hermes Project

Connection sequel racing to the next station.

****

About the time Morrissey and the SHIT Squad were piecing events together while Frank and Irina were dodging federal agents, Colonel Parva and General Pravum were getting an education in the true meaning of clandestine operations.

"That little So-of-a-bitch!" Pravum cursed aloud as he was just informed that Finley had changed the private key code to HERMES. "Are you sure?!" He demanded of the junior code writer on the other end of the phone line.

"Yes General. Altering the Private key is the only explanation. We've run through every other possibility."

Code systems are composed of Public keys and Private keys. Any change in the key system, of even one digit, renders the entire code useless.

What Colonel Parva and General Pravum were yet to discover was that Phil Finley may have been their subordinate in rank however, realising that Pravum's order to delete the firewall to HERMES was a suspicious order, he altered the private code rendering both the private and the public code useless.

Pravum's planned retirement nest egg with AstroCom depended on being able to bring HERMES with him, intact to AstroCom.

****

The secretary poked her head in through the door. "Chief, visitor here to see you."

"Send him in." Wachowski grumbled without looking up from his desk. However, the big Pole did a double take when Inspector Morrissey stepped through the door.

"Inspector Morrison! So glad you dropped by!" Wachowski made no attempt to mask the sarcasm in his voice as he came around from behind his desk, wrapped one arm around Morrissey's shoulders and guided him to the couch where he stood above him, hands on hips. "We have so much to talk about!"

"Yes we do actually. And it's Morrissey not Morrison. Inspector Morr-"

"Who gives a shit?! Where's my paperwork, where's Mahone and where's my God damned murder suspect?!"

"Detective Mahone is somewhere in route with Special Agent Kuksova and-"

"Who the hell is Special Agent Kuksova and what do you mean 'somewhere'?"

"Special Agent Kuksova works out of the Police Plaza offices Downtown and was investigating a political corruption case when-"

"Which explains why the FBI has been here twice and keeps calling me every couple of hours!" Wachowski again interrupted.

"I would assume so, yes. Now-"

"What do you mean by 'somewhere'? You mean you don't know where they are?"

"Somewhere indicates somewhere between our

present location and another, as of yet unknown location yet to be determined! But I believe-"

"What the hell does an FBI political corruption case have to do with Mahone's murder case?"

"Initially nothing, however-"

"Hold on a minute! Is Kuksova the Russian dame-"

"Chief this is not 1930, we don't use the word 'dame' anymore. And I believe she is Ukrainian not Russian."

"Oh, I'm sorry, please excuse my politically incorrect language! Do allow me to rephrase my interrogative! Is this the broad Mahone was playing hide the salami with over in London when you two were fucking around with that armored car case?!"

"Yes, as a matter of fact it is. The good news I have for you is-"

"So they're working together! Son-of-a-"

"The-good-news-is-we-believe-we-have-found-your-bloody-killer!" He quickly spat out.

Wachowski stopped, stared and returned to his dsek sat back, smiled and nodded in approval.

"That is good news!" He put an unlit, half-smoked stogie in his mouth. "But that don't mean Mahone can go tear-assing around the place and disappear for a week or more at a time!"

"Chief Wachowski, all I know is that when the Squad and I return to England I'm going to see about putting that man in for The King's Police Medal for what he did over in London!"

"Good for him!"

"Also Chief, there is something you need to

realize about this case."

"Yeah, what's that?"

"I've worked here long enough to observe that exactly like in England, police procedures here are contaminated with politics. In this particular case, quite high up politics! Particularly the people involved with this murder."

"I don't give a shit if he's King Charles, the the Prince of Siam and he's friends with the Clintons! He commits murder in my precinct he's going down!"

"Glad you feel that way Chief. I'm confident Mahone and I have the proof to build the case you need!"

"Yeah, I trust you do, now all we gotta do is find him!"

*

It was well past two p.m. as Nialls Reagan sat in the converted basement of the old tenement building on MacDougal Street in Greenwich Village tapping his fingers on the rickety table of the garishly decorated café.

Surrounded by hanging plants, 1960s posters and incense burners he stared at the lava lamp in the center of the table his third cup of gourmet, Brazilian coffee already gone cold.

Reagan heard the cursing from across the all-but-deserted café before he saw the man emerge from the dark shadows.

"Welcome to the fuckin' world of macramé!"

The Hermes Project

The man in the heavy overcoat sarcastically grunted of the décor as he took a seat at the secluded corner table with Reagan. "Can't believe I had to task the company jet to fly up to this shit hole just to meet you!" The NSA Director complained.

"How was I supposed to know she couldn't hold her booze?!" Reagan quietly but strongly defended.

"You're in the God damned intel game!" Pravum forcibly restrained the volume of his voice as he spoke. "You're supposed to know what the hell is going on around you at all times!"

"I'm a God damn biochemist, not an international spy!"

"No, you're just another schmuck who let's his little head do the thinking for his big head!"

Both men paused to settle down.

"We had a drunken argument that night. Not even an argument, a tiff. And it's a good thing too, otherwise we never would have found out what she was planning and that she threatened to expose us!"

"US?!" Pravum shouted before looking around to see if anyone noticed. The few patrons up by the front door didn't. "You mean expose **you**! And are you actually trying to say it's a good thing you killed her?"

"I just-"

"You have any idea what happens if this gets out and is traced back to us?! The fucking press are already comparing us to the Gestapo, Savak and the KGB fer fuck's sake!"

"I been thinking about it and I tell you what I'm going to do-"

"No! I'll tell you what you're gonna do! You're gonna take a vacation. You've got a sick relative out in California."

"I have no relatives in California!" Reagan protested.

"You do now! You're gonna disappear for awhile! I'll arrange something with the CEO at AstroCom. You'll be notified of the details!"

Pravum made no attempt to hide his anger as he stood and stomped back out the door and into the bright, afternoon sunlight, climbed into his Merc rental car and drove off.

****

It was early evening when the private home line of Mr J. Gutierrez, Assistant Director of AstroCom rang.

"Gutierrez here."

"It's me."

"Michael! What's so important you call me at-"

"You were right about Reagan."

"SHIT!"

"I need you to send him on a business trip down to our supplier's facility."

"On what premise? What will he do in Bogotá?"

"Tell him there's some kind of problem with the FARC cell leader that only he can fix. Tell him they want to renegotiate our agreement. Give him some spending cash and an all expense paid holiday weekend."

"Then what?"

"I'll take care of the rest. It's been almost a minute, I gotta go."

Had anyone been tapping the satellite phone, one minute was the allowable safe time to keep the line open.

Pravum's next placed a secure landline call to his adjutant, Colonel Parva.

"General Pravum! What can I do for you?"

"Parva, unfortunately I have recently discovered that one of our contractors has been engaging in illegal activity. Should his activities leak it would bring disrepute upon the agency."

"It was Reagan!" He deduced. "How do you want to handle it Director?" The Colonel asked.

"I believe I have it taken care of."

"As always sir!"

"However, I need you to do a few things in the morning. Can you be in at six?"

"No problem sir. And may I say well done on once again staying ahead of the problem."

"People are in your life for one of two reasons Parva; to help or hinder; if they are not there to help then they exist to be used!"

"I understand sir. And if they are there to hinder sir?"

There was no answer, the line simply went dead.

*

El Dorado Aeropuerto Internacional
Bogotá, Colombia

Stepping out into the glaring sun Reagan wiped a bead of sweat from his brow as he was briefly distracted by a six inch green gecko scurrying up the white stucco wall of the terminal.

Nialls Reagan's flight over the plushly forrested hilly terrain had touched down from JFK at 14:00 local Bogotá time and was met by two gentlemen.

The well-dressed one greeted him warmly with a handshake and instructed the farmer-type with him to take Reagan's bag.

"I am Victor Martinez I have been sent to see that you have no trouble finding your way." He explained as he led the way out of the terminal into the blazing heat of the glaring sun, across the road to another smaller tarmac and over to a red and white De Havilland Beaver, motor already running.

"Señor Havlo has sent you one of his private aircraft to take you to the meeting."

"But I'm booked at the Marriott Courtyard. I'm to meet señor Havlo at three in the hotel!" Reagan protested.

"Señor Havlo has been called to the north to Tabio. He explained as he stowed Reagan's bag behind the seats in the cargo hold.

"Where is Tabio? Reagan enquired as he climbed into the aircraft along with Martinez and the farmer.

"A short flight to a small village about 25 km north of here. There's been some trouble with the local government again. They claim your State Department is giving us trouble about exporting the frog venom."

"But it's for medical research."

"I know, we have explained that to them. If you ask me I don't think it's about exports. I just think someone is looking for more money. Once greed attains a certain level it can never be satisfied."

At 5,000 feet for the entire flight the ride was short but extremely scenic.

Flying just west of the village the plane landed on a well groomed, grass runway cut out of the jungle.

The men walked the short distance to an ornate but modest-sized hacienda where Reagan couldn't help but notice the lack of guard contingent he had seen when visiting Havlo and others of his ilk in the past.

Dressed in a cotton, brightly flowered shirt, khaki shorts and sandals Havlo emerged from the shadows of the casa and approached all smiles.

"Buenos dias señor Reagan! Welcome!" Havlo was short, stout and, as an atypical characteristic in this part of the world, cleanly shaven. "Would you like something to drink?"

"No thank you."

"Apology for changing of plans señor Reagan. There was a dispute and we had to relocate one of our operations to this new facility."

"I'm sorry to hear about your troubles Mr. Havlo. If you explain to me the details I'm sure we can work something out."

"No doubt in my mind Reagan. But first please allow me to give you a brief tour of the new lab facility. It will increase production by 40 to 50%!"

Led around to the side of the hacienda Reagan

thought it impossible that the small size of the new facility, barely larger than a residential two car garage, corrugated metal covered shack was enough to contain a single room much less an entire drug lab.

He reasoned the rest of the operation was likely located underground.

At first, when he stepped into the shade of the open structure, Reagan thought it was one of the myriad of insects infesting this country. But as he drew his hand from his neck he felt the dart and turned just in time to see the worker standing a few meters behind him smiling and lowering the dart gun.

Turning to see the four men dressed in rubber aprons, gloves and gas masks standing around a 55 gallon drum of hydrochloric acid Reagan came to understand the meaning of the word 'reality'.

A mere twenty minutes later Mr. Nialls Reagan had been erased from existence.

****

"Next stop Station Way. Station Way next stop!" The conductor called as he made his way through the car.

"Come on let's go." Frank instructed Irina as she was dozing off in the seat next to him.

"Go where?" She questioned as she yawned widely and peered out the train window. "This is still Jersey! I thought we were to going to Manhattan?"

"We are, just not by train. After the last reception committee there's a good chance they'll be waiting for us at Moynaghan Station. Instead of going into Midtown we'll take a ferry to the Battery."

Frank and Irina left the train and scurried over to the taxi stand across the road.

"Harborside Terminal." Frank directed and the Hispanic *Gemini Taxi* driver took off.

Unfortunately for the pair Irina Kuksova wasn't the only one who had been looking out the window.

Several seats back a young woman seated next to her snoozing father had been surfing her iPhone and stopped on CNN where a public alert had been running for the last 48 hours. A public alert featuring the photos of Frank Mahone and Irina Kuksova.

The police were called.

About five minutes into the 20-minute taxi ride Frank took advantage of his bilingual ability and initiated a superficial yet friendly conversation with the driver in Spanish.

Mahone asked where he was from, about his family and how long he had been in America. They both had a good laugh when the driver replied he was born in Brooklyn.

With the ice broken Mahone feigned having left his phone on the train.

When he explained he had to ring his brother to meet them in Manhattan the driver politely offered his phone.

Frank thanked him and called his precinct house where he asked to be put through to Wachowski's office.

"Chief Wachowski here."

"Chief its me." Wachowski immediately recognised the voice of the detective he hadn't seen in nearly a week.

"Hello there how are you? Everything okay? And by the way, there was something else. Oh yeah, WHERE THE HELL ARE YOU?!" The Chief yelled.

"Everything okay Bro?" Frank calmly asked.

"Okay?! Hello no everything's not okay! I got the entire U.S. government on my ass-"

Wachowski suddenly switched to an animated voice as two suits entered his office and took a seat on the couch.

"Yes dear, I won't forget. Milk bread and tea." The Chief cajoled with an exaggerated compliance.

"What the hell are you talking about? Milk and bread?" A confused Mahone asked.

"What time can I expect you home dear?" Wachowski asked.

"Home?!" This caused the wheels in Mahone's head to swiftly start turning. "There's someone in your office isn't there?" He Finally copped on.

"Yes dear, you're right as usual honey." The big Pole responded as he smiled across the room to the two dark suited men now sitting there. "I'll be home straight after work dear." Being married for over 26 years the big man was a master at controlling his emotions and portraying a deceitful demeanor.

"I'll meet you at the house between seven and eight." Frank signalled.

"Okay, see you then." The Chief responded.

"Love you snookums!" Frank teased. There was a long moment of silence. "Come on, aren't you gonna say it? I love you. Do you love me?" Frank pushed.

More silence.

It was between clenched teeth that the big Pole eventually uttered the words.

"Love you **dear!**"

The older of the two agents resumed reading his *Time Magazine* while the younger one continued playing the video game on his phone.

While Chief Wachowski went back to work the two Federal agents, who had been hovering around the police station most of the day, resumed their unusual stakeout.

From Harborside Terminal in Jersey City Frank and Irina caught a New York Waterways ferry over the Hudson to Lower Manhattan and from there they planned to catch the N train out to Queens.

CHAPTER TWENTY

A taxi to the ferry, the ferry to Manhattan and Canal Street to the N train out to Queens. At least that was the plan. However, as they say; 'The best laid plans of mice and men...'

Thanks to three things: iPhones, You Tube and bored teen Gen Z's, the plan didn't go as planned.

Of the 75 or 80 people on board the ferry there were perhaps a dozen or so teens each with his or her face buried in their phone.

On the south east shore of the very tip of Manhattan, known locally as the Battery, lies Pier 11. Unlike traditional ferry slips those on Pier 11 are wide open.

Approximately 100 yards out from the landing Frank Mahone took advantage of this and scurried to the top deck of the boat affording himself a view of nearly the entire shore of the east Battery. Unfortunately he saw what he didn't want to see. Two FBI agents milling around the various stands and booths.

"Bastards are thorough I give them that!" Frank mumbled to himself.

Returning to the lower deck he informed Irina of what he saw.

"What's the plan?" She nervously asked. He thought for a moment.

"If we get separated meet at the precinct house at six tonight, Got it?"

"Got it!"

With that he hustled back top side this time to the

pilot house.

"Sir you're not allowed-" A crew member blocked his path. The deckhand's protest was cut short as Frank flashed his badge.

"This is an emergency!"

The helmsman, only a few feet away in the small cabin, glanced over his shoulder while still manning the helm as he cut engines and they drifted towards the pier.

"My precinct just received a bomb threat that said they were going to bomb a ferry boat. I just spotted two suspicious men onshore outside your slip!"

"What do you want me to do?" The coxswain asked as he maneuvered the boat.

"Can you take your time docking?"

"I can't slow the docking but we can hold the passengers once we're tied up." He responded.

"Good enough. I'll go ashore first and check things out then signal you when its safe to let them off. I need you to notify Harbor Patrol and the parks authority to have those guys checked out!"

Of all the places on the planet where a bomb threat is taken seriously no where do people react as quickly as in Lower Manhattan.

Less than two minutes later, as the ferry tied up, a pair of squad cars pulled up from opposite directions of where the two suites stood. The two cars vomited police and moved to question the two men. Frank moved immediately to signal the pilot who allowed the passengers to disembark.

Lost amongst them was Irina Kuksova followed

close behind by Frank Mahone.

Just over two hours later they found their way up to Queens and into Astoria and the Wachowski household.

*** * ***

After having spent the night at Chief Wachowski's house where they spent several hours catching him up to speed, Frank and Irina rode into Manhattan from Astoria with Wachowski and headed for the precinct next morning.

Being Friday the traffic going into the City was unexpectedly light however became progressively more congested as they approached the east 20s and by the time they attempted to turn on to 21st Street they were compelled to stop the car. They were all three overwhelmed by the sight that greeted them.

Police barricades had been erected, apparently on both ends of the street, a sizeable crowd comprised largely of TV news crews and reporters were being held at bay by a line of uniformed officers blocking the precinct's entrance.

The officers manning the barricades at the east end of 21st Street recognised the Chief, slid the wooden barricade aside and waved him through.

His car had no sooner pulled up outside the precinct house when someone in the crowd yelled, "IT'S THEM!"

The tide of the crowd immediately shifted and the car was surrounded. Even before any of the three could exit the vehicle the feeding frenzy began

The Hermes Project

as they were bombarded with questions even before they exited the vehicle.

"Told you I'd make you famous!" Frank quipped to Irina as they moved to get out of the car and get to the front door.

"Thaaks for the favor!" Irina sarcastically replied.

Several of Frank's colleagues were able to barge through the crowd and get them safely inside.

Once inside Wachowski made for the front desk.

"Charlie, what the hell is going on here? Why is there a mob of reporters outside our door?!" He asked of the desk sergeant.

"Beats me Chief! One of the reporters said they got an anonymous tip the two fugitives were being brought in."

"An anonymous tip! Who the hell would call in an anonymous tip and would know where and when these two would arrive?"

Morrissey! was the name that immediately popped into Mahone's head.

"Hey Chief!" The Desk Sergeant called after them as they headed upstairs. "You'd better call the Mayor's office, He's been calling all day, yesterday and today. plus he sent his deputy over earlier."

"Thanks!" Chief yelled back from the staircase.

Upon entering his office Wachowski found a new pair of FBI agents waiting inside on the couch.

"Who the hell are you two?!" Wachowski demanded. They both stood,

"This is Agent Childs, I'm Special Agent Rakowski." He flashed his I.D. as he spoke. "We're here to take these two into custody."

"Not until I clear it with our legal guys in the Commissioner's office you're not." The Chief snapped back.

The Special Agent scowled, became incensed and pulled the warrant from his pocket.

"This isn't a fucking parking ticket, Pops! It's a federal warrant." He argued as he brandished the papers, "This is a a federal warrant, a FISA warrant signed by a federal judge!"

From behind his desk Wachowski leaned forward, folded his hands and made dispassionate eye contact.

"I don't care if it's a warrant autographed by Judge Judy, endorsed by Judge Wapner and co-singed by Steve Harvey! They stay here until I get the okay to transfer custody! And that ain't gonna happen until I talk to my boss. So **Special Agent**. . ." The Chief stood and stepped around from behind his desk. ". . . you and your little trainee friend here are gonna have a seat outside and wait for me to make some phone calls! Are we green boys? Because if not I've got a precinct full of cops, most of whom voted for Trump and would love to have a shot at putting a couple of Democrat appointed feds in the drunk tank!"

Rakowski foolishly initiated a brief staring contest with the Chief before the inevitable happened. The two agents exchanged glances with each other, turned and exited the office.

"No wonder the country's lost faith in those clowns!" Wachowski grumbled before he realised Special Agent Kuksova was in the room. "No offence intended young lady."

"None taken Chief." She responded. "After the last couple of weeks I'm beginning to feel the same way."

Just then the telephone rang. Taking a seat back behind his desk Wachowski answered it.

"Wachowski speaking." There was a slight pause. "Yes Commissioner. No Commissioner. Of course Commissioner. Yes Commissioner I have them in custody. Yes Commissioner, the FBI is here. Will do Commissioner."

Immediately after Wachowski took the call Frank casually stepped over to the couch, opened the office door, tepped part way out and called back into the office.

"CHIEF! IT'S THE MAYOR'S OFFICE ON LINE TWO!" He shouted across the office.

Kuksova smiled and shook her head as Frank provided Wachowski his chance.

"Commissioner I'm sorry that's the Mayor on the other line. Can I call you back? Thank you sir." The Cheif hung up just as Mahone took a seat on the couch.

"So who was it?" Mahone sarcastically asked.

"Not now Mahone!" The Chief was in no mood. "Get those two Hoover clowns back in here." He ordered to no one in particular. Mahone stepped to the door and directed them back in.

"Okay boychiks, here's where we stand, I just spoke with the Commissioner. These two are here until Monday morning 10:00 when there'll be a hearing downtown at the Federal Courthouse at which time a federal judge will determine their status. Until that time you two are free to frequent whichever Chelsea area gay nightclub you choose and we will see you Monday morning Downtown. Thank you for your service! You may leave."

Not at all happy they had no choice but to go.

Wachowski pressed his intercom.

"Darcy? Wachowski here, send somebody up here for drunk tank escort duty." Irina assumed a concerned look. Frank signaled her not to worry. "No booking's not necessary. Never mind why just do it!" Chief ordered.

Frank and Irina were escorted upstairs to the drunk tank.

"Sorry to have to do this Frank!" The escorting officer apologized as they were rought upstairs and to the 10X12 cell.

"No problem Jimmy."

"I don't know what they've got planned but there's something going on." Frank observed quietly to Irina as the guard walked away.

"How do you know?"

"It's against regulations to lock up men and women together. We have two separate drunk tanks, one male one female **and** we're not being booked!"

He waited until the guard locked the door of the cell and was out of earshot. "Besides. . ." He opened his coat as he spoke to reveal the fact that Wachowski hadn't confiscated his badge and gun.

"Maybe he just forgot!" She argued.

"He didn't forget. Have a little faith."

"In what?"

"In the fact that there are at least two

orgaizations in this town the left wing, P.C. crowd will never bring down. This isn't just another federal, bureaucratic, risk-averse organization. Here loyalty means something."

"What organizations?" She asked. Mahone hesitated as he flopped down on the wall bench before responding.

"The FDNY the NYPD!" He begrudgingly mumbled.

****

It was nearly seven o'clock that evening when the crowd outside had dissipated and the guard finally brought them something to eat.

He unlocked the cell door and handed them each a tray of food. As he did he was careful to make eye contact with Mahone and nod over to the door.

Unseen by Irina, Frank nodded back.

As he moved to pull the door over he spoke to Mahone.

"I won't be back to collect your trays. I'm the only one on the desk tonight. I only get a bathroom break at exactly 11:30 for fifteen minutes." He explained.

"We'll just stack the trays in the corner Jimmy." Frank said.

Digging into her food, distracted by hunger, Irina hadn't noticed but was suspicious of their stillted tone as they spoke.

Some time later Frank pushed up from the floor where he had been sitting, put his shoes back on and shook Irina awake where she had been sleeping on the single long bench.

"What? What time is it?" She drowsily inquired.

"Time to go!" Frank informed her. "Get your shoes on. It's nearly 11:30."

"What are you talking about?!"

"Time to leave."

"How?! Magically become Reed Richards and squeeze through the bars?"

"No." He checked that the overhead CCTV camera had been switched off then eased the unlocked door open. "You wanna come along or you wanna hang around til morning?"

"How did . . .?"

"Told you to have a little faith! C'mon!"

Taking her by the hand they made their way down the back stairs and out through the rear of the station.

Outside it was cold and windy but not uncomfortably so. They were able to make their way over to 24th Street where they were able to catch the PATH train under the river and over to New Jersey. Disembarking at the Hoboken station, correctly deducing that Frank's apartment was being staked out, they headed for the Squad's hotel.

At the front desk they rang up to Inspector Morrissey's room.

****

It was just after midnight when Colonel Parva manned the secure line and rang his boss.

The Hermes Project

"General Pravum, we just got a message in from the FBI. Their guys report that Kuksova and the cop are in custody in the city jail in Manhattan."

"Is that confirmed?" Pravum excitedly asked.

"Yes sir, I called the jail myself. They're being held at the 13th Precinct, Downtown."

"Well isn't that handy! Right close to the federal courthouse."

"And jail!" Parva added.

"Yes, and jail!"

"Apparently there's an emergency hearing scheduled for 10:00 Monday morning in the Federal Courthouse. What would you like me to do sir?"

"You've got the FISA summation drawn up?"

"Yes sir finished it yesterday. Former agent Kuksova is being charged with unauthorised access to a classified Top Secret NSA program with probable intent to sell it to an agent of the People's Republic of China all while on suspension."

"Good, that's good."

"What about the O'Neill case sir?" Parva pushed.

"It's already been ruled a homicide, will likely remain open indefinitely and eventually get tossed on to the 50% pile of unsolved murders in this country which accumulate each year."

"And Mr. Reagan sir?"

"Not an issue. He's been relocated and has taken up a new position in South America."

"Is there anything else sir?"

"Yes, come to think of it. I don't trust those NYPD clowns. Call Wray's people in the morning and tell them to send a couple of guys over there and get those two transferred down to Police Plaza and into federal custody."

"Will do sir."

****

Holiday Inn Express Hotel
Hoboken, New Jersey

Like a sophisticated, high level game of Chinese Whispers a flurry of phone calls ensued that weekend.

Not having formally checked into the hotel last night Frank and Irina had crashed in Inspector Morrissey's room.

"Wakey-wakey Sleeping Beauty! Lots of work to do today!" Mahone teased as he smacked Irina's duvet covered ass from under the covers that morning.

"What time is it?" She sleepily asked as she rolled over.

"Just after eight. Coffee's ready." Frank announced from the kitchenette as he shuttled a pot of coffee, cups and a box of Krispy Kreme doughnuts to the coffee table where he poured her a cup.

"What's the plan general?" She asked as she washed her face in the sink.

"You are going to get hold of that congresswoman you interviewed and set up a meet to tell her what we found out."

"How? All my contact information was in my

phone, with the phones you dumped!"

"Well I'm sure that with that machine over there called a computer, you can go online and find her contact number."

"What good will that do? Today's Friday, she's no office hours on Fridays!" Kuksova protested. "She won't be in her office and its for certain her home phone won't be listed."

"How did you people ever catch Al Capone?" He countered as he poured some coffee. "Find the Morristown police, call them, tell them who you are and explain there's a family emergency. Tell them you've got a 10-53 with a suspected family member involved and you need a home phone. If there's a problem tell them you have an NYPD officer with you to verify. If need be I'll take it from there."

"What's a 10-53?"

"Traffic accident."

"Then what, after I get her number?"

"Then call her and explain-"

"What can I do?" Nigel asked. As he emerged from the spare room and helped himself to a cup of coffee.

Minutes later having located the Morristown PD's number and using the room phone, Irina was about to dial.

"No wait!" Mahone snapped. "When you interviewed congresswoman Farmiga you posed as Sam O'Neill didn't you?"

"How did you know that?!"

"NYPD Baby! Just good police work!" He bragged.

"Yes, I did. Why?"

"Make the call anonymously."

"Okay, why?"

"When you want to catch a big fish . . ."

Using the room's computer Kuksova found the Morristown New Jersey P.D.'s number and eventually was given Cogresswoman Farmiga's private number.

"I've got her number."

"Good. Think a minute, before you call her we need to be sure she understands the magnitude of what we found."

"What do you suggest?"

"Make her think if she doesn't do something, take some sort of action she'll get caught up in it." Frank suggested.

"I get it." Irina considered for a minute before she dialled.

"Hello?" The phone was answered on the second ring.

"Natalie Farmiga?" Irina feigned a falsetto voice.

"Yes, who's calling please?"

"Cogresswoman Natalie Farmiga of the U.S. Congressioal Intel committee?" Irina repeated.

"Yes! Who is this?!"

"A friend, listen carefully! Early next week an article will go out over the UP wire which means it will reach all the national dailies. It will detail how you are involved with Senator James Burman in a pay-for-play scheme with South American terrorists and the PRC."

"That's ridiculous! I never even-"

The Hermes Project

"Your enemies won't care!"

"There's no way the Chairman of the Intel Committee is mixed up with the Chinese communists!" Farmiga countered.

"Are you quite sure about Burman?!" Irina baited. There was a long pause. "Isn't he the man who asked you to step down from the Intel Committee?"

"Why tell me about this story, if there even is a story?!" Farmiga finally challenged.

"You're being told because Sam O'Neill said you were a good egg!" At the mention of Sam O'Neill's name there was another long silence.

"Why should I care about a press leak?"

"To give you a life preserver before the ship gets torpedoed!" Kuksova abruptly hung up.

"You think she bought it?" Irina turned to Frank and Nigel as she hung up.

"Meryl Streep couldn't have done better!" Mahone congradulated.

On the other end Farmiga wasn't sure what to make of the mysterious phone call. After a short consideration she placed a call on her phone and left a message for Chairman Burman of the Intel Committee.

"Nigel, give us the use of your phone. I have to text Wachowski and let him know we think we've got the goods on Reagan for O'Neill's murder." Frank requested.

"I've already told him that when I visited him in his office."

"Great."

"In any case he'll want to know your plans before Monday." Nigel advised as he fiddled with his cell phone.

"I'll get back to you on that."

"Blast it to bloody hell!" Nigel cursed at his cell.

"What's wrong?" Irina asked.

"Bloody phone's out of credit!"

"There's a convenience store in the lobby. Should be open by now. I'll duck down and get a top off." Irina volunteered. She finished dressing and left.

As Irina went through the door Nigel turned to Mahone.

"Frank if you don't mind my asking, would it not have been safer to keep her in the city jail until Monday?"

"No, if the Feds managed to get the right judge they could finagle a federal transfer order in which case they could take her and hide her somewhere indefinitely."

"You mean they'd actually kidnap her?"

"They've done it before! More than once!" Mahone assured.

"Bloody hell! I thought the Whigs and Tories were bastards!"

Once on the ground floor of the hotel Irina was required to pass the reception desk to reach the convenience store. Across from reception, set up in the lobby, was a self-help breakfast bar with tea coffee and cereal.

It was over at the breakfast bar that Enfield and Little Tammy were loading up their trays.

"Agent Kuksova!" Tammy cried out catching Irina's attention who unsuccessfully motioned Tammy to hold it down.

Unfortunately the middle-aged receptionist that started each morning with an MSNBC broadcast featuring the story, details and photos of Frank Mahone and Irina Kuksova, at-large felons, also heard Tammy's greeting.

Craning her neck for a better look at the woman with the long blonde hair, the receptionist immediately realized Kuksova was one of the fugitives.

Visions of monetary rewards immediately danced in her head.

*** * ***

She may have been a freshman house member and not yet fully indoctrinated into the ways of The Swamp but she was no dunce.

Cancelling her few morning appointments and brooding in her home office it was only a short time after she received the call from Irina Kuksova that Congresswoman Natalie Farmiga eventually made the decision to rephone Senator James Burman. Before she could dial the number her cell phone rang.

"Miss Farmiga speaking."

"Natalie, glad I caught you at home."

"Senator Burman?"

"I got a message that you rang earlier."

"Yes, yes sir. I got a very strange phone call a

little while ago."

"Oh?"

"Someone warning me that a story would break next week concerning you and I being involved in a pay-for-play scheme."

"Really?! Did the caller identify themself?"

"No, no it was a woman and all she said was something about South American Terroroists and the PRC? That make any sense to you?!"

"Did you get her number or did she say she'd call back?"

"No. But if it makes no sense to you perhaps we should notify the Capitol Police?"

"I don't think that's necessary. Let's wait and see if she rings back and if not I'd just dismiss the whole thing."

"Are you, are you sure sir? With the elections coming up-"

"Representative Farmiga, Natalie, the Senate gets half a dozen crank calls a week. One fruit cake or another threatening this, that or God knows what! Either we'll hear back from her again or not. Until then let's not lose any sleep or start ringing alarm bells over it, shall we?"

"Senator Burman I really think-"

"Let me know if you hear back from her. Have a good afternoon."

No sooner had Burman hung up the phone when he was dialling a new number.

"May I speak with General Pravum please?"

In the background Burman could hear the female who answered as she called Pravum to the phone.

"Mike Pravum here."

"We need to talk." Burman barked into the phone.

"Jim! What are you doing calling me at home on the weekend?"

"You got your Thuraya X5 there at the house?"

"I always do, why?"

"Find some place you can talk and call me back on my Iridiu."

The fact that Burman wanted a call back to continue the conversation on their classified sat phones indicated there was a serious matter to discuss.

"Jim you sound stressed. What's going on?" Pravum probed once he was out in his greenhouse in the rear garden.

"Just what the hell happened between your asshole connection at AstroCom and that female journalist?" Burman angrily demanded.

"Why? What are you talking about?!"

"I'm talking about the phone call I just got from a former member of my Intel committee saying that someone is about to publish a story about FARC terrorists, me and the fucking PRC! That's what I'm talking about!"

"OH SHIT!"

"You'd better believe 'OH SHIT!'"

"Senator believe me everything is under control!" Pravum assured.

"Pravum when someone says to me 'everything is under control', not only do the hairs on the back of my neck stand up but I'm pretty God damned certain that **something** is **not** under control! Now what the hell is going on?!"

"Nothing serious! There was a slight problem."

"With Reagan?"

"Reagan and the girl."

"Well, can you get to her, offer her some money or something? Proof or no proof we can't let that story get out!"

"I've got it on pretty good authority she won't be releasing the story Senator."

"You mean you killed it?"

"In a manner of speaking, yes."

"How certain is your 'good authority'?"

"Trust me Senator, its a dead certainty!"

"What about Reagan?"

"I had AstroCom transfer him sir. He's out of the picture."

"I need you to understand Michael, with my stock in the Ming Tao company if this FARC thing gets out it will blow up and if I'm called to testify . . . I'll have no choice."

"No choice but to? -" Pravum didn't need to finish.

"Exactly! Clean this shit up or put in for early retirement!"

"But what would I tell the POTUS?!"

"I don't give a shit! Tell him you have a sick relative in California!"

The line went dead.

*

After more than an hour trying General Pravum

finally reached Colonel Parva by phone.

"We have an issue. Can you be at the office in one hour?"

"Yes sir. Is it about the Kuksova girl?" Parva reflexively asked.

"What about the Kuksova girl?!" Pravum demanded as he still stood in the backyard greenhouse.

"You haven't heard?"

"Heard what?!"

"It would appear she had some help and has flown the coop." Parva knew enough to hold his cell phone away from his ear after delivering the bad news.

"WHAT THE HELL DO YOU MEAN 'FLOWN THE COOP'?! I THOUGHT YOU SAID THEY HAD HER LOCKED UP IN A DOWNTOWN CITY JAIL?!"

His yelling was loud enough to reach the kitchen and attract the attention of his wife who was preparing dinner.

"As of this morning sir they did. Apparently she's escaped."

"So-of-a-bitch! Suddenly I'm in a B movie!" Pravum cursed. "Be in the office in one hour!"

"Yes sir."

Although completely in the dark regarding Pravum's illicit extracurricular activities, Parva was the ambitious type and knew better than to question his boss.

****

Little Tammy, sitting with Enfield having a coffee in the hotel lounge reached over and tapped Enfield as she nodded out the side window of the hotel café area. A pair of cops had pulled up in a patrol car.

The two watched as the large officers entered and headed straight to the reception desk.

Out of earshot but with a clear view across the lobby the two watched as the cops questioned the receptionist. It was when they presented what appeared to be a picture on one of their cell phones to the middle-aged woman that Enfield leaned over and whispered to Tammy.

"Stay here."

"Got it!" She nodded as he slipped away and made for the elevators.

The receptionist pointed across the lobby. Both uniforms made for Tammy's table where she sat slumped in her seat, feet propped up on an adjoining chair as she sipped her coffee.

"Excuse us miss. Can we speak with you?"

"You're wearing the uniform mate!" She happily answered.

"The receptionist tells us you know this woman." He handed her a loose leaf-sized printout which displayed a headshot, a description and details of Irina Kuksova.

"I don't know her, but I have spoken with her."

"What exactly did you speak about?"

"About our work. Claimed she was some kind of cop."

"She's FBI."

"Really?!" Expressig just the right amount of faux shock Tammy sat upright.

"When did you speak with her last?"

"Day or so ago. Didn't speak with her but for five maybe ten minutes most."

"You talk funny. Where are you from?" One of the cops challenged.

"Glasgow."

"I Love The Beatles!" The shorter cop said. Tammy nodded and smiled.

"You here on vacation?"

"Yeah."

"You said you spoke with her about your work?"

"Yeah."

"What exactly is your work?"

"Same as you! I'm a Peeler."

"A what?"

"A Peeler. John Bull. A copper."

"You're a police officer?"

"At's right. Sergeant MacIntyre, Scotland Yard. Glad to meet youse!"

"A detective?"

"Aye, I am." She leaned in more closely to examine their Sam Brown belts.

"I notice youse carry loads'a gear! Does it not get in the way when youse have to chase the knackers?"

"The what?"

"Knackers! Crimis, barkers!"

"I think she means the bad guys." The shorter one offered up to his partner.

"Exactly! Does it not bog ya down like?" Mindful of what she suspected Enfield was up to, she continued to stall for time.

"Not at all. We train for it." The short cop answered.

"Do ya mind if I ask youse another question?" She innocently queried.

"Not at all, what is it?"

"Ain't that your police car?" She pointed out the window as they all watched the rear of the patrol car pulling out onto the street, turn and head north, Mahone driving with Irina ducked down, unseen in the back seat.

A pair of teens across the room clapped and cheered as the two officers darted from the hotel, their Sam Browns jingling all the way out the door.

****

Weehawken public park several miles north of Hoboken overlooks the wide expanse of the Hudson River over to the northern most areas of Manhattan.

"What are we doing?" Irina asked as Frank steered the cop car into the small park, up onto the footpath and into a tunnel under the overhead highway. Once tucked away in the shadows he shut down the engine. "We should be good here for awhile while we concoct a plan of action."

Irina removed her coat and slipped it on backwards before sliding down in her seat as the late afternoon chill began to set in.

"You want me to turn the heater on?" Frank

offered.

"No, I'm okay." She unconvincingly replied. Mahone reached over, started the car and turned on the heater.

"I said I'm okay!" She protested.

"Well maybe I'm cold!" He snapped back. The fact that his overcoat was tossed in the backseat with their hastily packed travel bags belied his claim.

They sat for a while in silence and watched as the sun slowly slid behind the Manhattan skyline.

Perched on the high ground the park afforded a panoramic view from the George Washington Bridge across the river to Manhattan and as far south as the mouth of the expansive harbor.

"You can't really appreciate the magnitude of this place until you see it for yourself!" She quietly declared.

"You've never been to New York?"

"No, first time. I can see how people like it though." She mused. "Were you born here?" She asked.

"Saint Vincent's hospital, 14th Street. Mother was a nurse dad was NYPD."

"Just like you."

"Just like me. Just like his brother, just like his other brother who is FDNY. I guess you could say we're all incestuous, professionally speaking." He quipped.

"Nonsense! It's tradition!" She adamantly asserted. Frank gave no responce. "Something sadly lacking in this country, tradition." She strongly opined.

"How do you mean?"

"Nobody here carries on what was built by their forefathers. It's why the American middle class is shrinking so quickly and so many people are sliding below the poverty line. It seems the further Americans stray from their ethnic roots the more they lose their cultural identity."

"I don't know if I'd put it that way." He objected.

"Okay, I'll prove it to you! What do you call someone who speaks three languages?" She challenged.

"Trilingual." He immediately answered turning to face her.

"Yes. And what do you call someone who speaks two languages?"

"Bilingual of course." His curiosity was aroused.

"And what do you call someone who only speaks one language?"

"Monolingual naturally!"

"No! American!" She corrected.

"Okay wise ass I'm bilingual, how do you explain me then?"

"There is no explaination for you! You're an anomaly, an incongruity. A glitch in the Matrix!" Mahone wasn't sure how to take her comments. "A middle class working stiff who sacrifices everything to protect the little guy?" She continued. "That goes against everything contemporary society dictates." They exchanged glances and smiled.

Both momentarily considered verbalising their feelings out loud but decided against it.

"Anything else, Dr. Ruth?" He pushed.

"Yes, you're an altruist. Altruists are a dying breed!" She added.

"A middle class altruist?" He casually nodded. "I'll take that as a compliment."

"The middle class is the backbone of Western civilization." Irina continued. "Why do you suppose all those Third World countries are third world countries? They only have two classes, the very rich and the very poor. The prosperity of the Middle Class through its Constitution is America's gift to civilization. Why do you think communists, fascists and socialists hate it so much? It's why my father brought us here from Ukraine"

"I can see babysitting you for a couple days is going to be a very interesting experience." He opined.

"I don't need a babysitter, I need a good lawyer!"

"I'm working on it, trust me." He assured her.

Being the first she heard of this she smiled and took his hand.

"I appreciate everything you're doing for me."

By way of response he asked her a question.

"You ever think about what you're gonna do after the FBI?"

"You mean **IF** we get out of this in one piece?" She grumbled.

"Yeah, you know, aside from the being suspended, having a federal arrest warrant out on you, potential homicide charges and being hunted by the most secretive, rogue agency in the world. You know, little annoying things like that."

"To be perfectly honest, I thought I had my life set here in this country. But what I see now here compared to what my parents told me about the old Soviet times in Ukraine, kinda scares me."

"Don't let it get to you. We'll get through this, you'll have your badge again and be back working cases in no time."

"I hope you're right. When I put in to transfer out of the tech branch and work the streets I didn't bargain on the system I thought I was defending being turned against me!"

"It's a high-stakes game Sweetheart. The closer you get to the top of the social order the more vicious the players and the blurrier the lines get. The more people like Pravum, Parva and the yokels at AstroCom will seek to trample anything or anyone in their way, you and I included. And they have the power to do it."

"Well that's encouraging!" She chided. "You really know how to cheer a girl up!"

"Just because this is the best socio-economic system yet devised doesn't mean there isn't a downside." He added.

"And what's that, as if I didn't know?"

"For those willing to claw their way to the top everyone else is there as cannon fodder. For some of those people there are no rules. The worst crime you can commit is getting caught."

"It appears that's especially true in government!" She conceded.

"Now you're startin to sound like an American!"

"So what are **your** big plans after retirement?"

She ventured.

"I got my eye on something. After retirement I should be pulling in just enough to put a down payment on a small place on the Lower East Side with an apartment above it. Downstairs will make a good office space and I think I'll set up shop as a P.I."

"Wow, a P.I.! That has a certain poetic continuity to it." She conceded. "Sounds cosy."

"Yeah, no more eight a.m. roll calls, middle of the night alerts, mandatory overtime or union assholes tellin' me what I can and can't do."

She suddenly furrowed her brow and got quiet.

"I just thought of something." Irina blurted out. "Don't they fit cop cars with GPS tracking devices?"

"Yes."

"Then shouldn't there be one in this car?"

"Yes. Probably"

"So shouldn't we be worried?!" She asked with alarm. "I mean we certainly can't sit in this tunnel for the rest of the weekend."

As they spoke he glanced down the hill and noticed a second cruise ship, smaller than the first, moored on the Jersey side of the river docked next to the first.

"No, not really."

"And why not what, Mr. Cocky?!"

"Because we're in a granite tunnel, ten feet below ground and surrounded by power cables along the street, so the answer to your question is, probably not."

"**Probably** not?" She questioned.

"Never mind that, I've got an idea!" He put the car in gear and backed out onto the street.

"Oh good! Another brainstorm! Let's see where this one is going to wind us up at!" She complained. "Where're we going?"

"To catch a boat!"

"What kind of boat? What about the cop car? At least tell me what the plan is this time!" She demanded as he drove.

"I don't know I'm making this up as we go along! All I know is I have to keep you out of trouble until Monday morning."

"Now what are we doing?" She asked. He nodded down towards the cruisers.

"They feature Hudson River overnight tours north to Niagara Falls and then return to dock in Manhattan in the morning."

"Huh!"

"How much money you got left?" Frank asked.

"Not a lot! We've been spending like drunken sailors! They kept my purse back at your police station but I have plenty in my savings account if it's not blocked."

"I've got a couple of hundred left on my credit cards as well. If we can find an ATM we can pull some cash."

"But won't that leave a trail?"

"Yeah but they won't pick it up until morning, by then it'll be too late."

"What's the plan for Monday morning?"

"There's a hearing at ten at the Federal

Courthouse. I'm gonna call Wachowski and get him to arrange for a Police Union lawyer to meet us before the hearing."

"Make it a Jewish lawyer if possible. Two of them!" She added. "Now what?"

"We find a phone and an ATM."

As they cruised through town she spotted a bank with an outside ATM.

"You mean like that one?" She pointed out.

They parked and locked the car in a backstreet alley, withdrew some cash and walked the short distance into the town center where they found a payphone.

**

While the secretive illegal 'Extradition Flights' of the early 2000's in some cases were justified and only later declared illegal, they were never really removed from government policy altogether. They merely paved the way for the DOJ, NSA and the FBI, as well as the other 14 U.S. security agencies, to push the boundaries of what they could get away with as concerns their illicit activities.

Now with Irina Kuksova MIA and the federal Court hearing less than 48 hours away, it was in a somewhat panicked frame of mind that General Michael Pravum began to see his long military career begin to potentially evaporate. To this end Pravum turned to his last resort.

He had access to what was called a covert 'Black Team'. So covert in fact that less than half a dozen in the entire Intel Commuinty, the POTUS not included, knew of its existence.

The current team leader of the FBI's 'Team 21', 21 for short, was a former coordinator for the CIA managed, NSA directed, FBI assisted elicit extradition squads used to kidnap and fly suspects from foreign countries to go on to be stored in Guantanamo Bay.

From his office late that evening Pravum placed a classified call.

"Lieutenant, the DIRNSA here."

"Yes sir?"

"I need your team assembled and on the helo pad at Langley in one hour. Someone will be there to brief you. Can you comply?"

"We'll be there in 55 minutes Director. What's the mission?"

"A high value prisoner has escaped and is believed to be enroute to the Canadian border via the Hudson River. I'll text you the last known position via satphone as soon as I get it."

"Understood. Objective sir?"

"Retrieve and return said individual to the federal facility in New York City."

"Is the asset protected sir?"

"Prisoner is believed to be accompanied by one, semi-retired, older NYPD cop."

"Bring him in also sir?"

"Negative. However you are authorized to neutralize him if required. The asset itself must be brought in alive. Understood?"

"Understood sir. Consider it done. 21 Actual

out."

****

It was nearing sunset that evening when the four members of Team 21 in their twin inboard, center console Chris-Craft with attached dinghy were speeding north up the Hudson.

Through intercepted police reports, the use of Stingray tracking devices and a few phone calls it was a simple matter to track the stolen police car to the street just outside Weehawken, New Jersey.

From there CCTV cameras revealed Mahone and Kuksova making their way aboard the New York Waterways Hudson cruise linertour boat earlier that afternoon.

It was just before twenty-two hundred when the men of 21 spotted the slow cruising Hudson River tour boat just outside of West Point Military Academy.

****

As Inspector Morrissey was crossing the hotel lobby his mobile phone rang.

"Morrissey here."

"Inspector, this is Phil Finley."

"Mr. Finley what can I do for you?"

"Is something going on with detective Mahone?"

"Why do you ask?"

"I tried to reach him by phone but the line appears to be dead."

Morrissey stepped into an alcove to speak more candidly.

"I've no time to explain but there's been an incident."

"Anything I can do?" Finley offered.

"Yes there is. Is Parvum currently at the Center?"

"No. As a matter of fact he and Colonel Parva were in earlier this morning, dressed in civilian clothes and we're acting strange."

"Strange how?"

"Aside from the fact that it's a weekend and they almost never come in on the weekend unless there's a problem, they never come to the center in civies."

"I see."

"They seemed to be in a hurry but before they left they asked me to engage *Hermes* and track agent Kuksova one more time."

"What do you mean by 'one more time'? I thought she was under arrest in jail?" Morrissey feigned surprise.

"Apparently not. They rang the 13th Precinct from here several times. It seems she's disappeared."

A broad smile crept across Morrissey's face.

"Can you track Pravum using your *Hermes* system?" He asked.

"The system is active but I've had to install a new firewall code. Pravum wanted it completed with no code which made me suspicious. I still believe he wanted to bring *Hermes* with him when he goes to work for AstroCom."

"You're probably right, but can you track him

now?" Morrissey pushed.

"As long as he has his phone with him yes."

"Good! Call me back at this number in 10 minutes and let me know where he is now. Can you do that?"

"I'll call you in nine minutes!" Finley replied.

True to his word Phil Finley got to work and minutes later was able to pinpoint both Pravum and Parva at 32,000 feet in the air apparently enroute to New York City.

Morrissey, having also been informed about the Monday morning court hearing by Cheif Wachowski, assumed the two military officers were flying in only to attend the hearing.

His misjudgement would soon come to light.

*

It was late Saturday evening as dusk encroached when the FBI snatch team cited the pleasure cruiser about a half a mile ahead slowly meandering up the Hudson.

The 33 foot, SOC-R, Special Operations Craft-Riverine, boat could do 40 knots or about 75 km/h and so brought their target in sight a few hours after leaving the Brooklyn Navy yards.

The O.D. green craft was on loan from a Coast Guard SOCOM Reserve Unit on Governor's Island.

The captain and coxswain of the four man crew slowed engines to five knots and put in at a nearby clearing to allow them to finalise a boarding plan.

Meanwhile, out on the bow deck of *The Spirit of*

New York, the 134 foot, triple deck tour boat, Frank and Irina were finishing off the last of their after dinner drinks of the evening and were preparing to head off to their cabin.

Although the ordeal they had endured together over the last weeks had brought them closer together their relationship was still no more than what could be described as 'Friends with Benefits'.

It had just gone 23:10.

"What do you think will happen in court?" Irina asked.

"There's no sure way to know. It's a crapshoot as to which judge we get but if I had to bet any money I'd bet that whatever happens it's not going to be what anybody expects."

Noticing the concern in her face Frank reached across the table and took her hand.

"Whatever happens I'm confident you'll be cleared, reinstated, get your job back and things will be back to normal in no time!" He reassured. They gathered their things and headed up to their cabin.

Back on the the SOCOM swift boat it had been decided that the best method of attack would be for three of the men to board the cruiser under way, snatch the girl and remount the SOCOM craft from the port fantail where there was an emergency evacuation ladder.

Waiting until half past eleven when, with the use of NVG's, they could see most of the decks were cleared and the majority of passengers had turned in, they launched their operation.

Slowing as they approached the lumbering

cruiser so as not to arouse attention then pulling alongside the three man snatch team daftly hopped the ladder and climbed aboard.

Not only would Irina's strong eastern European features and long blonde hair make her stand out in a crowd, but each member of the 21 Team had been issued a copy of Kuksova's I.D. photo. Once aboard the search was on.

Part of the professional preparation for their mission had been to hack into the New York Waterways computer system, obtain the passenger list for this cruise and pinpoint Kuksova's cabin number. However no passengers under the names Kuksova or Mahone came up on the manifest.

What the misinformed commandos did find were half a dozen couples registered under various names. Three names were Hispanic, one Asian and two were Anglo thus giving them a 50/50 chance of getting the right cabin.

Once on the second deck one man posted himself at the entrance to the passageway while the other two made their way down the hall to cabin #17.

The cabin door was unlocked and so it was a simple matter for the two black-clad gunman to ease themselves into the room. Two people in colourful underwear stood by the bed passionately kissing.

The man, holding the long-haired woman turned, gasped and raised his hands. Wide-eyed the woman turned and followed suit.

A quick glance at the photos and the agents realised it was the wrong blonde.

Mahone and Kuksova were in cabin #19. With

foresight Frank had wisely made the reservations under the name O'Neill, Irina's occasional a.k.a.

Minutes later the FBI agents exited cabin #17 leaving the two lovers zip tied and tape gagged on the bed next to each other.

"'Is is wat ew meant by 'ig surprise night'? Asthole!" The girl cursed her boyfriend through the tape.

Down the hall it was to their luck that Mahone was in the toilet as one of them, 9mm in hand, eased the door open while the other took aim with a tranquilizer gun.

Irina, preparing for bed with her back to the door never saw it coming.

"Ow!" As the dart buried itself in her upper thigh.

"You say something?" Frank, Not yet fully undressed, called from the bathroom.

There was no answer only an empty room when he emerged from the toilet a minute later.

"Irina?" He called into the room. With no response he looked around the relatively small cabin and spotted her shoes and blouse on the floor next to the bed.

Alarm bells instantly rang and he had the presence of mind to snatch up his shoulder holster from the nightstand before bolting from the cabin.

As he ran down the passageway and burst through the aft door on the second deck and into the night he peered over the rail in time to see two men one deck below carrying the unconscious Irina heading across the fantail.

But as he reached the foot of the stairs he was

allowed two steps before being hit across the back of the head with something hard.

Grabbing the back of his head Mahone stumbled to the rail as he was aware of heavy footsteps scurrying away from him.

Recovering quickly he retrieved his 9mm from the deck, leaned over the stair rail and let off two shots. The first missed but the second hit his assailant in the lower back.

The kidnapper collapsed, began to crawl towards the emergency ladder but turned and let off one shot which missed Mahone. The wounded assailant continued to crawl.

He apparently ran out of steam as he reached the ladder, dropped his weapon, again collapsed and fell over the side into the inky black of the river.

Mahone recovered and made it to the rail in time to see the assault boat escaping down river aways then turning in towards shore. He carefully took aim as they sped away however for fear of hitting Irina, he hesitated.

By then it was too late.

Realizing he hadn't a prayer of catching them but knew he must leave the boat, he continued his efforts.

As the assailants sped into the night Frank looked back across the deck to see a handful of tourists who had emerged from their cabins and had been observing events.

"Hey mister I got their frames!" A young, pyjama clad girl boasted as she brandished her iPhone.

"Their what?"

"Their frames! Their pictures!"

"Show me!" Frank demanded as he grabbed the phone. "Give your contact details to the captain. I'll see that you get your phone back."

Much to the girl's chagrin Mahone quickly pocketed the device while the shocked teecn stared in disbelief as Mahone scurried down the stairway, to a lifeboat station on the fantail.

He struggled with the hydrostatic release unit but was able to disconnect it and access the painter rope lashing the large, white plastic capsule to the railing.

It took 20 to 30 seconds for the eight man rubber raft to inflate and for him to wrestle it over the side.

Meanwhile the SOCOM boat was vanishing into the dark.

Twenty-five minutes later Frank made it to shore on the unwieldy life raft by which time he had long lost sight of the kidnapers.

It was as he was dragging the raft ashore that Frank looked up to see a Black Hawk helicopter slowly rising up from the West Point compound up the hill above him.

Frank reached into his pocket and quickly produced the tourist phone he had snatched and scrolled through the girl's photos.

She had managed six to eight shots but only two frames were discernible, one of them of the thug Mahone tagged with his is 9mm the other carrying Irina

Making his way up the bank to the two lane blacktop Mahone watched the Black Hawk from a distance as it lifted into the night sky, turned and headed back down south along the river.

He instinctively knew Irina was aboard and where they were taking her. South back into the city.

****

Mahone walked west for near;y an hour in the cold and dark to the highway then traveled south to the City via Interstate route 87 before being picked up by a Canadian long-distance truck driver at an all night diner.

Once back in the city he briefly considered making it over to his apartment in Hoboken however decided it was likely that they still had it staked out.

In the meantime he puzzled over where exactly they could have taken Irina. There was no question who kidnapped her, it was merely a matter of where and what their next move would be.

CHAPTER TWENTY-ONE

It was right around seven a.m. that Sunday morning when Mahone was dropped off on the Manhattan side of the Hudson so he hopped the PATH subway over to Hoboken and made his way to one of his new haunts, Buddy's 24 Hour Diner on the corner of Washington and York in central Hoboken.

Using the cell phone he 'borrowed' from the cruise ship passenger, he rang Morrissey's room at the hotel.

Thirty minutes later Morrissey and the Squad were at the diner squeezed into a large back booth of the near empty eatery where Frank filled them in on the previous night's events.

"If the mission now is to find Miss Kuksova, my suggestion is we start by trying to find out where Pravum is." Enfield threw out.

"Why Pravum?" Heath asked.

"With the hearing only a day away and the fact that he and Kuksova have to be there, he can't be very far away." Enfield explained.

"In as much as guys like him feel no obligation to folllow the law I wouldn't count on him bringing Irina to court!" Frank interjected.

"So then how do we find them . . .? Him . . . her? All of them!" Heath asked.

"I spoke with Finley yesterday." Morrissey broke in. "He told me both Pravum and Parva were acting strange and appeared to be heading out somewhere, away from D.C. possibly this morning."

"They're coming here!" Frank suddenly realized.
"Apparently." Nigel confirmed.

Retrieving Phil Finley's number from Morrissey Frank called and, without revealing too much, had a brief talk with Finley explaining that he was trying to locate Irina. In the course of the conversation Finley confirmed that Parva and Pravum had headed up to New York City.

"Now all we need to do is find out if they've landed yet." Heath advised.

"And where!" Din added. "But how?"

"By ringing up the airports!" Mahone said as he dialled the cell phone.

Frank started with calls to JFK and Newark asking about flight info from Dulles. With the exception of two flights to JFK that were due in that evening and one flight booked at the last minute coming in D.C. to Newark there were no others that day. However, when he attempted to garner more details such as flight number and passenger count the young clerk shut him down.

"Sorry sir we are not permitted to give out that information over the phone." She politely explained.

"I understand." Frank quickly checked his watch. "I am Detective Lieutenant Frank Mahone NYPD. If you need to verify who I am my badge number is 5417 and I work out of the 13th precinct in Manhattan. I am with the security detail supposed to meet a passenger on that flight. That flight carries NSA dignitaries from Washington and was scheduled to land at 9 oclock. I make it to be 10:45. I'm just off the phone with D.C. and they told me the flight left on time. If there's a problem we need to know. "

"Please hold one sir."

A minute later a different, older woman came back on the line.

"Lieutenant Mahone?"

"Yes ma'am?"

"You must have been given the wrong departure time. Either that or they were somehow delayed. The flight your enquiring about is currently due to touchdown in fifty-five minutes."

"Fifty-five minutes. That's a relief, I'll tell the team. We were getting a bit concerned! Thank you for your cooperation."

"Not at all Lieutenant, glad I could help."

Frank turned to the group and issued directives.

"Okay, Heath and Tammy to Newark Liberty Airport. It's five minutes to the train, 25 minutes to the terminal by PATH. You should be there a half hour before they land. Get out there, find them and tail them."

"How will we know what they look like?" Heath asked.

"Use your phones, Google 'NSA Director' on the way out, his picture is no doubt on line." Enfield advised. "They're probably travelling in civilian clothes." He added.

"We're going to need a base to work from. Nigel, okay if we use your room?" Frank asked.

"By all means."

"I have a better idea." Enfield spoke up.

"Talk to me." Frank prompted.

The Hermes Project

"The locals have already made us in that hotel. There's a cheap motel just down the road. Din's not signed into a room at our hotel, he's essentially anonymous. By me registering a room in the motel down the street we can have a place to work out of and not worry about the cops showing up again."

"Yeah, Bloody Cops!" Tammy joked.

"Sounds good to me!" Frank backed. "Din, collect everyone's key card, get back over to the hotel, pack up everyone's belongings and stage them in the Inspector's room."

"Should I go with and check us out of the hotel?" Enfield voluteered.

"No that might tip our hand. Just consolidate the luggage. Questions, comments snide remarks?" He glanced around the table and waited. "None? Okay, everyone to their battle stations! Meet back here in an hour!"

Heath and Tammy hopped to it and headed for the door.

"Text us as soon as you two make contact!" Frank called after them. Tammy shot him a thumbs up as they passed through the door just ahead of Din and Enfield leaving Frank and Nigel alone at the table.

"Have you given any thought to what we're going to do if and when we locate her?"

"Yes quite a lot of thought actually." Frank replied.

"Care to share exactly what you're going to do?"

"Whatever I have to to get her back!"

****

Heath and Tammy arrived out at Newark Liberty a full twenty minutes before the NSA agents were due to land. But as they inconspicuously watched from the side of the gate as the United Airlines flight spilled it's passengers out into the terminal no men fitting the description of Pravum or Parva appeared.

When the last of the passengers filed past Heath quickly phoned in to report. Morrissey took the call and relayed the message to Mahone.

"Tell them to check the private or restricted tarmac. They might not be flying commercial." Frank instructed.

Minutes later they located the reserve tarmac where a government Lear jet was parked and they where able to pick up Pravum and Parva at the luggage claim carousel.

Being professional London detectives Tammy and Heath where now in their element.

From a safe distance the two Scotland Yarders followed the agents to the outside taxi rank where they climbed into a cab.

The entire way across the terminal Tammy constantly bugged Heath.

"Come on let me do it!" She insisted.

"No! This isn't a bloody movie!" Heath argued.

"Come on just once! PLEASE?!" She pleaded.

"What are you twelve years old all of a sudden?"

"I'm gonna do it anyway! You know I am!" She threatened.

"Alright damn it! You can do it." He relented.

As soon as Pravum's taxi pulled away Heath and Tammy climbed into the next one.

"Follow that car!" Tammy proudly instructored. The driver turned and stared at the two in the backseat.

"Yes, she's serious!" Heath resigned himself to acknowledge. "Follow that car." He lethargically echoed.

They tailed Pravum & Parva through the Holland tunnel into Manhattan and watched as they were dropped off outside the Hilton on West 24th in the Chelsea district.

The two detectives left their cab across the avenue.

"I'll lay you odds that place is near 500 quid a night!" Heath quietly uttered as he perused the exterior of the swank hotel. "Keep an eye out, I'm going to duck around the corner and call in."

Ordering two coffees from a luncheonette Heath called Frank who instructed them to stay on it as the two marks checked in. He further informed them to maintain observation and that the team would be there in forty-five minutes to an hour.

"500 quid a night? Why not?" Tammy mumbled to herself as she watched from across the street. "If you're goin' slip it to them what pays the candle wax might as well slip it in up to the hilt eh?!" She swore as she watched the two enter through the brass plated revolving doors of the opulent lobby of the luxurious hotel.

Paddy Kelly

****

Describing the Motel 6½ as shabby would be like describing Jeffrey Epstein as a matchmaker. And even at that one could be considered being polite.

However, as dilapidated, rundown motels go the 1960s chic, two story cinder block building, featuring alternating powder blue and bright orange doors was more than a runner-up for pole position.

The 'Truck Divers [sic] Must Shower Before Using Pool' sign prominently displayed on the green, chain link fence surrounding the dead leaf and grease-coated pool water was the first hint as to the reason for the $39.95 per night price tag flashing out on the partially burnt out neon road sign.

Having temporarily shifted over to the Motel 6½ Mahone had no sooner hung up from talking to Heath when he and The Squad were on their way over to Manhattan.

As predicted Frank and Nigel showed up at the Woolworths luncheonette over in Midtown about an hour later bringing the rest of the crew, Din and Enfield, with.

After a quick briefing to include a physical description of the two marks, Frank ordered Din & Enfield to take over surveillance duty from Tammy & Heath.

Just as they did . . .

"Marks' are on the move!" Din quietly declared as he watched the two federal agents exit the hotel and head east down 24th Street.

"Nigel, you Tammy and Heath go grab a quick cup of coffee and meet back here." Frank instructed. "We're going to tail those two. since they're on foot they're likely only going for lunch but we have to be sure. Din, Enfield with me."

At that Mahone, Enfield and Din moved out to follow Parva and Pravum.

Using the hopscotch technique of tailing a suspect where-by the police spread out and alternate positions, they commenced their moving surveillance.

However their well-trained, well-executed, Cold War styled manoeuvre was cut short as a half a block away the two agents turned north on 6th Avenue and turned again back west only a block away on 25th Street.

This is where Mahone and the crew got a lucky break.

Halfway up 25th Street Pravum and Parva had settled on a restaurant. Mahone's team halted then spread out up the block where Mahone made a quick decision.

"Enfield, you graduate the police academy?"

"Of course! 18 weeks at Merseyside. Top of me class!"

"Okay, here's your big chance to show us what you learned at the police academy in Merseyside!" Frank chided as he dialled his phone and nodded across the street to the Smithfield Hall, a 150 seat, privately-owned, English-styled sports pub and restaurant.

Being only a few blocks north of the 13th

Precinct, Frank had gotten to know the owner, also a former Marine, quite well after having eaten there on and off for the last seven years.

Someone answered the phone after two rings.

"The Hall, O'Connor speaking."

"Liam! Frank Mahone here! How're they hangin'?"

"Low and to the left Brother! Wachowski still lettin' you out durin' the day to collect bullet holes?"

"Only so's I can visit your wife!"

"Not this one Brother! The other two before my second divorce maybe, but not this one! What can I do for you?"

"There's a couple of jamokes in your place right now having lunch. They're a critical link to a murder case I'm working on."

"Okay. What do you need from me?" O'Connor answered as he perused the long room.

"I need to get a guy in there and hover around the table, see if we can pick up what they're talking about."

From his perch sitting at the end of the bar Liam scanned the restaurant and spotted the only pair of men, both in suits sitting at a two top near the back.

"I think I see them. Grey suits, dark hair both? One a little older?"

"You got 'em. I'll slip my man through the literary agency office hall next door-"

"I'll save you the trouble." Liam offered.

"How?"

"Stand by one." At that Frank heard Liam call

over to someone. "Stacy!"

A minute later an attractive thirty-something blonde was busily bussing and cleaning tables surrounding the two NSA agents. Her slow efforts were quickly rewarded. She reported over to Liam.

Back on the phone Liam again picked up the conversation with Frank.

"Sounds like they work for the government."

"Give that man a cigar!" Frank jokingly said.

"Stacey says they're talking about something about an island."

"An island?"

"Yeah, something about one of them has to get down to Police Plaza and the other one has to get out to 'The Island', wherever that is."

"Anything else?" Frank pushed.

"No, they finished their drinks, no food, and ordered their checks. Looks like they're getting ready to shove off."

"Thanks Liam, I owe you a pint! And slip Stacey a 20 for me, I'm good for it next time I'm in."

"You got it Frank, watch your ass!"

Mahone went back to meet up with Nigel, Tammy and Heath after he assigned Din and Enfield to maintain a tail on Pravum while Heath and Tammy took Parva.

****

On their way back to the Hilton Pravum explained his plans for the upcoming week.

"I want this female off the FBI and behind bars

for a minimum of 15 to 20!"

"What's our back-up if you're not granted a FISA warrant?"

"Not to worry! After tomorrow's hearing the judge will want to know why this Kuksova broad hasn't been caught earlier! And by the time we get back down to D.C. on Wednesday to appear before the FISA Court I'll have them thinking she's a double agent and connected to the Steele Dossier!"

"And if you're **not granted** the warrant?" Parva pushed.

"Don't worry! With the judge we're gonna get tomorrow-"

"Neuhouse!" Parva realized. "How'd you manage that sir? If you don't mind my asking."

"Back before she was on the bench, when she was just a prosecutor, she needed some information on a subject. I helped her out and she got her conviction. We've been sort of working together on and off ever since."

"And Finley and the Hermes project?"

"First thing when we get back to D.C. I want you to get the paperwork done to change the name of that program to something more appropriate."

"Like what?"

"Like Backdoor." He proudly declared. "And schedule the skiff for a week from Monday. I'll have to brief the Gang of Eight on my new Backdoor anti-spy program. "

"Backdoor it is sir!"

****

Just over a hour later, back at Motel 6½ Mahone and The Squad, painfully aware that time was running out that afternoon, were huddled together in their rundown room debating the significance of the single word overheard by Stacy the waitress, 'island'.

All were unanimous in their agreement that it must be one of the many islands in the Greater New York City area, however with over 40 dedicated islands within the boundaries of the Big Apple, it was anyone's guess as to on which of the islands they might be able to locate their missing comrade.

"Liberty Island? It's government owned and controlled by the feds!" Tammy said aloud.

"To high profile, too many tourists." Frank objected.

"Randall's Island has a prison, doesn't it? Morrissey suggested.

"They closed it down on humanitarian grounds." Frank countered.

"Roosevelt Island maybe? It's bigger, more places to hide her." Heath tossed out.

It was just then that Morrissey's cell phone rang. It was Enfield calling from the ferry piers on the Manhattan Battery.

"Talk to me!" Frank answered as he signalled for the room to be quiet.

"Lieutenant, it's me. Pravum just boarded the ferry to Governors Island."

"You sure?!"

"I'm watching him climb the stairs to the upper

deck as we speak." There was a long pause. "What do you want me to do, they're getting ready to push off?"

"How crowded is the ferry?"

"Pretty crowded."

"If you think you can follow him without being made go for it." Frank instructed.

"Right! Enfield out!" He quickly signed off as he pocketed his mobile phone, dashed across the dock to the passenger ramp and hopped aboard just as a crewmember pulled the safety gate across the fantail.

"It's Governors Island!" Frank declared to the rest of the room.

"I thought that was a public park?" Morrissey questioned.

"It is. But part of it is still owned by the government at Fort Jay."

Less than forty minutes later Endfield texted Mahone:

> Pravum carrying portfolio into Fort Jay.
> 15 minutes. Back out minus portfolio.

*

Fort Jay the 18th Century fortification on the northern end of the island was, Frank noted, temporarily closed since 2001 which raises the question what would the head of the NSA be doing going there?

"Not an unusual situation given the reputation of the bureaucracy of New York City." Morrissey observed.

"We still have no way to know if she's definitely being held there." Tammy pointed out.

"No but, if he does show up in court with her no doubt she'll have the opportunity to take the stand and tell her side of the story in which case it will cast doubt on his story. If things go that far the police union lawyer I've arranged for will get her bail or at least transferred into state custody."

"Either one will muck up his plans!" Heath observed.

"Exactly!" Frank agreed.

"But if this judge is a real hard case as you suspect he might be, it could all turn into one big crap shoot!" Tammy again threw in.

"Pravum is in town for one reason, the hearing." Frank countered. "I'm convinced he has no intention of producing Irina in court. He'll throw out some bullshit excuse as to why she can't be produced, about it all being classified and that she's being held in a secure facility!" They all silently agreed. "It's too late for us to do anything else of any significance now. Either we take our chances on Governors or show up at court empty-handed leaving Pravum all the cards."

Various expressions circled the room until suddenly a voice broke the silence.

"I have an idea!" Enfield spurted out.

*

It was 16:00 that afteroon as dusk was setting in

when Mahone, Morrissey, Tammy and Enfield crossed into Manhattan and took a ride on the tourist ferry over to Governors Island.

Din and Heath took up positions at a dock-side café on the Manhattan side near the ferry port to act as rear guard and lookouts.

At a mere 800 meters off the Manhattan Battery it was a short fifteen minutes until the ferry docked on the north shore of the tear drop shaped island.

Being the second to last shuttle boat back to the mainland for that afternoon, a considerable crowd waiting to board had gathered so, as soon as the four stepped off the ramp they spread out through the crowd so as not to be seen as a group.

As they did Mahone was careful to take a mental inventory of the few boats moored along the dock.

Maintaining their distance apart Enfield pointed them the short 200 meters to the west wall of the red stone fort and to the central, above ground tunnel he had seen Pravum enter earlier in the day.

Frank entered the tunnel while Morrissey stood outside pretending to use his cell phone.

Tammy, pretending to take pictures with her phone, peeled off to one of the oversized cannon mounts 150 meters away affording her a position between the docks and the tunnel as Enfield slowly circled his way back to the dock area taking a seat on the breakwater and eyeing the collection of small boats moored there.

Mahone walked slowly through the long tunnel carefully assessing the half dozen, over-sized, heavy oak doors to each of the tunnel's branching passageways.

All were closed over and appeared to be padlocked shut. All except the third door. Noting that the door's hasp featured no lock and that the dirt in front of the threshold had recently been disturbed, Mahone believed he had found what he was looking for.

As he reached to open the door he heard a voice out at the far end of the tunnel.

"Sorry sir, we are closing. I need you to make your way back towards the ferry dock. We close at five." It was a uniformed Parks Department ranger addressing Morrissey.

Frank quickly slipped in through the door.

"Sure, no problem. I'll go find my friend and we'll head over." Nigel replied.

Unseen by the ranger Frank, the door cracked open, peered through the shadows to spot a small empty table and chair. The items on the table, a half read novel, a partially filled ash tray with a burning cigarette and a cell phone clearly indicated he had stumbled on an improvised guard post.

Enfield still sat on a pier piling back over in the docking area nervously checking the time and spotting no sign of his colleagues.

Tammy peered out from between the black iron struts of a 4,500 lbs Rodman gun as she hid under the west-facing cannon mount while a pair of Parks rangers leisurely strolled past gossiping about their supervisor.

It was well after five o'clock as the minutes slowly passed and the skies grew darker. Enfield moved to hide in the public toilets until fewer and fewer park rangers roamed the grounds and the last ferry load of tourists had long sailed away from the island.

Now with no rangers or other foot traffic in sight Tammy cautiously peered out over the ramparts to see that the ferry had docked across the river at the Manhattan piers.

Her phone suddenly vibrated and she read the text:

Third door on right. No lock.

Mahone, from back just outside the door, shook his head when he saw that she had texted back a smiley face.

Cautiously but swiftly she scurried across the 150 meters of open ground to the tunnel area and, guided by Frank pointing, quietly entered the only door without a lock.

Mustering her best 'frightened' face as she looked around, a wide-eyed Tammy approached the military guard now seated at the small table. With her natural Scottish accent the tall, uniformed MP easily believed she was a lost and disoriented tourist.

"Sorry Miss, this is a restricted area!" He informed as he lay his pulp fiction novel aside, rose from the small desk and stepped towards her.

"Sorry but I was trying to make me way back to the wee ferry boat!" She pleaded.

"Well you'll have to go back outside and to your right. But you might have a problem, I think the last one to the mainland has left." He suggested checking his wrist watch.

"Perhaps I could call a water taxi?"

However, before anything else could occur Frank appeared in the doorway a pistol levelled at the sentry. The MP raised his hands and shot Tammy a nasty look.

"Looks like me ride is here!" She smiled and shrugged.

"Lawrence?!" They were surprised to hear an unseen voice as just then a second guard strolled around the corner eating half a cheese and bologna sandwich.

"Lawrence, who are you talking-." The second MP immediately read the situation, dropped his sandwich and foolishly fumbled for his side arm. However, when Nigel stepped into the doorway alongside Frank, also brandishing a 9mm, reality struck home and MP#2 thought it wiser to also surrender.

Tammy assumed a smiley face as she moved to confiscate their side arms.

MP#2 looked down in dismay at his half-eaten cheese and bologna sandwich in the dirt.

"Here, keep them covered." Morrissey instructed as he handed off his formerly FBI-owned 9mm to Tammy.

"Reach for the sky lads!" She growled loudly pointing the weapon at the two nervous sentries. Mahone turned and looked over at her as he and Nigel vanished around the corner to search for Irina.

"That woman does not have both oars in the

water!" Frank mumbled.

"Which is why she fits right in!" Morrissey replied.

At the end of a short hallway a second, larger room greeted them in the corner of which they found a narrow, wrought iron, spiral staircase going down.

"Stay here!" He ordered Morrissey. "In case they get past Tammy!"

"I don't see that happening mate!"

With Mahone going down the iron staircase alone into the 18th Century dungeon he found Irina in the center cell of three narrow, dimly lit stone chambers, sitting on a wooden bench, a wool blanket draped over her shoulders.

"Hi sexy! Come here often?" Mahone quipped.

"FRANK!" She sprang to her feet, ran to the door and kissed him from between the bars. Her expression suddenly turned serious as she pushed him away.

"About time you showed up!" She admonished.

"What?!"

"I could have been shipped off to Guantanamo Bay by now!"

"SHIT!" Frank swore loudly as he patted himself down.

"What?!" Irina suddenly panicked.

"I just remembered, I don't have the keys to your cell! We might have to come back tomorrow." He stepped away as if to leave.

"Very funny wiseguy! The keys are hanging on the wall, over there!" She nodded to a wall hook

The Hermes Project

below the stairs.

Letting her out they moved to the stairs.

As she was preparing for bed when she was kidnapped, Irina was still in her underwear so Mahone removed his brown leather bomber jacket and gave it to her leaving her now only barefoot.

"NIGEL, WE CLEAR?" Mahone called up.

"HAVEN'T HEARD ANY GUNSHOTS YET!" He called back down so, with Frank leading they started back up.

Tammy, having already cuffed the two MP's back-to-back, sitting on the floor Mahone quickly relieved Tammy of their side arms, ejected the magazines and cleared the chambers tossing the weapons down the stairs.

Morrissey followed on by collecting their walkie talkies and smashing them open.

"What size shoes you wear?" Frank asked looking down at the smaller soldier.

"What?!" He barked back which earned him a kick in the side.

"You heard me! What size shoes you take?"

"Seven and a half!"

Minutes later as they exited the building into the dusk Irina was sporting a brand new pair of loose but spit-shined combat boots.

"I see why you Yanks are always on about these things!" Morrissey complimented hefting the pistol as the four of them hustled towards the docks.

Enfield had already untied and started one of the 225hp, six man Stabicraft launches and with Mahone taking the helm they all piled in and shoved off.

"SHIT!" One of them said loudly.

"What is it?" Frank called back over his shoulder as he steered. Tammy was pointing back to shore where a Parks ranger flanked by the two MP's stood growing smaller as the boat sped away.

"How the hell-?" Frank mumbled aloud.

When he turned to look, the ranger turned back and ran in the direction of the main building but the two MP's piled into another motor boat.

Meanwhile, five miles north up river, on Randall's Island, the NYPD Harbor Unit had been alerted and had redirected a high speed patrol boat already in the vicinity off Liberty Island to divert to the scene.

Through the diminishing light and intermittent mist of the encroaching evening the lights of the MP's chase boat continued at pace north west towards the Manhattan Battery.

From Mahone's boat the lights across on the tip of Manhattan started coming into view silhouetting the distant shoreline when a blue flashing light appeared in the distance off their port side.

"Is that a police boat?!" Kuksova demanded of Frank.

"Probably."

"We'll never outrun them!"

Now with Mahone's boat at about 300 meters out from shore it was without warning that he swung the helm hard to starboard and headed the craft around in a wide arch east away from the tip of Manhattan.

The Hermes Project

"Where'a you taking us?" Irina questioned.

"To the Batcave!"

He appeared to be taking them back to the island but at the last minute headed for a long slender out cropping holding an unmarked tall, narrow concrete structure.

Easing the boat around and on to the cement landing of the five story building which lie about fifty meters off the north shore of Governors, Mahone quickly unloaded his passengers, faced the getaway boat out towards the north east, tied off the helm and slipped it into gear where it would head out and across the channel harmlessly drifting into the Red Hook docks in Brooklyn.

The last thing Mahone could make out as he entered the building behind the others, was the harbor police boat stopping the MP's Stabicraft and boarding her.

Once everyone was below ground, past the giant ventilation fans and noisy generators it was a simple matter to head single file along the two foot wide catwalk next to the west bound lane of traffic and towards Manhattan.

"Where the hell are we?" Irina asked as she walked right behind Frank.

"Ventilation building of the Brooklyn Battery Tunnel. Runs from Red Hook to the battery entrance of the Westside Highway. It's an emergency personnel catwalk alongside the west bound traffic lane. From here we can make our way under the harbor to Battery Park."

"How did you know about this?" She asked.

"NYPD Baby! Just good police work!"

"Why do you always have to be such a smartass?" Irina, in the no mood for banter, snapped at Mahone as they made their way along the catwalk.

"Hey, a smartass is better than no ass!" Frank shot back.

"Sounds like them too are at each other." Behind them Enfield commented as he turned back to Tammy.

"Must be the sexual attention!" She casually responded.

CHAPTER TWENTY-TWO

**Federal Courthouse
1 Saint Andrews Plaza
Lower Manhattan, New York
Monday, 09:47**

Having first made their way back to the hotel, Morrissey and the Squad had arrived at the courthouse nearly an hour ago.

Frank and Irina on the other hand couldn't chance returning to the Motel 61/2.

Instead, following a quick breakfast at an all night diner they bought some clothes for Irina at a second hand store on Canal Street.

With no shoe stores in walking distance Irina's distinguished pantsuit and blouse were topped off with a pair of shiny MP's combat boots.

After briefly stopping by a street vendor to buy a long scarf, Frank and Irina turned the corner and took the sprawling granite steps of the Federal Courthouse two at a time only to be stopped at the front door to the lobby by an armed guard.

"Lieutenant Mahone, NYPD. Escorting a witness to trial." He informed as he flashed his I.D. and was allowed entrance.

"Some fucking vacation!" Little Tammy grumbled as they sat on the long wooden bench in the expansive courthouse lobby.

"Quit your bitchin'!" Enfield countered. "At

least we're not chasing knackers across the East End!"

From across the decoratively marbled lobby Frank spotted Nigel on a bench, the SHIT Squad seated around him. Mahone and Irina scurried over.

"Nigel! Glad to see you guys!" Frank greeted.

"About time you two showed up! It's ten til!" Morrissey chastised.

"Sorry! But we had some domestic chores to sort out."

"Is that what they call it over here? 'chores'?" Tammy quipped. "Sure in Glasgow we just call it shaggin'!" She nudged Heath who didn't laugh.

"Stand by one second." Frank instructed as he turned and made his way over to the reception desk in mid lobby.

"Excuse me, I'm due in court this morning at ten."

"Yes, Judge Esther Neuhouse's court. Courtroom number three One flight up and to the right. It's in the west wing." The desk clerk informed.

"Thanks." He made his way back over to Morrissey.

"How are we looking?" Heath asked.

"Not good!" Frank replied.

"Why not?"

"We're in Esther Neuhouse's Court."

"So who's Esther Neuhouse when she's home?" Tammy challenged.

"The most left wing, liberal prick in the district! Hates men, been passed over twice for Supreme Court nomination. Thinks The Constitution is completely outdated and even most of her own democrat colleagues can't stand her."

"Other than that we're okay though, yeah?" Enfield jibbed. The fact that no one laughed was indicative of the situation's seriousness.

Once upstairs and before entering the courtroom they were surprised to see a battalion of press, TV cameras included, lining the back wall.

"I thought this was supposed to be a closed hearing?" Irina said.

"Apparently somebody leaked it to the press." Heath observed as they stood outside.

"Imagine that?! A leak about a classified Washington D.C. hearing!" Mahone bitched.

"Inspector, you and The Squad take Irina and sit in the back row." He instructed as he handed Irina the scarf he bought off the street vendor. "Here, put this on and keep your face down! Morrissey you and The Squad crowd around her to keep her out of sight as much as possible."

"Got it!"

"This is shaping up to be a bloody circus!" Enfield commented.

"Most American courtrooms are." Frank added. "First Century Rome had the Circus Maximus. 21st Century New York has the courts."

"Now I know why there are so many courtroom TV shows in this country!" Din emphatically added.

"Exactly! People like to see other people getting fucked over in the name of Lady Justice." Tammy chimed in.

"England's not much better." Morrissey quietly

added.

They took their seats and from the front of the court a bailiff appeared followed by a judge.

"Hear ye, hear ye, hear ye! All rise! The first District Court of New York is now in session, the honorable Judge Noreen William-Simmons presiding."

At the announcement of a different judge Morrisey and Mahone exchanged surprised glasses.

"What happeed to the hanging judge?" Morrissey whispered.

"Deus ex Machina baby!" Frank quietly declared. "Looks like we get a break!" Frank whispered back.

"High time!" Nigel echoed.

Mahone stepped forward and took a seat next to the Policeman's Benevolent Association union lawyer who sat alone at the defence table.

The union lawyer gave a quiet but brief explanation that judge Neuhouse was involved in a fender bender on the way in from Long Island that morning. As he did he glanced over at the prosecution bench to see the three lawyers, two assistants and a clerk busily shuffling papers and arranging files. Along with Pravum himself.

This being a hearing and not a trial it was not unusual to pull a substitute judge for the proceeding. Unusual or not Frank made a mental note to track down the driver involved in the accident and send him a bottle of scotch.

"Is the prosecution ready?" Asked the judge.

"Yes your Honor."

"Is the defence ready?"

"We are your Honor, however at this time I would like to move for dismissal." The PBA union lawyer challenged.

"On what grounds?"

"To save the court time and money by avoiding a mistrial."

"Councillor, you do understand this is just a preliminary hearing?" The judge sought to clarify.

"I do your Honor however given the fact that not only is the defendant not present as mandated by law, but we have yet to be allowed to meet with her for the first time this morning as promised, not even by phone. Not only were we not briefed on the case before our promised, consultation with Special Agent Kuksova during which were told we would not be allowed any recording devices, note taking material or access to the prosecution's evidence through discovery. I am not a constitutional lawyer your Honor but at the very least we should be allowed-"

"Yes, yes, point taken counsellor. Are these statements accurate?" She queried the prosecution causing the head prosecutor to rise and address the bench.

"Your Honor you must understand we are dealing with highly sensitive material and top secret information. We intend to prove the actions of miss Kuksova may have had severe detrimental effects on national security."

"Your Honor. I have extremely important evidence-" Much to the annoyance of the PBA lawyer Frank stood and interrupted.

"And who are you?" She asked. The PBA lawyer also stood to answer, staying Mahone with one hand has he sought to reply.

"Your Honor this is homicide Lieutenant Detective Frank Mahone. He has-"

"Of the NYPD?" The judge interrupted.

"Yes your Honor."

"Hold up, hold up! You the same Frank Mahone what took five bullets three different times in the line of duty?"

"Three bullets on two separate occasions, judge."

As Frank answered the lawyer took him by the shoulder to straighten up as he addressed the bench.

"And you still on active duty?!" She more declared then queried.

"Yes judge."

"What the hell's wrong with you boy? Why ain't you sittin' on a boat down in the Bahamas sippin' margaritas and fishin'?" The judge commented half in chastisement and half in admiration.

A ripple of laughter drifted across the courtroom as the TV cameras kept rolling.

"I guess it's a matter of barbarians at the gate, Your Honor." Judge William-Simmons allowed the hint of a smile to eek out. "Your Honor. If you have time I have extremely important-"

"Hell yes I got time for you! Step up to the bench!" Mahone complied.

"Objection your honor!" The senior prosecutor demanded.

"Overruled! Be quiet while I talk to this man! Go on Lieutenant."

"Your Honor, I have extremely important evidence relevant to this case."

"What kind'a evidence?"

"A key witness has been kidnapped and was being held by rogue federal agents whom these lawyers represent."

"And who is this key witness?"

"Your Honor, the reason Special Agent Kuksova's not here is because she was the one kidnapped."

The judge's face registered shock.

"Kidnapped by who?"

"By men I strongly suspect were working for General Pravum, or at least are able to be traced back to the NSA." Mahone posited.

"Do you have any evidence of this Lieutenant Mahone?"

"I'm fairly certain if you have your bailiff take the time to contact the Orange County Sheriff's office upstate they'll confirm that a body, killed with a 9mm, was fished out of the Hudson in the vicinity of West Point sometime late Saturday evening or early Sunday."

"Interesting! Rather specific details!" William-Simmons muttered as she perused the table where Pravum and his lawyers sat.

Mahone then produced the cruise boat tourist's cell phone he had snatched and scrolled to the photos several of which, dark but discernible, showed two men in black hauling an unconscious Irina, easily identifiable by her long blonde hair, over the side rail. But more clearly photos of the man Frank shot.

The judge looked at the obviously wounded man lying on the deck.

"That your handy work lieutenant?"

"I'm afraid it is judge." He admitted.

"Bailiff, have one of your men contact the Orange County Sheriff's office upstate and see if he will verify the lieutenant's story."

"Yes judge." The bailiff replied Before he left the room.

"Does the prosecution have anything to add?" William-Simmons asked.

The reaction of the head prosecutor to this news clearly indicated he was unaware of these facts. A reaction which did not go unnoticed by the entire courtroom.

"Your Honor may I have a moment alone with my client?" The caught off-guard head prosecutor requested.

"Make it brief counsellor, I have a full docket today!"

The TV cameras zoomed in as the NSA lawyer signaled for Pravum to follow him. They both walked to a small consultation chamber just off to the side of the courtroom, the lawyer glancing back at the cameras as they disappeared behind the heavy oak door.

Once inside the room the lawyer made no pretense of his mood.

"One question Mike." The lawyer started off.

"What?"

"Have you lost your **fucking mind**?!"

"What?! I-"

"Kidnapping an American citizen on U.S. soil?! And a federal agent to boot?"

"You have no idea what's at stake here!" Pravum angrily countered.

"And I don't want to know! But I do know one thing, I know the shit this is going to stir up between the Agency and the FBI! How its going to tarnish our rep and future dealings with the guys at Langley! Not to mention DHS, DEA and the White House!"

"I don't give a damn about all them other alphabet agencies!" Pravum shot back. "Hell, half of, most of the intel they get comes from my office! And I damn sure don't give a shit about that relic of a fossil taking up space in the Oval Office! We'll be lucky if he makes it to the midterms! Guy's so old he still sees in black and white fer Christ's sake!"

"Mike, you need to understand that in this country nobody is above the law! Well, almost nobody. You need to-"

"Who in the hell do you think you're talking to you? I'm a goddamn Major General in the goddamn United States Air Force! Director of the most powerful spy agency in the goddamn world! All them other wanna-be spy agencies are working for me! Including you!"

Out in the courtroom everyone waited patiently as the private consultations progressed. Everyone except Frank Mahone.

"Nigel, I need to borrow your phone." Frank requested of Morrissey sitting in the gallery directly behind him.

Pravum's unrestrained hubris took the lawyer off balance leaving him unsure of how to react. The seasoned counsellor patiently listened to Pravum's rant then, folding his arms across his chest, quietly nodded, looked down and, without uttering a word, motioned Pravum back into the courtroom.

As Pravum's private pow wow with his lawyer continued Mahone stepped out into the hallway and used Nigel's cellphone to place a brief call before returning to his seat.

Minutes later Pravum and his lawyer also stepped back into the courtroom.

"Are we ready to proceed?" Asked the judge.

The NSA lawyer stood, cleared his throat and replied.

"It would appear that the accused is curretly in protective custody Your Honor."

"Protection from what, from whom?"

"Your Honor, under the Patriot Act-"

"Son, I was born durin' the day but it weren't yesterday! I'm gonna find out the whole story here sooner or later so you and your team better come clean while you can, know what I mean? Where exactly is this all-important defendant?"

The lawyer leaned over and whispered to Pravum who whispered back. A huddle of the prosecutors followed.

William-Simmons was clearly losing patience.

"Do you wish to add the additional charge of terrorism?" The judge asked. Pravum turned to his lawyer who gently shook his head no.

"Not at this time Your Honor."

"Then you are required to produce the defendant. Where is she? Has she absconded?"

Pravum stood and answered.

"No Your Honor. I'm sure you can understand that due to the sensitivity of the on going investigation-"

"Don't give me that 'on going investigation crap!' This isn't some congressional hearing where you can dodge questions by answering with vagaries and employ innuendo. Where is Agent Kuksova?!"

"Your Honor-"

"I presume General you have heard of the defendant's right to face their accuser?"

"Yes your Honor but-"

"And don't give me any of that disinformation nonsense! This isn't the Senate floor where you can evade questions that make you uncomfortable! Is she in custody or isn't she?!"

In the rear of the room Irina fought desperately to suppress her joy at Pravum's squirming in front of the court.

In fact, most parties present appeared to be more than happy that Pravum was allowed to continue to make a fool of himself.

"Well . . . she was Your Honor."

"What do you mean she **was**? Was where?"

"In a city jail."

"Which city jail?"

"On 21st Street when we intended to move her to Police Plaza."

"And if she's not there now where is she?"

"She seems to have escaped judge." Pravum half mumbled.

"Escaped from the city jail or from Police Plaza?"

"Um. . . essentially both Your Honor."

"Both?! Who exactly is this woman, Houdini's sister?"

The long silence was interrupted when the head bailiff approached the bench.

"Judge, we just received word back from the Orange County Sheriff. Lieutenant Mahone's story appears to check out." He reported aloud.

"Appears to? Can we not verify it 100%?"

"Well, the sheriff says they did recover a body from the river but the coroner no longer had it for less than two hours when two men from the Federal Government showed up and took possession of the corpse."

"In the immortal words of Arte Johnson, 'verrry interesting'!" The judge quipped. "Counsellor, you or your client have any clue about these mysterious government agents who appear in the dead of night and confiscate dead bodies?"

The federal prosecutor and the General exchanged glances.

"Not at this time Your Honor."

"I thought as much. Counsellor, your client has until one o'clock today to produce the defendant otherwise I have no choice but to dismiss your case due to lack of evidence. In addition to which I will issue a subpoena to the Director of the FBI to either find and produce this agent Kuksova or launch an immediate investigation as to her whereabouts!"

"In which case Your Honor we will be compelled to file an appeal." Pravum unexpectedly countered much to the chagrin of the prosecutor.

"Which is your perfect right gentlemen! This court is in recess until one o'clock."

As reporters, observers and participants filed out of the courtroom, Frank met up with Morrissey and the Squad.

"Well, what do you think?" Morrissey, keeping Irina under wraps, asked Frank once out off to the side in the vestibule.

"Not sure what to think but one thing is certain, they're trying to pull something!" Frank replied.

"Don't fool yourself!" Frank contradicted.

"What's that mean?"

"That means a son-of-a-bitch like him is not going to give up!" Frank declared.

"Wait until we come back at one, let's see what happens." Morrissey counselled.

"Nigel, I'll go back in at one o'clock. You guys get Irina back to the motel. I'll be over as soon as they're done here."

Inside judge William-Simmons' chambers the head bailiff entered and handed her a sealed message.

"It's from a senator in Washington!" He said with little attempt to hide his surprise.

Upon reading it the judge smiled and shook her head.

"Any response, judge?"

"No Carl, its all taken care of!"

*

The stroke of luck Mahone and The Squad were dealt that morning was luckier then they could have known.

On return to court that afternoon at one o'clock, judge William-Simmons wasn't surprised to not see Agent Kuksova present in the courtroom.

The 52 year old judge was pleasantly surprised at the message she had received earlier which concerned Kuksova. It would give her a modecum of pleasure to deliver the news that she had received earlier that morning to the NSA Director and his lawyers.

Ester Neuhouse may have been what could only be described as a left-wing judge however, William-Simmons was also one of those 'political' judges that weren't supposed to exist. However, she was one of those rare 'less government' and more a people's politically oriented individual.

On return to court that afternoon, once everyone was settled in and the bailiff had called the court to order and before the prosecution could resume judge William-Simmons adderessed the litegants first.

"Certain details relevant to this case have come to my attention through a third party. General Pravum, has this agent Kuksova stolen any secret documents from your agency?"

"Your Honor we-" Pravum began but was cut off

by his lawyer. "Not that we have been able to determine, Your Honor."

"Has she passed classified information to an enemy of the state?"

"Not to our knowledge Your Honor."

"Then the court finds through this hearing that not only is there a lack of clear evidence to proceed but that the plaintive, having previously attempted to circumvent the grand jury procedure by filing a FISA request, the plaintive lacks standing or authority to prosecute but may himself be in violation of *The Secrets Act*.

Given these facts I am ordering the following: Prosecution, you will instruct your client to immediately reveal the exact whereabouts of agent Kuksova and order her release. To insure compliance your client will be held in custody until the confirmation that this order has been carried out.

Additionally I am directing the New York State District Attorney's office to review this case pending additional charges."

The look on Pravum's face was a melange of confusion, anger and disbelief as the bailiffs approached.

"Bailiff you will escort the General to a holding facility to be released on my order only."

"Yes ma'am!" The bailiffs moved to escort Pravum out.

"Your Honor, I respectfully request you set bail."

"Your client is not under arrest councillor. He is merley being held in protective custody." She replied before leaving the courtroom. "This hearing is dismissed." The judge declared before stepping down from the bench.

"This isn't over! I'm the God-damn Director of the God-damn NSA!" Pravum yelled as he was led out.

Tammy and Enfield high five'd, Morrissey smiled while Heath slumped in his seat and quietly muttered, "Finally!"

Meanwhile, at the prosecution's table, there were no such revelations.

"And you two wanted to move for a new hearing!" The head prosecutor chastised his team as he gathered his things and Pravum was led away.

CHAPTER TWENTY-THREE

Pete's Tavern
Hoboken, New Jersey
West Bank of the Hudson River

It was with the intent to have a farewell drink together that Frank and Irina had hired the upstairs function room at Pete's Tavern the Sunday night before the Squad were scheduled to fly back to London.

Seated at a back table Morrissey and the crew were debating details of the events of the previous weeks while they waited for Frank and Irina to arrive.

"How do you hide millions of dollars from the FBI?" Din took his turn at the improvised joke sesstion which had spontaneously evolved to pass the time and get the first couple of pints out of the way

"Give it to the CIA!" Heath answered. "I hear the number of serial killers has seriously declined this last decade." He added.

"Goddamn millennials, can't commit to a single thing!" Enfield threw in.

"My cousin just told me that she taped up the camera on her computer because she's afraid of being spied on by the NSA." Enfield then relayed.

"Really?"

"Yeah. I laughed. She laughed. Her smartphone laughed."

"If we can pause the *Amateur Hour* auditions for

a bit, there's something bugging me." Din interrupted.

"What's that?" Heath ventured.

"If that Chinese spy fella they shot in the park was some kind of high-speed espionage agent, why in hell did he have blanks in his gun?" He asked.

"One of two reasons; either he didn't know or he didn't want to hurt anybody, civilian-wise I mean." Heath speculated. "Killing an innocent civilian in a foreign country'd be a damn site more difficult for the embassy suites to clear him of! Remember what the Inspector told us back at the museum last week."

"According to Agent Kuksova, from the shocked look on his face right before he died, my bet is he not only knew but was told the FBI agents would be firing blanks." Din added.

"In which case he was probably being used by his people as a disposable patsy." Heath suggested.

"And another thing, why was the FBI guy they busted mixed up with Colombian terrorists?" Din questioned further. Enfield took up the answer.

"Same reason university professors and senior military personnel get mixed up with the Chinese commies; MICE." Enfield offered. Din still looked puzzled. "Money, Ideology, Compromise or Ego." Enfield clarified.

"Exactly!" The Inspector added. "The four most common motivations for treason."

Enfield, Din and Heath were by now working on their second pint while Tammy had relocated to the end of the bar and was engaged with a group of three rough looking locals.

"Right!" She offered to the largest of the three burly dockworkers she had been trading shots with for the last twenty minutes or so. "Barkeep! Two more shots and give us the lend of two empty shot glasses as well please." With that she produced a $10 bill and slapped it on the bar.

The bartender brought the glasses and the drinks and set them in front of her at which time she added her shot then lined up all five glasses in a straight row with the three full shots side-by-side flanked on either end by the two empty glasses.

As no one had followed suit by laying down their money she reiterated her challenge.

"Well, what'a youse waitin' for, engraved invitations?"

Two of the longshoremen quickly matched her bet and laid down their money. The third, the biggest of the three, declined.

"Right, the challenge is," she explained, ". . . in one move make it so you have one empty glass, one full glass, one empty glass etc. . . . alternating through the entire row without sliding any glasses around or pourin' any out!"

Without hesitation the smallest and burliest of the dock workers lifted the full glass in the very center threw back the shot and sat the empty glass back down in place.

All the men laughed.

"Oh! You're the sharp one of the group, so you are!" Tammy obseved.

About that time Morrissey approached from

behind and had, out of curiosity, wandered over to the bar.

"Tammy, as a sworn officer of the law tell us you're not taking advantage of these honest, tax paying members of the working class, are you?" Morrissey chided.

"At the moment Inspector it seems I'm giving them the opportunity to avoid payin' a bit of tax!" She said. As she slid the stack of tens over between them the man who had won the bet, easily a foot taller than her, smirked as he reached for the money but was stayed by Tammy.

"Hold on Mongo! Sure you're gonna give me a chance to get even, aren't ya?" She half assumed half pleaded. Morrissey, suspecting what was coming, drifted away back over to the table to sit with Enfield and the others.

Tammy re-challenged the trio.

"I'll bet I can drink two pints before one of youse can finish two shots." She offered. "Any takers?"

The three men exchanged glances.

"What's the catch?" The largest one, who had yet to bet asked.

"The only catch is we can't touch each other's glasses." She then slapped a $20 bill on the bar on top of the three tens. They then matched her bet, all except the one big fella.

Having already had a couple of full pints on the bar as back-ups, she selected two of the pints herself and slid the two shots over to the big man who hadn't yet bet.

"How about we let the big fella in on this one?"

She cajoled. The three men again exchaged glances. "Now I'll need a wee head start on one of the pints, agreed?" She asked.

"No problem little girl! I'll even let you you **finish** the first pint!" The big fella declared as he still hadn't slapped down his twenty.

"That's mighty sportin' of ya Louis, but we are yet to see the color of your money." She gently reminded.

"Come to think of it Louis, has your wallet ever seen the light of day in a bar?!" One of his friends sarcastically quipped. Louis was shamed into producing a twenty and sliding it across the bar, however reticently.

"Right!" Tammy said lifting the first pint and toasting the others, drank slowly but steadily and just as she had drained the last drop Big Louis lifted the first shot and downed it.

Unfortunately by the time he set the first shot glass back down Tammy had used her empty pint glass to cover Louis' second full shot glass. The workers erupted in laughter at her stunt.

All except Louis.

The big man slowly grew visibly angry as he watched Tammy attempt to scoop up the $120 from the bar slapping his huge paw on top of hers.

Heath, who had been paying attention from across the floor after Morrissey informed them what was happening over at the end of the bar, tapped Enfield, nodded and stood then, along with Din headed over to Tammy.

As they approached the bar Louis looked over

and noticed. He slowly removed his hand.

"Hi ya Tammy!" Heath greeted. Being roughly the same height and size as Louis Heath was sure to make direct eye contact with him. "Who are your new drinking buddies?" He asked in his best Yardie gangster dialect.

"Guys, this is Frankie, James and this is Big Louis." She cheerily introduced. "They all work down on the freight docks."

"Inspector wants you over at the table." Heath informed never losing eye contact with Big Louis.

"Inspector?!" James the dock worker repeated. "Youse is all cops?!"

"James, Frankie, allow me to introduce sergeants Enfield, Rankor and Heath of Scotland Yard." Forced yet polite nods were exchanged. "And yes, we is all cops. Cops of the Special Homicide squad." She finished.

"So what?!" Louis challenged. "Youse are all English!" Big Louis confidently spewed out. "You ain't got no weight here!"

Just then Frank without Irina came through the front door. Tammy smiled and nodded.

"Oh, and coming up the aisle is the man we all work with, Lieutenant Frank Mahone of the NYPD Homicide Division." Tammy winked at Big Louis. "He's got weight!" She assured him.

Snatching up the money Tammy tossed a twenty back on the bar. "Have a round on me boys!" She offered as the Squad all headed back to their table.

"Where's Irina?" Morrissey asked a concerned looking Frank Mahone refused a seat.

"I had to leave her in the apartment. Nigel, I think we may have a situation."

Frank informed him that he had spotted a suspicious van down around the corner through his bedroom window when it arrived nearly an hour ago.

"Why do you suspect it?" Morrissey asked.

"No one has gotten in or out since it parked."

"Are you certain?"

"The doors are labelled 'Anderson Cable, Jersey City, N.J.'."

"So?"

"There is no Anderson Cable listed in Jersey City. I checked."

"Well that is suspicious. What do you want to do?"

"If they are who I think they are, there's only one thing I can do."

"What's that?"

"Take them out!"

****

It had been well over a full hour since the black panel van labelled, 'Anderson Cable Jersey City' had parked a block away from Frank Mahone's apartment just off Sinatra Drive.

Earlier, a short time after observing Mahone exit the apartment house and watching him disappear around the corner while knowing that Irina was still inside, two men in the van, dressed in dark civilian clothes, climbed out while a third climbed from the back and sat next to the man behind the wheel. The first two made their way across the intersection up to the rear of the apartment house and over to the unlocked wrought iron gate to the back yard.

Back at the table inside the pub Frank Mahone was handing out assignments.

"And why are you wearing a heavy jacket underneath your Mackinaw?" Enfield asked Mahone.

"Because we're about the same size." Frank replied as he stripped off his black Mac.

"Oh."

"And because you are going to be me."

"Does that mean I get to to sleep with Irina?" Enfield excitedly asked.

"Sure! If you can get past the 9mm Glock she keeps in the hip holster behind her back." Mahone answered. "Now be a good little detective, put this coat on and make your way past the van parked over on Sinatra. Stay on the other side of the street, and make your way down to the waterfront where the James Bond wanna-bes can see you." He instructed as Enfield slipped on the Mackinaw.

"What do you want me to do there?" Enfield asked.

"Just sit there on a bench and have a cigarette. Nigel you and I are going to play hide and seek." As he reached over and raised Enfield's collar Mahone further instructed.

"But I don't smoke!" Enfield objected.

"But I do!" Frank corrected handing him a pack

of cigarettes and a lighter.

A short time later and a few blocks away, as Frank Mahone was setting his plan in motion, the driver of the van decided to dispatch the third thug to an overwatch position. As he did, it was from the corner of his eye that he spied Mahone descending the steps down to the recreation area of the waterfront park

"What about him?" The thug asked.

"You go, I'll take care of him." The driver directed.

As his man disappeared around the corner, the driver was shocked to see, through his large side mirror, a second Frank Mahone standing to the rear of the vehicle waving at him mockingly.

"BASTARD!" He cursed as he drew his service weapon and sprang from the van.

No sooner had his feet hit the black top when he felt the muzzle of a weapon pressed against the rear of his scull.

"I doubt you've taken a stupid breath in your life mate! I wouldn't start now!" The rough English voice of Inspector Morrissey filled his ears. "I'll have that pistol! Very dangerous, you might get hurt!" The driver obeyed and Mahone stepped forward nodding to Morrissey as he took the gun from the driver.

"Son-of-a-bitch!" Frank declared as he stepped into the light. "If it isn't the future organ donor Colonel Parva! What happen, your puppet masters decide to boost their pawns with a queen?"

"Laugh now Mahone! Its only a matter of time

before we nail you!"

"Sure it is! Get in the the van, asshole!"

Once inside the van they hustled Parva to the back, handcuffed him to the steel floor stanchion of the passeger's seat, searched him and prepared to leave.

"Lookie what I found here!" Morrissey suddenly declared as he produced a small box from under the driver's seat. Inside it they found zip ties, a roll of industrial duct tape and a black hood.

"Just here for a routine arrest, hey Parva?!" Frank taunted before he backhanded the handcuffed Parva across the face.

A few minutes later Nigel was off down to the waterfront to retrieve Enfield and Frank was off back towards his apartment.

Parva was left feebly mumbling the word 'HELF' through his taped mouth and hooded head.

Frank made his way across the intersection to the rear of his apartment building and started his climb up the fire escape to where he had seen the other two thugs enter his place.

Down on ground level, from his concealed position in a doorway across the street, the third thug watched Frank climb the fire escape.

Gingerly easing himself through the open hall window, up on the third floor, Frank could hear Irina struggling with the two NSA agents out in the living room.

With his Glock at the high ready as he moved up the narrow hallway, Mahone wheeled around the corner and drew a bead on the two agents who had Kuksova on the floor attempting to handcuff her.

"I told you assholes before, this is a sanctuary city!" Frank barked out.

The one holding Irina by her cuffed wrists cleverly stepped in front of the other one giving him concealment to draw his weapon. However this was not as clever as he calculated.

Mahone's first shot hit the front thug square in the chest driving him back into the second. Irina had the presence of mind to duck as Frank was able to land three rounds into the number two man.

Observing that number one was still breathing and deducing they both wore Kevlar PPE, Mahone fired another round into his leg causing him to howl loudly while the other, gasping for breath, raised his hands in surrender.

Irina quickly scrambled to confiscate both their weapons.

Suddenly and without warning, the front door burst open, Frank spun around and watched Morrissey come through and let off two rounds straight down the hallway towards the back window.

A loud grunt was heard followed by a single shot from the rear window which hit the ceiling above Nigel.

Down the far end of the hallway, thug number three was struggling to stand and raise his weapon.

Three more shots from Morrissey pushed him back through the window, breaking the glass, cracking the frame and sending him out onto the fire escape.

They watched as he fought to stand upright but only managed to fall backwards over the fire escape rail to tumble down and hit the pavement three stories below with a muffled 'thwack'!

"Good shootin' Tex!" Mahone complimented over the agonized moans of the agent writhing on the floor.

"At least we planted him in the right place!" Morrissey quipped.

"Where's that?" Irina asked.

"In the garden!"

Suddenly an older man in a plaid evening robe, brown slippers and brandishing a .357 Magnum darted through the still open front door, weapon at the high ready.

Irina flinched, Morrissey jumped and took aim. Frank smiled as he stayed Morrissey's weapon.

"It's okay Nigel, he's one of us." Frank informed as he raised a hand to lower the newcomer's weapon.

"Everybody okay?! I heard shots!" The stranger declared looking around.

"It's okay Andy! Everything's under control." Frank assured.

"CHRIST! Is everyone in this bloody country **armed to the bloody teeth?!**" Morrissey swore as he fought to catch his breath.

"Half the building's occupied by former military and ex-cops!" Irina informed as Frank undid her cuffs. The wounded agent continued moaning as he and his mate were hadcuffed together.

"God damn it!" Mahone swore.

"What, what's wrong?" Irina asked.

"I just had that rug cleaned!" Mahone complained about the blood-stained carpet.

CHAPTER TWENTY-FOUR

**New York Times Building
620 8th Avenue
Manhattan, New York
Monday 3rd April, 09:18 a.m.**

The twelve junior editors filed into the meeting room that morning to receive their marching orders from the Editor-in-Chief who was the last to take his place and as usual stood and leaned forward, both hands on the table as he kicked off the meeting.

"Okay boys and girls, welcome to another day in paradise! European desk, what are you working on?"

"Shooting in Germany. Seven people killed, at least 25 injured at a Jehovah's Witnesses center in Hamburg, Germany."

"Give it to the Crime Desk. Give me something on the Paris riots. What else?"

"Georgian protests."

"Who cares? Home Desk, what'a you got?"

"The Matamoros kidnappings. FBI reports they're leaning toward a drug deal gone bad."

"Any new leads?"

"No."

"Okay lead with that. Anything else?"

"LGBT rights in Uganda." Another journalist spoke up. "Their government is considering the death penalty for gays."

"LGBT rights, that's important, that'll get clicks.

Page two." He directed. "Olsen!"

"Yeah boss?" The reporter answered.

"You send me another story as poorly written as the piece on the big New York department stores you sent me last week and I'm sending you to Uganda!"

"I'd look forward to the vacation Chief!" The openly gay journalist replied causing a ripple of laughter to blanket the room.

"What else?" The Chief Editor pushed.

"Capital punishment in Belarus."

"Commies, who cares? What else?"

"The Russian invasion."

"That's not going away anytime soon!" He opined. "Political Desk what'a you got?"

"Chief, I wanna do an op ed on DeSantis and how he's likely gonna run." The thirty-something woman responded.

"You know something the rest of us don't?" The chief challenged.

"With all due respect Chief I probably know many things you don't!" She fired back. "But I don't want to show off, so for now I'll just say I have an inside source that tells me he's going to announce by May."

"We ate our Wheaties this morning didn't we Amanda dear?!" The Chief shot back by way of commenting on her confidence. "I want you on DeSantis' new bill. Angle it, 'Florida tries to take away right to free speech', something like that."

"I'll have a draft on your desk by Thursday." She responded. "Meanwhile I'll work up a draft on how DeSantis will likely announce by end of May." She quietly mumbled aloud.

The Chief Editor looked up from his notes before passing comment.

"You see that Olsen?" He said. "That's how you shoot back!" He advised. "D.C. Desk, what's the news from inside the Beltway?"

"Apparently another story about the NSA is making the rounds on social media."

"Yeah? Talk to me."

"Word on the street has it that the NSA is getting a new director." Another journalist threw in.

"What happened to Pravum?"

"Apparently he took early retirement and arranged for a job at a company called . . ." He flipped through his note pad. "AstroCom. Also my source tells me the NSA will be the subject of a Congressional hearing which is presently convening."

"Those guys in the Congress must be going deaf! All they do is have hearings!" He opined.

"Just what we need another five or ten million of the taxpayers' money down the drain!" Amanda the journalist commented.

"Any word on what they're investigating this time?" The Chief pushed.

"Apparently when Pravum went over to AstroCom he brought some guy named Hermes with him. Two of his workers at the NSA filed a grievance about something with the GAO."

"And what happened?"

"The usual FBI scenario. Their houses were

raided, all their electronics confiscated and two weeks later it went to court and was dismissed when it was shown that the 'evidence' presented to the court by the FBI was fabricated along with several false or forged statements. All their confiscated devices were ordered returned."

"Were they?"

"Yes but they were found to have been purged of all data even their Word apps. All hard drives and phones had been wiped clean. The two complainants were fired. Surprisingly they weren't blacklisted."

"They will be." The Chief added. "Tamp that part of the story down." He quickly ordered.

"What do you want to put in its place to fill the column?"

"With the up coming midterms and better start digging up some Trump stories, never too early for those."

"Already started Chief!"

"And Jessie, see how much you can coordinate with *The WoPo* and *CNN*. Talk to Sally's people, find out what they're gonna run this week."

"Will do Boss!"

"And while you're at it, see if you can get us at the same table next week at the annual Press Club dinner."

"Considerate it done."

*

Propped up against the headboard of his bed that

morning, TV remote in hand, Mahone was channel surfing as Irina climbed out and off the other side of the bed and slipped into her green satin robe.

"Ha!" Frank loudly declared.

"What are you ha'ing at?" She asked as she drew back the curtains to reveal the sun-soaked, panoramic view overlooking the Hudson River and the Manhattan skyline before heading across to the bathroom.

"The CNN chyron just scrolled that the former Colonel Parva will be the new expert political commentator for CNN!"

"Sounds like a step up for Parva!" She sarcastically quipped.

"Or a step down for CNN. Everyone will rise to their level of incompetence!" Frank quietly uttered.

"You say something?"

"Just talking to myself."

"Well, as long as you don't answer!" She added as she brushed her hair in the bathroom mirror. "Can't believe we have a whole two weeks off!" She joyfully declared. "You want to go out for breakfast or you want me to cook something up?"

"Check the fridge see what I have."

Minutes later Irina stood, one hand on the open fridge door, staring at a half carton of orange juice, one egg and an open box of baking soda.

"I vote for going out." She called from kitchen.

"Sounds good." He called back in response.

Irina returned to the bedroom and started to dress.

"According to an article in the *New York Post* Farmiga was reinstated to the Intel Committee."

Kuksova informed.

"Really?"

"Yeah. Apparently Burman humbly explained; 'On second thought perhaps it was a mistake' to ask her to step down." Irina informed with her best Foghorn Leghorn voice.

"That's good. I liked her." Frank confessed. "She seemed like a good woman."

"What about the Reagan guy?" She asked. "Any word?"

"Nialls Reagan is believed to be out of the country and is now listed on an open warrant," Mahone explained as he briefly paused on the TCM channel in the middle of an old black and white film before moving on.

"You think they'll ever catch him?" She wondered.

"I have a feeling a guy like Pravum isn't the kind of guy to leave any lose ends if you get my drift." Frank replied.

"What about Reagan?"

"Knowing what I have been told about O'Neill, she was no doubt playing him to get a story."

"That fits." Irina agreed.

"Apparently he found out and had no sense of humor about it is my guess." Frank added. "So you're off suspension. I knew it would work out." Frank encouraged by way of moral support. "Did the Director at least apologise for doubting you?"

"Two chances of that, slim and none. And slim just left town! But at least he gave me credit for the FARC intercept!" She added.

"Well I suppose the Bureau would look pretty foolish if they kept you on suspension after that. Not that they'd need any help in that department." Mahone opined as he switched off the TV and headed to the bathroom.

"At least they're debating new rules vis-a-vie limitations of contracts between federal retirees and contractors!" Irina offered as she finished buttoning up her blouse.

"Rules which they will dutifully ignore!" Mahone added as he finished shaving.

"And new rules for the FISA court submissions." She posited.

"Which they will also dutifully ignore!" Mahone said as he took a seat on the bed to put on his socks.

"Just out of curiosity, during the hearing who did you contact with that mysterious phone call while Pravum and his lawyer we're fighting it out in the back room?" She asked as she made her way around the bed to where he sat.

"I kind'a got lucky on that one."

He only got one sock on before she pushed him over onto the matress, climbed up and straddled him. He continued to explain. "I had no idea if I could get through but I rang around until I found Senator Burman's office number." He replied as he reached up and started to slowly unbutton her blouse.

"You called the actual Senate Intel Committee?!" She said in genuine shock.

"It was a brief conversation." He slid her top down off her shoulders and off before tossing it aside.

The Hermes Project

"About what?"

"I made him an offer he couldn't refuse." He reached around to unhook her bra but she stayed his hands.

"What exactly did you think would happen?" She insisted.

"Simple, if you just keep going high enough-" He explained as he methodically walked his fingers up her bare belly. ". . . sooner or later you reach the big guy." He massaged her left breast through her bra.

"And who is 'the big guy'?" She asked guiding his hand off her chest.

"The guy who has the power to flip the switch, turn the knob. Press the button!" He pressed her other breast as if it were an elevator button. "In this case, Senator Burman."

She grabbed both his hands, held them away from her breasts and with mounting anticipation pushed further.

"What'd you say to him?!"

"I informed him that there was a critical case in New York's First District Court that he might be able to help out on. Then explained to him how complicated his life might become if the Press were to learn about his stock ownership in a company supplying a terrorist organisation with potentially deadly technology."

Spurred on by yet more excitement her curiosity mounted.

"MING TAO! You told him you knew about Ming Tao!" She realized loudly, taking off her bra.

"What did **he** say?"

"He said the public will never believe it."

"He was right you know. Those guys in D.C. pull shit all the time and get away with it clean! It's culturally ingrained."

"True, but certified hard copies of his bank transactions and a handwritten note to him from the Deputy Head of FARC would be hard for him to dispute." Frank casualty informed. Her mouth dropped open.

Lifting her off him and onto her back he straddled her.

"Where did you get hard copies of. . . never mind I don't want to know!" She said looking up at him.

"Okay, I'll keep it a secret." He teased as he kissed the nape of her neck, "By the way, Phil Finley says to say hi."

"Finley!" She declared as she pushed him up with two hands. "You're a sneaky bastard, you know that?!" She playfully punched him in the chest.

"Yeah, but I'm a lovable sneaky bastard!"

With a warm smile she returned his kiss then laid back and stared up at him.

"What are you looking at?" He smiled back.

"I was just thinking, if you had a TV on your forehead and could breathe through your ears you'd be the perfect lover!" She quipped.

Frank briefly considered her comment before he lifted up off her, climbed out of bed and ducked out of the room.

"Hey! Where you going?!" She angrily

demanded.

A minute later he returned wearing a Yankees ball cap with his Iphone held on his forehead with a thick elastic band. The phone was set to a woman's talk show.

"You need serious help detective!" She giggled.

He climbed on top of her and placed the hat on her head resetting the phone to a baseball game.

"Much better!" He nodded in self agreement.

She grabbed his head as he began to kiss between her breasts.

"I thought we were going out for breakfast?!" She softly protested.

"Breakfast?!" He continued to kiss. "What breakfast? We dun need no stinking breakfast!" He said in a mock Mexican accent as he removed his sock and renewed his attack.

It was over two hours later until they got around to going out for breakfast.

THE END

Paddy Kelly

Also by Paddy Kelly

Operation Underworld

The Wolves of Calabria

Broad in the Kimono

The American Way

American Rhetoric

Politically Erect

Children of the Nuclear Gods

When Two Tribes Go To War

Spicer's Circus

The Galileo Project

The Hermes Project

There's an App For That!

Kelly's Full House

Synopsis & option info available online at:
paddy.incanto@gmail.com
https://www.amazon.co.uk/Paddy-Kelly/e/B002XP4N9O/ref=aufs_dp_fta_dsk

Ingram Content Group UK Ltd.
Milton Keynes UK
UKHW042023130723
425110UK00001B/20